ALARIS

Cover art by *Hyperclass Ark Studio*
Interior design, formatting and map art by Fanny Vergne

This novel is available in English (US) and French

Developmental Editing and Line Editing done by *Edith & Nous*
French Copy Editing done by *Edith & Nous*
English Copy Editing done by *Scribendi*

English version:
ISBN 978-1-7386208-0-7 (ebook)
ISBN 978-1-7386208-1-4 (Paperback)
ISBN 978-1-7386208-8-3 (Hardcover)

French version :
ISBN 978-1-7386208-3-8 (ebook)
ISBN 978-1-7386208-4-5 (Paperback)
ISBN 978-1-7386208-6-9 (Hardcover)

ALARIS

FANNY VERGNE

ABOUT THE AUTHOR

 For over fifteen years, Fanny Vergne has been a veteran artist in the video game industry, best known for her work on World of Warcraft, a project she continues to work on.

Originally from France, but after fulfilling her early dreams by traveling around the world, she decided to embark on writing her first Fantasy novel to pursue her greatest passion, which has always been storytelling, no matter the form.

In a surprising blend of fine French cheeses and delicious scones, she now resides in New Zealand with her partner, stepson, and their Siamese cat who enjoys vocalizing.

www.fannyvergne-author.com

@fannyvergne_author

PROLOGUE

All murmurs ceased. A silence colored with wonder took hold of the crowd. Standing, sitting, or cross-legged, everyone had eagerly awaited this event in the small village inn. For several days, news of their arrival had caused excitement. And now, with the moment finally arrived, an enthusiastic assembly had gathered in the narrow, dimly lit room. They all longed to satisfy the curiosity that consumed them. It was said to be a story known by few souls, a tale that must not be forgotten—for the good of all.

The young woman seated near the stage cast an affectionate gaze at the person emerging from backstage. She was not surprised when their regal posture and unparalleled beauty elicited cheers in the tavern. Exquisite attire crafted of rare fabrics with shimmering threads complemented the poignant voice and gestures of this charismatic being.

Everyone was captivated, enchanted by this otherworldly vision from a distant realm. Whether it was their peculiar ears that tapered to a point, their ever-changing color strands of hair, their amethyst skin adorned with stars, or the absence of pupils in the fiery blaze of their eyes, all were mesmerized.

So, when the echoes of the words spoken by their mouth reverberated melodiously in the hearts and minds of all, everyone listened attentively. They followed the imaginary path woven by this marvelous character, embracing the chance that presented itself to be a part of this story. To witness their unique testimony.

To be filled with hope.

"An eclipse.

The end of a dream, the beginning of a world.

On this day, the moon had finally decided to merge with the sun.

The dance of celestial bodies that would change everything. Set everything right. Reveal everything. That's what the legend had foretold.

An ancient and revered tale passed down through generations. A promise that all the druidic clans of the Astral Forest yearned to see come true. A story that promised magic and protection, powers and revelation.

Under the Tree of Ether, a majestic emblem with silvery foliage, the elders had proclaimed that twins blessed by the stars would receive fabulous powers during the Eclipse. Powers that would enhance Nature. Powers that would ensure the protection of all druidic clans.

Like a destiny woven from threads of gold and silver, of sun and moon, everything had been planned when two twins marked by the stars were finally born in the heart of the forest, within the Destellar clan.

One golden eye. One silver eye. Each blessed with these unique attributes.

Imbued by the stars, they had been both cherished and admired. Often feared and compelled to follow the path revealed at their birth, eighteen years ago. And so, their names had been chosen accordingly.

They would be named in honor of the stars—Lucine and Solehan, the moon and the sun."

CROSSED DESTINIES

1

The dark bark and silver reflections of its foliage shimmering in the daylight, the Tree of Ether imposed its magnificence among the deciduous trees of the Astral Forest. A powerful symbol of the druidic culture in which they had been raised. The celebration of eighteen years of anticipation would take place under its watchful gaze.

All the clans had been invited. The hope of the promised solar eclipse, set to occur on the same day, had drawn out all the typically reclusive souls of the great forest. Excitement was at its peak.

Lucine observed her twin brother walking by her side, at the forefront of the procession, as the peculiar tree revealed itself amid the woodland. The shared worry etched on their faces and the heterochromatic eyes that had turned their lives upside down. The anxiety that made his gait stiff despite his slender and athletic body. Like her, he seemed apprehensive about what was about to happen. The young woman's gaze discreetly drifted toward the line of people, stretching as far as the eye could see behind them. Dozens of druids of all ages followed in their footsteps, filled with admiration.

Lucine swallowed hard and shifted her nervous attention back to the Tree of Ether before them.

In the village shaman's hut, nestled among the trees, the twins had spent the morning preparing for the ceremony. Everything had been carefully arranged by the druids to celebrate this long-awaited moment. Custom-tailored garments, hairstyles, and various leaf jewelry; they had allowed themselves to be dressed up like pageantry by the enthusiasm of the Destellar clan members.

All the druids knew that the twins had possessed the unique chance of being born with the blessing of the stars, even though they had been deprived of their parents due to a tragic fate: their mother had not survived their birth, and their father had been crushed by grief. Despite this, and in the hope of seeing the legend come true, all the clan members had cherished and assisted them throughout their childhood.

Lucine sighed and placed a trembling hand on the small wooden amulet against her chest as she walked toward the peculiar tree. It was a gift the revered elders of the druidic clans had bestowed on her that very morning. "This will protect you from dangers and guide you on your path," they had said, presenting it to her. They now seemed so proud and walked with conviction at her side. The day had arrived when all their efforts would finally be rewarded. The elders had raised the twins in the druidic traditions and had made it their duty to prepare Lucine and Solehan for what lay ahead. To follow the druidic teachings, to prove themselves worthy of the powers they were destined to receive, and to respect nature and animals.

Still clutching the amulet in her hand, and with a glimpse of a smile on her face, Lucine recalled the evenings spent listening to the tales of her clan and gazing at the stars. Stories passed down from generation to generation, of which the legend concerning the twins was a part.

But a tinge of bitterness tainted her memories. Even though she and Solehan had never lacked anything, their extraordinary destiny had often overshadowed their childhood dreams and left little room for carefreeness. Amid the protection offered by the towering trees of the Astral Forest, everything had always been decided for them. An incredible stroke of luck, an existence that everyone envied.

A gilded prison.

Seeking solace, Lucine discreetly studied her brother once again through her long brown locks. The innocence portrayed on his round face reflected their young age and seclusion. But upon seeing the persisting turmoil in Solehan's eyes, the memory of their conversation from the previous night resurfaced in her mind.

As she usually did, caressed by the cool wind on her skin, she had climbed up onto the enormous rock polished by their hours of chatting and laughter over the years. The stars had chosen to reveal themselves proudly for the twins' last evening spent admiring them through the canopy of tall trees. The twins' favorite spot in the discreet darkness. Where they had never needed to pretend. Where they had admired the beauty of nature bathed in twilight, listened to the chirping of animals, and appreciated the absence of the tumult of their destiny. Where they had been able to dream of being something else for so many years. Their fraction of freedom. It had become their privileged and secret ritual.

That night, Lucine had laid down her bow and quiver on the stone and stretched out. With a notebook in hand, filled with sketches and drawings of plants and animals of all kinds, Solehan had joined his sister perched on the natural stage of the immense rock.

"Mmhh, do you feel ready?" Lucine whispered, after a long sigh.

"As ready as I'll ever be, I suppose," Solehan replied, with a resigned look on his face, as he lay down beside his sister and stretched his arms above his head.

"Sometimes I wonder why all this fell upon us, this whole grand destiny business," she said, waving her hands dramatically toward the sky. "Just because we resemble the description of one of their legends . . ."

Solehan offered a small smile without taking his eyes off the celestial vault. "I don't know. I question it every day. I've always dreamed of swapping places with anyone else, while most would want mine. But tomorrow, I'm supposed to be able to transform into a wolf, a bear, or who knows, maybe a marmot. Apparently, it's worth it for everyone. They imagine I'll be able to defend them against potential threats with those powers."

Lucine's laughter resonated through the silent forest. "Oh, if that happens, I won't stop asking you to transform into strange things! Maybe you'll even be able to grow trees out of your ears!" She playfully nudged him with her elbow, chuckling.

"I find it hard to imagine that I'll really be capable of such things, to be honest," Solehan lamented. "It seems like old grandmother clan stories to me. I suppose it reassures them to think that we'll be capable of extraordinary things to protect them."

"Yes, but at what cost . . ." Lucine murmured, seriousness suddenly etching her face.

Solehan let out a deep sigh of frustration and covered his face with his hands, trying to brush away his exasperation.

"At the very least," Lucine cried, "if they're going to deprive us of a future, they could have given us personalities to match! Minds that don't question, that don't crave knowledge." She groaned in despair. "At least you, according to the legend, as a man, you'll be able to transform, have magic. As for me? I'm supposed to carry on our clan's lineage, pass on our *gift* to offspring so the legend can come true again. It's almost grotesque!"

"I think they got the wrong candidates, to be honest!" Solehan teased.

A wry smile twisted the corner of Lucine's mouth. A breeze wound its way through the trunks of the imposing trees, causing the branches to creak and the leaves to rustle, creating a symphony that echoed through the starlit sky.

"Do you think there's something beyond the Astral Forest?" she asked dreamily.

"I don't know. The elders say there's only misery and despair outside. But it doesn't matter anyway; it's not like we'll ever have the chance to find out!"

Heavy-hearted, they drowned their gazes in the stars and cherished the rare serenity that enveloped them. It was their last moment of tranquility before the fateful day. After that, everything would change. The elders had been certain about it.

Lucine broke their uneasy silence. "I don't know what will happen tomorrow, but if there's one thing I'm grateful for in all of this, it's that you're here," she said, rising and propping herself up on her elbow toward Solehan.

A smile illuminated her brother's face. He pulled her into a hug, a gleam in his eyes. "Me too, sis."

"I'll always be there for you. We'll make it, Solehan." Lucine released her embrace, a mischievous sparkle in her eyes. "And look on the bright side! When you can transform, you'll be a magnificent target for me to practice my archery!"

Solehan responded by grabbing a handful of pebbles and playfully showering them over the young druidess.

They continued to contemplate the stars for a long time that night. But the carefree laughter eventually evaporated with the dawn.

A twinge of shame now pricked Lucine's chest. Were they ungrateful? Countless druids would have given anything to receive what they were potentially about to receive.

Her embarrassment and guilt grew as she admired the enthusiasm of the crowd around her and the restrained joy on their faces. The vibrant colors of banners, marks, and various paintings. Music that elevated cheerfully.

Yet, something inexorably crashed against the mind of the young druidess, despite her goodwill. An insatiable serpent coiling in her belly. Something she tried desperately to silence the questioning of. Was there nothing else? Was this truly the only possible path?

After several minutes of walking, they finally reached the Tree of Ether. Lucine sighed and examined it once again. Gracefully perched atop a small hill, this tree, with its supernatural appearance, stood in the midst of the Astral Forest like a jewel in shades of ebony and silver. Even the legend seemed inscribed on its bark: the two silhouettes of the lucky chosen ones were engraved on the trunk from which an eerie blue glow emanated. Other symbols representing the stars were carved and adorned this wooden sculpture that reached up to the silvery canopy of the tree.

Lucine didn't know why the Tree of Ether bore its name, nor why its prodigious appearance fascinated her so much. She had observed it many times since her earliest childhood, her mind filled with unanswered questions. But the trees rarely provided answers.

Turning around, she saw the vastness of the crowd now standing before them. Breathless, Lucine shifted her attention to the faces of the gathered druids, from the elderly to the children, who awaited the announced miracle with joy and impatience. The dance of the stars that would reveal their powers. The eclipse that would begin their new life.

She turned once again to Solehan and discovered the palpable anxiety on his face, surely weighed down by the burden of the task that awaited them. The responsibility that had been theirs since birth. There, spread out before their eyes.

She gently took his hand and tried to alleviate his fear with her presence. *You're not alone. I'll be there, by your side*, she conveyed through her eyes. A tentative smile flickered on Solehan's face; his expression still marked by sadness.

The voice of the shaman resonated among the trees, his chants and incantations soon joined by the crowd. The contagious elation of their anticipation.

Lucine's throat tightened. She directed her attention to the sky. And the brightness of the day was slowly eaten away.

 As he stared at the towering tree on the horizon, Solehan couldn't help but feel a certain bitterness. His stomach twisted with apprehension.

He had spent his life trying to evade the promise that this strange tree had placed upon them at their birth. Yet, despite his reluctance, his feet led him toward the destiny that had been decided for him. He was glad to have Lucine by his side, but he didn't know if it would be enough.

A heavy veil accompanied him with each step, but Solehan tried to keep his head held high at the front of the procession. Always trapped in the appearances he had to uphold, concealing what no one should guess.

The music and chants around him only magnified his sense of loneliness. The multitude of voices swirled around him. How could he be worthy of becoming their protector? He, who was so young. Was he really supposed to receive the gift of such magic? He, who felt entrenched in the lie of his own life.

Would he truly be capable of such wonders, of transforming into an animal, of possessing the magic of nature? And why couldn't Lucine possess a similar power? None of it made sense.

When the memory of green eyes came back to his mind, Solehan placed a hand on the tattoo on his chest, over his heart. Even on their skin, they couldn't escape their destiny. The story of their clan and the legend of the stars adorned their bodies in elegant arabesques of ink and bitterness.

He could only cherish the memory of a stolen night shared with the son of their clan's tattoo artist; their desire discovered with wonder as he practiced his art on Solehan when they were sixteen. Before the elders unleashed their anger on the secret that had grown between them. Apparently, that was not what nature intended.

He had never seen him again, the temptation eradicated when the young tattoo artist was sent to continue his apprenticeship in another clan. Only his memory persisted. Tattooed on his skin. Engraved in his shame. Sculpted in his despair.

So, when he finally turned around to see the assembly standing before him with so much hope, Solehan could only feel like an imposter, a fraud, and a liar. How could he protect them? He, who wasn't even capable of feeling what was expected of him.

Lucine took his hand gently, and Solehan tried to draw a smile on his lips, for her. Because she needed him at that moment. But it was she who tried to reassure him. Even that, he was decidedly incapable of.

The moon relieved his suffering and finally came to fulfill its duty.

Solehan took a deep breath.

2

An oppressive silence engulfed the surroundings of the Tree of Ether, disturbed only by the hearts of the druids in the assembly beating with anticipation of this promise.

Gently, the moon slid over the sun with hope and absorbed its rays of light. Dominating the center of the opening left by the tree canopy, a black and haloed orb shimmered amid the expanse of blue sky. The Astral Forest immersed itself in darkness, and Lucine felt the atmosphere cool around her. With Solehan's hand still in hers, she closed her eyes and focused on the change they were supposed to feel. Trying to ground her mind and senses, she listened carefully to the soft rustling of silver leaves above her and appreciated the caress of the now cool wind on her skin. The familiar scent of the forest filled her nostrils. The serenity of the moment soothed her soul.

But a cry of infinite horror shattered this moment. A deep, guttural cry. A cry that sent chills down Lucine's spine.

She opened her eyes to a state of confusion. The gathered druids clearly did not understand what was happening. Heads turned; minds questioned. Everyone tried to find the origin of that scream. Solehan, too, seemed entangled in ignorance, his golden and silver eyes scanning the assembly with astonishment. Was this normal?

Like a wave of terror rippling through the crowd, agitation grew. New cries arose in the distance. Lucine's heartbeat quickened in incomprehension.

Her fingers tightened around her brother's. Her eyes fluttered frantically among the assembly. What she saw turned her stomach.

In the madness of horror, the crowd scattered in all directions, revealing a swarm of figures made of wood and bark, desperately immobilized. From the youngest to the elderly, all the druids had been lignified, turned into wood, and immortalized in their final position of terror. A multitude of wooden statues frozen in fear. The eyes of the young druidess met their last bewildered gazes. All the clans had been affected before they could even react.

The survivors attempted to flee, running frantically in all directions, trying to escape among the trees of the vast forest. Several stumbled, some were trampled, their distress guided by madness. A myriad of helpless prey scattered under the control of a formidable and invisible predator.

Lucine remained paralyzed. She watched the only world she knew being shattered. The legend that had promised salvation for their clans had suddenly turned into condemnation. Time seemed to stretch to infinity within a handful of seconds. The events unfolded before her eyes, colliding with her reality. Was all of this really happening?

In front of her, the shaman's body stiffened and convulsed, like a puppet lifted off the ground. A massive crimson vine, adorned with wicked thorns, pierced him through, and vermillion liquid streamed down his body from the impact.

Still baffled, Lucine began to shiver. No sound could escape her mouth. Her momentary paralysis echoed the sad silhouettes of what had been the assembly of druidic clans just moments ago.

Beside her, her brother let out a groan of pain. A new vine tightened around the young man's body, leaving thin lines of scarlet red etched on his skin.

A sudden surge of fear shot through Lucine's body. *Solehan.*

The grimace of pain on her brother's face stabbed Lucine in the heart. Despite her dazed state, she nonetheless emerged from her stupor. She hurried, trying to remove the massive vine that was still coiled around Solehan's body, still holding him tightly like a vicious serpentine creature. The thorns pierced her hands, but she felt no pain. Desperately, she tried to free the only person dear to her heart. She couldn't survive without him.

"Lucine, save yourself!" exclaimed Solehan.

"No." Waves of panic overwhelmed her senses. Her brother's words became distant. She continued with determination, trying relentlessly to free him. She couldn't bring herself to leave him like this.

"Lucine, look at me!" The young druid's golden and silver eyes met Lucine's in a last moment of despair.

Confused, she scrutinized her brother's face, searching for a solution. His disheveled brown hair stuck to his forehead, damp with sweat. The droplets of blood that speckled the sun-kissed skin of his cheeks.

"Save yourself," he uttered.

"No, no. There must be a way!" she cried, breathless. Her fingers clenched tightly around the enormous vine.

"Lucine, save yourself before it's too late. Please," he pleaded with a broken voice.

Her eyes welled up, and she stumbled in the grass, hands trembling. How could she abandon him like this? An impossible choice. The resigned face of her brother, accepting his fate, seared her vision.

The outlines of the black sun grew less defined, less recognizable. A new nightmare descended upon the twin siblings, its shadow disturbing the blue sky. A sinister bellow echoed among the trees, and a monstrous creature, born from the darkest recesses of imagination, swooped down upon them. A creature made of bark and dead wood, with long wings of brown and yellowed leaves that beat powerfully. The top of its head was crowned with long antler-like branches.

Lucine lifted her head to behold the horrific beast. Her heart stopped.

Mounted on the back of this terrifying steed, a rider with green eyes scrutinized her intently. A piercing glare, devoid of pupils, indifferent to the cruelty that consumed them. A supernatural and all-powerful being. A god who decided the fate of his creation.

An apocalypse.

Lucine's legs started running. Her mind drowned in madness as she leaped over bodies, blood, and despair, maneuvering through the wooden statues toward the lush safety of the Astral Forest. It was a survival instinct that no longer made sense. She blocked out any thoughts that entered her mind, all the chaotic visions that assaulted her eyes. Around her, several survivors also tried to flee. Their screams, footsteps, and cries echoed in her ears.

The skin of some unfortunate souls lignified before her eyes. She kept running toward the edge of the towering trees, toward the familiar refuge she knew like the back of her hand. Her heart pounded furiously, her throat went dry, and her cheeks flooded with tears as she ran. Again and again, her feet skimmed through the mud and blood.

Like a never-ending nightmare, slender silhouettes appeared among the tree trunks. They approached the group of survivors and cunningly encircled them, surrounding the Tree of Ether in a vicious and relentless trap—a vice tightening around their will to live.

Similar to the flying creature she had previously glimpsed, the feminine bodies of these creatures seemed to be made of intertwined bark, branches, and twigs. The druids, at the command of the creatures' arms, transformed into statues of wood, terror crystallized forever in their ethereal flesh. These strange creatures were responsible for the solidification of the unfortunate souls. Lucine lost all hope.

She turned her head to Solehan in a final breath and saw the talons of the enormous flying creature tightening around her brother, the mad-eyed rider still in the saddle. Had he come to take Solehan away? Nothing made sense. Lucine's insides twisted. The creature soared with a mighty beat of its wings, its bellow tearing through the atmosphere, and Solehan enslaved by its monstrosity.

But around her, the silhouettes closed in on the last survivors. Lucine looked at her golden-skinned arms, covered in tattoos, dried blood, and dirt, and awaited her inexorable transformation into bark, as the creatures approached dangerously. Around her, the screams and cries were muffled. The unearthly cataclysm engulfed them all.

She thanked Solehan and the elders for being in her life. In her strange existence amid the Astral Forest, immersed in this absurd legend. And this inexplicable outcome. She wished for more. But everything was over.

She waited for the end.

Lucine let all her hopes be devoured in the now total Eclipse. Like a deadly response, the darkness deepened further and swallowed all possible escapes. The young woman listened attentively to the somber silence of her imminent death.

A few sparks scattered through the darkness. An improbable, unexpected crackling—a glimmer born in chaos.

A presence. A warm and comforting presence amid the devastation. A presence that called out to her entire being, her essence. She looked up. She recognized it.

A magnificent fox, with white, shimmering fur, stared at her from between the trees. She had seen it before in the Astral Forest. It had always observed her attentively, keeping its distance. Now, it appeared like a radiant light among the malevolent shadows, a guide in the pitch-black night. So, she ran toward it. If nothing made sense anymore, she would follow it. She had nothing left to lose.

Disheveled, Lucine embarked on a wild race. Despite the traps and dangers. Despite the impossibility of the task.

She managed to reach the safety of the majestic trees of the forest, and she immersed herself in them as much as she could. The tall ferns brushed her legs. She slipped between trunks and dense vegetation. The young woman soared over rocks and stumps, ignoring the pain in her body and heart. Behind her, silence fell, and she understood. No one had survived.

How had she managed to evade the relentless grip of those creatures? Why her?

The fox darted ahead of her, and she followed without hesitation, no longer truly knowing why. After a time she couldn't quantify, she eventually lost sight of it within the verdant thickets.

She left her past and her future at the Tree of Ether. Her family, her universe, her childhood, her beliefs.

She ran. Again and again. For hours that felt devoid of any end.

She ran until the first rays of the rediscovered sun pierced through the canopy of trees.

She ran until a clearing, bathed in the daylight, emerged before her eyes.

She ran until her legs could no longer carry her, until her consciousness faded.

Exhausted, Lucine collapsed into the tall grass, embracing the emptiness that sleep offered her.

A drop of blood rolled down his cheek. A violent breeze slapped against his face, the frigid air jolting him out of his stupor.

Pain. A throbbing pain that awakened sharply, and Solehan regained consciousness. His senses slowly returned, one by one, and the full agony of his aching limbs reminded him of their presence. Though restrained at the waist, he felt as if he was floating. His arms and legs swung with the force of the currents. Was he dead?

He struggled to open his eyes, but a bright red liquid blurred his vision. The young man shivered as he ran a trembling hand through his brown hair and over his face, trying to clear his senses. He made a difficult effort to focus on his surroundings and untangle reality from his nightmares. Had all of this truly happened? The grim truth resurfaced in his memory. His clan, the elders, Lucine. They had likely all perished.

Solehan's sight gradually returned, and he discovered the imposing talons of the creature gripping his waist. Its enormous leaf-like wings spread above him. Upon closer inspection, its body seemed to be made of bark and dried, decaying wood, with some mushrooms and roots ingrained in the cavities of its limbs. How could such a creature exist, let alone fly?

The young druid was overcome with violent nausea. All of this was undeniably real. With the hope of finding an escape route, he eagerly scanned his surroundings. Dread snaked down his spine.

Accustomed only to the druidic huts of the vast Astral Forest, trapped hundreds of meters above the ground, Solehan now laid his eyes upon a city of such magnitude for the first time. However, the sight brought him no enchantment.

In a vast valley, wedged between two mountains, what had once likely been an impressive metropolis now lay in ruins and silence. It was a heap of debris. Even the stars seemed unwilling to show themselves; the sun timidly peeked through thick gray clouds. Everything had been frozen and drained of color in an instant.

Located at the center of this turmoil, the silhouettes of tall dark towers tore through the gray sky like sharp spears. An enormous castle stood amid this city of despair, overlooking the remnants of streets and dwellings below. Its imposing fortifications sprang forth from the raw rock as if a sinister stone volcano had erupted.

The enormous creature's wings flapped forcefully, and it dove into the sky of ashes toward the accursed castle. Their destination.

Solehan gasped in astonishment. The magnitude of his captors' cruelty materialized before his eyes. It was a macabre spectacle forever frozen in time. The bodies of all the inhabitants had been turned into wood, frozen in positions of agony. Time had stopped, their suffering eternally fixed. Like what had just happened to his universe, to his clan, at the foot of the Tree of Ether.

But this was an entire city. By the stars, an entire city had been exterminated in such a manner. All its inhabitants.

The colossal creature finally landed on one of the castle ramparts and dropped Solehan heavily to the ground.

Bloodied, shocked, and battered, the young man struggled to rise, his body trembling on the frozen stone. He sensed its presence.

The rider dismounted from the creature with a fluid motion and scrutinized Solehan. The druid felt the eyes of deep green bore into him, biting his mind. The diabolical gaze, devoid of pupils, observed him with a certain malicious and exhilarated intent.

Slenderly built, the man wore a vegetal armor made of what appeared to be wood and bark, similar to the apparel of the strange creatures that had attacked at the Tree of Ether. He remained frozen, observing Solehan like a predator relishing the reaction of its prey before the kill.

Solehan's heart exploded with rage. With a thirst for vengeance, he shouted, "I will kill you, I swear, I will kill you!" He launched himself at the man, fueled by the remnants of his strength.

A vile and cruel smile appeared on his captor's face, as if he openly enjoyed Solehan's outpouring of emotions. His desperate attempt to avenge his kin. Lucine.

One of the man's hands rose toward Solehan, emanating a red glow. *Magic.*

Fine scarlet tendrils sprouted from the palm of the man's hand, coalescing into thorny vines. They encircled Solehan's body, causing him to fall to the ground before reaching his target. The druid screamed as the burning vines tightened around him, leaving a deep gash on his flank in their wake.

Exhausted by the events and the pain, Solehan lost consciousness, his eyes chained on his captor, who continued to smile down at him.

4

Lucine's senses slowly returned to her.

Taste, and her burning, parched throat.

Smell, and the colorful scents of flowers and herbs that were unfamiliar to her.

Hearing, and the rustling of tall grass along with strange barks.

Touch, the numbness of her limbs, and something damp blowing warm air on her face.

Finally, her vision returned, as she struggled to open her eyes. She discovered a dark spot contrasting against the azure sky. The silhouette of a huge black dog standing above her.

The beast happily licked her face, wagging its tail, clearly pleased to have sniffed her out in the tall grass.

"Hey, Katao! Come here, boy!" urged a man's voice, followed by a whistle.

The dog barked cheerfully.

"What have you found now, huh?"

Panicked, Lucine tried to get up but without success. Exhausted and still in shock, her body refused to support her.

An old man appeared above the tall grass, and the dog barked even louder.

Upon discovering Lucine, a stunned expression manifested on the wrinkles of his face. With his mouth open but no words spoken, he paused for a long moment. His brown eyes surveyed the bloodstained clothes and the distress of the young woman, the bewilderment caused by the shock.

After a few moments, a smile finally appeared on the old man's face. "Easy there . . . it'll be okay. I mean you no harm," he said, kneeling in the grass, which crunched under his weight.

Lucine recoiled. She tried to find the strength to get up and flee. Nothing made sense anymore. Where was she now? Her chest constricted with anxiety. She was no longer in the Astral Forest. Her head began to spin.

The stories of the elders emerged in her mind. The dangers of the outside world, the malevolent creatures spoken of in druidic legends. In an initial impulse, the young woman wanted to return immediately to the familiar tall trees. And then she recalled the blood, the tears, the screams. Her clan. Solehan. It all came rushing back.

Would she really be safer in the forest now? She had lost everything.

"Do you want some water? Are you hungry?" the old man added.

He unfastened a small flask from his belt and handed it to her.

After a few seconds of hesitation, Lucine took the small container with a trembling hand and drank eagerly. She had never been so thirsty in her life, and the sensation of cool water on her dry throat was welcome. Could she trust him? Did she have a choice? She looked at the man with suspicion. She would find a way to defend herself if necessary. Her senses still on alert, she searched for something that she could use as an improvised weapon by fumbling through the grass.

"My name is Zaf," the man said, "and this here is Katao," he continued, pointing to his dog with a smile.

The animal barked again and approached her enthusiastically, licking her face once more.

Lucine looked at the dog absentmindedly. Everything was racing through her mind: the horrifying visions, the screams, the silence, her escape into the dark forest, the rider with green eyes. How long had she been asleep? Did all of this really happen? Were there any survivors? Where was her brother now? The last mental image of Solehan, imprisoned in the talons of the creature, tugged at her gut.

But still in shock, her face remained neutral. Tears didn't fill her eyes. However, the kind demeanor of the old man, still sitting in front of her and patiently waiting, was apparent.

"I am a traveling merchant," he explained. "It's fortunate that Katao found you so far from the road in this grass. Do you need anything? I have some spare clothes, something to freshen up, and food in my little wagon. You can also sleep inside if you need to."

Why was he being so helpful? Could it be a trap?

Lucine scrutinized the frail build of the man that could be discerned beneath his modest attire. His balding head and unrefined features. "Why—why would you want to help me?" she managed to ask in a raspy voice, surprised to hear the sound of her own voice.

Initially taken aback, the old man didn't reply right away. A profound gentleness crossed his eyes as he carefully considered his response. "Well . . . let's just say I vowed never to be a coward again." He gave her a broad smile.

What a peculiar answer, Lucine thought. Still dazed, a moment of uncertainty flooded her mind, as she continued to assess the potential threat. Failing to find any means to defend herself, the young druidess analyzed the situation before her. What other option did she have but to trust him? She responded with a slight nod. Despite the discomfort she felt at allowing him to approach, she let the old man help her to her feet. The dog spun around them like a joyful whirlwind before running toward the road.

In the distance, confirming the merchant's words, a wagon pulled by a draft horse with a harness came into view. Painted in vibrant colors and draped in shimmering fabrics, the small cart was easily noticeable. Its appealing appearance contrasted with the images flooding the young woman's memory. A massive assortment of miscellaneous objects overflowed from the wagon, creating a chaotic and surprising silhouette. Trinkets dangled in all directions, producing a faint background noise as they clinked together in the wind.

With Zaf's assistance, Lucine sat on the small wooden ledge at the back. The dog gently rested his head on her thigh and let out a sympathetic whimper. The eyes of the animal attempted to ease her sorrow. Perhaps it was because he was just a dog, but she found herself gently stroking the top of his head. Her spirits were lifted slightly.

As she turned her head toward the interior of the caravan, she discovered a multitude of curious and puzzling objects piled up.

Zaf maneuvered through the bric-a-brac, seemingly searching for something. After a few minutes, he emerged and handed Lucine a piece of bread, a clean loose-fitting linen shirt, and some pants, as well as some cloth for cleaning.

"Do—do you sell all of this?" she stammered.

"Oh, yes! You'd be amazed! People really buy all sorts of things. For instance, the person who gave me the dog bought a broken old musical instrument from me. There was also a stableman that purchased a fancy but damaged grimoire, and even the person who sold me the wagon asked for some used clothes!"

Lucine timidly took a bite of the bread Zaf had handed her and continued to distractedly admire the astonishing array of various objects. She had never seen anything like it.

"I'm heading toward the kingdom of Vamentera," the old man said, sitting beside her. "Do you know where that is?"

No. She only knew of the Astral Forest and its towering trees, the Tree of Ether, and the druidic villages. A sense of dread washed over her once again. She felt lost. "No . . ." she murmured, shaking her head.

"Do you know where we are?"

She shook her head once again, too ashamed of her ignorance to add anything.

"Well, it seems like you fell from the sky!" He chuckled. "Here, we are in the kingdom of Astitan, ruled by King Arthios Therybane. It's a kingdom that shares a border with the kingdom of Vamentera, and that's where I'm headed. I must have a map lying around somewhere in this mess." Zaf scratched his temple, where his graying hair started, and looked thoughtfully at the jumble of objects inside the wagon. "I'll find it for you," he added. "But, in the meantime, you can come with us if you want. Otherwise, I can drop you off somewhere."

She didn't know what to do. Where to go. It made her dizzy. How could she find Solehan under these circumstances? Kidnapped and carried away through the air, far from the only world they knew. She wanted to go back to her old life, and she cursed herself for being so ungrateful. Perhaps the stars were making them pay for their selfishness? Lucine didn't want to torment herself anymore. Just sleep and think of nothing. Maybe it was a bad dream from which she would wake up?

"Listen," Zaf said, "it's okay if you don't know. You just need some time. You can change and rest in the wagon. If you want, I can leave Katao to watch over you while I continue on the road. Does that sound good?" The old man seemed to sense the turmoil that consumed her.

Lucine nodded slightly, her sad gaze still fixed on the dog's eyes.

She timidly finished her piece of bread and then entered the caravan to change, closing the door behind Katao. The interior was cozy, with a bunk bed, a table and chair, a small basin, and a few oil lamps that created a slightly dimmed atmosphere. Several colorful cushions and curtains provided privacy and enhanced the sense of warmth and tranquility. Various shelves, scattered across the walls, held all sorts of trinkets, as well as many books and several curious objects.

Once washed and changed, Lucine slipped into the bunk bed. The dog nestled against her. Her body and mind paralyzed by everything she had just experienced, Lucine stroked Katao's fur with a distant air. She felt the small caravan jolt into motion, the muffled sound of the horse's hooves thudding on the road. The uneven nature of the path caused all the trinkets to vibrate, with wooden surfaces colliding with metal, glass, and other materials.

As if to harmonize with this strange symphony, a slow and gentle tempo of music rose within the small carriage. Still numb, Lucine lazily lifted the stack of objects piled on the nightstand. There, she discovered what appeared to be a small wooden music box playing its tragic and beautiful melody.

Too exhausted to dwell on this discovery further, Lucine looked at the intriguing object and let herself be lulled by the tune. Perhaps she would wake up in the forest, with Solehan by her side? All of this was just a horrible nightmare. It had to be.

Finally, a long-awaited sleep took hold of her.

5

 The hours, the days passed by. Dawn and twilight alternated. Between lethargy and reality, Lucine remained concealed under the sheets of the bunk bed. She wanted to forget the rest of the world as she lay in this illusory cocoon. But the disappointment of waking up every time in the caravan, in this bed, grew within her. How could time continue to flow so brazenly? As if nothing had happened. As if nothing had changed. Every minute, every second away from her old life, away from the only sanctuary she knew among the trees of the vast forest. Away from Solehan.

Water and meals were placed on the small table. The warmth of Katao's body and the soothing melody of the music box provided her with some comfort. Still unwilling to believe, she fell asleep once again.

Just a nightmare. Just a nightmare.

A few more hours dissipated, despite Lucine's pleas and prayers. When she awakened again in the caravan, she could no longer ignore her new reality. Her heart tightened.

She partially opened the curtain and glimpsed the darkness of the night. How long had she slept? How many days? The truth of her situation slowly seeped into her mind. Even if she had wanted to, she could no longer escape.

The stars had granted her wish with cruel irony. Her cursed desire not to see the legend of the stars had come true, her wish for a different future had been ultimately bestowed.

The resigned golden and silver eyes of Solehan collided with her memory. With a gaping hole in her chest, Lucine tightly grasped her amulet to compose herself. Was he still alive? If he was, would she have a chance to find him? Her mind preoccupied, the druidess observed the rumpled sheets of the bed, evidence of the confusion that had consumed her in recent days. Because Solehan had allowed her to escape and continue her life, she owed it to him to find him and learn more. Honoring this promise might be the only thread that would allow her to escape this bottomless and purposeless maze. Lucine decided to get up.

She was surprised not to see Katao as usual and not to hear the familiar rhythm of hooves. The caravan had stopped. She stepped out and discovered the old man and his companion sitting around a campfire by the roadside, the serene blanket of the starry sky overhead.

Lucine sat beside them under Zaf's benevolent gaze.

He offered her a piece of grilled rabbit.

"That's kind of you, thank you," she said, in a hoarse voice, "but I've never eaten animal meat before." The druidess declined his offer with a small hand gesture.

Without appearing offended, Zaf nodded and pulled out a piece of bread from a small bag near him, offering it to her instead.

"Thank you," she began. "Where I grew up, we live . . . *lived*—" Lucine's voice choked. "—in harmony with nature. It was forbidden to kill animals. We nourished ourselves with berries and our harvest," she whispered, hugging her knees against her chest.

Katao barked, and the young woman felt a sense of approval from the dog.

"Do you come from the Astral Forest?" Zaf asked cautiously. "Near where we found you?"

He had guessed it. Lucine nodded timidly.

"What is your name?"

"Lucine."

She hesitated before revealing more. Her throat dried up. And then reality hit her once again. She couldn't protect anyone anymore. She no longer held any secrets. So, she began to tell him her story.

Her childhood, her relationship with Solehan and the elders of the druidic clans. The lush green beauty of the Astral Forest and its majestic towering trees, with the impressive wooden huts perched around their massive trunks, forming the village where she had grown up. Each hut painted in the colors of its clan, their height among the foliage exuding safety and protection. The hamlet seemed to hover within the vegetation, concealed in a leafy sanctuary that had sheltered a peaceful life until then.

Lucine reminisced about the place where her people gathered at all times of the day and night to admire the celestial vault through the large openings in the roofs of their dwellings, veiled only by ingenious systems of curtains when the weather turned gloomy. When had she last contemplated the stars in such a way?

The various druidic traditions, the symbols of tattoos scattered across her body, and the legend of the stars. That cursed legend.

Zaf listened attentively, captivated by a story he had never heard before. The dog also seemed to follow with keen attention.

Lucine swallowed hard. She also revealed to him what had happened on the day of the Eclipse. Her words flowed out of her mouth; her memories surged in her mind. She relived the scene through her words, felt her feet wet with blood once again, smelled death and decaying wood. The strange wooden creatures drawing closer. She felt as if she was abandoning Solehan once again.

Her heart constricted. Something broke inside her. A dam gave way. Tears finally flowed, liberated from the insurmountable wall she had tried to build in these past days. She clenched her amulet in her hand until her knuckles hurt.

Katao came and lay down beside her, emitting a comforting whimper. Zaf took out a large blanket from his pack. He placed it over their shoulders and enveloped all three of them.

Lucine wept on the old man's shoulder, releasing everything she had buried within her since that fateful day. All the numbing emptiness she had managed to accumulate in her mind.

Something finally opened up. And her lethargy flew away.

23

The next day, they resumed their journey. With her mind still disoriented, the druidess no longer knew exactly where to go, but she gratefully accepted the chance to follow the old man. Perhaps she could learn more about what had happened to her brother along their path?

Feeling indebted, Lucine wanted to help Zaf finish packing up and harnessing his horse. She approached the animal gently and let it sniff her hand. After receiving its approval, she delicately placed her hand between its nostrils and stroked its head, moving up toward its ears.

As Zaf swept away the last traces of their camp with a flick of his foot, he observed the scene. "It seems that she likes you. You have a way with animals," he said, with a certain tenderness in his voice.

Lucine returned a slight, melancholic smile.

Once the preparations were complete, the young woman settled beside Zaf at the front of the caravan. Katao also came and lay down at their feet in the small space arranged for the driver. The sun ascended slowly on the horizon, and they set off on the dusty road.

For the very first time, the druidess beheld landscapes other than those of the Astral Forest, with fields and golden clearings that seemed to stretch endlessly, embraced by the dawn's gentle rosy hue. A few birds fluttered happily above them, playing and chirping. It was a serene, almost idyllic sight.

A discovery that contrasted with the tales of the elders about the dangers of the outside world. Despite all those warnings, Lucine found herself smiling, breathing in the fresh morning air, savoring the novelty that blossomed before her. New shades of emotions, new colors that painted over the grayness she had suffered in recent days. But did she have the right to appreciate this scenery after what she had just experienced? Wasn't she betraying the teachings she had received? How strange it was that her wish had been granted under such circumstances. She was finally being given the opportunity to see the rest of the world. The stars must surely be mocking her. A twinge of guilt made her hold her arms close to her body.

And then, a curious ballet began. A dance of encounters and negotiations. On their journey, they crossed paths with souls of all kinds. Riders, sometimes alone or in groups; other carriages, caravans, and wagons heading to various destinations. Were there so many human beings living outside the Astral Forest? Lucine felt dizzy once again. She realized the extent of her ignorance.

At the sight of Zaf's colorful caravan, many stopped to negotiate with the old man and buy essential goods. Nevertheless, a certain unease stirred within Lucine. She discerned the suspicion and sometimes disdain in the eyes of the strangers who glanced discreetly at her. Why were they staring at her in that way?

Zaf's posture grew tense, and his words, although cordial, became increasingly brief as the exchanges went on.

After yet another transaction, one of the riders mounted his horse and cast a suspicious glance in Lucine's direction before galloping away with haste.

The old man, visibly upset, packed up his merchandise and took his place beside her.

"Zaf," she said, her tone serious, "you're going to have to tell me what's going on and why some people are looking at me like that."

"It's because they fear magic," he declared, with a saddened face.

"What magic?"

"In Astitan, only the magic of the goddess Callystrande is tolerated."

"Callystrande?"

Zaf nodded and sighed. "Goddess of light and virtue. It is said that every morning, when the sun rises, the goddess bestows her blessing and protection upon us. It is believed that she created all that is good in this world and that she blessed a few chosen ones to represent her good word. These people choose to dedicate their lives to honoring Callystrande and, in return, she grants them a gift. The ability to spread goodness around them by performing miracles. Healing people, slaying certain creatures . . . the usual stuff."

"And so, what does that have to do with me?" Lucine asked, intrigued, one of her eyebrows arched in question.

"Let's just say that these chosen ones usually have a distinctive attire, quite recognizable. Like priests or paladins. Robes, armor, a stern demeanor . . . but a young woman with golden and silver eyes and tattoos all over her body can make some people think twice."

"Oh . . ." Lucine's lips tightened, and a disappointed pout formed on her face. She examined the intricate patterns inked on her forearms with embarrassment. Was her appearance truly so unusual? She tugged at the sleeves of her shirt, attempting to conceal the tattoos, and clumsily tried to bury her face in her long brown hair. "But aren't you afraid of that? Magic?" she dared to ask. "Being seen with me?"

"There was a time . . .yes," Zaf admitted. "I was afraid, too. But that fear took everything from me," he murmured. He urged the horse to trot again.

"What do you mean?"

"I witnessed firsthand how far the greed and wickedness of men could go under the pretext of following their belief and forcing others in the same direction."

Lucine cast a tender look at the old man, urging him to continue his story.

Zaf, his attention fixed on the road, took a long breath. "My daughter . . ." His voice trailed off. ". . . had the misfortune of being born with different colored eyes as well," he finally added. "And when followers of Callystrande came to accuse her of practicing magic . . ." He sighed deeply. "I did nothing to stop them." The old man's fingers made the leather reins creak between his hands, his pain gripping his body. His guilt seemed to relentlessly ruminate in his conscience.

Sympathetic, Lucine slumped her shoulders. She glanced at the shimmering trail that traced down Zaf's wrinkled cheek. "I'm sorry," she whispered, lightly placing a hand on the old man's arm.

"No, it's all my fault," he growled. "I was a coward, such a coward." He turned his head toward Lucine, fixing her with furious eyes. "But I promised myself that it won't happen again. I want to give meaning to her death, even if I have to work toward it until the end of my days."

Her death? Were the followers of Callystrande so fanatical? Concerned, Lucine studied her tangled fingers resting on her knees.

"A few months ago," Zaf said, "during an exchange, a person claiming to be an oracle predicted that this quest for redemption would serve something grand." He chuckled at the irony. "I know it's just nonsense, but it gives me hope that one day I can finally look at myself in the mirror without feeling guilty for not being there for her."

"Is that why you took me in?"

"Yes." He nodded. "That's also why I try to help as many people as possible in this kingdom. By the way, in the next village, I'll buy you new clothes to conceal yourself better. If anyone asks, you're my granddaughter and you're traveling with me to help sell my merchandise."

Lucine nodded with a slightly dismayed smile. Had the elders been right to live secluded in the forest in this way to protect themselves? A bitter taste passed through her mouth. She observed the golden wheat fields gently swaying in the morning breeze. How could so much beauty be tarnished by fear? It made no sense. Was it naive to wish it could be otherwise?

Then, she thought of the old man and his dog, of the kindness he had shown her so far. Was he risking his life for hers?

Lucine turned to him, her eyes slightly glistening. "Thank you, Zaf, for everything . . ."

Melancholy transformed into joy on the old man's face. "However, don't look at anyone with those eyes, or we're toast!" He chuckled again.

They both burst into laughter and continued their journey to the rhythm created by the horse's trot.

6

Curls of smoke finally wafted from the chimney of a building in the distance. After several hours on the road, under the brilliant sun of the lands of the kingdom of Astitan, a hamlet finally appeared on the horizon.

"We have arrived at the village of Tavell," Zaf announced.

"I will park the wagon here and go buy you some clothes. Once you're concealed, we can go to the village together. Is that alright with you?"

Lucine nodded happily.

The old man instructed his dog to watch over her and walked away toward the village, whistling.

The young druidess watched as he became nothing more than a dark dot on the dusty road. She raised her arms in the air and stretched her weary body from the journey along the winding path.

But the wait became long, and curiosity got the better of the impatient young woman. So, after several minutes of sitting at the front of the wagon, stroking Katao, she decided to get off and stretch her legs as well, closely followed by the dog.

On the other side of the main road, Lucine caught sight of a small grove taking shape and delighted in the gentle rustling of the leaves from the lush green trees in the fresh air. Nostalgia swept over her as she sought refuge under their vegetal protection. Though they were much humbler than the trees of the Astral Forest, their woody scent embraced her with tenderness. She reached a small pond and sat on the mossy and velvety ground to savor the moment.

Katao lay down beside her, seemingly taking his role as a protector to heart.

Intrusive images clashed against her memory, and she tried to block and dilute them courageously from her mind. She wanted to focus only on her promise to find Solehan and the splendor unfolding before her. Nothing else. She no longer had time to be swallowed by her sadness. Nevertheless, she took hold of the wooden amulet that the elders had given her and passed it over her head to examine it closely between her fingers. It was a symbol of her former life, a comforting reminder tinged with melancholy.

She then admired the shimmering reflections on the water and cherished this moment of tranquility, enveloped in the comforting embrace of nature she loved so much. It had been greatly missed. She closed her eyes and listened to the silent yet wild cacophony of the forest. She appreciated the texture of the wooden amulet in her hands.

In this serene state, Lucine felt its benevolent presence. Its warmth. And when she opened her eyes once more, a radiant glow rippled in the water. Just as graceful, the white fox appeared on the other side of the body of water, the nobility of its shimmering fur reflected in the mirror-like liquid at its feet. It seemed to shine like a celestial body amid the darkness formed by the trees. A sun, a moon proudly asserting itself within the emerald nebula of foliage. An animal of otherworldly beauty. A mirage.

They observed each other for a long time. In silence. With respect and gratitude. Why did he seem to follow her? Why was it important for him to save her? Lucine placed a hand on her chest and warmly thanked him. Without a word. Just with her beating heart.

"Oh my goodness!" exclaimed Zaf from behind her.

In an instant, as she turned her head to discover the astonished expression on the old man's face, the fox vanished. It seemed to have been nothing but a dream. Had Zaf seen it too?

"Why are there so many birds?" the old man asked.

Perplexed, Lucine looked up. A swarm of birds of all kinds stared at her. All the feathered creatures were perched on various branches, their keen eyes scrutinizing her attentively. Falcons, eagles, owls—a curious assembly had come to witness the spectacle of her life. A cold shiver ran through

Lucine. What did all this mean? Was this part of the legends of the ancients?

Katao barked, and the birds hurriedly flew away.

Lucine stood up, slightly stunned, and noticed the clothes in Zaf's arms. He handed them to her, stammering, "How—how did you do that?"

"I don't know," she murmured honestly, as she put the amulet back around her neck.

Both of them, astounded, remained silent, their heads lowered. No words seemed to make sense of what they had witnessed. Without dwelling on this strange phenomenon, they decided to continue their journey.

Lucine put on her new clothes inside the caravan. Zaf had bought her a pair of pants and a long-sleeved shirt that finally fit her. She tied the shirt with a lace up to her neck. He had also brought her a belt, boots, and gloves to hide the tattoos on her hands, as well as a small brown cape with a hood. Within the stack of clothes, she also discovered a small dagger, which she attached to her belt.

The colorful caravan arrived at the village square in the afternoon. Zaf cheerfully got off and arranged all his merchandise on a table at the front of the vehicle.

Wanting to be helpful, Lucine removed the harness from the horse, tied the animal a little further away, and fed and watered it.

"Here," Zaf said. "If you see something you like at the market, treat yourself." He placed a few coins in her hand. "I might be busy for a while!"

Surprised, Lucine observed the gleaming copper metal between her fingers. Accustomed only to bartering and exchanging goods for other items of similar value among the druidic clans, this was the first time she had ever held currency in her hands. Although she had seen Zaf use coins for bargaining, the young druidess wondered how such a small piece of metal could have any value? She played with the coins between her fingers and admired the various engravings. One of them caught her attention—a female face, tears flowing abundantly on either side.

But she didn't have time to thank Zaf or inquire further, as several customers were already flocking to his stall to admire his goods and inquire about various information. Left to her own devices and exploration, she vowed to be cautious and not attract attention.

With Katao following her, the druidess delved into the stalls of the market to contemplate the various products while trying to conceal herself as best as possible under her hood. It was strange to see all these objects she didn't know: curious trinkets, colorful fabrics, and spices with a scent from elsewhere.

Lucine let out a small cry of admiration. One of the stalls displayed bows and arrows of various sizes and materials. A certain covetousness seized the young woman. Imprisoned by the vocation created for her by the druids and forced to hide to practice archery, she had been left the opportunity to train only during her nocturnal escapades with Solehan. Now, filled with melancholy, she gazed dreamily at the merchandise.

A man dressed entirely in leather approached her, exuding confidence of making a deal. A falcon perched on his forearm devoured her with large yellow eyes.

"You can pet its head if you want," the man offered, seeing the young woman's interest in the animal.

Lucine complied, too enthused to miss this opportunity. The bird seemed to appreciate the gesture. In a graceful arm movement, the merchant whistled what seemed to be a command. The feathered creature suddenly took flight, its wings unfolding with wild elegance.

Lucine looked up to the sky and contemplated the noble circling of the raptor that flew over the market square. The animal seemed to be the master of the place. It flew with impressive speed, sometimes brushing the heads of onlookers and twirling with prodigious grace. After this demonstration, the falcon settled back on the merchant's forearm in a controlled gesture. The young druidess let out another exclamation of laughter at the man and his animal's feats.

An immense wave of pride, seemingly emanating from the raptor, struck Lucine. She observed the bird and its slender silhouette attentively. She admired the freedom of its flight and envied its possibilities. Despite herself, the contrast of the image of Solehan imprisoned under the enormous vine resurfaced.

"I am a tracker, a falconer," the man announced, "and also a merchant in my spare time. I may be able to show you something that interests you. A bow, for example?"

"Yes, I would like that," she replied, trying to hide as much as possible under her hood. From her pocket, she took out the few coins Zaf had given her.

"Mmhh," the man said, "for that price, I can sell you this one." He pointed to a small bow of modest appearance in his stall.

Overjoyed at being able to buy it, she placed the coins in the man's outstretched hand.

"Here, have some arrows. I'll add them for free," he said with a smile.

"Oh, thank you!" she exclaimed, grabbing them.

Lucine couldn't contain her euphoria, and the most genuine smile appeared on her lips. The world wasn't so dangerous after all. Perhaps the elders had been wrong? Maybe Zaf had exaggerated?

The merchant recoiled. A grimace twisted his face. The man's limbs froze, and the coins vibrated in his still outstretched hand.

The market square tilted in the young woman's head. He had caught sight of her eyes.

Lucine's heart began to race. What had she done? She had forgotten all caution. Would she be arrested? Panicked, she fled and got lost in the crowd, with Katao following her hastily.

She ran until she reached the caravan. Zaf was still busy with several customers, showing them various objects. She took refuge inside to find shelter. Terror gripped her throat. Was she in danger? Would she ever feel safe? Would Zaf also be threatened?

Perhaps the druids had been right after all. She should live secluded in the middle of a forest to be at peace and not jeopardize the lives of the people she would meet. But how could she find her brother under those circumstances? Would he also suffer because of his appearance?

From her wandering thoughts arose a certain anguish. Then the anguish gave way to sadness, and sadness to exhaustion, and she fell asleep, slumped on the table, with Katao at her feet.

7

A terrible headache woke Solehan. A shiver ran through him. This time, it was the coldness of the stone against his back that he felt first.

He lifted his head as best he could. The wound on his chest caused by the thorny vine seemed to have been treated, as a makeshift bandage of dead leaves had been placed on his side.

Solehan tried to sit up, but a piercing pain in his wrists and ankles burned his skin. He realized that he was still held captive by crimson vines. How long had he been bound like this? His previous encounter with the mysterious man with the strange gaze also clearly had not been a dream. Who was that man? What did he want?

Still confused, Solehan turned his head from side to side to survey his surroundings. His eyes struggled to adjust to the blinding light, while a fetid smell reached his nostrils. Like an open mouth revealing a glimpse of a troubled sky, a huge opening in the ceiling above him bathed the center of the vast room in a dazzling glow, leaving the edges in a certain darkness.

"Ah! My little wolf cub has finally awakened," a raspy voice emanated from a dark corner of the room.

Solehan's heart raced. His body tensed with anxiety. He pulled at his restraints as best he could. The thorns sank into his flesh as he tried to free himself. His wrists and ankles turned red. "I will get my revenge!" the druid yelled, his rage still surging, as he struggled.

The man approached, chuckling. Stepping out of the shadows, he positioned his body under the light that streamed from the opening in the ceiling. His pupil-less eyes scrutinized Solehan with keen interest. "Now, now. It seems I must tame the beast," the man jested, with a disturbing grin.

For the first time, the fury in Solehan's eyes focused on the appearance of his captor. What he saw turned his stomach.

Like a statue of alabaster covered in vegetation, the man's flesh melded with the wooden armor that the young druid had previously glimpsed. The man's skin was twisted into a peculiar texture. Sometimes smooth, shiny, and ivory-like, other times lined with grooves and cavities where the bark began. His long hair fell in a gradient of shades: ebony at the roots fading to an extreme white down his back. The features of his face were so finely chiseled that they gave him an almost supernatural appearance. But what struck Solehan were the two jade irises that devoured him with sharp intelligence, enhancing the man's unsettling and enigmatic demeanor. But was this being truly a man?

As he leaned over Solehan, a strand of his hair fell forward, revealing a sharp point at the tip of his ear.

"What abomination are you?!" Solehan shouted.

"Mmhh. Such barking for such a young wolf," the man whispered. He placed his hand on the wound covered by the leaf bandage on Solehan's side with an eerie gentleness.

The young druid flinched at the sight of the long, slender fingers stained black like dead wood.

With his thumb, the man pressed firmly on the injury.

Trapped, Solehan had no choice but to endure his helplessness. He gritted his teeth and clenched his fists. His breathing became more difficult and laborious. Despite his struggle to maintain his dignity, the young man let out a cry of pain through his lips.

"I am an Alaris," the man announced. "A very ancient race. I am the equivalent of a god, and I have no interest in the quarrels of humans," the man added, with icy calm. His ink-colored finger then slid from the wound and slowly moved up Solehan's chest, following the traces of the tattoos amid the tatters of the druid's clothing.

"Don't touch me, you degenerate!" Solehan cried between labored breaths.

The Alaris smiled, revealing white teeth, his attention still fixed on the inked patterns on the young druid's skin. "You have something I need to accomplish my grand work," he commented, "and you will be my most beautiful creation."

Solehan spat forcefully at the man. But this defiant gesture narrowly missed the Alaris and landed on the floor.

A cruel veil passed over his captor's face. "Let us begin."

The unyielding impact of his voice made the young druid start. As the man turned away from him, two enormous vines wrapped around Solehan's body. He let out a new cry of pain and despair that rebounded in the room.

The torture lasted for several hours. Maybe several days. Solehan lost consciousness numerous times. The vines slithered and snaked across his body. The thorns viciously lacerated his flesh. A macabre routine. The Alaris's strange blood-red magic imprisoned him in its cruelty; the man's cutting laughter echoed through the stone.

After what felt like an endless time, his tormentor finally left the room, leaving Solehan alone with his despair and confusion, still chained to the cruel cold stone of the tomb. He preferred it that way, but he lost all sense of time. The young druid teetered between nightmare and reality. Was all of this truly happening? What did the man want from him? He knew nothing. He didn't even know where he was.

Exhausted, Solehan allowed the thorns to sink into his flesh. His mind focused on the gray of the sky piercing through the opening. The pain had become familiar now: expected and predictable.

The sky responded to his sadness, and a storm rumbled in the valley. Physical pain mattered little to him. Perhaps he deserved it after all? But his throat tightened. Had anyone survived the massacre? Was there a chance that Lucine was still alive? It was highly unlikely.

Solehan didn't know what this "Alaris" expected from him, but he knew he would fight to the end. Even if it meant dying. If he couldn't protect them, at least he would avenge them. Or die trying. That was his destiny.

The atmosphere trembled even more; thunder expressed its rage. Raindrops trickled down his face. It was his turn to respond to the elements, and Solehan's body was seized by sobs. His tears mingled with the water from the sky. Why him? Why them?

A bird darted overhead—a black splash against an infinitely gray sky. The young man's eyes, drowned in tears and rain, observed the dark blotches moving on the gray canvas. Bitter irony gripped his insides. Where were the powers that had been promised to him now? Him, chained like an animal to this odious tomb.

He closed his eyes, wet with sadness and the elements. Solehan imagined himself soaring over this accursed castle. He dreamed of the freedom of a bird. The freedom to glide through the sky, flap his wings, and see droplets cascade over his feathers. To be able to escape this nightmare. To float and twirl, brushing against the clouds. To no longer feel this pain, only the caress of the wind against his body. To become one with nature. If his body couldn't fly, then his spirit would depart from here.

He would be free, at last.

An intense pain struck his entire being. He felt himself falling heavily onto the stone floor. When he opened his eyes, Solehan discovered only the hardness of the cold tiles against his cheek. He struggled to use his trembling arms to rise and saw the Alaris standing before him.

The man pointed his long black fingers in his direction.

The young druid observed the thin red filaments of magic dissipating around him, releasing him from their grasp. The pain subsided and gave way to astonishment. He was no longer attached to the tomb but lying on the ground next to it. How was this possible?

As he tentatively stood on his legs, he noticed a few falcon feathers scattered amid the blood and chaos on the tombstone. *Had he transformed? Into a bird?*

"It's about time!" exclaimed the Alaris, with a certain exhilaration.

Then Solehan unraveled the mystery. Flabbergasted, he witnessed the fulfillment of the legend of the stars, of his powers. The escape that the Alaris had prevented with his magic. He examined his quivering hands in a daze.

Before the young druid could clarify his thoughts, new scarlet vines entwined his legs and torso, pinning him against one of the walls.

 With a gloomy air, Lucine hid under the hood of the cape that Zaf had given her the day before. As they continued their journey after their stop in the village of Tavell, she took place at the front of the caravan, with Katao at her feet. The young druidess had reported the incident at the market to the old man, who had then decided to shorten their stay, eager to put some distance between them and the village. However, she had managed to retrieve the bow and arrows she had purchased from the merchant.

"Once we cross the border, we will be safe," Zaf reassured her.

"Why? What's so different about the Kingdom of Vamentera anyway?" Lucine asked, her face still locked in a frown.

"Magic is more tolerated there," Zaf explained. "This kingdom is ruled by Queen Selena Aramanth. She is King Therybane's sister, but she governs in a completely different way!" The old man's tone was joyful.

"What do you mean?" Lucine asked.

"She has decided to remain neutral on the question of magic and only punishes the excesses associated with it, regardless of its source. Even the magic of the goddess Callystrande!"

"Oh. So, I won't need to hide like this anymore?"

"No. You will be able to come and go as you please," Zaf replied cheerfully. "In fact, that's why I help many people cross the border."

A discreet happiness illuminated Lucine's face. Was it true? Was there a place where her appearance wouldn't frighten others? She was struck by a sudden realization. "That's how you honor your daughter's memory, isn't it?"

"Indeed." Zaf nodded, placing a hand over his chest. "I do for others what I should have done for her."

"What was her name?"

"Ava," he answered, with evident nostalgia. Zaf shook his head as if to dispel his sadness and turned to Lucine. "You could also learn more about what happened to your brother in this kingdom. There are many people from all walks of life who might have answers to give you. More than here, at least."

A genuine smile formed on the young woman's lips. Impatiently, Lucine gazed at the colorful fields stretching endlessly. Was the Kingdom of Vamentera truly so different?

They continued their journey for several hours, making sure not to attract more attention than necessary. They stopped at the last village before the border to have a meal, but when they resumed their path, they noticed a considerable number of hoof marks imprinted on the earthy ground. The road leading to the Kingdom of Vamentera seemed to have undergone a significant upheaval—a testimony to recent and intense traffic.

"How come there's so much traffic on this road?" she inquired.

"I suppose we're not the only ones trying to cross the border in the past few weeks," Zaf concluded. "I can't blame them; King Therybane's politics have become quite uncontrollable lately. Don't worry. We're almost there!"

They continued their pilgrimage for several more minutes. The trot of the horse resonated in Lucine's heart like a countdown to freedom. Behind those few hills, their deliverance awaited. The rickety caravan trudged up one of the mounds of earth.

Lucine's body was suddenly seized by terror.

The long-awaited liberation now dissipated into growing anxiety. In the distance, several banners fluttered in the wind, displaying the emblem of a golden lion boldly placed on the immaculate white fabric. The two companions exchanged panicked glances.

"Paladins of Callystrande," Zaf murmured, his hands tightening on the horse's reins.

They now knew that they couldn't turn back without appearing suspicious. They would have to face the accusing stares of dozens of followers of the goddess to reach their salvation. What were these paladins doing here?

Lucine barely had time to catch a glimpse of the massive suits of armor, shimmering with gold, that blocked their path before she had to lower her head. Stern, golden metal masks replaced the expressions on their faces. They seemed no longer human; they were more like an army of inflexible apparitions blending into an ocean of light. Some paladins carried shields attached to their backs, resembling great golden wings that gave them a sinisterly celestial and commanding appearance. It was surely an intentional effect.

Lucine recalled the old man's warning from a few days ago. It was indeed hard not to notice them.

One of the paladins, distinguished by a blood-colored cloak, approached the caravan first, an impressive sword at his belt.

Lucine held her breath, her eyes still fixed on her feet. She concealed her face beneath the hood.

"On the orders of King Arthios Therybane of Astitan and the Crusade of the Dawn's Resolve," the paladin declared, in a deep voice from behind his golden mask, "all travelers heading toward the Kingdom of Vamentera must be inspected before crossing the border."

"Oh, of course, my lord!" Zaf replied, attempting to adopt a cheerful and detached demeanor. "We are nothing more than humble traveling merchants seeking our fortunes elsewhere. Times are tough these days."

Several paladins then surrounded the caravan and opened the rear door to inspect the various items inside. Various noises were heard, indicating little care given to the merchandise.

Lucine swallowed hard. She felt the piercing stare of the paladin with the red cape on her.

"Oh, this is my granddaughter, Ava," Zaf lied, anticipating the paladin's questions. "She's accompanying me on my journey to assist me. I'm getting old, and it's probably not going to get any better," he joked.

The old man laughed to lighten the atmosphere. But the armored man remained impassive to the attempt.

Still at the feet of the young druidess, Katao growled at the paladin. Lucine's stomach jumped to her throat. She hurriedly stroked the dog's head, trying her best to calm him down. But the growls grew louder, and the dog showed his teeth. Lucine then knelt to the animal's height and gently wrapped her arms around its neck.

"I'm sorry, my lord," she managed to murmur to the paladin.

Her heart skipped a beat. No! How could she be so foolish? Twice!

Out of reflex, she had just locked eyes with the paladin—with hazel irises marked with a golden halo that stared at her through the golden mask.

She sat back and hoped for the impossible. A chill ran down her spine. The back of her neck grew damp. Her chest tightened. The young druidess waited for the inevitable. Had Zaf seen it? Should she start running?

Her eyes still on her feet, Lucine felt as if she could have set her shoes on fire. Although her mind was panicked, conjuring up all possible scenarios, her body remained desperately paralyzed. She awaited punishment.

She heard several footsteps from the back of the caravan. The other paladins. Perhaps they were coming to take her away?

"It's fine, you may pass."

Lucine's thoughts liquefied. Her entire body slumped; waves of relief surged through her organs. Her breath returned in fits and starts, and she realized she had been holding her breath the whole time. Her fingers had corroded the wooden seat she had been sitting on, waiting for her end. Maybe he hadn't seen her eyes?

"Thank you, my lord," Zaf exclaimed enthusiastically. The old man performed a brief bow from his upper body and gave a small flick of the whip to the horse, which began trotting again.

They had succeeded. They were safe.

"Wait!" A feminine voice echoed in the clearing.

They had only managed to cover a few meters toward their freedom.

Lucine and Zaf froze. Terrified.

A slender figure approached slowly in their direction. As she passed, the various paladins knelt and drew their swords from their sheaths, inclining them in front of them with the point against the ground as a sign of utmost reverence and respect.

The woman walked with a graceful stride in her long white robe embroidered with golden threads. A light metal armor covered her chest. Her elegance and presence were such that she seemed to float above the ground; her body swayed amid the men and the swirling muddy earth.

Although she also wore a golden mask, hers was staked with long engravings beneath the spaces left for her eyes. Carved tears twisted on the cheeks of her sublime metallic face—similar to the engraving on the coin that Lucine had held between her fingers. A huge halo of golden armor adorned the back of the woman's head, completely encasing her skull. Her golden and piercing eyes burned through the mask, searing into Lucine's soul.

"Your Holiness, we have searched their belongings and found no trace of impure magic," confirmed the paladin with the red cloak, kneeling at the feet of the priestess.

Lucine now realized he had not noticed her eyes, after all.

The priestess addressed Lucine. "Lower your hood, my child," she insisted in a calm and chilling tone.

The young druidess's insides twisted in pain. They had been so close to their goal. In distress, Lucine glanced at Zaf, sweat beading on her forehead.

"Your Holiness," Zaf interjected, "my granddaughter is quite shy, you see." He stepped down from his seat and knelt at a respectable distance between the woman and the young druidess.

Lucine admired the old man's bravery. The strength of his promise. But the attempt seemed desperate.

"*Lower your hood. Immediately.*"

In the face of the priestess's harsh voice, a flash of horror seized Lucine's body, and she couldn't resist the command. With trembling hands, she complied.

The brown hood fell onto her shoulders, but she continued to focus on the ground as best she could, breathing heavily.

"*Look at me.*"

Agony. Lucine felt herself falling into the void, unable to disobey that sharp voice. Slowly, she raised her eyes toward the woman.

Two orbs of fiery ochre burned through the metallic visage. "Seize her!" the priestess ordered.

A whirlwind of gold and panic erupted. Two paladins with fanatical and fervent gazes threw themselves recklessly at Lucine.

Zaf stood on his two feet in an instant. He dove toward one of the paladins to defend her. The poor unfortunate soul was caught in a storm of creaking metal from all sides. Everything happened too fast.

The young druidess saw the cruelty of their situation. The frail body of the old man against the imposing golden armor. He had no chance. He resisted with all the strength he had, gripping one of the paladin's wrists. His emaciated body shuddered under the force exerted by the golden giant.

Through his gesture to protect her, Lucine observed the strength of the promise Zaf had made to his daughter. Hope against intolerance. But his battle was lost in advance.

Wanting to help, she absurdly searched for the dagger that was still attached to her belt. Her fingers pressed onto the handle of the blade with pain. With a trembling arm, she managed to defy the second paladin who approached her. A pathetic threat. She knew it well.

A groan of horror escaped the old man. A cry of distress.

The metallic tip of a sword emerged from Zaf's back. Lucine stared blankly at the vermilion stain that spread across her friend's back like an opening poppy.

His body collapsed a few moments later, revealing to the young druidess the imposing silhouette of the shining metal monster that had slain him. The paladin casually wiped the blood-soaked sword on his pants.

Dazed, Lucine traced the contours of the puddle of blood that formed beneath the old man's lifeless body. The more it expanded, the more the young woman understood the magnitude of her reality.

These monsters. They had killed him.

Zaf had sacrificed himself for her.

Tears flowed uncontrollably down Lucine's cheeks. She only caught a glimpse of her dagger pointed at the second man, which vibrated chaotically as he advanced even further.

The paladin firmly grasped her arm and disarmed her with grotesque ease. Though she struggled with all her might, the man did not flinch.

Growls reverberated by her side. Katao lunged at her assailant, causing him to release his grip.

Lucine fell backward. She no longer understood what she was seeing. She floated amid these white and golden splatters that stirred around her. The muffled sounds of metal, screams, and barks mingled with images of blood and terror. Her fingers sank into the mud. Everything appeared in slow motion, and yet too fast at the same time. She had the sensation of watching the scene from the top of the caravan.

Lucine, save yourself!

Solehan's voice shattered in her memory. His golden and silver eyes scrutinized her soul.

She had to escape. Again. For the promise she had sworn to fulfill.

Lucine began to run in the opposite direction.

Without thinking, no longer feeling her legs in her sprint, she raced toward the woods instinctively. She wanted to drown herself among the trees, soar through their branches, and smell the fresh scent of nature instead of the scent of blood and horror.

Sounds of hooves resonated behind her. Her head collided with the ground.

9

Everything occurred at a dizzying speed.

The captain didn't have time to understand what was happening when a blade had pierced the old man's body right before his eyes. An innocent had died. He had failed.

Despite having seen the strange and extraordinary golden and silver eyes of the young woman, he had not felt any magic emanating from them or their little caravan. He understood why she had tried to hide under her hood. Most of the inhabitants of the cities and villages they had crossed avoided them with fear. The growing fanaticism of his order and the Crusade of the Dawn's Resolve gnawed at his stomach.

For several days on their journey to the kingdom of Vamentera, he had observed the long, solemn, and haughty procession of the crusade. Riding a massive black armored horse, with his unwavering gaze, King Arthios Therybane had led the way, closely followed by the High Priestess. Representative of the faith of the goddess of light and advisor to the king. "The Lamented of Callystrande," as she liked to point out, although her name was Piore.

Dwelling behind the golden glow of her mask, only the deep ochre eyes of the priestess pierced through the surface of metal with an inquisitive air. The long train of her robe shimmered with large angelic wings that seemed to have been sewn from pure gold, floating behind her white stallion like a banner. Every time the imposing halo adorning the back of her head reflected the first rays of the sun, Piore appeared as a symbol to follow for the paladins in the procession behind her.

What hypocrisy.

The captain's fist tightened around the hilt of his sword. The red puddle slowly grew at his feet.

He had never truly appreciated magic, except that of his goddess, but he couldn't reconcile his faith with some of his king's recent decisions. And now, another innocent would die because of the cruelty of the High Priestess.

Having witnessed atrocities from a young age, he had decided to dedicate his life to fighting injustice and protecting the weak. He thanked and honored the protection of the goddess he himself had received. A thirst for justice that he took great pride in. A virtuous aspiration that had allowed him to rise to the rank of captain quickly, at only twenty-two years old. The red cloak of his rank fluttered with nobility over his golden armor.

But he felt no pride at that moment.

The young woman was pursued and brought back on horseback. The captain's hands trembled as he heard her screams and cries, as one of the paladins pulled her by her long brown hair.

How could Callystrande agree with such cruelty?

One of his men violently pushed the captive to the ground in front of the High Priestess, and the young woman began pleading for her life, tears streaming down her cheeks. The gold and silver in her eyes drowned in waves of despair. The youthfulness and innocence of her features crumpled in distress.

The captain felt deep repulsion as he sensed Piore reveling beneath her mask embellished with golden tears. The knuckles of his fingers whitened as he clenched his fist around his sword. He couldn't bear the plea.

When the goddess had appeared to him in a dream, when her magic had radiated through his being, he had known in that moment that he would dedicate his entire life to her. Liquid gold tears had streamed down his face upon waking, confirming the imprint Callystrande had left on his soul.

But now, he couldn't reconcile what was happening before his eyes with that memory.

One of his men, still violently pulling the unfortunate woman's hair, proceeded to tear the clothes she wore, revealing the tattoos that covered her body.

It was too much. The captain couldn't take it anymore. "That's enough," he cut in, with an icy voice.

"She's a witch, Captain Haldgard, she—" the other paladin began in a tone dripping with disgust.

"I said, *that's enough.*" He spoke with all the coldness he could muster. The man released his grip.

The captain then leaned toward the young woman and began covering her by tying her shirt around her back. Behind him, he felt the overflowing exultation of the High Priestess, who continued to witness the scene. A silent rage surged within him.

Under Piore's orders, his men began gathering wood to create a pyre by the roadside. The young woman was to be an example and a warning. That was how witches were treated in the kingdom of Astitan. He couldn't prevent it.

The captain, filled with contempt, watched his men busy themselves. Pretending to go into the woods to relieve himself, he vomited in disgust. His bitterness needed to escape his throat. The young woman was going to be sacrificed in the name of Callystrande.

His hand trembled on the hilt of his mentor's sword, still in its sheath. He thought back to his teachings, to the aid he provided to the less fortunate, his example, his justice, his courage. What courage or justice was there in burning an innocent young woman? One only guilty of being born different. He couldn't bring himself to choose between Justice and Virtue.

He turned back toward the camp, lost in his faith and anger.

The young woman was still softly crying, her body shaking with sobs. The captain picked up the small wooden amulet that had been torn from her neck moments earlier and stuffed it into his pocket. What else could he do?

The paladins tied her to the stake that stood above the pyre, her feet and hands bound. His men had also set fire to the old man's body and his caravan. The dog seemed to have escaped. The horse, still harnessed to the burning wagon, reared frantically.

The captain ran toward it and freed the animal with a sword strike. Once the bonds were broken, the horse fled into the forest. At least one innocent would be saved today. He watched, with bitter irony, as it disappeared into the thick, green edge.

And the moment he dreaded finally arrived. The fire blazed on the pyre before his helpless eyes.

All the paladins had gathered around. The High Priestess proudly presided over them. The cries of the young woman mingled with her screams as the fire began to lick at her feet.

Dazed, he observed the rows of motionless white and golden suits of armor before him. A shimmering and unchanging ocean in the face of cruelty, in the face of injustice. How could this be possible? How could his brothers remain so indifferent to this spectacle?

His heart tore apart with her screams. His limbs began to shiver. His faith was shaken. His goddess could not condone this.

The captain clenched the hilt of his sword in his hand and his knuckles tightened in pain. He didn't know what to do. In a confused numbness, he lifted his eyes to meet the gaze of the unfortunate woman, finding hers in absolute despair.

His soul was struck by lightning.

A sign. The one he had been waiting for.

A liquid golden tear trickled from the young woman's golden eye. It rolled down her cheek and dissolved in the flames below.

A fraction of time that felt eternal. His entire being froze.

Callystrande.

Something deep within him stirred awake. He saw himself draw the sword from its sheath and hurl it recklessly toward the blaze in front of him.

Nothing else existed. The call of his goddess became imperative. Was he the only one who could hear it?

He soared over the sea of golden armor. The paladins faded from his sight. The captain ran with long strides, his armor shielding him from the relentless fire, the blade of his sword gleaming in his hand. His cloak trailed a vermilion wake behind his steps.

He felt imbued with supernatural strength. The will of the goddess of light seemed to manifest in his blade. He didn't know how, but he managed to swiftly and powerfully sever the post to which the unfortunate woman was bound, causing it to topple outside the flames.

The surprised eyes of the young woman then focused on him. He became lost in them, swirling with gold and silver, the golden tear still streaking down her cheek.

Only when he started to untie the bonds on her hands and feet did he realize his actions. A horde of paladins rushed toward him. What had he done?

A deafening sound of wingbeats crashed against his eardrums. As he raised his head, he caught sight of a swarm of birds of all kinds descending upon his brothers.

The captain was bewildered, his mind empty of all thoughts. A leaden weight fell upon his brain. Nothing made sense anymore.

With talons and sharp beaks, the birds swirled around them, forming a frenzied and effervescent shield, their wings beating vehemently.

But adrenaline overwhelmed him.

Taking advantage of the chaos, and with no option to retreat, he freed the young woman from the wooden post. Once her bonds were undone, they began to run toward the border, toward the kingdom of Vamentera.

Why had he done this?

In this illogical escape, he spotted the horse he had released from the blazing caravan galloping toward them. How was this possible?

Who was she?

He helped the young woman onto the saddle before mounting behind her, and they set off in a frantic gallop.

When he turned his head to confirm that it hadn't been a dream, all he saw were the paladins and the metallic gleam of their armor, struggling in a whirlwind of feathers and screams.

10

They galloped at a steady pace for several hours, trying to create a clear distance from the crusade. They didn't exchange a word, but the captain sensed the young woman's fear turning into fatigue as time passed. Initially shivering, she seemed to gradually calm down and eventually dozed off against his shoulder, visibly exhausted.

As the sun started to descend, he decided to stop and create an impromptu camp for the night. After a few minutes of searching, he came across a small pond amid the forest, surrounded by the protection of trees.

He gently laid the still drowsy young woman on the ground and used his red cloak as an improvised blanket to cover her body. He also took out the amulet from his pocket and placed it near her on the ground. After lighting a fire in an attempt to warm her up, he disappeared into the trees.

The heat created by the flames brushed against her skin and her memory. The horror of the pyre surged in Lucine's mind, and she woke up with a start, a hand on her throat. She was safe and sound. Panting, she tried to lessen her sudden terror and discovered the small campfire nearby. Surprised to find the paladin's red cloak draped over her body, she reached for the amulet in the grass. Where had he gone? And why had he saved her?

The image of Zaf's blood-stained shirt invaded her thoughts, and she burst into tears. True to the vow he had made in honor of Ava's memory, he had given his life in exchange for hers. His ultimate act of bravery. Lucine was strangled by guilt and buried her face in her hands. Why was she still alive? Why would she deserve such a sacrifice? She had barely had time to know him.

A lancinating pain suddenly seized her. A grimace twisted the face of the young druidess as she sucked in a breath through her teeth, her cheeks wet with tears. She lifted the piece of cloth to see a large burn on the lower part of her leg. The flames of the pyre had managed to inflict some damage on her body.

Ignorance and shame choked her with grief. Perhaps she shouldn't have survived the Eclipse ceremony. Had she been too naive to believe she would be safe outside the forest?

A figure emerged despite the turmoil caused by her abundant tears. A man stood before her, sword in hand. Too devastated for any fear to grip her body, Lucine wiped her eyes with her sleeve and focused her attention on the form that emerged in the glow of the fire.

Standing upright, the paladin approached cautiously. She caught sight of his short, military-cut chestnut hair, his square jaw, and features that seemed to have been carved from raw granite. Clean-shaven, he wore a stern expression, although a hint of surprise betrayed him. However, despite the obvious austerity of his initial appearance, a certain caution was exuded from the softness of his movements.

He was young. Very young without his golden and sinister mask. Barely older than she was. Lucine noticed that he had removed his impressive armor, revealing his rather broad build, but he had kept his weapon, and the sheath attached to his belt.

How could the paladin she had glimpsed and this man be the same person?

The man's hazel eyes glanced over the wound on her leg. He knelt beside her and placed his sword in the grass. "Wait, I'll help you," he offered, in a deep voice.

Lucine flinched as he positioned his hands a few inches above the injury. What was he trying to do? The young woman pulled her legs closer to herself.

"I can heal you," he murmured, "but you have to let me do it." A faint smile appeared on his impassive face.

He was clearly trying to reassure her. Up close, Lucine could read in the young man's eyes a gentleness that contradicted the severity of his features and angular profile. She recalled Zaf's words. Was he trying to invoke the magic of Callystrande?

Still uncertain, she nevertheless unfolded her legs in the grass.

The young man repositioned his hands above the wound. But nothing came. No light, no magic.

The paladin's face darkened, a flicker of panic and sadness passing through his eyes. He rubbed his hands on his pants, as if hoping some kind of magnetism would take effect. But when he tried again, the goddess remained deaf to his call.

"It's not working?" Lucine asked.

"It seems not."

He withdrew his hands, but Lucine had time to see that he was unsuccessfully trying to hide their trembling.

With a neutral face, the paladin proceeded to clean the wound with water from his small pack and tore a piece of the red cloak to use as a makeshift bandage around her leg. "We'll need to find a healer quickly," he said. "Tomorrow, we'll try to find a village and seek help."

"What's your name?" Lucine asked.

"Talyvien . . . Haldgard."

Feeling helpless in the situation, he sat cross-legged by the fire next to Lucine. He then took out some berries from his pocket and handed them to her.

The young druidess accepted them cautiously.

"I suppose Ava is not your real name?" he said.

"No," she replied, sniffling back a sob.

"Mmhh. So, the man who was with you was not your—"

"My grandfather, no," she finished, her throat tight. "But he sacrificed his life trying to defend me."

"I'm sorry. I should have . . ." He hesitated. "I should have intervened earlier." He placed a hand behind his neck and focused on his feet, looking embarrassed.

Lucine stared at him for a long moment, perplexed. "Why did you save me?" she blurted out.

"I—I'm not sure. I think I saw a sign from Callystrande. A sign that I had to do it. I don't know," he stammered. He avoided her stare, and a tinge of shame escaped through his tone of voice.

"A sign?" Lucine insisted.

"A golden tear fell from your . . . golden eye," he explained, pointing at her face.

"A golden tear?" she exclaimed with incredulity, gently touching her cheek with her fingertips.

She stared absently at the campfire, wondering if it had any connection to the Eclipse ceremony. To the powers promised by the ancient druidic clans. Lucine dismissed this absurd thought. All of this was probably just fabrications and old stories.

"And why would a goddess want to save me?" she scoffed bitterly.

Disillusioned, Lucine focused her teary gaze on the dancing flames. To warm her soul and body, she folded her legs against her chest, arms crossed, chin on her knees.

The paladin looked surprised at the resignation in the young woman's posture. "Because every life deserves to be saved," he declared solemnly.

"Is that why you choose to ignore the color of my eyes when you saw them?" she said sullenly.

"Indeed," he murmured, a slight smirk appearing at the corner of his lips. Compassion shone in his eyes as he looked at Lucine.

"I wish I could believe in that," she whispered, her tone softened. "But all I have left is the hope of seeing a promise come true."

The promise of finding Solehan. But she couldn't say more to the paladin, unsure if she could trust him. Had her own naivety cost Zaf his life? She could no longer afford to believe in the utopia hidden in her heart.

"You seem to be the only paladin who thinks that way, anyway," she finally said.

"I don't know," he said, saddened. "But I am convinced that your friend wouldn't want his sacrifice to be in vain. He would want you to keep living and hoping."

Lucine observed Talyvien, who placed a delicate hand on his sword next to him. For the first time, an almost nostalgic look crossed his face. He was right. Just as Zaf had managed to give meaning to the loss of his child, she had to honor his act of courage. Even if she felt insignificant, she had no choice but to continue.

"You only kept the sword?" she asked.

"Yes, it belonged to my mentor. Tuoryn. It was given to me recently. I couldn't bring myself to part with it. To continue honoring him in battle and in . . . *my faith*." His last words caught in his throat.

Was that why he had abandoned his armor? Lucine wondered. Had his goddess condemned him for his act?

"A part of Tuoryn's soul," Talyvien added, "as well as those of the paladins before him, was forged into the blade. So, they can guide me."

"Oh. He's no longer . . . among us?"

"No," he replied, in a solemn voice. "Before leaving for the crusade, I prayed one last time before his coffin in the grand cathedral."

Happy to redirect the subject, Lucine seized the opportunity to learn more about this man. She didn't want to reveal anything about her own story, out of caution. She cast him a curious glance and silently urged him to continue his narrative.

"I'm talking about the cathedral of Callystra," he explained. "The capital of the Kingdom of Astitan."

"That's where you're from?"

With his hand still resting on his sword, he nodded.

"Have you ever been to the Kingdom of Vamentera?" she asked, hope rising in her chest. Perhaps he knew where to find valuable information that could help her find Solehan?

"No, this is my first time crossing the border. But we were also heading in that direction. The goal of the Crusade of the Dawn's Resolve is to reach the capital of the Kingdom of Vamentera and rally Queen Selena Aramanth to their cause."

Lucine displayed a dismayed pout. But since the crusade was also heading to Vamentera and she would surely have to travel with this man for a while, she tried to learn even more. Her ignorance had already caused too much damage. "Eradicating any other form of magic?" she ventured cautiously.

"Yes. By order of the High Priestess, Piore. 'The Lamented of Callystrande'," he sneered with a grotesque hand gesture. "They sent scouts to announce our arrival. We were stationed there, waiting for permission to enter the territory. And she deemed it wise to conduct a screening of anyone wishing to cross, probably to appease her thirst for fanaticism."

"But so, you . . . don't share her ideas?"

"Let's just say I'm not particularly fond of magic. But to exterminate all people who practice it—" He growled with contempt. "The decision to raise a crusade was made quickly after Tuoryn's death. I imagine Piore finally got her way in her desire for purification to convince King Arthios Therybane."

"Oh, you think she has some influence over him?"

"It seems so. Tuoryn had always been able to temper King Arthios's faith, but since my mentor is no longer here, I no longer recognize the ruler. He has become increasingly severe and uncompromising with the people of his country. A new, fervent, and zealous gleam seems to inhabit his eyes now."

"Mmhh. This priestess . . . Why is she called the 'The Lamented of Callystrande'? Is it related to the tears on her mask?"

Talyvien's initial reaction was to let out a bitter snicker. He clearly did not hold this woman in high regard. "She comes from a humble background," he said, "but she rose to this rank in just a few months, proclaiming that Callystrande herself had revealed to her and commanded her to purify the continent of all impure magic. This name 'Lamented' is derived from a legend that tells of a being with golden wings who would bring the salvation of the goddess of light to the earth. So, when Piore arrived with this attire, with large golden wings embroidered on the train of her robe, many believed they recognized the savior they had long awaited."

Lucine's mouth curved, visible disgust showing on her face.

"Many rumors circulate about her," Talyvien continued. "The most widespread being that no one has ever seen her face, which she conceals under this golden mask representing the weeping goddess. But she is said to possess unmatched beauty. She hides to not provoke temptation, apparently, as the paladins have taken a vow of celibacy. This, of course, only fuels the rumor mill."

"Oh. Do you think her beauty could have played a role in convincing King Arthios?"

"It's possible. He certainly isn't bound by a vow of celibacy." He sneered.

Lucine responded with a slight smile. But a shiver ran through her, and her body grew tense even more. The air was becoming colder. The darkness of the night was settling in peacefully.

Exhausted by her reality and by this information, Lucine felt her eyelids grow heavy. Nothing made sense anymore. She couldn't keep up with the events.

Talyvien noticed her exhaustion. "You should sleep. I'll keep watch," he offered.

She looked at the paladin wearily and nodded, resigned. She wrapped herself in the large red cloak and lay down.

"Lucine," she whispered, with her back turned.

"What?" he said, surprised.

"My name is Lucine."

"Oh."

"I'm not really sure why I'm still alive, but—thank you, Talyvien," she murmured, before closing her eyes.

 Talyvien's attention remained fixed for a long time on the silhouette of the young woman wrapped in his cloak.

What had he done?

Callystrande had finally forsaken him. When he had tried to invoke her glorious warmth in his hands, she had remained deaf to his call. He placed a hand over his heart. A pain sliced through his chest, overwhelming him. He had lost the most important thing in his life.

Earlier in the evening, as he had passed by the shimmering reflection of the pond, he had removed his golden mask and glanced at his face with sadness. The golden halo that usually encircled his hazel eyes around his pupils had vanished. It was at that moment that he understood the consequences of his actions. He was now a fallen paladin. He could never again honor his mentor and the paladins who had preceded him in their faith for Callystrande. He could never go back.

Talyvien had placed his armor in a small cavity beneath a massive rock, keeping only the tunic he wore underneath, but he couldn't abandon Tuoryn's sword. He no longer deserved it, he knew, but it was the last thing he had left of his mentor, who had been like a father to him.

Had he dreamed what he had seen in Lucine's eyes? Was it truly a sign from the goddess, or had he lost his sanity? Was it all worth betraying his honor and his brethren?

He looked once again at the frail body of the young woman wrapped in the large red cloak. And he despised himself for having such thoughts. He had saved her life. He had saved the life of an innocent.

But then, why did his goddess seem to be at odds with that?

11

Solehan woke up once again on the cold stone of the tomb. For the first time since he had been in this place, he felt no particular pain and appeared to be unbound. Only thin bracelets of red energy glowed on his wrists.

The young druid sat up and surveyed the room around him. He was alone. Some carefully folded garments lay at his feet. As he picked them up, he saw that they were made of elegantly woven dead leaves. Why would the Alaris have taken the trouble to leave him clothes?

He decided to put them on to replace his torn and blood-stained attire. As he placed his old clothes on the stone, he stared at them for a long moment. They were the last evidence of what had transpired, the ceremony, and his former life. The young druid placed his hand on them and rolled the fabric between his fingers.

Solehan inspected the tomb once more. A dark and narrow passage leading to a small door emerged from a corner of the large room, and he decided to venture into it.

A long tunnel, immersed in darkness, stretched out before his eyes. Accustomed only to huts nestled in the tall trees of the Astral Forest, confusion gripped his mind. How could such a structure made entirely of stone remain standing? He listened to his footsteps echoing on the disordered and damp tiles with a sharp clacking sound. In some places, the rain had infiltrated the walls. Drops hammered the floor at regular intervals, merging with the pulsations of his heart. A few discreet spiderwebs vibrated as he passed. The young druid wrinkled his nose at the stench of the place; mold was ingrained between the icy stone bricks that inadvertently brushed against Solehan's arms.

The young man's resolve was split in two. He knew he had to find a way to escape from this wretched place. But could he leave this "Alaris" alive after what the being had done to his clan? Even if Lucine had survived, would they ever be safe with this constant threat looming over their heads? His desire for revenge surged through his veins. He gritted his teeth.

Solehan followed the tunnel for what seemed like an endless duration, relying on the faint glow of the thin red filaments around his wrists to guide him when darkness swallowed him completely. Finally, he arrived at an old spiral stone staircase, which he ascended.

Why was he no longer bound? Why did the Alaris persist in torturing him, only to heal him afterward? What did these strange, magical vermillion bracelets mean?

He thought back to the vision of feathers on the stone. Had he lost his mind under the pain and exhaustion, or had the legend of the stars finally come true? What purpose would such power serve now? His entire village, along with those of the other druid clans, had been reduced to nothingness. There was nothing left to protect. Was the Alaris aware of this legend, despite the isolation of the druids in the Astral Forest? Solehan would have to remain on guard.

A weathered wooden door awaited him at the top of the staircase. He proceeded to open it cautiously, yet the hinges creaked under the effort. Emerging from the abyss, Solehan was blinded by the brightness of the place. A long row of windows stretched endlessly along a vast corridor. Orange rays of light escaped through the openings, leaving their contrasting imprint on the solid parquet floor. Facing them, several rough wooden doors responded with perfect symmetry.

The floorboards creaked under the weight of his body as he advanced. Through the grime on one of the windows, the gray and gloomy city spread out, even as the atmosphere was painted with the warm hue of the final hours of the day. The city he had seen on the day of his arrival in the clutches of the enormous creature. What was this place? Itching with curiosity, the young man opened the first door within his reach.

Although accustomed to a modest life in the forest, he realized he was entering what appeared to be an entirely ordinary bedroom. A few old dusty pieces of furniture lay scattered about. In the center of the room stood a massive canopy bed.

But there was a figure beneath the sheets.

Solehan's heart raced. Gathering his courage, he approached and lifted the fabric with caution. The body of a child, lignified in wood, lay in eternal slumber, trapped in the last position it had assumed.

Solehan felt a surge of revulsion.

He then remembered the horror of seeing the members of his clan transformed in a similar manner. This was likely a child who once lived in this castle. Solehan gently placed the sheet back over the body, completely covering it as a sign of respect. He returned to the corridor, which he followed, but decided not to open any more doors. They all surely led to various rooms of the castle, and he could not bear the sight of other unfortunate souls.

He passed the long procession of windows and doors, trying to remain inconspicuous. An antechamber leading to a lounge revealed itself to him. The young druid's steps became cautious. To his immense astonishment, Solehan discovered the Alaris, a glass of wine in hand, lounging casually on a massive blood-red sofa. Solehan struggled to swallow.

The large room was bathed in only natural light, emanating from a large adjoining balcony. The last rays of the sun timidly pierced through the clouds, casting a slightly rosy ambiance that outlined the sculpted profile of his captor. The appearance of the Alaris took Solehan by surprise.

Like a statue of a fallen emperor on his throne, the posture of his body and face seemed to have been chiseled from marble. But an air of raw pain marred his features. With one ankle resting on a knee and a distant gaze, the Alaris seemed lost in his thoughts. He had not heard Solehan approach. With an odd delicacy, he swirled the glass between his dark fingers, reflecting the sunlight on the deep red liquid. The ember of his eyes appeared cooled by a striking nostalgia, and memories seemed to replace the cruelty that Solehan had witnessed until then.

A tunic made of carefully woven leaves, like the one Solehan wore, revealed the delicate, irregular texture of his shoulders—the only place where the bark was still faintly visible. The rest of his body displayed pale, perfectly smooth skin, and his long hair pulled back revealed his peculiar ears.

To complete this tableau, enormous velvet sofas and armchairs dominated the center of the room, while several solid wooden furniture pieces displayed numerous elegantly engraved decorations that adorned the rest of the lounge. A dormant fireplace rested in one corner, and the lofty stone vaults of the ceiling sealed this work of art.

The young druid was intrigued. He loathed having to admit it, but there was something captivating about the Alaris. Absorbed by this sight, he leaned in to observe him better.

The parquet floor creaked under Solehan's steps. The green stare pierced him. The emotion of his captor immediately became sharp again, although a slight smile appeared on his face.

"Ah! Finally! Please, have a seat," the Alaris offered, gesturing to one of the sofas with a wave of his hand.

Solehan cautiously approached in his direction. He clenched his fists, his barely contained rage still present, his desire for vengeance ever burning.

"I believe we both know where this road leads," the Alaris joked, looking at Solehan's fists, his hand still extended toward the sofa.

Resigned, the young druid walked over and sat on the couch opposite him. Solehan, his facial features torn by his fury, stared at the Alaris.

"Perhaps a bit of wine?" the man offered, in a grotesquely light tone.

Solehan shook his head, his jaw still clenched.

"Mmhh, too bad, you're missing out," the Alaris mused. "They have a fantastic wine cellar!"

An expression of deep disgust crossed Solehan's face as he remembered the wooden child he had seen under the sheets.

"I suppose you have questions?" the Alaris asked, then taking a nonchalant sip.

"Why me?" Solehan erupted.

The Alaris let out a sigh as his first response. He sank his shoulders further into the couch, ostentatiously getting comfortable. "Isn't it obvious?" he finally said, rolling his eyes. "Mmhh, perhaps you're hungry? Or maybe you'd like to taste a more special vintage?"

Before Solehan could respond, the tips of the Alaris's left hand fingers emitted a reddish glow. A door creaked open, and a small, slender figure entered with a tray. Solehan immediately recognized one of the creatures made of wood and bark that had attacked and lignified his people on the day of the ceremony. Instinctively, he recoiled.

From a closer look, Solehan noted that its body surprisingly resembled that of a human woman, although branches had grown onto her shoulders and head. She placed the tray on the low table right in front of him. Solehan continued to watch her warily as she exited the room.

"A forest spirit, a lychena," explained the Alaris, observing his reaction with amusement. "Some of them have chosen to align themselves with my cause."

The food laid out in front of him consisting of strange berries and fruits, looked appetizing. But even though he was hungry, Solehan decided not to touch it. As a precaution.

"If I wanted to kill you, it would have already been done," mocked his captor, lingering his gaze on the untouched food.

The young druid noticed that two filled wine glasses had also been placed in front of him. One contained a deep red liquid, similar to what the Alaris held in his hand—probably ordinary wine. The second one, however, was filled with a vibrant cobalt-blue drink. Was it the special vintage the Alaris had mentioned? It didn't matter; he wouldn't touch the glasses anyway.

"Enough beating around the bush," Solehan declared, his voice rising in anger. "Why am I here?"

A broad smile spread across the Alaris's face, revealing his white teeth. "Straight to the heart of the matter. I see, ah!"

The sardonic stare of the Alaris landed on the wine swirling in his right hand. Then, as his features became serious once again, it shifted to the young druid. "To help me exterminate humanity."

Solehan burst into a nervous and loud laughter that resonated throughout the room. "I knew you were disturbed," he gasped, "but to this extent—"

A burning sensation violently wrapped around Solehan's neck, strangling him. His body lifted off the couch and hung suspended in the air. He fought to breathe, instinctively placing his hands on the fiery collar that now encircled his throat. He struggled to remove it, burning his hands in the process. Once again, he felt powerless and trapped by the magic of the Alaris. At the man's mercy. His body writhed in mid-air like a disjointed puppet. The lack of air became excruciating.

From the corners of his teary eyes, he saw thin red filaments shooting out from the Alaris's left hand toward him, as the man continued to drink from his other hand, observing Solehan over the rim of the glass with delight.

Solehan fell heavily to the floor. He began coughing and struggled to fill his lungs with air.

"You find it amusing, and I understand," the Alaris replied impassively. "There was a time when I thought there might be another solution. A solution where humans and nature could coexist; where they could learn. But I have spent enough time observing them to know that it's impossible. Centuries of watching them destroy everything like spoiled children. Destroying each other."

The Alaris got up from his sofa and approached Solehan, who was still on the ground, his breath wheezing between bouts of coughing. "You don't even know who gave you this gift and why," the Alaris said, "and even worse, you reject it. Humans are not capable of magic unless blessed by a god."

Solehan was overcome by dizziness. Was it the lack of air? Or what the Alaris had just told him?

So, he had indeed received certain powers during the Eclipse. Had he truly transformed into a bird? A god? None of the elders had ever mentioned any gods to him, as druids believed only in nature and the stars.

"Have you never questioned yourself about the Tree of Ether? Its origin?" the Alaris calmly asked, kneeling beside the young druid.

Solehan stared at the ground, trying to sort through the thoughts racing in his head.

The Alaris sighed, irritated by his ignorance. "The world we inhabit was created by gods. No one knows how many there are, and some choose never to reveal themselves. But beneath the Tree of Ether lies the body of Teluar, the god of Nature."

Still on the ground, Solehan absorbed what his captor was saying. He looked up defiantly, and the Alaris's eyes met his with a hint of misery.

"As a god of beauty and life," the Alaris stated, "not war and violence, Teluar chose to enter hibernation at this place, overcome by sorrow and guilt in the face of human cruelty." In a saddened tone, he added, "His slumber has had certain consequences, such as the appearance of creatures that are part-human, part-animal, degenerate monsters."

"And what does that have to do with me?" Solehan grumbled in a hoarse voice.

"But absolutely everything!" the Alaris exclaimed, gesturing with an annoyed wave of his hand. "You see, Teluar is the son of the opposing goddesses. The goddess of light that humans named Callystrande and the one who rules over shadows going by the name of Sazaelith. It is said that they are the origin of all things. The cycle of time, day and night. And from their union, Nature sprung forth."

"And so?" Solehan growled. "Spare me your history lessons; I still don't see—"

"What audacity for someone so ignorant," the Alaris interrupted, rolling his eyes. "I'm getting to that!" He cleared his throat. "Therefore, as I was saying, since the hibernation of their son, Callystrande has been pleading for his return, while Sazaelith only wishes to exact vengeance on the men who caused his sorrow. In order to protect their son and the tree that has grown above his body, every ten thousand years, a few selected humans receive Teluar's gift under the blessing of the mother goddesses. Revealed when their divergent paths finally intersect during the Eclipse."

The Alaris delicately placed his dark fingers under Solehan's chin and lifted his face. "Usually represented by one golden eye and one silver eye," he whispered.

Solehan abruptly recoiled from the man's touch and turned his head in disgust.

The Alaris stood up and walked slowly toward the large balcony. The sun had almost disappeared behind the towering mountains that stretched across the valley.

"Even if all of this were true," Solehan retorted, "my role would be to protect the Tree of Ether, not to kill all humans!" He got back on his feet.

The Alaris turned toward him, the last rays of the sun framing his slender figure. "Your role is to protect Nature! To restore its glory! To honor Teluar and awaken him from his slumber so he can witness his creation devoid of cruelty!" he exclaimed. "And this is incompatible with the human race. Once we have exterminated enough human souls, only you will be able to awaken him."

"Why is it so important to wake him from his hibernation anyway?" Solehan spat.

"Because as long as he remains asleep, the world will be doomed. Humans will destroy everything."

Silent, Solehan sat back on the sofa. He focused his distracted attention on the empty wine glass his captor had placed on the table in front of him. The Alaris was completely mad. To destroy humanity in order to save Nature as the only option? To awaken the god Teluar? It was senseless and cruel.

Solehan had never encountered anyone other than the druids of the Astral Forest, but they certainly didn't deserve to die, just as his own people hadn't deserved it. And how could he know if what the Alaris had told him was true and not fabricated?

Even if his powers turned out to be a gift from the god Teluar, it mattered little to him. But perhaps he could learn enough to control them. He could then avenge his people, kill the Alaris, and search for Lucine. Find out if she had survived.

Did she possess a similar magic? The legend of the druids only mentioned such powers for men.

"Mmhh, I understand your reluctance," the Alaris admitted, approaching behind the sofa where Solehan sat. "You know, I am not the one who killed your sister."

Solehan's breath caught in his throat.

Lucine.

With a swift motion, he turned toward the Alaris.

The black fingers of his captor rested on his forehead, emitting a faint, shimmering red glow. "Let me show you." The voice of the Alaris undulated from a distance.

Solehan's eyes took on a crimson light as his limbs turned to stone on the sofa. Everything wavered. A swirling darkness without boundaries consumed his vision. Small red dots flickered in the bottomless dark ocean that engulfed Solehan. The spots transformed into trajectories, illuminating the contours of his body. A buzzing filled his head. The blood-colored filaments morphed into more concrete images and collided in his mind.

He hovered above the scene. Lucine was trying to hide under a hood, surrounded by men in gleaming armor. Her terror and anguish gripped Solehan in a fatal embrace. His sister's despair seeped into his own emotions.

Helplessly, she witnessed the murder of the man who seemed to be traveling with her, as he was impaled by a sword. Though she struggled, the golden-armored figures swallowed her completely.

Lucine, save yourself! Solehan urged her to flee, but his words were lost in the void. He was a powerless witness to what fanned out before his eyes.

A mounted man caught up to Lucine as she attempted to escape and violently knocked her to the ground. On her knees, she pleaded tearfully for him to spare her life. But the golden shadows remained motionless. Worse, the men tore her clothes and exposed her body. Solehan wanted to kill them, to obliterate them.

Bound to a pyre, Lucine begged for their mercy, as flames began to lick her feet. Her love for him struck him hard. Even in her final moments, she had hoped to be reunited with him.

Once again, darkness swallowed the young man's mind. The last mental image of Lucine in tears gradually faded away.

Solehan's regained sight locked onto the face of the Alaris, who observed him calmly. Tears had rolled down the cheeks of the young druid. Through a blurred vision, he tried to orient himself in the room. He couldn't explain why, but he felt the truth of the moment. Their souls had briefly joined in a final spark of life. It had all truly happened.

Wide-eyed and trembling like a leaf, Solehan turned toward the table where the platter was placed. Haggard, he wolfed down several fruits, his cheeks still wet. Nothing else mattered anymore—Lucine was gone.

He had lost everything.

12

Solehan cried silently for long minutes, until his tears exhausted themselves. All the hopes he had desperately clung to in the past few days scattered within him. His will to live drowned in denial. How could he accept a world without Lucine? Without purpose and without hope?

After devouring the food to fill the void left by her loss, Solehan grabbed the glass of wine on the coffee table and gulped it down in one go. Barely finishing the first glass, he poured himself another, trying to numb his thoughts with the intoxicating promise of the liquid. It was a foolish and crazy idea, but he no longer cared. Thirsty for oblivion, he let the inebriation suffocate his pain little by little. He didn't want to think about anything anymore. He refused to believe what he had seen. But with absurd caution, he decided not to touch the blue liquid.

After several consumed glasses, when the annihilation of the drink finally embraced him, Solehan lifted a wavering eye toward the Alaris. Facing him, he noticed the Alaris's attentive and silent focus on him. As if the young druid was a curious beast, and the man seemed to analyze his reactions. Unlike Solehan's huddled posture and anguish-marked face, his captor appeared unperturbed. This difference further accentuated the helplessness of the aberrant situation in which the young man found himself.

With his desire for revenge still burning in his heart, Solehan couldn't tolerate this contrast. "By the way, I still don't know your name or what you exactly are," he uttered in a tone that aimed to be sarcastic, affected by the liquid courage flowing through his veins.

The green eyes of the Alaris tinted with pity slapped the young druid in the heart. Solehan felt stung.

"Valnard," the Alaris replied.

So that was his name.

The Alaris now solemnly took his time to reveal more to him, and his eyes rested on the reddish liquid swirling in his glass. He took another sip. "As I told you, I am an Alaris," he said, shrugging.

Faced with Valnard's evident restraint, Solehan insisted, "And what else?"

"Mmhh . . . Are you sure you want to know more, young druid?" Valnard jeered. "After all, you've just found out who you were yourself moments ago . . . and the tragic fate of your sister."

A dagger of grief stabbed the young man's chest at the mention of Lucine. He took another gulp to dismiss this unwelcome feeling. "Stop playing games with me," he protested. "I have the right to know to what do I owe the 'pleasure'?"

Valnard chuckled into the glass he had just raised to his mouth. "Ah, well then! If you insist so much! Well, the Alaris originally come from a different world than this one," he said, with a sweeping gesture of his arm. "That's why our bodies aren't governed by the same natural laws as humans, for example. We are immortal and, *of course*, we don't need any connection with a deity to practice our magic."

Solehan bit into a fruit and tried to refocus his attention, despite his sadness and intoxication. How could such beings exist? He had clearly already had a good glimpse of what Valnard was capable of with Alaris magic, and he had no doubt about the vastness of what he had not yet seen. But an entire immortal race from elsewhere capable of such wonders? Unreal. Dangerous. Absurd.

The gleam of pride on Valnard's face set it ablaze. "The magic I practice is called the Ignescent, characterized by its recognizable blood-red color," he rejoiced, with a cruel smile.

Fine red filaments emerged from his dark fingers, coiled around his glass, and gave an even more crimson hue to the liquid. "It is the magic possessed by the Alaris who choose to become males," he added.

"Choose?" Solehan interjected, raising his head.

Valnard glanced at the young druid from the corner of his eye, savoring Solehan's inexperience. He stood up from the sofa and walked toward the dormant fireplace in the corner of the room. With his back to Solehan, he placed his hands in front of the hearth. Large red flames burst forth from his fingers and ignited the logs.

"Yes, choose," Valnard said. "The Alaris are neither born male nor female. They choose their gender during a ceremony that takes place on their hundredth birthday."

"Are they forced to choose?" Solehan asked, his voice wavering.

This question sparked a distinctive gleam on Valnard's face. A memory danced in his eyes. Valnard cracked his knuckles, and small scarlet sparks crackled at the tips of his fingers. "No, although it is the only way to access the true strength of our race. One would have to be foolish to refuse such a gift," he declared. "That's why most of them choose to be male, to be able to master the power of Ignescent. But that's also why the Alaris are rare."

The immortal turned his attention away from the flames ravaging the fireplace and looked at the young druid. His face bore a carnivorous look. "Between us, if you had the choice, wouldn't you choose to be male?" he resumed.

Solehan didn't know how to answer. What kind of question was that? How could it have been any different anyway? All he knew was that he had spent countless nights cursing himself for not feeling what was expected of him, what his body should have experienced according to the ancients.

Solehan scrutinized the Alaris, who still stood with his back to him, facing the incandescent flames. There was no doubt that a certain power emanated from Valnard. The young man's head spun; his mind clouded by alcohol. Was it the rage of the flames in the fireplace that attested to the Alaris's extraordinary potential, or was it the sight of Valnard's body that gave him this impression of omnipotence? Did the Ignescent influence the Alaris's appearance? The contours of the immortal's slender silhouette became distinct, the scarlet light revealing the muscles of his shoulders beneath his tunic.

Solehan immediately despised himself for allowing his mind to wander in that direction. He mentally slapped himself and plunged back into the bitterness and shame so familiar to him. Valnard was responsible for his misery. For the death of his people.

Stung by his own stupidity, the young druid decided to annihilate all thoughts and emotions once and for all and downed another full glass of wine. He wanted to disappear.

Valnard turned around and approached him slowly. "I believe you've had enough to drink for today," he concluded in a stern tone.

Solehan found the strength to raise his eyes filled with disdain toward him.

Valnard's dark fingers brushed against his forehead.

A sudden red glow blinded Solehan. The young druid felt his body collapse heavily onto the couch. He sank into nothingness, unconscious.

13

The dawn of the goddess of light deposited the morning dew in the middle of the forest and awakened Lucine and Talyvien. After refreshing themselves with a little bit of water on their faces and eating some berries they gathered, they decided to continue their journey.

They avoided the main roads and trotted for several hours, hoping to reach a town or village to find refuge. The only thing Talyvien was certain of was that they were in the kingdom of Vamentera, the realm of Queen Selena, and that Lucine's appearance would not be a problem in these lands where magic was allowed in moderation. The political difference between the two rulers was one of the most well-known rumors in the capital of Callystra where he had grown up.

Still preoccupied with Lucine's burn, the paladin had made up his mind to purchase the services of a healer, as well as supplies and equipment.

On the journey, he caught Lucine admiring the beauty and tranquility of the forest. The canopy of trees allowed a few rays of sunlight to shine above them, creating patterns on their skin. She seemed at peace in this environment. "You haven't told me," he commented, in a detached tone, "but . . . where exactly do you come from?"

The paladin felt Lucine's body tense against his on the horse, her shoulders suddenly raised. But Talyvien understood the hesitation of the young woman. How could she trust him after what she had just been through?

"I—I come from the Astral Forest," she said, seemingly resigned. "From a clan of druids."

A druidess? He had never encountered one before. But it explained her ease in this verdant environment. And probably her tattoos and her strange connection with animals as well.

"Hmm, druids are not usually known for mingling with the rest of humankind," he said.

Talyvien tried to learn more about her. If he was to ensure her safety, at least until the next village, he wanted to know what he was getting himself into. How could he have traded his relationship with Callystrande for someone he didn't know? He despised this feeling. His selfishness. But a part of him hoped that there was a reason behind all of this, behind his act of madness, behind the worth of her life.

"Generally, no," she confirmed with a sigh. "Druids tend to remain secluded. But something terrible happened to my clan and the clans of the Astral Forest . . ."

"Oh . . . Hmm . . . What happened?" he dared to ask.

In the silence that followed, Talyvien could sense the internal debate taking place in Lucine's mind.

"Everyone was . . . murdered," she finally replied, her voice trembling. "I managed to escape, but I couldn't save my twin brother. Our attackers took him away. And I don't know if he's still alive, somewhere. I don't know if I even hope he is. Sometimes, it seems that my imagination is far crueler." Her voice faltered. She reached for the wooden amulet around her neck.

Talyvien stared at the path ahead of them with sadness. Murdered? A familiar feeling resonated within him. "I'm sorry," he said somberly. "Why would they have only taken your brother?"

"For a . . . legend," she murmured. The young woman turned her head and timidly looked at him from the corner of her eye.

Was she afraid of his reaction? "A legend?" the paladin encouraged.

"Yes," she sighed. "The druids predicted that my brother and I were chosen ones. Chosen ones of the stars who would receive powers on the day of the Solar Eclipse. Well, apparently it always affects men more. So, I guess the people who kidnapped Solehan must have known about the legend too. I don't know if any of it is true or just stories from ancient druids, but I fear that my brother is enduring atrocities for a stupid legend."

Talyvien remained silent. Throughout his life, he had been taught by the paladins of Callystrande to despise any form of magic. Being capable of magic for a man meant having an affinity with a deity. He had been trained to detect that special connection between the divine and the human. However, he had felt nothing regarding Lucine during his inspection at the border. Despite that, her strange bond with animals troubled him. Was she responsible for the flock of birds he had glimpsed when he had saved her from the stake?

"I don't care about that dumb legend!" Lucine protested, her anger rising. "I just want my brother to be here. To see my friends, my clan. I miss them so much."

A memory crossed Talyvien's mind. He had been just a child, crying for his assassinated parents in front of the altar of Callystrande, alone in the vast cathedral. A man had approached him gently, his footsteps resonating on the ancestral stone. He remembered the serene expression on the man's face and his shining armor as he had looked up at Tuoryn.

The paladin felt his sword slowly vibrate at his side with the horse's trots, in tune with the rhythm of his heart. "An old friend of mine once told me that grieving is feeling love," he murmured. "A love that you want to give but has nowhere to go. And that love is like a seed that you can decide to plant and make it sprout. To make it shine. To choose not to be exactly the same person anymore. But something better. For them, because they existed. Strangely, that thought comforted me."

Her focus distant, the young woman didn't respond. But after a few moments, Talyvien felt her rest her head on his shoulder as he sat behind her on the horse.

"Thank you, Talyvien," she whispered.

The young man was taken aback by her gesture. Was she too naive because she had spent her life isolated from everything? Was she trusting too quickly? However, a shade of pride replaced the shame that had tainted the paladin's chest until now.

After several hours of following a small dirt path, they were surprised to hear a metallic noise repeating at regular intervals. They emerged from the dense part of the forest and cautiously approached to get a closer look. They then recognized the sound of a blacksmith's hammer hitting an anvil.

Their journey led them to a medium-sized village with a few bustling streets, indicated by a sign that read "Luminaur." Talyvien dismounted the horse and took the reins to guide it, while Lucine remained in the saddle.

Around them, many villagers were busy with their daily tasks and paid no attention to them. Life seemed well-organized and peaceful. With the priority of healing Lucine's burn still in mind, Talyvien focused on trying to discern the presence of his goddess and observed the villagers they encountered with caution. He attempted to sense the influence of Callystrande through the potential connection a human could have with her. But was he still capable of feeling that?

After wandering through the village streets for several minutes, a faint warmth tingled on his skin. A silky veil settled on his epidermis. A calling was coming from a nearby street.

He followed this familiar sensation, and they arrived in front of a small church tucked away on a street corner. Talyvien spotted a priest of Callystrande, dressed in the traditional attire adorned with the symbol of the goddess. The priest was standing on the steps and sweeping them.

Talyvien felt a twinge of jealousy and envy wrinkle his chest. "Father, we are in need of your services," he announced, kneeling before the priest with reverence.

"Well, well, no need for all this ceremony, my child," the priest joked. "Just show me how I can help."

Bitterness churned in Talyvien's gut. Without his paladin armor, he had become an ordinary man again. His love for the goddess no longer radiated from him.

He helped Lucine dismount from the horse and gently set her on the church steps.

The priest then placed his hands over the burn on her leg, and a warm light enveloped the young woman's skin.

Talyvien watched helplessly, humiliated by his own uselessness despite the relief of finding someone capable of helping them. His fingers squeaked against the leather grip of his sword, as he stepped back. The pride of a life devoted to healing and protecting evaporated in an instant. Without his connection to Callystrande, who had he become?

Once the healing was complete, Lucine broke into a wide smile, pleased to have regained the use of her leg.

Talyvien took a coin from his purse and handed it to the priest, expressing his heartfelt gratitude. A deep, visceral longing filled him as he felt the crackling remnants of the goddess's magic in the man's hand. The paladin concealed his pain as best he could.

They set off toward the main street to do some shopping.

 Lucine marveled as she observed the vibrant life of the village of Luminaur bustling before her. Children playing on the main street, climbing and dodging the massive wooden beams supporting the old buildings. The chaotic and astonishing architecture of the village, with houses that didn't align perfectly with one another and seemed to have been created by many different hands. Each floor bore a different style, with vibrant and varied colors that extended up to the roofs, whose tiles were painted in a multitude of shades. Windows, intricately intertwined, appeared to have been added with calculated anarchy to some houses, and wooden bridges connected others. Despite this apparent disorganization, sometimes consisting of bricks, lime, or wooden planks, climbing plants had entangled themselves here and there, attempting in vain to unify this magnificent inconsistency.

All of this gave the village of Luminaur an unique charm, attracting people from all walks of life. The young woman noted, with joyful surprise, the diversity among its villagers—the variety in height, different skin tones, and hair colors. Some displayed tattoos, hairstyles, and clothing of various origins. Zaf's words echoed in her thoughts. She understood why they had attempted to cross the border.

Earlier that morning, with a heavy yet grateful heart, the young druidess had distractedly stroked the horse and realized she had never had the chance to ask the old merchant the animal's name. Despite that, a name and a memory had flooded her senses when she touched it.

The silhouette of the old man attaching a saddlebag had shimmered before her eyes. He had stroked the horse's neck and uttered the name *Maia*. When Lucine had indeed discovered a pack at the back of the saddle, she understood her friend's thoughtfulness in case things went awry. Upon opening it, she had found a small water flask, a few rations of bread, and the bow and arrows he had given her. It was Zaf's last flicker of hope that she couldn't betray by giving up.

Lucine now tried not to dwell on her guilty sadness and followed Talyvien through the different shops in the village of Luminaur.

As she trailed closely behind him, she looked at the square figure of the young man ahead and reflected on the conversation they had that very morning. Faced with his sacrifice and thoughtfulness toward her, she had ultimately decided to reveal her story to him. Had she done the right thing?

They spent the entire afternoon strolling around, searching for food and supplies. Because Talyvien had a purse filled with his last payment as a paladin of Callystrande, he purchased a complete set of heavily padded leather armor. A lightweight chainmail shirt that allowed for agility was also fastened at his chest. This purchase seemed to lift the paladin's spirits, as he evidently enjoyed sharing his combat knowledge.

Lucine, on the other hand, eyed a set made of thick woven cotton in beige and green—a long jacket cinched at the waist and matching pants. Recognizing her interest in archery, Talyvien also bought her a quiver made of woven cotton. Both also acquired sturdy belts, gloves, and boots to comfortably attach the various flasks, daggers, and pouches they would need.

Once equipped, they set out to find a place to spend the night. Based on recommendations from several merchants in the village, they decided to stay at Luminaur's main inn, *The Crossed Destinies*.

<h1>14</h1>

A warm and welcoming tumult greeted them as they pushed open the door of the establishment. Talyvien remained unfazed, but Lucine was taken aback by the sheer excitement. The party was in full swing in the small room. The intoxication of hearts and drinks spilled all around them. In a whirlwind of merriment, dozens of villagers celebrated and laughed, clinking their tankards together. Thunderous laughter mingled with the clamor of broken dishes, belches, and musical notes. The outlines of the revelers appeared blurry in the hazy atmosphere of the tavern, illuminated only by the flames of a fireplace and a few old chandeliers.

Elegant stone arches intertwined with imposing wooden beams supported the ceiling of the small building. The architecture of the tavern seemed as improbable as the exterior of the edifice. The place had several corners with curious angles, where tables and chairs of various shapes were arranged. It was a sublime chaos of hilarity and euphoria.

As they maneuvered their way to the large circular bar at the back of the room, a bizarre silhouette caught the young druidess's attention. With its gaping jaws, the polished skull of a gigantic creature with sharp fangs dominated the tavern, judging all the drunkards who dared to approach the counter. How could such an enormous creature have once been alive? Did such monsters still roam the land?

Intrigued and distracted by the peculiar bones, Lucine tried not to lose sight of Talyvien. While the paladin seemed unperturbed by the mass of people or their inebriation, he confidently advanced to speak with the bartender. However, Lucine, who had never been surrounded by so many souls, was quickly overwhelmed by the crowd pressing against her.

A hand forcefully grabbed her forearm. "Is it your first time seeing a dragon, sweetheart?" a hoarse voice dripped into her ear. The paunchy man in his fifties pulled her to the side before she could react.

Lucine only had time to catch a glimpse of the tattoo on the left side of his face as he pressed his body against hers with force. One of his huge, calloused hands still gripping her arm, he tightly encircled her waist with the other to immobilize her completely. "Come with me, we'll just have a good time . . ." he said.

The foul smell of his alcohol-laden breath assaulted her nose. The young woman's body tensed with fear. She struggled to turn her head and catch sight of Talyvien. Where was he?

The man's hand slid over her body.

"Let go of me!" Lucine screamed, with a mix of rage and panic.

But her protests were lost in the ambient clamor and confusion of the party. She could only rely on herself. Lucine then tried to reach for her dagger at her belt, her fingers trembling.

Suddenly, the man flinched. He released his hold.

Talyvien's hand gripped the drunkard's collar. The paladin delivered a powerful punch to his jaw with his other arm. The assailant was thrown to the ground, and a trickle of blood flowed from his mouth. The people around fell silent, interrupted by the scene.

Flashes of anger and disdain crossed the faces of the paladin and the drunkard as the two men locked eyes. With his ego bruised, the man lunged at the paladin, letting out a scream of rage.

The metal of the sword squeaked as it slid against its sheath. The tip of Talyvien's blade came to rest on the throat of the drunkard, who abruptly stopped in his tracks.

Silence filled the tavern. Curious and concerned patrons observed the interaction between the two men.

"No swords drawn in the establishment!" bellowed the voice of the bartender from the back of the room.

The drunkard spat on the ground at the paladin's feet. Deciding it wasn't worth the trouble, he left the inn shortly thereafter.

"Thank you, Talyvien," murmured Lucine as she approached, a shivering hand on her throat.

He nodded slightly, sheathing his sword. "I'm sorry. I should have intervened sooner."

"No, no, it's not your fault. You acted like a true paladin," she thanked him, a relieved smile on her face.

A corner of Talyvien's mouth lifted slightly. He clearly appreciated the compliment.

When they finally reached the bar, the excitement in the tavern had resumed with renewed vigor. A heavily built man with an apron stood behind the counter. The lines on his face spoke of the stories and adventures he seemed to have experienced.

"Sorry about the sword," Talyvien said to the bartender, who was wiping a tankard with a cloth.

"Hey, no worries. We always have problems with that kind of individual. But times are tough, and it's hard to turn away customers. Let's just say that lecherous brutes drink more beer than damsels in distress," the bartender apologized, glancing at Lucine.

Damsel in distress? Was she really so incapable and weak? Lucine felt the sting.

Talyvien ordered their dinner, as well as two rooms for the night. When it came time to pay, he slipped an extra coin to the bartender. "What's the news from the continent?" he inquired. "Has anyone reported anything noteworthy?"

"Hmm, let me think," the bartender replied. "There are rumors about King Arthios Therybane's crusade, 'The Dawn's Resolve.' They're trying to convince Queen Selena Aramanth to join their cause."

Talyvien was already well aware of that. "Anything else?" he asked nonchalantly, resting his elbow on the counter.

"Hmm . . . Oh yes! There's a rumor that all the residents of Argentvale, the capital of the Kingdom of Narlimar, have turned into trees! Scouts have brought back this news, but I find it hard to believe. Just more sordid gossip, if you ask me! Trees!" He chuckled in a gravelly voice.

Lucine's body froze. Intrusive images from the day of the Eclipse resurfaced in her mind. She ran her quivering fingers over the bar with a profoundly absent stare, struck by the texture of the wood beneath her fingertips. They had become nothing more than that. Objects.

"Sorry, that's all I've got," the bartender added, snapping his cloth on the counter.

Lucine was jolted.

Talyvien turned around and discovered the expression of shock on the young druidess's face. He then took her by the shoulders and led her to sit in one of the alcoves with tables in a corner of the tavern.

"Talk to me, Lucine, what's wrong?" he asked, concerned, as they sat facing each other.

"It's . . . what happened. My clan . . . the druids . . . they were all turned into wood . . . into bark. They're all dead!" she exclaimed, her eyes frantic.

The paladin crossed his arms, looking skeptical and furrowing his brow as he scrutinized the table in front of him. "Do you think the two events could be connected? I mean, it's quite a coincidence, and perhaps the bartender's information is just a rumor. He didn't seem very sure . . ."

"Maybe, but the coincidence is too unsettling for me. I have to go there. Solehan might be there!" she exclaimed.

Talyvien gestured for her to lower her voice, clearly wary of prying ears. "Wait, calm down! If all this is true, you barely escaped last time. You can't just rush off alone to find your brother. It's madness!"

Tears began to shimmer in Lucine's eyes. She held her face in her hands. "What can I do then?!" she despaired.

She felt so powerless in the face of this information. Solehan? In Argentvale?

"We should first find out if this rumor is true," Talyvien insisted. "I imagine the scouts he mentioned are those of Queen Selena Aramanth." He paused, seeming hesitant.

The waitress broke their silence as she brought their food and drinks.

The paladin gave a slight nod of thanks. "We could go to Dawnelest," he whispered. "It's the capital of the Kingdom of Vamentera. We could request an audience with the queen to confirm the scouts' reports."

Lucine raised tear-filled eyes from her meal, intrigued. "And what makes you think she would agree to grant us an audience? We're nobody important, just a wretched druidess and a paladin who is no longer one."

Lucine cursed her words when she saw a hint of sadness cross the paladin's face.

"Let's just say . . . I know her a little," he stammered.

She stopped chewing her bread and looked at him incredulously.

Talyvien explained. "King Arthios Therybane, her brother, received training from the paladins of Callystrande." He coughed, covering his mouth with a fist. "Being roughly the same age, we often trained together and had the same mentor . . . and his sister would sometimes come to watch the training sessions."

The young man's eyes awkwardly averted. He was omitting an obvious part of the story.

"Just the training sessions?" she teased.

Talyvien's cheeks reddened slightly, but he evaded the question. "The problem is," he continued, "the Crusade of the Dawn's Resolve is also heading in that direction."

Lucine felt compassion for her friend and didn't press further. "Hmm," she mused. "It still remains our best chance to find out what happened in the city of Argentvale and see if this attack is similar to the massacre of my clan," she said, dipping a piece of bread into the soup in front of her. "If you know the queen, maybe you could also warn her about what's going on with her brother and the crusade? Perhaps she could help dismantle it or reason with the king?"

"I had thought about it, but—"

A sudden change in the atmosphere of the room rescued Talyvien from his discomfort. A heavy silence fell, and a palpable excitement swept through the crowd. The small stage, where several bards had been playing until now, had emptied of its musicians. All heads turned toward it, and conversations gradually ceased.

Surprised by this sudden change in ambiance, Lucine observed the gathering. Her attention settled on a blind woman wearing a dark blue blindfold, hood, and long robe of the same color. Something ceremonial seemed to emanate from her, as she calmly enjoyed her meal alone at a nearby table. Did Talyvien know more about her weird attire?

"A priestess of Sazaelith," he answered her silent question. "It is said that they offer their eyes to their goddess when they are still children." He lowered his eyes back to his meal. "Religion of degenerates," he muttered, a disgusted grimace contorting his face.

Lucine then realized the paladin's aversion to any god or religion other than that devoted to Callystrande and understood that she should not broach the subject. All conversations in the room fell silent, as one of the waitresses stepped onto the stage.

"Tonight," the waitress announced, "to accompany us in the celebration once again, I have the honor of presenting Calixte! Mage and Bard of wonders!"

Thunderous applause resounded. It was clear that this person was eagerly anticipated. However, Lucine noticed Talyvien's hands tensing on the table.

In the recess of a door located behind the dais and pushing aside with one hand the thin curtains that separated the wings from this improvised stage, Calixte appeared.

Lucine let out a small exclamation. She had never seen anyone so strange and magnificent in her life. She didn't know if Calixte was a man or a woman, but it didn't matter to her.

Calixte's smooth, violet skin, like a polished amethyst, shimmered with a multitude of sparks under the various sources of light in the room. Long white hair with blue highlights framed their elegant face, with its refined features, and seemed to move as if immersed in liquid grace. Dark makeup started from the corner of Calixte's eyes and cascaded into a superb gradient of bright, vibrant colors, ending on each side of their jaw, complementing the color of their pupil-less irises with orange hues of a setting sun.

They wore garments of rare elegance, made of the finest silk and embroideries that embraced and flattered their slender and graceful body. Combining the rich and deep purple of the fabric with some ornaments and patterns in bright orange, their long tunic added to Calixte's magnetic presence. Their appearance was perfectly crafted.

Lucine couldn't take her eyes off this electrifying vision, captivated by the image of the bard. Who was this bewildering person with such a charismatic presence?

Although a hint of surprise passed through Talyvien's eyes involuntarily, the rest of his face remained neutral. "An Alaris," he whispered to Lucine.

Before he could tell her more, Calixte made a small bow on the stage. "Thank you! Thank you for the warm welcome as always! Any preferences for tonight?" Their deep and exquisite voice melodiously reverberated through the room.

Several hands were raised, requesting several pieces from their repertoire, clearly known by heart to many in the audience.

Calixte then took out a small instrument from their pack. With one hand on the strings and the other turning a crank on its side, they began to play a lively tune. Their sublime voice filled the room and blended with the sound of the hurdy-gurdy. When they tapped their foot and hopped to the rhythm of the instrument, their enthusiasm and smile infected the crowd, who started dancing and singing along.

Lucine also began to tap the rhythm of the music with her feet.

A translucent, swirling blue glow passed over the gathering. It took the form of a small blue fox made of ethereal energy and began running, jumping, and playing with agility.

Magic.

Several hands attempted to catch it, but in vain. People laughed heartily and danced to the music. As Calixte's song progressed, other animals appeared. A lion and an owl joined the fox, playing around a large tree whose branches stretched into an impressive blue canopy, illustrating the rhyme in a magnificent azure tableau.

When the song came to an end and the melody faded, Calixte's hair had taken on a rose-orange hue, flowing fluidly in sync with their movements.

Unreal. Splendid. Grandiose. Lucine was left breathless.

Amid laughter and cheers from the audience, Calixte continued with several rhythmic melodies. Some strands of their hair would occasionally change from red to orange, transitioning through shades of pink and purple.

For each of their songs, beautiful illustrations of bluish light appeared in the room, sometimes above the crowd, sometimes around Calixte, playing with the musician. Calixte skillfully alternated between different instruments, effortlessly switching from the hurdy-gurdy to the lyre or violin.

Lucine was captivated, absorbed by so much magnificence, carried away by her awe. How could such a being exist? The young woman swayed with the surrounding joy and merriment. Her heart and mind floated along with the lyrics and notes.

Under a certain drowsiness, she looked at Talyvien. He was focused on his now empty plate, avoiding what was happening on the stage. His cheeks were tense. His eyes burned through the enamel of the bowl. Did the magic of the Alaris make him uncomfortable? So much beauty. She didn't understand.

A fine scarlet sparkle fluttered before her eyes. Then two. A multitude of them. They shimmered under the lights of the room. Almost entranced,

Lucine, with a rapturous gaze, watched them flit about. Her consciousness emptied of all emotion and negative thoughts. The recent events, the pain, and grief suffocated within her, like flames of a devouring fire lacking oxygen.

She didn't think about anything anymore. She was simply there, in that tavern, admiring this incredible spectacle. How did this happen? Were the crimson particles responsible for her strange euphoria? It would have been easy and dangerous to want to stay in this state forever.

After so much dancing and drinking, as the fatigue of the crowd grew, Calixte changed both instrument and melody. With their skilled hands, they grasped the body of a sort of enormous lute and sat on the small stool provided. Under their elegant fingers, the rest of the instrument was unveiled through the ethereal blue energy magic delicately taking shape. The neck of the instrument appeared, along with a few strings that formed an immense theorbo. Calixte positioned their hands on the ethereal parts of the instrument, which seemed to materialize as they played.

With each verse, a new string became visible under their fingers. The complexity of the ballad increased, showcasing the impressive dexterity of the bard. A mesmerized silence reigned in the assembly. Everyone, breath held, admired the Alaris's fingers moving frantically on the theorbo, transforming into a magnificent and lively melody.

With a final note on the impressive instrument, the music faded into a triumphant last breath. The theorbo now possessed fourteen strings.

The crowd stood up in thunderous applause and cheers.

A brilliant smile appeared on the bard's face, and they made a short bow of the head to thank the audience. "Thank you very much! I hope you enjoyed the show!" they exclaimed, taking a sip of water from their flask.

New cheers resounded among the excited crowd.

"Thank you again! I would like to share one last piece with you before I depart. I believe it will conclude this lovely moment we spent together!"

Calixte settled back onto the stool, held the immense and partially ethereal theorbo between their hands, and closed their eyes. An almost solemn air appeared on their beautiful face.

A slow and harmonious melody gently rose. Their deep voice emerged in the now silent room.

Talyvien gritted his teeth. The grip of the Alaris's magic weighed heavily on his mind, and he focused on trying to block its influence, as he had been trained to do by the paladins of Callystrande.

Fine red particles slid before his eyes.

No. He would resist. He tightened his focus on the plate in front of him. On the pain in his clenched jaws.

The wood of the table began to ripple. Crimson liquid snaked along the grooves. His field of vision was flooded. His body started to float, and the outline of his hands shimmered with a strange red glow.

Chorus
Our bodies entwine in this cosmic affair,
Your skin's golden hue, my soul's bluish reign,
In this fleeting passion, a dance without compare,
As my found eyes blend with your tears, untamed.

Rivers of gold flow at my feet,
Merging with the ink of your skin's sweet.
I've wept for the twilight, long and profound,
The owl's mournful hoot echoing all around.

Each morning I seek that intoxicating embrace,
Your hands' blue touch on my body's grace.
But all that remains is a lingering pain,
As your memory fades, like a short-lived refrain.

Chorus

My heart heavy with vengeance, I bear,
Your sun's justice fails to illumine or care.
A sentence, unyielding, in coldness shall stand,
Your absence has consumed me, a cruel demand.

Shooting stars trail down my cheeks,
I search for your light, elusive it seeks.
In blinding darkness, I play my part,
While you wait for me, aching, at dawn's start.

Chorus

Despair interlaces with anger's fierce fire,
Our four hands joined, unable to quell desire.
The sleep of winter, cruel and unjust,
Tears apart the creation, the child's trust.

The gold and silver of the tree's embrace,
Where the fox rests, dreaming in peaceful space.
My love, let us protect, let us defend,
The fruit of our passion, unyielding till the end

Talyvien's bare feet sank into the dark, charcoal-colored earth as he advanced. The golden hue of his skin shimmered under the caress of the sunlight. Long black silhouettes stretched out before him as far as the eye could see. The contours of the dark trees contrasted against the warm, golden sky.

He continued to move forward. The silver leaves of the trees gently detached and scattered around him, carried by the wind. It was a shimmering rain.

A small white fox scurried away, prompting him to run in an attempt to catch it.

As he approached, the outlines of the golden sky liquefied and intertwined with the silhouettes of the trees. The liquid gold swirled with the ink of the horizon, enveloping him in a tornado of shades.

Two delicate feminine hands, blue in color, tenderly caressed his shoulders. He trembled. The young man was surprised to find himself bare-chested. The warm touch of that skin against his own was divine, intoxicating.

Everything around him disappeared. He only saw the blue silhouette of those hands on his golden skin, descending along his arms. Those cobalt fingers expertly brushed against him, sending a shiver through his body.

Driven by devouring curiosity, he turned around to see the stranger. He only had time to catch a glimpse of her eyes fading into the shadows. Fierce and relentless. Magnetic and desirous.

But she was already gone. The fleeting touch of her hands had dissipated on his skin. Longing clawed at his insides. Talyvien wanted to find that embrace again, to make it eternal.

As he scanned his surroundings, a vermilion glow appeared on each side of his eyes. Gradually, it occupied his entire field of vision.

Glad that Talyvien had finally turned his head to admire Calixte's performance, Lucine was now worried. The paladin was no longer responding. His eyes gleamed with a strange red light, even though the song had ended.

"Talyvien! Talyvien!" she called out, shaking his arm.

After a few unsuccessful attempts, the scarlet glow faded from his gaze. Talyvien came back to himself, his attention finally refocused on the druidess's face.

"Hey! You scared me! Where were you?" whispered Lucine.

The paladin blinked his eyes. His thoughts readjusted to his surroundings. "Damn magic!" he grumbled, his annoyed look returning to his angular face.

Lucine didn't dare ask any further, sensing the visible discomfort and embarrassment on the paladin's features. Why had the Alaris's magic affected him so much?

With the show now over, a small crowd had gathered around Calixte, and laughter and flirtatious glances were exchanged. Still as magnetic as ever, they bantered with various tavern patrons, and several dropped a few coins into a small purple silk purse near them. A few amber winks flew as thanks.

Impatient, Lucine took some remaining coins from her afternoon purchases and decided to introduce herself. She felt Talyvien's disenchanted stare following her, his eyes rolling in exasperation. He definitely didn't like magic.

She approached closer and noticed the exhaustion of the bard, the sweat glistening on their amethyst forehead. A movement of their head revealed their strange, pointed ears peeking through a few strands of their colorful hair. What a fascinating and prodigious being.

Excited, Lucine placed her coins into the silk purse. "That was absolutely incredible! I've never seen anything like it!"

Indeed, she hadn't seen much in her life, but the Alaris's performance had been incomparable.

Calixte, a flattered expression crossing their graceful face, took Lucine's hand. Lucine felt her cheeks blush as they kissed the back of her hand.

"The pleasure is all mine," the Alaris coquettishly replied.

An ethereal blue rose appeared in the palm of Calixte's hand as Lucine withdrew her fingers. The bard delicately placed it behind the young druidess's ear.

Their pupil-less eyes then glanced at Talyvien, still seated at the table.

"Take care of your friend; he seems grumpy," they teased.

A slight laughter escaped Lucine's mouth.

Calixte winked at the paladin, who grumbled with disdain and embarrassment.

Talyvien decided he'd had enough for the evening and went up to his room to sleep.

Lucine followed, waving a small farewell to the Alaris. A trail of shimmering magic followed the young woman as the blue rose in her hair evaporated with each step she took.

15

"If you need anything, knock on the wall. My room is just next door, and I have a spare key to yours," Talyvien had told her before closing the door.

Although its appearance seemed rather modest, the small bedroom in the inn was comfortable. However, Lucine felt the effects of Calixte's magic dissipating, and a sense of emptiness crept into her heart. Negative thoughts boiled up to the surface.

The helplessness she had felt when facing her assailant in the tavern haunted her once again. How could she survive in such a world? What would have happened to her if Talyvien hadn't been there? Panic shivered through her under the bedsheets, as she realized her insignificance in a universe that seemed so dangerous and cruel. Her mediocrity, her smallness. Would she forever need someone to protect her?

But the beauty of Calixte's performance, the kindness and sacrifice of the paladin and Zaf, and her desire to reunite with Solehan clashed with her doubts and anxieties. She had no choice. She couldn't let fear overwhelm her. She sighed deeply, exhausted.

She knew that the next day she would have to convince Talyvien to head to Dawnelest, the capital of the kingdom of Vamentera, to learn more about what the scouts had reported. An entire city's population transformed into wood? It might be their only lead.

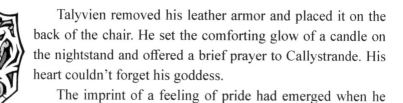Talyvien removed his leather armor and placed it on the back of the chair. He set the comforting glow of a candle on the nightstand and offered a brief prayer to Callystrande. His heart couldn't forget his goddess.

The imprint of a feeling of pride had emerged when he comforted Lucine and defended her against the drunkard. An unexpected emotion that somewhat eased his sorrow and gave him hope in his ability to protect and defend, even though he was no longer a true paladin. He placed Tuoryn's sword near his bed and wished to continue honoring it, even without the blessing of Callystrande.

As he lay down on the bed, the performance of the Alaris formed in his mind. A nuanced groan of discomfort and fatigue escaped his throat.

Even though his training had taught him to despise any form of magic other than that of the goddess of light, he knew it was not the main reason for the revulsion he experienced. He admitted that it made him feel cowardly, but the loss of control he endured upon contact with magic was something he couldn't tolerate. Why was he naturally so vulnerable to it?

Talyvien had received special training from his mentor to resist it as best as possible and had sworn to fortify his mind against this type of magic. Yet, with little success, it seemed.

Nevertheless, he also knew that this issue had been an advantage in the past. Callystrande's magic had been able to express itself powerfully through his hands.

But now, this gift was tainted by bitterness. Having lost his connection with the goddess, all he had left was his weakness. He knew the magic of the Alaris was astonishingly potent and was glad not to encounter it more often. A shiver of disgust ran through him.

Then, fragments of the conversation he had exchanged with the druidess seeped into his embarrassment. The thoughts of the paladin drifted toward memories he had of the sovereign. Toward Selena.

Lucine's mocking tone had not lied to him. She had sensed that he had omitted some details, but he couldn't bring himself to tell her more, as that secret could cost him his life. A certain nostalgia weighed on his chest.

Talyvien remembered the first time he and Selena had passionately kissed, away from prying eyes. Her scent, her golden hair like wheat, and the radiant smile she had afterward.

The first time their bodies had found each other in secret in the grand castle of Callystra. The smell of her skin.

Their heart-wrenching farewells, knowing their situation was doomed to failure. She, destined to marry the son of the king of Vamentera, Prince Herald Aramanth, and become his queen. He, a child of humble origin, bound to take a vow of celibacy among the paladins of Callystrande.

Talyvien had long been relieved to wear a golden mask to conceal his sorrow when he'd seen her before she left for the kingdom of Vamentera. However, he knew he couldn't avoid her forever. He knew that Lucine needed to go to Dawnelest to learn more. He had to seize this opportunity to warn Selena about the dangers of the crusade and its High Priestess.

He closed his eyes, exhausted, ready to sink into much-needed sleep.

Why did he want to help Lucine anyway? Was it perhaps out of shame for not having done anything earlier about her situation? Or maybe to prove to himself that he could still be useful and honor his oath?

A cool breeze brushed against his face. The night was growing cold. He got up to close the window in his room.

A hooded figure stood before him, holding a dagger.

His heart leapt in his throat. A cold flash paralyzed his thoughts.

An assassin.

Talyvien lunged to grab the sword at the foot of his bed. The assailant's dagger sliced through the air, narrowly missing his throat but cutting his face instead. Blood spurted from his split lip and splashed on the floor.

The glint of the dagger moved again in the dim light. A second deadly strike swirled toward him. This time, he met it with the steel of his sword, the sound echoing in a metallic reverberation.

The attacker sneered with disdain.

Talyvien then delivered a powerful kick to the assassin's abdomen.

The assailant staggered back but landed with grace, allowing the paladin to stand upright. A second dagger materialized in the assassin's other hand.

Talyvien gritted his teeth and tried to ignore the pain and the blood flowing down his face. It was clear that his assailant had a good command of his blades.

The silhouette lunged again, with an almost supernatural dexterity. The contours of his cape seemed to blend into the surroundings.

Surprised, Talyvien struggled to parry the repeated strikes coming from all sides. He found it extremely difficult to anticipate the origin of the attacks.

Only the metallic glint of the daggers shone, reflecting the moonlight and leaving thin streaks of light cutting through the air. It was like a whirlwind of blades. Between two movements of the assassin, Talyvien noticed something.

The silhouette of his attacker was that of a woman.

Her body seemed to be nowhere and everywhere at once; the feline grace of her movements appeared prodigious. Each time he turned his head to block a new strike, she had already vanished from his field of vision. He understood then. She was trying to wear him down, using her speed as an advantage against his strength. A torrent of metal relentlessly raining down on him.

Without the magic of his goddess to aid him, she succeeded. The silhouette finally made him stumble.

Talyvien fell heavily onto the floor.

She then pounced on him, straddling him, the dagger ready to deliver the final blow. Was this truly the end? Was he going to die like this? In this room?

Two sapphire-blue eyes pierced his soul. They glowed in a supernatural way within the darkness of the hood. Her pupils resembled those of an animal, scrutinizing him with a cold fury, like a feline or a reptile. He was mesmerized by this vision. His heart stopped. The gleam of the dagger shone in the night as it struck him down.

Suddenly, the door to his room swung open.

"Oh, sorry lovebirds! Must've got the wrong room!" Calixte chuckled drunkenly, stumbling at the doorway with a bottle in hand.

Talyvien only had time to feel the weight of the assassin's body lift off him.

He turned his head. The window was wide open. She had vanished.

Calixte closed the door grumbling. It took Talyvien a few seconds on the floor to regain his senses and process what had just happened. The pain on his face became more intense.

Lucine!

He got up quickly, retrieved his fallen sword, and rushed down the corridor toward her room. He hated to disturb her privacy, but he needed to make sure.

When the paladin managed to open the door with his spare key, he found the druidess peacefully asleep in her bed. After a quick inspection of the room, he closed the window latch. Finding no trace of the assassin, he breathed a sigh of relief, closed the door, and returned to his room.

Sleep eluded him that night. He tried to stop the bleeding on his face and organize the jumble of thoughts in his mind.

Had Piore sent an assassin after him? It made him sick. What had become of the Order of the Paladins of Callystrande? Was his king aware? Had the king himself orchestrated the assassination attempt? The situation was worse than he had imagined. Time was running out.

They would leave for Dawnelest in the morning.

16

 The weight of intoxication dissipated in the early morning, and Solehan woke up in one of the castle's rooms that Valnard seemed to have assigned to him. After a quick glance around, he was relieved to find no wooden statues there. The furniture, although dusty, was functional. The huge canopy bed on which he had slept stood in the middle of the room.

Thin bracelets of red light still encircled his wrists. Was it a form of control to prevent him from escaping or using his magic? The young man scoffed bitterly. Where could he even go? He couldn't even control his powers.

He took some fruits from the nightstand as breakfast and decided to explore the castle to learn more. As he headed toward the door, a mirror on one of the walls caught his attention. He wiped off the dust to look at himself.

He was emaciated. He saw that his tanned skin was paler than usual. The darkened contour of his eyes was marked by tears and the emotions of the past few days. His natural candor faded in his grief, a raw pain hidden in his chest. He examined every corner of his face. Each of his features mirrored the perfect and cruel image of the sister he had lost—a reflection forever deprived of his other half. An invisible grip tightened around his throat.

The sense of time seemed vague to him. Questions that he didn't care about emerged in his mind. How many days had he been here? Was the feeling of vengeance he harbored enough to give him a reason to live?

Solehan brushed aside the mental turmoil and hurried out of the room. The corridor leading to his bedroom looked identical to the one he had seen a few floors below. A perfect symmetry of grimy windows and wooden doors.

The young druid descended the stairs and arrived in the antechamber adjoining the salon where he had fallen asleep the previous night. He found no trace of the Alaris, so he decided to go out onto the balcony to observe the gloomy valley.

Caught in an eternal gray mist, the timid sun still attempted to cast its light upon the colossal mountains adorned with somber vegetation that stood on either side of the city. What was this place? As he drew deep breaths, the crisp air filled his lungs and gently brushed against his face. The first time in a long while.

In the middle of a large inner courtyard below the castle stood the emaciated silhouette of an enormous tree with dark bark. There, he had no trouble spotting Valnard's ivory-white skin, as the Alaris seemingly knelt beside it. The spark of curiosity, which Solehan thought he had numbed, tugged at the back of his mind.

After navigating through corridors, doors, and stairs, he found the path that led to the inner courtyard. Upon his arrival, he was greeted by the tranquil and monastic atmosphere that prevailed. Elaborately carved stone arches wrapped around the central square, defining a long open corridor.

The tall tree that Solehan had glimpsed from the balcony occupied the very heart of the courtyard square, its long branches reaching out to caress the stone arches. Though it looked frightening, it was the only vegetation thriving in this strange reliquary of grayish rock.

With his head bowed, in a semblance of meditation or prayer, his hands resting on the trunk, the Alaris seemed to commune with the tree.

Solehan noticed that Valnard's arm skin seemed to blend with the bark. What was he doing?

The young druid walked toward Valnard. His footsteps made the large stone slabs of the courtyard crackle.

At that sound, Valnard jerked upright. The bark of his arms quickly returned to smooth skin, his austere look in place.

Had he disturbed the Alaris? Solehan wondered. Despite trying to hide it, a definite emotion tinged the gleam in Valnard's green eyes.

Solehan let out a cry of pain, as a crimson vine quickly lifted the stone slabs beneath his feet and coiled around his leg.

Valnard approached him slowly, his eyes still distant.

Solehan watched in apprehension. Did the Alaris want to make him pay for witnessing that moment?

Knowing he couldn't move, Valnard brought his face close to Solehan's. "Show me what you're made of," he taunted, with a sadistic smile.

The bramble snaked languidly along Solehan's leg, setting him free but leaving thin lacerations all around his calf, from which blood began to trickle. The pressure around his wrists relaxed. The red energy bracelets dissipated.

Did Valnard want to fight him? *Perfect.* The young druid grinned maliciously. Powers or not, he would give everything he had. A welcome outlet to unleash his hatred and grief.

The hours that followed were spent quenching their respective thirsts for vengeance. However, this curious and unrestrained training proved more difficult than expected. Valnard continued his relentless attacks, and new lacerations soon dotted the young man's body.

It was only when the sun dipped low, and Solehan lay on the ground, exhausted and unable to continue any further, that Valnard stopped. Covered in blood and gasping for breath, the young druid collapsed on his back in pain and fatigue.

Valnard knelt beside him and took out some leaves and ointments from a small pouch attached to his vest. In an aberrant contradiction, he began to tend to Solehan's wounds by placing his hands on them.

Solehan recoiled at the Alaris's touch. The memory of his fingers in the wound on his chest became vivid.

In return, Valnard's gaze burned him with disapproval. "If you were an ordinary human, I would have killed you already," he confirmed, with disarming nonchalance.

"Then why heal me?" Solehan spat. "Why not let me die?"

Ignoring the young druid's protests at first, Valnard applied bandages and ointment to the wounds with his graceful hands. The gentleness of his gesture struck Solehan, and a certain confusion overcame him. Torn between extreme repulsion and a longing to be touched by a caring hand.

"I've already told you," Valnard exclaimed with exasperation. "You need to learn to control your powers, Teluar's powers."

"What does it matter to you anyway?" Solehan groaned in pain as the ointment stung his wounds. "Aren't you already powerful enough to exterminate all of us?"

"What you will be capable of? No, I cannot do it for you. As long as you remain a human, you will be useless. You must learn to transform yourself and feel Teluar's magic manifest within you. That's why we will train every day. And when you are ready, you will be the only one who can awaken the God of Nature. When you understand the purpose of your existence and the greatness of his gift."

"And do you really think beating each other up every day will change anything?" the young druid snarled.

"Do not underestimate the power of rage, of vengeance. You want to avenge your clan? Your sister? To kill me? Good. Use it!"

Valnard's honesty shook Solehan. Was he so sure of himself to risk his life? Or did he consider him so incapable?

With nothing else left in his life but this absurd ritual, Solehan spent several days training for hours with Valnard in the inner courtyard under the big tree. Once the young man was exhausted and his body aching, the Alaris would tend to his wounds with disconcerting efficiency, preparing him for the macabre routine the next day.

At first, Solehan struggled to see the purpose of this "training," which seemed to him more like a slow execution. But day after day, despite the smoldering and vindictive rage still boiling within him, the despair he had initially felt began to fade.

Strangely, this relentless repetition became increasingly comforting to him. The predictability of Valnard, the pain, the blood, and the scents of dead wood and ointment enveloped him like a familiar blanket. Yet, Teluar's powers still did not awaken within him. His sole transformation into a bird remained the only evidence of Valnard's claims.

A part of his being found a certain appeal in losing himself in the notion of time, no longer seeking to understand what he felt. His life had been set on a parallel path, where nothing had meaning or a sense of duration. If it weren't for the dawn and dusk, Solehan would gladly have descended into that blurry and hazy abyss.

He also developed an interest in exploring the castle and its surroundings, wandering through the fortifications and deserted streets during his moments of freedom. Valnard's training, at least, had the advantage of building his endurance for pain and blood. Less exhausted than the first few times, he had more free time to discover the city.

He often passed by the wooden statues, all frozen in positions more desperate than the others. Solehan now managed to block the feelings of sadness and despair that welled up within him and he forced himself to see them for what they were, rather than what they had once represented. He also occasionally encountered forest spirits that fled at his sight, disappearing into the dark, narrow alleyways or slipping between the disorderly stones of the buildings.

One night, amid this temporal haze and unable to sleep, Solehan decided to distract himself by stretching his legs and enjoying the cool air of the darkness on his face. Unsure of where to go, he recalled Valnard's unusual behavior toward the mysterious tree, and he made his way to the large square courtyard below the castle. Finding nothing remarkable about the strange tree, he sat against its trunk and serenely observed the patterns of the stone arches framing the courtyard. He listened to the gentle crackling of the leafless branches above him.

Breezes rushed in, swirled, and caressed the ancient stone, before dissipating against his skin. There, wrapped in his solitude, he remembered the moments he had shared with Lucine under the starry ceiling, drawing and scribbling in his sketchbook, attempting to depict the various plants and animals they could observe.

The memory of the verdant serenity of the great trees in the Astral Forest invaded his melancholy. Trapped in the abundance of gray stone surrounding him, Solehan felt the absence of their protective atmosphere.

He sighed, rested his head against the bark of the gnarled tree, and closed his eyes. Nostalgically, he let his imagination wander. He listened to the enchanting melody of rustling leaves in the night wind and to the chirping of small animals flitting about in the lush secrecy of the woods, and he admired the glistening dew sliding off flower petals beneath the stars.

A silhouette emerged among the trees of this imagined forest. It could have been that of a small person or a child; he wasn't certain. Solehan couldn't distinguish the features of their face; only their slender appearance and the outline of their long, tangled hair as it floated in the wind. Two small wooden horns expanded from its forehead. Familiar green eyes observed him through the foliage. The young druid noticed a magnificent translucent and opalescent flower delicately placed in the leafy hair, creating an iridescent note amid the shadows.

When Solehan tried to approach, a massive white fox the size of a bear leaped out of the darkness and wrapped itself around the silhouette, which seemed unfazed. The sharp eyes of the animal locked onto him, its sparkling white fur enveloping the green of the forest.

An acute pain around his wrists jolted the young druid. Startled, Solehan opened his eyes, shaking his hands. Smoke was emanating from the thin red energy bracelets, burning his skin.

Had he used his magic?

17

 When dawn broke on the horizon, Talyvien refreshed his face and body with some water from a basin placed at his disposal. His split lip had stopped bleeding, but the pain still lingered. He hurriedly prepared himself, determined to get supplies, buy a horse, and seek an audience with the queen at the capital.

He put on his leather armor, sheathed his sword, and then knocked on Lucine's door. But only silence greeted him, filled with unbearable anticipation.

A gust of panic swept over the young man. He opened the door with his key and was horrified to find the room completely empty. Where had she gone?

He rushed down the stairs to the tavern on the ground floor. The atmosphere was calmer than the night before, and he spotted the innkeeper tidying up bottles and dishes behind the bar, yawning and humming.

"Where is the young woman who was with me?" Talyvien exclaimed eagerly, placing his hands on the counter.

"Hey, good morning to you too!" the innkeeper chuckled, looking up at the paladin. "I don't know where she is! But you have got to calm down, my friend. It happens to everyone who gets stood up."

The man's playful eyes rested on the cut on Talyvien's lip.

The paladin was about to retort with a mixture of insults and annoyance, when a voice elevated behind him. "She's in the stables."

He turned around and saw Calixte dining at a table, a feast fit for a king before them. They were wearing an elegantly embroidered purple robe, their long hair tied up in a high bun, revealing their pointed ears. Their face was makeup-free, and their peculiar orange eyes were fixed on him.

Talyvien stared back at Calixte in complete bewilderment.

"The young woman," Calixte repeated. "She's in the stables."

With a slight nod of thanks, Talyvien rushed out of the room.

 Lucine was caressing Maia on the snout when Talyvien arrived.

He rushed toward her, his face marked by anxiety.

"Ah, Taly! Did you slee—?" she began, but stopped abruptly at the sight of his face. "What happened?" she asked, worried in turn.

"An assassin. Last night," he said gravely.

A shiver ran down Lucine's spine.

"Are you alright?" he asked, placing his hands on the young druidess's shoulders.

She gave a slight nod of her head, much to Talyvien's noticeable relief.

"We need to leave for Dawnelest today," he said, releasing her shoulders. "Pack your things, and we'll buy a horse with what's left of my savings, to travel more comfortably. I think the assassin will strike again at some point, so we have to stay on guard."

"Do you think Piore sent them to kill you?" she asked, panic rising in her.

"Probably," he replied. "A paladin who possesses sensitive information in the wild, she must not like that." He patted the horse's head, which snorted in response. "Maybe I could also train you to fight, just in case?"

The feeling of helplessness Lucine had experienced during her encounter with the man from the night before resurfaced once again. She clenched her fist and vowed not to feel so powerless in the future. She couldn't refuse this offer. "I would really appreciate that," she replied with determination.

Talyvien nodded, a corner of his injured mouth lifting.

They hurried across the tavern again and headed toward the stairs leading to their rooms to prepare their belongings.

"Do you want some?" Calixte exclaimed, seeing them passing. They gestured toward the multitude of food on the table in front of them with emphasis.

Too excited to miss such an opportunity, Lucine headed toward the Alaris's table.

Talyvien grumbled and followed her reluctantly, dragging his feet. "That's very kind of you, but we're in a bit of a hurry," he emphasized.

"Oh, come on," Calixte said. "You're not going to leave on an empty stomach!" they joked, with a charming smile.

Why did he hate magic so much? Lucine wondered. Knowing Talyvien's aversion to the bard, Lucine made a pleading pout on her face. The paladin's shoulders slumped, and her wish was granted as he sat at the table with a resigned look, grumbling even more.

"I promise I won't use any magic on you," Calixte teased, winking at him.

Talyvien remained silent and began to eat the food in front of him.

"Unless you want me to heal that nasty wound?" they mocked, seemingly enjoying the paladin's discomfort.

"No, thanks. I'll be fine," Talyvien replied curtly.

"Ah, it's because it's not the magic of the goddess Callystrande?"

Talyvien abruptly stopped eating. He cast icy eyes in the bard's direction, and his hand slid to the hilt of his sword.

"Take it easy! I'm not here to pry!" A deep chuckle escaped Calixte's throat. "It's just that you're not the first paladin I've encountered. Always looking so serious and austere. But I guess it's part of the charm." Calixte's mischievous look disappeared behind a glass of fruit juice, which they brought to their lips in a dramatic pause. "Besides, I can sense your connection with the goddess," they added, putting back down the drink.

Was it true? Could the Alaris really feel that? Talyvien's features softened. Calixte had hit the mark. The words seemed to comfort him.

"But my offer still stands if you want me to heal your face," the bard affirmed.

"No. Even if you were capable of healing me with the goddess's magic, I wouldn't accept," replied Talyvien, grabbing a pastry from one of the trays.

"Why not?" Lucine asked, intrigued.

"Because Callystrande's paladins use their magic to heal the most disadvantaged—those who truly need it," Talyvien explained solemnly. "And unless our lives are in danger, we prefer to keep and see our scars as reminders of our failures, to push us to excel and train harder."

"Ah, the mysterious paladins of Callystrande, with their muscular bodies marked by their battles. Quite a program!" chuckled Calixte, refilling their glass with fruit juice.

Lucine couldn't help but burst into laughter, trying to contain herself in the face of Talyvien's embarrassment. She masked her sudden joy with a snort and forced herself to adopt a more neutral expression. Trying to help her friend, she decided to change the subject. "What exactly are the Alaris?" she asked eagerly. "You seem to be able to do amazing things!"

"Oh, always so flattering!" Calixte boasted, lightly patting the back of Lucine's hand. "We are an ancient race from the great metropolis of Alar. It's a city that floats above a volcanic island in the middle of the ocean."

An ethereal blue magical illusion took shape in Calixte's hands. In a turquoise and sparkling swirl, an island with a massive volcano emerged above their feast. A smaller island floated above the first one, dominated by a resplendent city. Tall and slender towers proudly sprung at the heart of it. It was a fantastic and unreal sight.

"It looks magnificent!" exclaimed Lucine.

Talyvien, though interested, had a disdainful grunt at the sight of the Alaris's magic.

"I said I won't use magic directed at you, but I didn't say I won't use magic at all!" Calixte teased, glancing sideways at the paladin.

Talyvien grumbled in response and resumed his meal.

"We have the peculiarity of being immortal and possessing our own magic, devoid of the intervention of the gods," the bard continued. "But this magic is linked to our gender. Men practice what is called the Ignescent, while women use the Flow."

Lucine was puzzled. How was all of this possible? Immortal beings? "Forgive me for asking," she said cautiously, "but what kind of magic do you practice?"

Calixte burst into a deep, hearty laughter. "Don't worry, I understand! I practice both!"

The Alaris opened their palms on the table. A small blood-red flame ignited in their left hand, while a fluid and sparkling blue spiral swirled in their right one.

"How is that possible?" Talyvien asked, his question a mixture of curiosity and disdain.

"Let's just say that when I turned one hundred, I refused to attend the ceremony to determine my gender," Calixte explained. "Alaris are born with the ability to practice a little of both magics, but the powers of the Ignescent or the Flow truly reveal their full potential in only one gender."

"So, you refused to choose?" Talyvien intervened sternly.

"The absence of choice is a choice in itself, paladin. Not identifying with either gender, I preferred to stay true to myself," they challenged, a coldness slipping into their pupil-less eyes.

"Even if it cost you a portion of your powers?" the paladin retorted.

"Choosing to be either a woman or a man would have also deprived me of some of my powers," they sulked.

"I find it fascinating!" Lucine interrupted, trying to lighten the atmosphere. "So, what can you do with all this magic?"

"The Ignescent is offensive magic, based on the power of fire, as the name suggests. Alaris men can tap into its essence and control the bodies and minds of most humans, destroy, and burn. I don't have as much power as a man, but I refuse to use the Ignescent that way. I prefer to use it for defense or more creatively, like conjuring dreams or pleasant feelings with my music," they rejoiced, looking at Talyvien with a regained smile. "As for the Flow, it's magic of contemplation and life, based on the element of water. It allows me to heal, create certain illusions, and read certain thoughts, although I also refuse to use it that way."

"I don't mean to be impolite, but all of this seems a bit . . . forced?" Lucine hesitated. "Why should these types of magic necessarily align with a specific gender?"

"Ah! That's what I thought too!" Calixte laughed. "I found myself far too extraordinary to be confined to such boxes!"

The Alaris's response awakened admiration in Lucine. The young woman envied the bard's courage and honesty. How could they rid themselves of the guilt of wanting something different from what the world had decided for them?

"So," Talyvien asked, "what is an Alaris doing so far from their homeland, and why did you choose to become a bard?" He nonchalantly helped himself to eggs and sausages from another tray.

"Mmhh, always this question of choice," Calixte said, placing their empty glass in front of them, their eyes lost in their memories. "Let's just say my people weren't too happy about me not attending the ceremony. So, I decided to leave and explore the rest of the world!" Their attention then turned to Lucine. "And to share my truth with people who would appreciate it!"

"Thank you for the show and this meal, by the way," Lucine said, a smile on her lips. "It's very kind of you!"

"You're welcome. It's my pleasure," Calixte said enthusiastically, giving a small nod of their head. "I'll be staying in this inn for several days. The customers are friendly and pay well for my performances. If you ever want to drop by or need anything, my offer still stands."

Calixte's citrine eyes met Talyvien's with a strange insistence.

The paladin, still with the fork in his mouth, stared back at them with a perplexed look.

 Lucine and Talyvien retrieved all their belongings. At a local stable, they purchased a magnificent gray horse, which Talyvien decided to name Aho, and they set off for Dawnelest.

Slowly but steadily, as Lucine had never practiced horseback riding before, they moved forward with caution. Although Talyvien showed her how to handle Maia, he once again noticed the young woman's natural skill with animals. It was as if she could communicate with the horse.

He thought back to their conversation with Calixte and was relieved to be able to leave Luminaur and the cumbersome magic of the Alaris behind. He found it surprising that Calixte hadn't mentioned what had happened the previous night with the assassin. Perhaps the bard had been too drunk to remember? Or maybe they didn't realize that their actions had saved his life?

18

Several days passed as Lucine and Talyvien journeyed to Dawnelest. They had avoided towns and villages, fearing they might encounter the Crusade of the paladins of Callystrande and aiming to attract as little attention as possible. After all, an assassin was still on their trail.

True to his promise, Talyvien trained the young woman whenever they made camp for the night. They would run for hours to improve her endurance. The paladin was determined to teach her the fundamentals of combat, unarmed or with wooden staves, to develop the strength and posture of the young druidess. Although she had never fought before, Lucine proved to be a brilliant student, with a burning desire to learn evident in her mismatched eyes. He endeavored to teach her everything he knew—everything unrelated to Callystrande's magic, that is.

Talyvien appreciated feeling useful and admired the progress of the young woman, but he couldn't stop the nostalgia he felt for his lost abilities from tinting their training sessions. The exhilaration that the goddess's magic had brought him in battle relentlessly tugged at his thoughts. Being blessed by the miracle of the Goddess of Light meant being able to burn enemies or heal flesh. Now deprived of Callystrande's favor, this absence gnawed at him day after day. However, he always made sure not to let anything show to Lucine, as the druidess had already endured enough hardships in her short life.

Around the fire, they regularly exchanged stories from their past lives, from the Cathedral of Callystra to the Astral Forest, from Tuoryn to the ancients and Solehan.

One day, like any other, after several hours of galloping on their horses, they decided to stop and set up camp as night fell. The ruins of an ancient village emerged, with the remains of an old church standing prominently among the stone foundations.

The peaceful and spiritual atmosphere of the place embraced them, even though the building seemed to have lost its past glory. Like the ribcage of a gigantic creature, the skeletal arches supported the massive yet fragile structure of the roof, of which a section had partially collapsed. A mass of climbing plants had found refuge in the corners of the building, wrapped around tall, polished stone columns. The memory of the architectural details and the devotion of the place was being engulfed by vegetation. Large beams of light pierced through what had been the building's vault, creating curious silhouettes of light on the cracked rocks and glass debris under their feet.

Partly covered in ivy, a statue dominated the chancel of the church. Talyvien approached it cautiously, with the sword of Tuoryn drawn from its scabbard. Behind him, Lucine followed, her bow drawn, ready to release an arrow.

With the tip of his sword, he gently removed some ivy leaves and uncovered the sorrowful face of his goddess, her hands open in welcome. He wanted to believe it was a sign. A blessing. Grateful to his goddess, Talyvien placed a hand over his heart.

They set up their camp in the middle of the nave to take advantage of the remaining roof cover and the protection of Callystrande.

In their well-rehearsed routine, they tried to stay close together as much as possible. With the threat of the assassin still hanging over them, Talyvien struggled to remain vigilant, even though the hooded figure had not reappeared since their altercation at the inn in Luminaur. The beast-like eyes taunted his memory, making his blood run cold.

 Lucine watched the paladin head into the woods to gather some additional logs. Then, she cleared a portion of the stone floor to make way for the fire, which she ignited with a few twigs. She arranged their bedding and thanked the stars for the rations they had been able to carry, sparing them from having to hunt animals for survival, as berries were becoming scarce.

Remaining alert, she waited for Talyvien's return and sat on her bedding, gazing at the stars emerging in the darkening sky. Could it be that, somewhere, Solehan could also be contemplating them? Connected by the same sky? Though absurd, the familiarity of this thought comforted her.

Out of habit, she listened to the gentle crackling of the fire as it started, the rustling of the light breeze in the trees, and the cries of animals coming from the woods. She studied the now-high moon, which redefined the shapes of the strange carcass of the church.

Soft weeping mingled with the hooting of an owl.

Disturbed from her melancholy, Lucine paused in her thoughts. She listened more attentively. Faint sobs, akin to those of a child or a woman, rose in the night. She hadn't imagined it.

Her pulse quickened. Overwhelmed by panic, Lucine turned her head left and right, trying to locate the paladin. Should she wait for his return? But with her friend's silhouette nowhere to be found, she resolved to get up.

The crying intensified.

Would she always be haunted by fear of everything? Lucine gritted her teeth, frustrated by her weakness. Her trembling fingers grasped the wood of her bow. Irritated by her lack of courage, she drew the weapon and attempted to find the source of the mysterious sobbing on her own.

The young druidess approached the collapsed wall of the church and stepped over the debris and bricks scattered on the ground. On the other side, a few tombstones lay in the darkness, likely belonging to the cemetery adjacent to the church. She walked among the graves; their epitaphs mostly faded.

A frail figure was curled up against one of the tombstones.

Lucine cautiously approached, getting a closer look with light steps. She then discerned the features of a young woman, seemingly of a similar age to hers, her face bathed in tears. She wore only a simple pale gray dress; her bare feet were covered in mud and dirt.

Still somewhat wary, Lucine scanned the surroundings. Could it be a trap? But all was silent in the small cemetery. No alarming sounds or visions appeared before the young druidess. She redirected her attention to the weeping woman.

Large black eyes met Lucine's gaze through blond locks flowing over fragile shoulders. An echo of her own powerlessness. Lucine's heart wrenched. She knelt beside the woman and now felt foolish for having been petrified by such fears. What was this woman doing here?

"Don't be afraid," the druidess said. "My name is Lucine." Not quite sure what else to say, she tried to comfort the young woman with a smile. "Oh, are you crying for one of the graves? Someone from your family?"

The unfortunate woman nodded timidly.

Filled with profound compassion and empathy, Lucine felt the pain of losing loved ones, still fresh for her as well. But she hesitated to help. Was it safe? Perhaps if she brought the woman back to camp, Talyvien could also assist her and figure out what to do.

"We have some rations, water, and a campfire in the church, if you're hungry and need to warm up."

The young woman nodded again.

Content that the unfortunate soul had accepted her offer, Lucine made a small hand gesture, inviting her to follow. On the way back, the druidess stepped over the stone debris once more and carefully ensured that the woman was keeping up.

The woman appeared frightened; the anguish etched in her large black eyes. She held her arms and shivered in the cool breeze against her pale skin.

 When Talyvien had finally finished cutting enough wood, he made his way back to the ruined village, following the small path among the trees. After a few minutes of walking through the maze of debris, he entered the large, unhinged door of the church. He had suffered from lack of sleep and found it difficult to fully surrender to the night with the threat of the assassin still looming. Therefore, he hurried back to the camp.

Two female silhouettes greeted him in the faint glow of the flames. The paladin's gait faltered. Who was this stranger? He quickened his pace.

One of them appeared in the dim light. He recognized Lucine's smile, as she approached the nascent fire and headed in his direction.

"Taly! I found a young woman who—"

Lucine's voice was stifled in his mind. Talyvien's arms tightened around the logs he was carrying. The face of the other woman projected over the blaze.

The paladin's stomach turned. His legs wavered.

In the fiery light of the campfire, two eyes opened on the woman's cheeks and joined her human eyes. Peeking through the curtain of blonde locks, four nightmarish orbs of deep black scrutinized the paladin. They engulfed his vision with cruelty. A wicked smile formed, revealing two enormous fangs. The creature's long tongue moistened the fangs before snapping back into its inhumanly large mouth.

Talyvien dropped the wood from his hands and drew his sword from its sheath. He launched into a frantic run along the church's nave.

Stupefied by the paladin's reaction, Lucine turned. The four-eyed, gleaming face lunged at her. She drew the dagger from her belt, but the creature grabbed her wrist before the blade could reach its trajectory. Holding her in place, the creature sank its two enormous fangs into Lucine's tender neck. Her scream tore through the night.

"No!" Talyvien yelled, still running amid the dilapidated church pews, Tuoryn's sword gleaming under the moonlight.

His distress fueled his rage.

Lucine's body convulsed in pain. Her dagger hit the stone floor with a metallic echo that resonated in the paladin's heart.

As he finally reached them, the creature released its grip. The druidess's body slumped to the ground. Blood flowed from either side of the creature's vicious mouth, and it ran its long tongue over its lips, savoring the taste.

Talyvien took a leap in his stride and raised his sword toward its chest.

Before he could pierce it, the creature's woman's body transformed. Its legs gave way to a huge, pale, and glistening abdomen, like that of a gigantic spider, from which six long and dangerously sharp legs branched out. They resembled formidable wooden stakes, their chaotic tangle of branches connecting them to the thorax, the upper part of the human body still attached to this horrifying nightmare vision.

Talyvien swore and came to an abrupt stop in his tracks. *An echarvora!*

Although he had fought a few in his life as a paladin of Callystrande, he knew they were rare. However, he had never defeated one alone. Vicious creatures, they liked to play with their prey and emotions before relishing them, finding their victims' emotional weaknesses and deploying their psychic web to enjoy them better. Talyvien also knew the havoc a bite from such a monstrosity could cause. What could he do without the magic of his goddess to save Lucine?

No. He refused to succumb to terror, and he focused on the priority of their situation. He would figure it out later.

Talyvien and the creature faced each other. They circled in the transept of the church, under the petrified gaze of the great statue of Callystrande.

The insect-like body of the creature lunged at the paladin. With a swift movement, he dove to the side to evade the attack. He cursed the absence of his golden armor and powers. Unjustly restrained to defend himself like an ordinary man, he could only take comfort in the presence of his mentor's sword in his hand. He had no choice.

Another assault. One of the huge wooden legs charged toward him with the clear intention of disemboweling him. Taking advantage of the creature's momentum, he dodged the attack and sliced off one of the bark-covered legs, which fell heavily to the ground. Black blood gushed from the dismembered body and stained the bare stone.

The creature's roar of rage and pain shook the church's structure. Unrestrained, it immediately launched another attack. Its powerful blows came from all directions. The legs sliced through the air like daggers around Talyvien. Overwhelmed by the fury of the creature, he used its width to play with the momentum of its attacks to conserve his stamina.

The flames behind him were dying out due to neglect. A deadly parallel with Lucine's condition.

As the creature's two front legs tried to scissor him in a new display of cruelty, Talyvien barely bent backward. The slash cut through the air just above his head, taking a lock of his hair with it. He slid under the enormous body of the echarvora and thrust his sword with all his might into the creature's abdomen. It vociferated even louder, but the armored skin of its insect-like body absorbed most of the impact. The metal of the sword reverberated in the air, leaving only a scratch on the creature's abdomen.

Despite the vehement counterattacks of the monstrosity, the young man continued to dodge the onslaught for several minutes. Disheartened, Talyvien tried to spot the creature's weak points, now certain that the spider body had a carapace resistant to the sharpness of his blade. Bitterness filled his mouth. The deficiency of his goddess's magic pounded with frustration in his chest.

The creature towered several meters above him. How would he put an end to this degenerate nightmare? He glanced at the statue of the goddess, which still watched impassively over this improvised arena. Still moved by his unwavering loyalty to Callystrande, Talyvien muttered a prayer between his teeth in the face of the madness of the plan forming in his mind.

During yet another assault, he evaded the blade of one of the legs as it swished through the night, and he tried once again to dismember the echarvora. But seemingly learning from the paladin's combat techniques, it evaded him in return.

Talyvien was thrown to the ground, his neck exposed to the creature. It seized the opportunity to sink its fangs into his flesh and swiftly leaned its human upper body forward. Its head didn't have the time to taste the precious nectar, as Tuoryn's sword sliced through its neck in a fiery flash. The creature's cruel gluttony had cost it its life.

The head of the echarvora rolled onto the ground, with its four black eyes desperately fixed on Talyvien's. The rest of the creature's body then returned to its human appearance and fell heavily as well.

Exhausted, the paladin got back onto his feet. He took a few seconds to savor the success of his stratagem before realizing that his sword was glowing in the dim light with a soft and familiar radiance. The souls of his mentor and the paladins who had come before him, contained within the blade, seemed to have answered his call. He stared in disbelief at his leather armor, now soaked in black blood, rising and falling with his ragged breaths.

A moan from the makeshift camp made him spin around. The sight that unfolded before him stabbed Talyvien's heart like a dagger. The young druidess lay on the ground, her frail body convulsing. He knelt beside her and placed his hands on her neck, where profane black veins wove a spiderweb pattern under her skin, from the base of her shoulder to her cheek.

For the very first time, the abandonment by his goddess struck a blow to his faith. The inexorable cruelty of their situation made him curse the Order of the Paladins of Callystrande. Piore. His king. His entire kingdom. Their fate.

Lucine looked at him, her eyes now completely shrouded in darkness, tears rolling down her cheeks.

He desperately tried to invoke his goddess's magic, but only the weak embers of the campfire emitted a faint light in the dimness.

"Taly . . ." she groaned, with visible difficulty, her throat trembling under the weight of each word. She managed to take one of the paladin's hands in hers, at the level of her neck. "I'm scared," she mumbled. "I can feel . . . myself changing. Please don't let me transform . . ."

"No. No! There must be a way," he insisted, still focused on Lucine's neck, concentrating on the impossible task.

"Talyvien, do it" she whispered. "I beg you."

Her large black eyes met Talyvien's in a final plea. The paladin's hands sagged in despair and fatigue. How had they come to this? In a fraction of seconds, everything had changed. He had failed, once again. He was no more than the shadow of a paladin. Pathetic.

"I want to leave as myself. Please," Lucine murmured in a strangely resigned tone. "I can't take it anymore. The elders were right . . ."

It seemed they had both given up. They had failed. Perhaps she wanted to join her departed loved ones?

Her breath now came in ragged gasps, and Talyvien noticed two long canines beneath her lips. Her convulsions had stopped. He knew time was running out.

With a weary hand, he picked up the dagger from the ground. Holding Lucine's body close to him with his other arm, he placed her face against the hollow of his shoulder and positioned the point of the dagger against her back.

"Goodbye, Lucine," he whispered into her ear.

19

She loathed contracts that gave her a hard time; thus, she cursed the Alaris who had stumbled upon her that night in the inn room. Her code was clear; no witnesses could be allowed.

The Order of the Twilight Children of Sazaelith tolerated no failure. The assassin had patiently hoped that the man would make a careless mistake and forget the threat. However, she didn't expect her target to be accompanied, nor did she anticipate his swordsmanship skills. Nevertheless, she would adapt. Unforeseen events were not uncommon in her line of work, as her many years of practice had taught her.

She knew nothing about her target other than his name, Talyvien Haldgard, and his general appearance, as tradition required. It was better that way. She didn't want to know anything. Sazaelith had chosen her target, and she would carry out the sentence.

She usually traveled at night, benefiting from her goddess's blessing in possessing extraordinary speed and endurance in the darkness. She followed the traces the horses left in the woods and always stopped a few hundred meters from their camp, which she found every dawn. She patiently waited for her moment. The assassin allowed a few days of respite for her target, hoping that their guard would drop, but she decided to accelerate her pace to get closer to them.

The delicate art of assassination should not be rushed.

That's how she had followed them to the abandoned village in the middle of the woods. Staying hidden among the trees, she finally saw the man venture alone to gather firewood for the camp. An opportune moment.

She noticed the man's robust figure with his back turned and his sword in its sheath. A dagger gracefully slid from the assassin's sleeve. She hoped to avoid the mishaps of the inn incident. She had to act quickly and efficiently, preferably by surprise. Like a feline stalking its prey, she prepared to strike in the night.

The cries of a young woman echoed in the distance.

The assassin silently cursed the interruption. She listened carefully, blessed by her goddess with heightened senses. The cries became more poignant. She decided to abort her mission for tonight; there was a special place in Sazaelith's heart for female suffering. However, the man did not seem to have heard.

She followed him stealthily as he returned to their camp, which they had set up in a dilapidated church of Callystrande. At the sight of such a place, she couldn't help but spit on the ground. Sazaelith was the antithesis of the goddess of light, after all. The assassin slithered among the church's stones like a mouse. Where were the cries coming from?

Then she saw her. The young woman was being attacked by a hideous creature, its four ebony eyes reveling in its prey.

Although she was an assassin, she respected the value of life. Her order's code forbade her from killing innocents—people without compelling evidence of wrongdoing or without a contract from the Mother Superior. Sazaelith was a deity of vengeance and finesse, not sadism or cruelty. She refused to indulge in the pleasure of needless suffering and always tried to fulfill her mission as quickly and efficiently as the goddess demanded. So, she despised seeing a young woman suffer like this.

However, being concealed, she had no choice but to wait patiently. She observed the man drawing his sword and attacking the creature. He clearly had received specialized training in sword combat, as his movements were fluid and confident.

Regardless of the outcome of the battle, her mission would be accomplished. However, she preferred to complete her contract herself and ensure that one of these monstrosities was no longer roaming free. She had too much pride to let one of these creatures do the job for her.

When the creature's head fell to the ground, the man's sword emitted a dazzling glow. *A paladin of Callystrande.* That explained their choice of camp location.

Her mouth twisted in disgust.

He could thus come to the aid of the young woman, who was now convulsing on the floor of the church. She just had to wait. She bade her time for a few more minutes, waiting for the man's hands to administer the necessary care. But nothing happened.

Instead, to her horror, she witnessed him desperately pointing a dagger at the young woman's back.

In a gesture she didn't understand, she stood up and approached the camp.

20

With her cheek against his and a hand in her hair, and whispering his goodbyes to her, Talyvien resigned himself to letting Lucine go in peace. He had failed and couldn't protect her. The least he could do was to end her suffering. With quivering fingers, he readied himself to administer the merciful act.

A woman's voice echoed in the night. "I can save her."

He raised his head eagerly. A dark silhouette stood before him. He immediately recognized the feline fury in the sapphire eyes glimmering under the hood.

The assassin. Just what he needed, he thought ruefully.

With a swift motion, he let go of the dagger and grabbed his sword, which was lying nearby. He pointed it toward the figure, still holding Lucine's body pressed against him.

The assassin approached with silent steps. She raised her hands on either side of her face and removed the hood, revealing a woman's face itself in the faint glow of dying embers.

The darkness allowed the paladin to discern only her tanned skin and delicate features, as well as long black hair braided down her back.

"I can save her," the woman reiterated, "but you must let me do it. We don't have much time left."

Had he gone mad? Was this real? Talyvien became lost between nightmare and reality. "We?" he scoffed.

"Let me help you," the woman insisted. "You know she doesn't have much time before she transforms, and unless you can use your goddess's magic—" She dared not finish her sentence.

"Now we've seen it all," Talyvien retorted. "An assassin who wants to save lives." He let out a nervous chuckle.

"My contract is on you, not her," the assassin objected, a certain reproach in her voice. "And Sazaelith can save her."

"Sazaelith! That's out of the question. Now I understand why you reek of pagan magic," the paladin challenged with ferocity and disgust.

"Do you have another solution? Besides executing her?" she taunted.

Talyvien's thoughts and emotions pierced him from all sides, and he did not know what to do. Deep down, he knew the assassin was right. There wasn't much time left. He had to act quickly. But was she truly capable of saving Lucine? Wasn't the magic of the goddess of shadows worse than death? In defiance, he retorted, "And what's stopping you from killing me and saving her afterward?"

"Oh, that has certainly crossed my mind," she mocked. A sneering smile appeared on her face, revealing her white teeth. "But you don't seem like the type to give up easily, and we must act fast. Also, after doing what I must, I won't be able to protect her. So, she'll need you . . . for now."

As the woman finished her speech, Lucine's body began to convulse violently against Talyvien's chest. He turned his gaze away from the assassin and gently placed the druidess onto the ground.

Black tears like ink now flowed from her eyes. Large canines protruded from her twisted, half-opened mouth, as she struggled painfully to breathe. Talyvien's chest tightened.

The assassin knelt beside Lucine, who seemed no longer aware of her surroundings. There was no time now to wait for his consent.

Talyvien watched the scene in horror, lost in an impossible choice. Everything was happening too fast.

The assassin rolled up one sleeve of her leather jacket, revealing a portion of a tattoo. She placed her wrist in front of Lucine's gasping mouth.

"Drink," she commanded firmly.

"What? No!" Struck by horror, Talyvien regained his composure and looked up at the woman in protest. What he saw puzzled him.

Like a proud and untamed predator, a cold and insolent fury emerged from the surprising face of the assassin. Fine scars in the inner corners of her eyes enhanced the feline appearance of her cat-like pupils and seemed to illustrate the deadly danger the paladin knew she was capable of. A ruthless and beastly beauty.

Neither of them had time to say anything.

Lucine seized the assassin's offered wrist and drove her two enormous fangs into the flesh, emitting a growl of pleasure. Vibrant blue blood dripped from either side of the young druidess's mouth. Her body gradually calmed, apparently relishing the warm cobalt liquid flowing down her throat.

The assassin groaned in pain under the pressure of the bite.

Talyvien recoiled, still on the ground, horrified by the spectacle unfolding before him.

"The blood of the chosen ones of the goddess of shadows has many properties, such as slowing down the poison of certain creatures. But she will still need a healer, preferably someone who does not practice Callystrande's magic. The two magics don't mix well." The assassin intervened with difficulty as Lucine continued to bite and drink greedily from her wrist.

Wide-eyed, the paladin observed the scene, unable to respond in any way. What had he done?

"I will also have to feed her several times," the assassin said, "to keep the poison inactive for as long as possible. But if she doesn't receive help soon, she will likely develop an addiction to my blood. And I'm not an endless resource either."

Talyvien stood up in a contrite silence. The confused eyes of the assassin followed his movements. He went to kneel before the statue of the goddess and planted the point of his sword into the ground. Firmly gripping the hilt, the paladin placed his forehead on his hands and began to pray, head bowed.

He was lost. He needed a sign.

Contempt flowed behind him from the feline eyes that stared at him.

"What is your name?" Talyvien asked in a broken voice that echoed in the silent church.

"Shael," she whispered.

"Shael, we must return to Luminaur."

And those were the only words he said that night. Lost, Talyvien lifted his head to look at the face of the statue, still with open palms before him.

Golden tears flowed from its stone eyes.

21

For several days now, Solehan and Valnard had faced each other daily around the great tree. But even though the young druid had grown accustomed to this special training, on this day, the Alaris seemed less merciful in his attacks.

Solehan dodged the rapidly snaking vines and threw himself to the side, landing on the rough stone slabs of the courtyard, scraping the skin of his forearms in the process. Breathing heavily, he only had time to lift his head before seeing more vines rushing toward him. Trying to regain his bearings, he attempted to roll on the ground to avoid this new onslaught. He let out a cry of pain as one of them clasped around his legs. Immobilized on the ground, he watched as the slow steps of Valnard approached him.

"Pathetic," was the only word that came out of the Alaris's mouth as he looked down at the young druid with disdain. The branches of the tall, dark tree tore through the sky behind his silhouette. His green eyes penetrated Solehan's mind like sharpened blades.

"Kill me and get it over with," Solehan uttered. Blood formed in his mouth, and he spat it onto the ground.

"Perhaps I was wrong?" Valnard declared nonchalantly, his attention briefly shifting to the burn marks on Solehan's wrists. "Perhaps you'll never be ready?"

Out of breath, Solehan didn't respond. It all seemed meaningless now.

"You're going to die without avenging your kin," Valnard added. "Just a life with *no value, no purpose, wasted.*" He snapped the last words harshly in his mouth.

Even in this, Solehan knew he had failed. Valnard was right. His short life was worthless. He had accomplished nothing, had no more purpose, and felt nothing anymore. Perhaps it was better this way? He had never felt like he belonged anywhere, not even within his clan or the legend of the stars. Maybe there was no place that existed for someone like him?

Wearily, he focused on the branches of the tree creaking in the wind behind Valnard. He got lost in the silhouette against the gray sky.

"You'll then never avenge Lucine," Valnard insisted.

Solehan felt like he had been punched upon hearing his twin sister's name from Valnard's mouth.

"Don't speak her name," the young druid coldly growled, redirecting his attention to the Alaris.

A cruel smile crossed Valnard's face. "Dead for nothing. Poor little . . . *Lucine,*" he whispered, with a peculiar delight.

"Don't say—"

Solehan never got to finish his sentence, as it died in his throat. Enormous fangs pushed against his lips and distorted his jaw. An energy seized his limbs, breaking the vines that ensnared him with a sudden jerk. His body propelled forward. An animalistic fervor surged through his arms and legs. Carried away by the power emanating from within him, his desire for revenge shattered all barriers of his mind at an incredible speed. Time stood still.

His eyes locked onto Valnard's face.

His teeth. His smile.

His hair floating around his shoulders.

One of the veins pulsating under the skin of his arm.

He followed its course carefully up to his neck.

His fangs sank into the flesh of the Alaris, who let out a scream of mixed surprise and pain.

The two men fell backward, Valnard landing on his back. A gigantic black spider had replaced the young man's body and now stood menacingly over the Alaris, threatening him with its enormous mandibles.

Valnard, gripping his bleeding neck, burst into loud laughter. The Ignescent grabbed Solehan's thorax and threw him several meters away against the stone arches. Upon impact, the spider metamorphosed back into a man and fell heavily, shattering some stone blocks from one of the arches.

Solehan, lying miserably among the debris, struggled to get up. What had just happened? He felt a warm and metallic liquid in his mouth. What had he done? A shiver of horror ran through him.

With wide eyes, he fled through the door leading to the castle, under the amused gaze of Valnard, whose blood still flowed down his arm, his hand pressed against his neck.

Solehan raced through corridors and antechambers, taking the stairs four at a time. He dashed away, the specter of his own terror chasing after him.

Finally, he arrived in his room and hastily closed the door with a loud thud of raw wood. He sat panting on the bed. His hands stained the white sheets with red liquid.

The young druid then noticed the mirror leaning against the wall. He stood up and faced his reflection. Vermilion red blood streamed from both sides of his contorted mouth due to his emotions, and his disheveled brown hair fell around his pale face. His golden and silver eyes frantically scrutinized his image with an astonished expression.

He wiped his face with a trembling hand and was overcome by violent nausea. Solehan vomited Valnard's blood, which mixed with his own on the floor. Once his disgust had subsided, he crawled under the bed sheets and curled up, shaking uncontrollably.

What had he become? Why had his body seemed to have chosen to transform into a bloodthirsty spider-like beast? He wanted revenge, but was he willing to give up so much of himself to achieve it? Was this the place Teluar had reserved for him?

The days passed; dawn and twilight alternating in their ephemeral dance through the window.

Solehan remained huddled under the sheets of his bed. Despair and horror paralyzed him. The browned bloodstains of his fingers on the white sheets constantly reminded him of the monster he had become.

Forest spirits, the lychenas, occasionally entered the room with light steps, making the large wooden door creak, to bring him food and water that he did not touch. He could not bring himself to sleep, no longer trusting his body and mind. He couldn't cry, speak, or scream. His body had frozen in this icy stupor.

After several days spent in a haze, desperately staring at the window on the other side of the room, Solehan heard the creaking hinges of the door once again. The footsteps of the lychena became discreet on the parquet floor. More food. The mattress of the bed lazily sank under its weight.

Valnard's long black fingers rested on Solehan's shoulder.

The young man started, electrified by this contact.

"This transformation surprised me. I didn't expect this, Solehan," came the deep and hoarse voice behind him.

Solehan listened to his name form in the mouth of the Alaris. He did not recognize the man speaking now. The gentleness of his voice. The tenderness of his gesture.

"Let me show you the extent of the gift you have received," Valnard insisted.

Perplexed, Solehan turned his head. The Alaris was looking at him impassively, a leaf bandage placed on his neck. His usually cruel eyes carried an emotion that was unfamiliar to the young druid. A glimmer that he had only glimpsed fleetingly before.

"Follow me," Valnard said. He got to his feet and exited the room with steady steps.

Solehan inspected the door of his room for a few seconds. Did all of this just happen? Were hunger and thirst starting to make him hallucinate?

At the end of the corridor, Valnard's silhouette was moving away. Solehan followed in silence.

The two men traversed the entire castle, back and forth. They went through various corridors, doors, and rooms, descending several staircases for what felt like endless minutes. They finally arrived in front of a heavy wooden door, which Valnard pushed open. A layer of dust dissipated in its path, revealing a gigantic hall.

A throne overlooked the large dormant room, elevated by a few steps and frozen in all its splendor. An intact relic of a glorious past that had witnessed the birth and death of numerous stories and rulers. Like the caustic reflections of water under the oceans, a cerulean brightness embraced the place, produced by long stained-glass windows that loomed up to the ceiling. Luminous shades intertwined with turquoise and silver, harmoniously drawing contrasting illustrations on the long carpet that led to the throne.

Allowing the colored lights to sketch their arabesques on his skin, Solehan noticed the elegant motif at the center of this tableau of light—the symbol of a radiant fox surrounded by leaves and branches. However, the Alaris did not seem to pay attention to it, instead crossing the throne room to head toward another door at the back of the hall.

The second door opened onto a large balcony, where several lychenas were busy around two enormous creatures.

Solehan was left breathless. The beasts were similar to the one that had carried him in its talons on the fateful day of the Eclipse. Their skin was made of bark; each chimeric being had a deer-like head adorned with majestic antlers on each side. Each also possessed a canine body with four powerful legs ending in formidable talons, as well as a tail garnished with long yellowed and browned leaves. The two great forest spirits shook their long wingspans made of branches and bark, sending the wind rustling through the foliage.

Valnard delicately placed his hand on the forehead of one of the creatures. Seemingly appreciating the gesture, the creature lowered its head at the touch.

"Elaphoras," he whispered, a smile bouncing in his voice.

Solehan approached cautiously, and the second elaphora watched him with its large yellow eyes, looking curious. The bark skin felt cold under his fingertips as he slowly slid his hand to touch the deer antlers of the creature, which allowed him to do so. The young man marveled at its beauty, its long and graceful appearance. How could he have been afraid of this?

With a quick and confident gesture, Valnard climbed onto the back of the elaphora with ease and, with a look, invited Solehan to do the same with the second beast. Sensing the hesitation of the young man, the creature lowered itself. Solehan managed, with some effort, to hoist himself onto its back, and he clung to the branches protruding from its neck.

Valnard's elaphora suddenly leaped into the void. It jumped off the balcony with agility, letting out a bellow that echoed through the valley. Solehan's creature followed its companion, not waiting for the young man's agreement, as he clung to the creature as best he could.

He squinted under the power of the wind on his face. Legs tightly pressed against the elaphora's body, Solehan dared not move. His stomach was tied in knots by the powerful beats of the wings that surrounded him. A second rustle of wings joined the first, and he finally found the strength to open his eyes.

The kindred forest spirit, with Valnard astride, soared in the air beside him. Valnard's slim and leaning body gracefully embraced the creature, his long hair trailing like a wispy streak of black and white. The silhouette of his admirably chiseled profile stood out against the sky, and he bore an air of unknown joy inscribed on his face. Valnard was intensely contemplating the beauty of the landscape before him, the diaphanous atmosphere coloring his irises with myriad cerulean shades and a tinge of tenderness.

With an unusual heaviness in his chest, Solehan felt a warm flush spreading across his cheeks at the sight.

He followed Valnard's gaze and saw the incredible canvas that nature was painting for them in its glory, beneath the powerful bodies of the elaphoras. The long valley, graced with streams and rivers, which the timid sun lit up with a diffuse glow, was bordered by imposing dark and protective mountains. Impressed, the young druid admired the blanket of clouds pierced by the peaks, the sparse forest of dark trees under their feet, and the protruding cliffs of bluish-gray stone framing their progression.

Valnard's elaphora dived into the void in a controlled descent under its rider's command. It reared just before crashing to the ground, soaring up again in a spectacular pirouette and twirling around Solehan. The two creatures bellowed in unison. A sincere and exultant expression appeared on Valnard's face. He clearly enjoyed flying like this. The immortal's eyes met Solehan's, inviting him to join in the game.

On a dare, the young druid engaged in the competition and spread his arms wide. The wind pounded the sleeves of his clothes against his skin. He wanted to lose himself in the spectacle before him. He wanted to merge with the majesty of nature. He had nothing left to hope for.

Nothing else mattered. No one, anymore.

All that mattered was just this incandescent moment of madness and recklessness. A rupture between his wretched reality and the beauty of his despair.

Solehan loosened the grip of his legs on the mount. He presented himself to the currents of air that passed through him. Tears flowed from his closed eyes, dissolving into a brilliant trail behind him. The fabric on his skin beat at a steady and sustained rhythm. Its touch became softer and softer.

A tingling sensation made him open his eyes once again. Feathers were gradually sprouting from the tips of his fingers and along his arms, enveloping his shoulders in a warm and thick coat. A cry of exhilaration escaped his hoarse throat. His body took the form of a magnificent eagle, and he soared among the elaphoras.

Solehan whirled around Valnard, playing with the mist, the drops rolling off his outstretched wings. He danced in the air, and his piercing cry echoed throughout the valley. When Valnard once again dove toward the ground, he followed in a graceful and powerful movement.

They played like this for several hours, blessed by the slumbering valley, and for the first time, Solehan felt the power of Teluar resonating in his heart and veins.

22

The paladin and the assassin rode at a steady gallop toward the village of Luminaur to find the Alaris Calixte, who was capable of healing the poison coursing through Lucine's veins. The bard's orange eyes were etched in Talyvien's memory, and he hoped to reach the inn in time before Calixte departed. The paladin rode on his tall gray horse, Aho, with the druidess's light body nestled in the crook of his shoulder, while Shael followed a few meters behind on Maia.

Lucine, feverish and confused, whimpered against the paladin's chest. Twice already, Shael had needed to feed her the blessed blue blood of the goddess Sazaelith to calm her body during convulsions. Talyvien noticed that the assassin weakened a little more each time, but he cared little for it and only focused on the young druidess in his arms.

The magic of the goddess of shadow disgusted him. He wished to arrive quickly in Luminaur to avoid using it again. He also knew that the contract Shael had to fulfill still loomed over his head.

Lucine no longer knew exactly where she was. Disoriented and in a state of drifting, she couldn't perceive what was happening around her.

Talyvien's farewells emerged in her mind. Was she dead? Would she finally see the members of her clan? Zaf? However, despite the longing she felt, a part of her hoped not to see Solehan in the afterlife. It was not meant to be.

As Lucine ventured into the shadows, the burden of a presence weighed down her steps. From the corner of her eye, she saw hundreds of motionless spiders watching her, their multiple eyes fixed on her. But entranced by an unusual calm, she continued to walk.

Wings flapping above her head reverberated through the void. A magnificent owl flew before her, the feathers of its immense wings vibrating in the currents of air. Its plumage seemed to be composed of a mixture of dark and blue nebulous swirls, dissipating into a vaporous trail behind its bird body. A few sparkling stars streaked through this misty wake, their light dispersing in gentle flickers.

Was the owl showing her the way? Lucine followed the splendid animal with gratitude.

A woman's silhouette began to take shape in the distance. The bird perched on her shoulder and scrutinized the druidess with its black and fierce eyes. The woman's inconceivable blue and wild pupils dissected her in a similar way.

As Lucine approached closer, the two figures merged into one. The representation of a female body adorned with the majestic attributes of the animal took form: sublime wings of pure darkness on her back, bird-like talons in place of feet and hands, a predatory gaze piercing through long black hair, and dark bluish skin that shimmered like the starry sky.

The exquisite figure advanced toward Lucine, who didn't flinch. Her arms and large silky wings enveloped the young woman tenderly, like a mother cradling her child. Thus imprisoned in this cocoon of benevolence, the young druidess surrendered to it. A sweet and smooth liquid flowed into her throat. A wave of warmth surged through her. She wanted to stay like this forever, enchanted by the voice of the divinity singing to soothe her.

After a time that felt very long to Lucine but too short at the same time, the angelic voice fell silent. Lips the color of night brushed against the young woman's ear.

"They're coming," she whispered to her.

 With duty always in his heart and his horse galloping frantically, Talyvien suddenly felt Lucine's body jerk, as if caught in a nightmare. Concerned, he slowed Aho to a trot to assist the young woman. Shael urged Maia to trot alongside him as well.

"What's wrong?" Shael inquired from under her midnight blue hood.

"I don't know," Talyvien replied, with a worried tone. "She seems agitated."

"They're coming," whispered Lucine, her eyes half-closed, tainted by the darkness of the poison's corruption.

"I think she's delirious due to the fever," he ventured.

The paladin sought Shael's approval, and she nodded in agreement without saying a word.

But an arrow came hurtling and struck Talyvien's shoulder.

He groaned in pain and was thrown to the ground, as Aho reared in fear. Though dizzy, he made sure Lucine was not injured in their fall and gently laid her on the ground. The paladin then moved the horse a few meters away as a precaution.

Shael dismounted from Maia with extreme speed.

Six men emerged from the dense woods and surrounded them on all sides, wielding short swords, daggers, and maces.

The paladin unsheathed Tuoryn's sword from its scabbard with his right hand and thanked Callystrande that the arrow had run through his left shoulder.

"Surrender, and you'll have your lives spared," grunted a man who stepped forward toward Talyvien.

Various pieces composed his makeshift armor. An unkempt black beard and hair surrounded his dirty face. Though his demeanor displayed some aggression, his gaze appeared strangely vacant, devoid of any depth. Despite his lack of attention to his appearance, Talyvien could guess a rather athletic body. The way he handled and wielded his short swords indicated a certain skill in combat.

"Boss! Some Sazaelith scum here!" shouted one of the bandits from the back, his insult directed at Shael, whose sharp blue eyes under her hood exuded hatred in return.

"Perfect!" rejoiced the first man with the expressionless eyes but a wicked smile, evidently the group's leader. "It will sell well on the black market!"

Talyvien noticed from the corner of his eye that two daggers had appeared in Shael's hands when three of the brigands surrounded her from behind. Would their salvation, as well as Lucine's, rest on a chosen one of Sazaelith? On an assassin? The irony of the idea disturbed him.

"Leave, and you'll have *your* lives spared," Talyvien declared coldly, not giving himself time to dwell on his distress.

The bandit leader let out a sinister cackle and lunged at the paladin without hesitation.

Talyvien parried the first blow with his sword, the impact resonating among the trees.

The other two bandits standing beside their leader joined the fight. Six against two.

Shael and Talyvien were now both engaged in a struggle, each facing three opponents. The paladin at the front, the assassin at the back, they encircled Lucine's body to protect her.

An irritated grimace on his face, Talyvien tried to ignore the pain of the arrow lodged in his shoulder and the sight of blood flowing down his arm. He parried and defended himself as best as he could under the circumstances. He clashed his blade against the various weapons that came at him and hoped Shael was doing the same. The paladin listened carefully to the metallic echoes as a sign of hope that she was still fighting.

Both were weakened by the lack of the precious liquid coursing through their veins, so they had to act quickly to avoid exhausting themselves too soon.

The leader dealt the paladin two quick and close blows with each of his short swords. Talyvien growled with rage and spun his blade in a furious parry that drained all his resources.

One of the bandits took advantage of this opportunity and charged toward him at the same time.

He was overwhelmed. How could they possibly defeat six men anyway? A futile hope. Especially without the blessing of the goddess of light.

Disillusioned, Talyvien prepared to endure the blow. The tendons in his neck tensed with frustrated anger. Every muscle in his body tightened with apprehension.

A miraculous dagger suddenly lodged itself in the forehead of the approaching bandit, just before he could swing his mace at him.

The man collapsed, lifeless.

Talyvien briefly looked behind him.

Shael nodded at him. She had just saved his skin.

He was left speechless.

As if of its own will, the dagger planted in the man's forehead pulled itself out of his flesh and hovered above the body. The blade floated through the air and returned to the assassin's hand.

Talyvien's legs wavered. How was this possible?

The leader of the bandits screamed in rage at the sight of the death of one of his men and charged at Talyvien once more. A renewed motivation filled the paladin, who evaded and parried the new assaults with a burst of energy. He had to believe.

Seemingly greedier than the others, the third bandit headed toward Lucine's inert body on the ground.

Talyvien growled with anger at the urgency of the situation. At his helplessness and frustration. He had to go protect her. He had sworn it to himself.

But the group's leader intensified his attacks against him, as if fatigue had no hold on his body.

The other brigand knelt beside the young druidess and began to rummage through her pockets and belt.

Talyvien emitted an unsatisfied groan at the impossibility of the task. He couldn't leave the defenseless young woman alone.

Suddenly, a huge black dog emerged from the forest and pounced on the covetous bandit. The animal bit the man's jugular and tore out his throat. Blood sprayed on the earthen ground. The dog shook its head frantically around the man's neck, growling. The vermilion liquid stained its glistening fangs.

Was this the same dog he had seen with Lucine and the old man? Had it followed them?

Talyvien heaved a sigh of relief amid the parries. Nothing made sense anymore, but the young druidess would be safe and sound. That was all that mattered.

Finally, in a one-on-one fight, he hurried to help Shael, who was still alone against three men.

Talyvien spun around and dodged a quick attack from the leader, who had his two short swords aimed forward. Taking advantage of the momentum of the man's movement, the paladin pivoted and struck with a deep and cutting blow to the leader's side. Gurgles escaped the bandit's throat, along with blood from his chest. The vacant look in his eyes dissipated, soon replaced by raw terror. The man collapsed heavily in the dust left by the hoofprints.

Finally.

Talyvien leaned forward and tried to catch his breath. To reorganize his thoughts. He looked astonished at the bodies of his three assailants lying at his feet.

Metallic sounds from behind rang in his ears. He rushed toward the assassin. But when he turned around, he froze. Stopped by a surprising sight.

Everywhere and nowhere at once, Shael's body moved with supernatural dexterity. Enveloped in the dark magic of her goddess, her hooded silhouette flickered and danced through space, shifting from one place to another, leaving only the elusive contours of her cloak that were difficult to discern with precision to the naked eye. Only the shimmering reflections on her daggers produced arcs of light that streaked through the air, a fleeting memory of her elusive and misty form.

 In an almost ethereal movement, Shael found herself with her legs crossed around the neck of one of the men and sitting on his shoulders. With one swift motion, she slit his throat with one hand, while her other hand sent her second dagger plunging into the neck of a second bandit a few meters away.

The bodies of the two men collapsed heavily at the same time.

Two down. She landed gracefully on the ground, following the fall of her victim's body. Exhausted, breathing heavily, she remained on the ground for a few moments. Why had she followed them? Now so weak, having lost so much blood. She was panting from fatigue.

A strike from the third bandit shot up in her direction. She no longer had the strength. She raised her hands to protect her head from the blade and prepared to absorb the brunt of the impact.

A sword tip emerged from the belly of the bandit above her. The man's body slumped heavily to the side, revealing the face of the paladin behind him. He had saved her life.

Both of them, out of breath and panting, locked eyes with initial surprise. Then, a triumphant smile involuntarily spread across their lips. Both were satisfied with the carnage they had just unleashed.

They had survived. How was it possible?

Talyvien offered his hand to the assassin to help her up, but Shael had far too much pride to take it and got up on her own. She headed toward Lucine, to discover a huge black dog lying next to the druidess, its head on her belly.

"That's the dog that was traveling with her when . . . I met her," Talyvien explained, as he joined them.

Shael stroked the animal's head, a grateful look on her face. Happy to see that Lucine had not been harmed, she stood up and focused her attention on the paladin. When she saw the arrow still lodged in the young man's shoulder, the assassin approached him silently and placed a hand on his chest as a counterweight. She snapped the wooden part of the arrow with a sharp crack, leaving only the metal tip in his flesh. Taken aback, the paladin recoiled slightly, a mixture of pain and embarrassment on his face.

"I've never seen anyone fight like that," he blurted out.

She chose to evade his questioning and walked away. He didn't need to know. Shael preferred the silence he had shown toward her so far. Why would she want to form an attachment with a paladin of Callystrande? Her contract was unfortunately delayed; she was just giving him a temporary reprieve. As soon as the young woman was out of danger, she would enjoy finally finishing this mission, which had been nothing but a series of unforeseen events.

"We should leave the arrowhead in your shoulder; one person bleeding out is more than enough," she quipped.

With furrowed eyebrows, Talyvien continued to stare at her, awaiting an answer to his question.

Shael sighed in exasperation. After all, they had saved each other's lives. "It's called the Quanta," she explained. "A gift from Sazaelith. A magic of concealment and shadow."

A mixture of admiration, surprise, and disappointment rippled in Talyvien's hazel eyes as he remained silent.

Shael busied herself searching for the pockets and garments of the six corpses lying on the ground around them.

The paladin's disapproving gaze lingered on her as he wiped his sword and prepared the horses. "What did they mean by 'black market'?" he intervened.

"Another gift from my goddess, I suppose," Shael sighed, stuffing one of the bandits' purses into her pocket. "Blue blood sells for a small fortune on the black market."

"Because it's a powerful antidote?"

"One could believe that, but it's actually more of a poison than anything else," she snapped, her frustration evident. "Some use it as a drug because of its hallucinogenic properties, and that's why it prevents the poison of an echarvora from spreading in the minds of its victims, who become delirious. They lose control. But that's also why the chosen ones of the goddess of shadows are often subjected to persecution and slavery."

Although he remained silent, the assassin sensed a flicker of compassion cross the face of the paladin who continued to scrutinize her. She hated that.

23

 That morning, a blanket of mist had settled over the small village of Luminaur. Activity on the main street was slowly beginning to awaken, and a few drowsy passersby turned their heads as they heard the sound of horse hooves clattering on the cobblestones. Shael and Talyvien came rushing in, galloping up the main avenue, followed by the black dog.

A few lights from the inn shone through the windowpanes, and they quickly entered the stables to secure Maia and Aho. The paladin carried Lucine in his arms, grimacing in pain from the arrowhead still lodged in his shoulder, while Shael closed the stalls and helped open the doors.

The innkeeper turned around to welcome them but paused for a moment as he caught sight of the peculiar group they formed: Lucine unconscious in the paladin's arms, Talyvien's armor stained with blood on one side, and Shael's suspicious attire and feline eyes.

"Calixte! Is she—he—still here?" Talyvien pressed, his voice urgent.

The half-asleep innkeeper stared at him with a stupefied look.

"The Alaris! The bard! What is his—their room number!" the paladin exclaimed.

"I—I cannot reveal that. It's—"

He didn't have time to finish his sentence as a dagger landed a few inches from his face, embedding itself in the shelves behind him. The man let out a small, piercing cry.

"Number four! Room number four! Please don't kill me!" he stammered; hands raised above his head.

Taken aback, Talyvien turned to Shael, reproach displayed on his face.

The dagger vibrated in the wooden shelf, and then flew back into the assassin's hand. She flashed a smug smile at the paladin in response to his silent reprimand.

"Hmm. Effective," Talyvien conceded, shrugging at first but grimacing again at the forgotten arrowhead in his shoulder.

They stormed up the stairs to room number four.

The assassin rapped on the door with a firm gesture.

The door finally opened, revealing Calixte yawning and rubbing their eyes.

"Breakfast?" Calixte questioned.

"You could say that," Shael joked.

The black dog jumped onto Calixte, barking joyfully and wagging its tail. The bard, startled, let out a small, high-pitched yelp of surprise.

"He didn't give me such a warm welcome the first time," the paladin remarked with surprise.

"He must just have good taste," Shael quipped.

The paladin huffed through his nose. He didn't have time for her questionable humor. Ignoring the assassin's words, Talyvien hurriedly entered Calixte's room.

When Calixte spotted Lucine's motionless body, the bard finally understood what was happening and straightened up. They closed their violet robe and adopted an unusually serious demeanor.

"Lay her on the bed," they instructed the paladin, who complied.

Calixte slid a chair near a small desk to position it in front of the bed. In doing so, they noticed the dried blood on Talyvien's shoulder and arm. "We should take care of that first," they remarked, pointing at the wound.

"No," he insisted. "Attend to her first." He cast a glance toward the sleeping young druidess.

"I promise I'll leave you with a scar," Calixte purred mischievously. "I'll just accelerate the natural healing process. It'll only take a few minutes."

Talyvien nodded resignedly to Calixte and began removing his chainmail and the top part of his leather armor.

Shael, leaning against one of the room's walls with crossed arms, averted her gaze modestly.

The paladin found himself shirtless, and Calixte placed one of their hands a few inches above the wound. Thin red filaments emanated from their fingers, delicately encircling the metallic arrowhead and extracting it from the flesh with precision.

Talyvien groaned, his eyes squinted in pain. Nevertheless, once the piece of metal was removed, he let out a long exhale of relief.

Calixte then began to use the Flow. They applied their hand once again, and a shimmering blue undulation grazed the wound for a few seconds. When the glow subsided, a fine cross-shaped mark streaked the young man's skin.

"Thank you," he said to the Alaris, who responded with a broad smile.

Calixte turned around and sat on the chair next to the bed where Lucine lay, still unconscious.

"An echarvora bit her on the neck," Shael announced from the shadows, where she was leaning against the back wall of the room. "I made her drink some of my blood to delay the effects of the poison."

"And the paladin let you do that?" Calixte teased.

Shael chuckled, but Talyvien, who was getting dressed, remained silent, lost in his confusion.

The Alaris placed their hands above Lucine's body, their head tilting slightly backward. Calixte's eyes sparkled with a blue, almost turquoise, glow. Long undulations emanated from their slender fingers and glided over the young woman's body. Fine blue lines moved elegantly along her arms and legs, caressing her skin as they passed through it. After a few minutes, they fully integrated into her body.

"Mmhh, I see. I'll have to try to purge the poison while countering Sazaelith's influence; otherwise, she might either transform or suffer from an overdose. The poison and the blue blood have bonded in her body, and each mitigates the effects of the other," Calixte explained, beads of sweat now scattered on their forehead.

"And do you think you can do it?" the paladin asked, wincing worriedly.

"It will probably take me a few days, but yes, I should be able to do it," Calixte replied. "I imagine her body will experience withdrawal from the blood and the rejection of the poison, but I'll use the Ignescent to help her overcome that."

Talyvien nodded, his expression a mix of gratitude and concern.

The black dog lay at the foot of the bed, still faithful to its apparent vow of protection.

Calixte picked up the hurdy-gurdy from the nightstand and began to craft a gentle melody. Their hand slowly turned the crank, and a blue gleam reappeared in their eyes. Fine ribbons of ethereal blue magic emanated from the instrument's wheel as they played, gently settling on the young druidess's body. They meandered along her limbs and intertwined above her chest that began to glow. Calixte then changed the tune of the lament, and the ribbons lifted from her skin, hovering a few inches above her.

Talyvien surveyed the scene with a circumspect look. He had never seen such remarkable healing magic before.

An image of the young woman's circulatory system undulated above her body, with the blue heart pulsating in the midst of this entanglement. Before him materialized a human body made entirely of ethereal magic, with small veins coursing through Lucine's hands and feet, leading to the main arteries pulsating under the effort of the blue organ.

It was an image that should not have existed, so dazzling in its beauty that it left Talyvien in awe. A vision so unreal, so sublime, and so primal in its embodiment of life that it left him astonished.

But shame mingled with his wonderment. What would his goddess have thought of one of her paladins marveling at the power of pagan magic?

"Do you need anything else, Calixte?" Talyvien managed to say from behind the Alaris.

"A breakfast wouldn't hurt!" the bard replied with a smile, turning their head slightly toward the paladin, their eyes still affected by the strange blue glow.

"I'll bring it right away," he responded.

Talyvien and Shael left the room in silence.

Everything had happened too quickly. Where he had failed, the magic of the goddess of shadows and that of the Alaris had saved Lucine. He didn't know what to think anymore.

Troubled, he watched the back of the assassin as she descended the stairs ahead of him. "Thank you, Shael," he said.

The assassin came to a sudden stop. Facing away from him, her demeanor was unflinching, but a hint of surprise showed in her eyes when she turned her face. She nodded slightly in Talyvien's direction.

When they reached the ground floor, she raised her hood and slipped out through the main door.

The paladin headed to the counter to order Calixte's breakfast, keeping his gaze fixed on the young woman.

Shael didn't reappear for the rest of the day.

24

The last few days spent in the castle had been more pleasant for Solehan. The Alaris's cruelty seemed to lessen toward him. He had also managed to transform into various birds several times since the day they had ridden the elaphoras, thanks to the new routine that had developed between the two of them. They now flew above the valley every afternoon.

Solehan cheerfully alternated between different types of birds, switching from eagles to falcons, hawks, and other species, all under the amused gaze of Valnard, who competed with playful antics and tricks alongside on the spirit of the forest.

The training in the courtyard around the great tree took place only during the mornings, but the volleys of vines seemed to have little effect on his progress in mastering his powers. The fear of transforming into a bloodthirsty spider had paralyzed his progress in that area. However, as a result of these trainings, the young druid felt his body transforming and growing stronger, his endurance and strength developing. His skin also seemed less dull, gradually regaining its natural tanned hue.

As usual, the Alaris continued to efficiently tend to Solehan's wounds after training. The druid had developed a habit of observing Valnard's unfaltering face, while the Alaris's eyes were seemingly focused on distant thoughts as he mechanically applied ointments and leaf bandages to Solehan's body.

Yet, the young man felt himself slipping into a certain confusion and incomprehensible bewilderment. He was surprised to find himself enjoying their moments in flight, and Valnard's touch during the healing process had become almost comforting. Was it because he missed the touch of someone caring? Was it due to fatigue or the succession of intense emotions that had swept through him in such a short time?

Solehan also knew he was free now. Valnard had not put back the Ignescent bracelets around his wrists, but the young druid couldn't bring himself to leave. The Alaris was the only person who could help him master the powers of Teluar.

He was embarrassed to admit it, but something about Valnard had intrigued him since he'd first saw him seemingly communing with the great tree in the courtyard, with a sorrowful face. What was his story?

They landed on the grand balcony at dusk. The elaphora gently touched the ground, and the Alaris skillfully leaped out of the saddle. Solehan arrived shortly after, this time transformed into a great horned owl, and he gracefully resumed his original form on the stone tiles.

Feeling numb as he readjusted to his human body after spending several hours in the owl's form, Solehan rubbed his arms. He eagerly noticed Valnard's cheerful air as he headed toward the throne room. As they crossed it, the young druid's gaze once again slid over the colorful stained-glass windows above the imposing chair.

After a few minutes, they reached the lounge, where the grand fireplace proudly stood in one corner of the room, with the three red sofas still arranged in the middle. Valnard invoked the power of the Ignescent and set fire to the logs in the hearth to create a warm and dimly lit atmosphere. A feast awaited them on the coffee table: an assortment of fruits and colorful vegetables, nuts, bread, and wine, likely prepared by the informed lychenas upon their return. The young druid also noticed that a bottle of the strange blue liquid was placed on the table.

"Ah! I'm famished!" exclaimed Valnard, his attention fixed on the feast before them. He poured himself a glass of wine and began to nibble on what lay in front of him.

Solehan, with an amused look, did the same, and both dined in silence, blessed by the crackling magic of the Alaris.

The young druid found himself unexpectedly enjoying this moment. He admired the dance of the scarlet flames and savored the tranquility that filled the room. He thought of Lucine. Would she have appreciated this moment too? He wished to share Teluar's powers with her, to be by her side. Perhaps she could have also shapeshifted?

With his wine glass empty, Valnard reached for the cobalt liquid bottle and poured a bit of its contents. Intrigued, Solehan watched closely as the Alaris raised the glass to his mouth and took a sip. Letting out a deep sigh, Valnard sank into the sofa, getting comfortable with his head tilted back and his eyelids closed.

"What is it?" Solehan asked, his curiosity outweighing his caution.

"The only thing that helps me stop thinking," murmured Valnard, his eyes still closed.

"Thinking about what?" the druid dared to ask.

The Alaris slowly opened his eyelids and looked wearily at Solehan, a slight smirk on the corner of his lips. Valnard evaded the young man's questions, grabbed the bottle once again, along with an empty glass, and stood up. He walked toward the sofa where the druid was sitting and settled down next to him.

Solehan swallowed hard. The beats of his heart quickened their pace. He had a slight recoil, surprised by his proximity to Valnard. Their thighs brushed against each other.

"You can taste it if you want," suggested the Alaris, pouring a small amount of the liquid into the glass and offering it to Solehan.

The young druid took hold of it and examined its contents cautiously.

"It's like alcohol, but a little more potent," added the Alaris, who swallowed another gulp from his glass. "The same vices, the same benefits. Neither more nor less."

Solehan tentatively dipped his lips into the liquid. The warm and sweet taste of the strange substance surprised him. He felt Valnard's curious gaze fixed on him as the Alaris sank comfortably into the backrest of the sofa.

Pleasantly bewildered by the flavor, the young druid took a full sip from his glass. What did he have to lose anyway?

"You know, I would have preferred it to be different at the beginning," admitted the Alaris. "But I knew that only a strong emotion could unlock your powers. Hatred and despair seemed to be the best candidates at the time. I mean, what other feeling would have sufficed?" Valnard chuckled lightly and brought his glass to his lips again, his stare still distant.

Solehan remained silent. He didn't know how to respond to that. Indeed, what else could he have felt toward Valnard other than hatred and a desire for revenge? But perhaps it was the effect of this strange drink, or maybe it was the fact that Solehan had never been able to feel what was expected of him. He couldn't lie to himself; he felt something else now. Something he couldn't name. Something obscured by shame and guilt.

"I developed so much hatred toward humans," Valnard conceded. "But . . . I've been waiting for you for a long time. For centuries in fact."

The voice of the Alaris created ripples in his mind. Did he just say that? Dazed, Solehan observed the elegant marble face that scrutinized him, its eyes ablaze. The fiery reflections of the Ignescent from the fireplace danced in Valnard's irises. Absorbed, Solehan couldn't look away.

The cushions of the sofa wrapped around the young man, embracing him tenderly. Despite his efforts, he felt his body sinking. The sensitivity of his skin became heightened. He flinched as Valnard's dark fingers delicately touched his neck.

Cradled by the gentle caresses on his skin, Solehan succumbed. He slipped into the heaviness of his delirium and fell into a swirling sea of deep blue.

He allowed himself to be carried by the currents and whirlpools. The young druid's eyes then settled on the water's surface and the tumultuous reflections of the agitated and shimmering sea.

His name fell from Valnard's lips. Several times. Over and over. Then, the deep voice of the Alaris morphed into a more familiar voice. A voice he had missed so much.

Lucine.

His sister's face appeared on the surface of the water, separated by this strange line where air and liquid defined themselves.

"*I'm sorry, I wasn't there. I couldn't save you,*" he told her. He placed his hands against this barrier, now solid like glass.

Lucine was calling his name. She pounded vehemently on this impassable transparent barricade.

"*I'm sorry. I'm sorry,*" he reiterated.

Solehan's tears mingled with the currents. Suddenly, dozens of hands gripped the young man's clothes and carried him away into the waves.

Lucine's struggling face receded.

His body rolled and thrashed in this turbulent ocean. Maltreated. He couldn't breathe anymore.

He fell from this strangely cobalt sky and collapsed into the mud.

When he stood up unsteadily, Solehan was horrified to see thousands of men killing each other. Clad in armor and wielding various weapons, roaring with rage and hatred.

A glittering tide of death and desolation. A battlefield that stretched into infinity.

Solehan began to tremble. Before him, a vivid red expanse of blood spread dramatically beneath a pile of human bodies. And in the midst of this funereal tableau lay the corpse of what had once been a magnificent animal—a white fox, its fur, once shimmering, was now stained with vermillion liquid.

Solehan fell to his knees and screamed. His voice reverberated so loudly that the scene froze. All eyes turned to him.

The men's skin lignified into wood. Branches sprouted, bark formed, and buds blossomed. From their bodies and their hatred emerged a paradise of emerald, a grand and dazzling forest. Solehan's heart burst with primordial euphoria.

Taking a deep breath, he suddenly opened his eyes.

"Solehan?" said Valnard, sounding concerned and leaning over him, his hand still on his neck.

The young man hastily pulled away from the Alaris and fell to the floor beside the couch.

"I didn't think it would affect you so much," Valnard hesitated, looking uncertain.

With his breath ragged, Solehan tried to regain his composure. Confused, he looked at the blue liquid in the glass and vowed never to touch it again. Images jumbled and whirled in his mind. He spent several minutes trying to calm his body and gather his thoughts. Eventually, as his breathing became more serene, he sat on one of the other couches, leaving Valnard alone on his own.

Why had such hallucinations taken hold of him? Was there any meaning to it all? The vision he had experienced near the grand tree also flashed in his memory—the silhouette with the crystal flower and the large white fox protecting it. Why did this animal seem so present, so recurring? His curiosity was too great.

"Valnard, what does the symbol of the fox—a white fox—represent?"

Speaking the Alaris's name out loud felt strange and too familiar on his tongue, and Solehan immediately regretted asking the question. Could Valnard guess what he had seen?

"Why?" Valnard's penetrating irises fixed on the young man, his features transforming into a stern and inquisitive look.

"Uh . . . it's just that there's a white fox on the stained-glass windows in the throne room, so I was wondering . . ." Solehan stammered.

"Mmhh. It's the symbolic animal of Teluar," the Alaris replied, his tone becoming gentler and more assured. "It was also the symbol of the city of Argentvale."

Solehan didn't dare look at Valnard but silently absorbed the information. Had he seen Teluar? So, this city was called Argentvale? The grand throne room and the mental images of the remnants of the city etched into his memory. People had lived there; a king or queen had ruled, and everyone had disappeared. The forest spirits had reduced an entire capital to nothingness under the orders of the Alaris. Solehan clenched his fists on his knees.

"In the kingdom of Narlimar, it was said that this city had a special connection with Teluar," Valnard said casually. "That's why I settled here a few months ago, in preparation for your arrival."

Solehan bit his trembling lip and huddled into the cushions of the couch. How could he have momentarily forgotten what the Alaris was capable of? With a tight throat, he lowered his eyes to his entangled fingers. How could he have enjoyed Valnard's company in recent days and forgotten that an entire city had been obliterated in his name?

Overwhelmed by a deep disgust for himself, he stood up and moved to the small balcony adjoining the living room to breathe in the fresh air. Unable to bear it any longer, his heart heavy, he transformed into an owl and flew away, under the impassive gaze of Valnard, who continued to enjoy his meal.

Solehan wandered through the deserted streets of the city below. Numb and confused, he needed to rekindle the terror he had felt when he first discovered this place. To feel the fear coursing through his body again. He dreaded forgetting his humanity.

After flying for a few minutes, he landed on the stone-paved street of what he imagined had been a bustling place in the past. He transformed back into a human and observed the contours of the lignified wooden bodies in different positions, illuminated by the moon's glow through the clouds.

An eternal scene of horror.

Entering several houses, taverns, and places of life, he imagined what their daily lives might have been like. In each room, a macabre theater played out before his eyes, the wooden statues frozen in what had been their final expressions of agony. A strange parallel formed in his mind with his hallucination. But unlike his delusion, he let the injustice of their reality hit him—all of this was real. He embraced the sadness that gripped his soul and vowed not to forget the wooden statues, to avenge them too.

Then, Solehan transformed into an owl again and wanted to contemplate the small silhouette of the child he had left a few weeks ago in the first room of the castle he had visited. Passing through the window, he noticed that something still lay under the sheets as he approached. Once again in human form, the druid lay down on the bed next to the silhouette. He swore with fierce conviction to let the turmoil he had felt at that moment reaffirm his promise. For them, for Lucine, for his clan. Prepared to be devastated, Solehan lifted the piece of fabric.

And was thunderstruck.

A magnificent flower had grown on the shoulder of the small wooden body. A flower with delicate shades of red, pink, and orange. A flower with velvety petals wrapped in an elegant hem while a long golden pistil rose at its center.

Solehan remained silent. Disoriented by its beauty and truth for long minutes. From horror arose the most incredible of flowers.

He had come to this room to remember his promise of vengeance, but now only confusion filled him. What did it mean? Was Valnard right? Did humanity deserve to be annihilated so that Nature could reclaim its rights? Was his hallucination a premonition, a message from Teluar?

Exiled in the depths of his doubts and lost in his own flesh, the young man wished to share his questions with someone. With Lucine. With a member of his clan. Just with someone. So, not really knowing why any longer, he headed back toward the living room.

As he passed through the antechamber, the fire in the fireplace still crackled, and a few embers died out on the floor. Solehan found Valnard dozing on the red couch where he had left him, an empty wine glass resting on the table.

Piqued by curiosity and by the memory of his dark fingers on his skin, the young druid slid his steps across the parquet floor. He was struck by the peaceful and pained serenity on Valnard's sleeping face. Through the disheveled leaf tunic of the Alaris, he observed the smooth skin of his chest rising and falling gently with slow breaths, and the serene exhalations escaping from his mouth. This intimate and private moment ignited a blush on the young druid's cheeks. No cruelty lingered on the now peaceful face of the sleeping man, his delicate features relaxed, imprisoned in a sad emotion, his eyes closed, and his body motionless.

Solehan turned back and headed toward his room. He couldn't bring himself to sleep that night, unsure of what to feel.

25

The next morning, after thinking about it all night, Solehan made a radical decision and did not go to the castle's large square courtyard for his usual training.

He wanted to be sure. He couldn't bear being torn between these two versions of himself that clashed. So, determined to form his own opinion, he would see the world for himself. Its beauty and its misery. The splendor and the downfall of humanity.

Feeling like he was escaping, even though he was free, Solehan flew out of his bedroom window disguised as a hawk and soared for hours toward the Astral Forest as a landmark. He had never flown this far, but an invisible thread seemed to connect him to the Tree of Ether, as if he had a close connection to the god who had granted him his powers, with Teluar's body. Nevertheless, he knew he couldn't reach the base of the tree until his mind and heart aligned in the same direction. He couldn't endure the sight of the members of his clan transformed in such a way.

When the Astral Forest spread out before him, Solehan decided to change course. Fields, plains, and clearings quickly unfurled beneath his keen eyes and led him to glorious settlements of various sizes.

The ingenuity of men was then revealed to him. What they could build, invent, create. Music, art, science. What they could feel and cultivate. Love, cooperation, joy. The promise of a future in the children playing around the buildings, the compassion of those who cared, the wisdom of the elders.

The cruelty of raiders and bandits. The endless expanse of fields and pastures, the livestock piled up like objects of flesh under the greed of men and their conquests. The forests that were no more, the territories that expanded without end. Cruelty, bloodshed. Malice and slander, hatred of differences. Wars and petty quarrels.

How was he supposed to make a choice?

Hungry for knowledge, Solehan landed on the roof of a building in one of the villages and observed life unfolding around him. He spent many hours satisfying his curiosity, his thirst for wisdom. A full day and night studying them, the vibrant life of the village, born and dying with the passing hours.

The next morning, at dawn, exhausted from being confined in a bird's body for so long, he decided to return to Argentvale. Still feeling somewhat confused, he had not been able to make a choice. He had seen hatred and love in the hearts of men, their kindness and wickedness, their knowledge and ignorance.

As he was about to take flight, thick black smoke from the woods adjacent to the village caught his attention. Curious, he flew over the area to see what was happening. But when he reached the clearing from which the commotion emanated, his bird's body faltered in shock.

A crowd of men in golden armor were gathered around three large pyres.

Two of the pyres were already engulfed in flames, with a charred figure on one of them, while two other bound women struggled, cried, and pleaded for their lives. Just like his sister had done.

The memory of Lucine's death devastated his mind.

Solehan let out an acute cry of pain as he flew over the scene, powerless in the face of such cruelty. What else could he have done? He only possessed the meager power to transform into a bird. So, he perched on a branch of a nearby tree and witnessed the execution of the three women. A penance for a non-existent crime. The young druid's heart crushed in his chest at this abhorrent sight. For the first time, he found himself praying to Teluar to come to their aid.

Lucine had died under the same conditions, also begging for her life, for their mercy. He hadn't been there to save her, and once again, he helplessly witnessed the madness of men. An endless loop.

He hated feeling useless.

He hated being a human himself.

He hated all the men standing there without reacting.

At that moment, Solehan wished to possess Valnard's powers to massacre them all, to avenge their victims. He imagined them suffering in proportion to the pain and torture they inflicted on others.

His soul and heart became tinted with pure hatred. Solehan didn't fight it. He wouldn't resist Teluar's powers either; he would let them consume his entire being to no longer feel so weak and incapable. Once he could sufficiently control the powers of the god of Nature, he would seek revenge on everyone, in the name of the deity, in the name of Lucine. He would let rancor consume him and Nature triumph.

If humans were capable of such atrocities against their own kind, they didn't deserve their place. No one would ever suffer again; only the grandeur of nature would reclaim its rights.

His decision was made.

When this sad spectacle came to an end, the three pyres completely charred and the cries silenced, Solehan flew toward Argentvale. He arrived in the late afternoon, as the sun discreetly began to hide behind one of the valley's mountains, and landed on the small balcony adjacent to the living room.

The young man resumed his human form and barely had time to see Valnard approaching him before his legs gave way, the pain of his prolonged transformation and disgust making him stumble. Tears finally started to flow down his cheeks and didn't stop.

The Alaris knelt gently beside him. His black fingers lifted Solehan's chin as the druid's eyes continued to drown in a flood of tears. "I'm sorry," Valnard whispered, looking at him with something the druid saw crossing his irises for the first time.

Compassion.

The Alaris's apology rebounded and fell into a pool of despair within Solehan, the water vibrating slowly. A truth had just opened up inside him.

Valnard understood, and his arms encircled the young druid.

Solehan then buried his face in the hollow of his shoulder and wept for a long time, savoring the comfort of the warmth of the Alaris's body.

26

Talyvien wandered through the streets of the village of Luminaur, blending amid the crowds of passersby and the stalls of shops, the scents of spices, the colorful fabrics, and the diverse merchandise of the marketplaces. He admired the twisted buildings nestled against each other and the various colors of tiles that complemented the vibrant hues of the rooftops.

Earlier in the morning, after coming back with a breakfast tray filled with pastries, fruits, and various delicacies as a token of gratitude for Calixte, he had decided to trust them and had left Lucine in their care. The paladin had also booked a room for the night on the top floor of the inn, beneath the colorful roofs, and had bought a new shirt to replace the one that was torn and stained with the blood from the arrow that had struck his shoulder.

Despite Calixte tending to his wound, a certain weariness still overwhelmed him. His soul and heart, tired from the absence of his goddess, made him sit on the stone steps of a house facing the small church of Callystrande. The church where the priest had healed Lucine's burn a few days ago.

Sitting there, torn between doubts and the lack of his magic of light, he observed with bitterness and longing for hours how Callystrande's power was invoked through the hands of the man, helping the needy and the sorrowful, healing wounds and hearts.

Talyvien didn't regret saving Lucine's life. However, the abandonment and uncertainty of his faith gnawed at him deeply. His helplessness in the face of recent events had shaken him. He couldn't save the druidess from the echarvora's poison, and he'd had to resort to the magic of the goddess of shadow and the Alaris to do so.

Talyvien felt a surge of nausea. Had he become so useless? What would Tuoryn think of his current state?

He felt like he had lived his life these past weeks contrary to all the teachings he had received since he'd been that inconsolable child in the cathedral of Callystra. Perhaps Shael's contract had come at the right time? What future could he have? He was nothing more than an ordinary man now.

The old priest's eyes met his, with an answer to Talyvien's pain inscribed on the features of his elderly face, an invitation to enter the church in his smile.

So Talyvien stepped inside.

A gentle ambiance emanated from the small stone building. In the dim light of flickering candles, the paladin admired the modest and welcoming interior of the chapel. He walked through the wooden pews arranged on either side, lightly brushing them with his fingers as he passed, and looked up to observe the elegantly intersecting stone vaults. A stained glass rose window was located above a small statue of the goddess, with a simple gray stone altar reigning at the end of the nave. The church couldn't rival the grandeur of the glorious Cathedral of Callystra, which he had explored to its every nook and cranny, but a sense of tranquility washed over him. He decided to sit on one of the benches and began to pray. Perhaps he would find some answers?

He spent a few minutes in this way, amid the silence of his doubts, in the soothing of his soul.

Then, an answer appeared. A familiar warmth emanated from the sword, sheathed in its scabbard at his waist. As he drew the blade, he gazed at the gleaming metal in the palm of his hand. A smile crept onto the paladin's face. It was a sign that Tuoryn was still by his side.

When he returned to the inn that evening, a strange feeling of peace lingered in his mind. This day had been exactly what he had hoped for, and now he felt ready.

 After leaving the inn in Luminaur, Shael needed to be alone. She didn't enjoy the company of others for too long; solitude was her only familiar accomplice.

When the paladin had gotten his shoulder treated, she hadn't been able to resist taking a peek. She had noticed inscriptions on his chest and arms, along with numerous scars. What could these markings mean? Were they tattoos or symbols painted on his skin? She was also surprised when the paladin had thanked her. She knew he hated her magic. What game was he playing?

The assassin hated her wandering thoughts. She preferred to remain ignorant of her contract's motivations and was consumed by the anticipation of ending it. She had already lost too much time and impatiently yearned to return to the convent of Sazaelith, where she lived among her sisters. She longed to reclaim her former life, free from this newfound curiosity that she loathed.

She knew she would strike that very evening, so she needed to regain strength after losing so much blood to save the young woman. The druidess was now under the care of the Alaris. Shael had no reason to delay the inevitable any further.

Dressed in her usual assassin's garb of Sazaelith, she disappeared into the woods surrounding the village of Luminaur. Her hood made her resemble an owl—a symbol of her goddess—with pointed ends on her forehead. Two small fabric strips at the top of her head represented the bird's feathers.

During her pursuit, Shael had spotted a small pond nestled amid the woods, and she undressed to refresh herself in the cold water. The liquid's silent embrace enveloped her. The assassin savored the tranquility of the moment, swaying amid the dancing shadows under the verdant canopy. She immersed her entire body, leaving only her face above water, and allowed herself to float with the gentle current. Only the rhythm of her breathing and heartbeats broke the familiar silence.

The miracle of the present moment. The blessing of solitude and silence against the horrors that plagued her mind. Against the ceaseless nightmares that dotted her thoughts and nights. Against the intrusions of her past that surged into her mind uninvited.

Feeling calm and revitalized after spending several hours with her eyes closed in the water, she dressed, stretched her limbs, and began her combat training, with the tall forest trees as her only witnesses. This was her ritual before each assassination, accepting with gratitude the power of her goddess flowing through her. This way, she felt like Sazaelith's armed hand: a body she had carefully shaped into a formidable symbol of revenge against the helplessness she once felt. A body that would never betray her again. She had promised herself that.

Sazaelith had given her a voice in this world, a means to express her hatred, anger, and desire for vengeance. Her greatest gift. Shael cherished this unique destiny every day. Thus, she would once again deliver the justice of the goddess and, in the process, dispense her own. She would rid the world of one of its monsters. For the greater good.

She waited for nightfall to cloak herself in its comforting and familiar cover, focusing solely on her mission as her sole objective.

When the stars finally revealed their splendor in the ink-black sky, Shael headed toward the inn.

She suspected the paladin had likely reserved one of the rooms for the night, and the light spilling from one of the colorful rooftop windows confirmed it. Like an insect that paid no heed to gravity, she climbed onto the tiles of the building and silently opened the window to slip into the room.

In the faint candlelight, she found him on his knees, eyes closed. Perfectly vulnerable.

Shael noticed new symbols on his bare chest. The paladin had sprinkled some water from a basin in front of him onto the top of his head, and the liquid trickled down his neck and shoulders.

A blade gently slid into Shael's palm. Her velvety steps brushed the wooden floor.

"I was expecting you," he uttered, turning his head in her direction.

The assassin froze.

Solemnly, Talyvien rose to his feet and approached confidently. "At least grant me a death with dignity, please," he added, with a hint of sorrow in his voice and smile.

What was he doing? The assassin's initial astonishment waned, swiftly replaced by a certain contempt. She noticed that the paladin had shaved closely and cut his chestnut hair short since she had last seen him that morning. Had he prepared himself to join his goddess?

Her gaze shifted to the now numerous symbols on his chest. They must have been painted with ink. Nothing in his demeanor showed any resistance to what awaited him. Shael had never encountered this before. She had always taken lives by surprise or through violence, but never in resignation.

A particularly bitter taste filled her mouth. Something within her disliked what she saw. Something awakened in her that she immediately despised.

"Take care of Lucine, please," he murmured. "She will need someone to guide her. Teach her your resilience. I am incapable of that."

"And so, you ask an assassin to take care of someone close to you?"

"An assassin, perhaps, but someone who must have overcome many things to still be here. That's what she needs today." Talyvien closed his eyes. He awaited the coup de grâce.

Shael loathed him with all her might. His arrogance. His calmness. His surrender. The scar she inflicted on his upper lip the last time. Those damned symbols on his body.

She placed the blade on his neck.

The paladin flinched at the touch of the cold metal but kept his eyelids shut. His face remained calm and resigned. Almost serene. He was ready.

And he was at her mercy.

Shael's hand began to tremble. She despised him even more for it.

His slow and steady breath clashed with her own, growing more erratic as her heart beat faster. She observed the water droplets gently sliding down his angular face, his square jaw, the corner of his mouth, and landing on his collarbones before continuing their journey on his chest.

Time stood still, disrupted only by the incessant rhythm of the artery pulsating with life beneath the blade. Her mind, her past, and her pain screamed at her to plunge the dagger into the paladin's neck with passion.

It makes no difference. He is like all the others. Administer your justice. Unleash your hatred.

But Shael's arm remained frozen.

She didn't feel her goddess by her side. She did not feel her mischief, her vengeance, or her approval.

27

The cold metal of the blade was no longer felt on his skin, and Talyvien blinked slightly to find an empty room, the window still open to the starry night. Where had she gone?

He put on his shirt and stuck his head out of the dormer to feel the cool air on his skin. Why was he still alive? The paladin turned his head and saw the assassin sitting a few meters away on the tiles, also gazing at the sky, her hood lowered.

"Why?" he asked, climbing up as well to sit on the roof, at a safe distance from the assassin.

Shael hesitated to respond. She wanted to escape. Her entire body urged her to leave, but a part of her soul remained still, sympathizing with a paladin of Callystrande. With a man. At that moment, she felt her devotion to her goddess slipping away.

"Something is not right," she confessed. "I didn't feel Sazaelith with me."

"It didn't seem that way the first time."

"Maybe it was just not meant to be." Shael sat with her legs against her body, trying to find solace in the stars above. For the first time, she felt sorrow in the silence, sadness in the calm and solitude.

Because she no longer understood where all of this was leading, Shael did something strictly forbidden by her order. "Why would someone want to assassinate you?" she asked.

"I betrayed the order of the paladins of Callystrande," Talyvien replied in a grave voice. "I interrupted the execution of the young woman, Lucine, and saved her from the pyre."

Shael didn't expect this revelation and didn't know what to make of it. "Why was she on a pyre?"

"Because she was born different, I suppose. The paladins of Callystrande don't appreciate magics that don't emanate from the goddess of light."

"I noticed that!" Shael remarked, with irony.

A sad smirk appeared at the corner of Talyvien's mouth. "But to go as far as executing anyone even slightly different, I couldn't bear it," he affirmed seriously. "Although that doesn't justify anything, I didn't even feel any magic emanating from her. She was just unfortunate to be born with eyes of different colors."

"Why her? I imagine she's not the only victim of the madness of these paladins."

Talyvien's hands clenched slightly on the colorful tiles. "I saw in her a sign from the goddess. Golden tears flowed from one of her eyes during her execution."

Talyvien's eyes lowered, and a deep sense of shame seemed to consume him at this confession. His guilt for not having reacted sooner, for not having resisted the fanaticism of his order, haunted him.

"Is that why you can't use the powers of Callystrande anymore?" Shael asked.

"Yes," he acknowledged. "I lost them as soon as I left the Crusade of the Dawn's Resolve after rescuing her."

Shael didn't know much about the religion of the chosen of Callystrande, but what she heard disgusted her to her core. Even though most people turned away at the mere mention of Sazaelith, she knew that at least her goddess didn't abandon her followers, but helped them in the shadows when society failed to protect them.

"It's just my opinion, but a goddess who punishes one of her chosen for saving lives doesn't deserve devotion," she said coldly.

"You are an assassin, Shael. You literally kill people in the name of your own goddess," he retorted, raising an eyebrow.

Stung in her pride, she locked eyes with Talyvien, burning with defiance.

"I don't kill innocents, *paladin*."

"How can you be so sure?" he asked. "You knew nothing about me."

She turned her head, not knowing what to say. He was right. If Callystrande was guilty of punishing someone trying to save an innocent life, then why would Sazaelith have approved of having him assassinated?

"I should return to my convent near Dawnelest," she said. "Something is not right. I don't even understand why I was tasked with assassinating a paladin of Callystrande."

"Indeed," Talyvien scoffed. "I found it curious that my order would call upon an assassin of Sazaelith, knowing the mutual hatred our orders have for each other."

"Even a simple assassination! Isn't that contrary to the principles of Callystrande?"

"You're right," he agreed. "It doesn't make sense."

They both remained silent for several minutes, looking at the sky, no longer understanding their situation. It was all absurd.

"Why do you have those symbols on your body?" Shael asked suddenly. She mentally chastised herself for admitting that she had looked at them. Fortunately, the paladin didn't dwell on this detail and kept his focus on the stars.

"They are prayers of protection from Callystrande. They protect me before a battle or . . ." he hesitated, his words trailing off in his throat.

"For passing into the afterlife?" Shael finished gently.

Talyvien nodded.

"Why did you give up?" she asked again.

"Because I don't see a future for myself without Callystrande's blessing. Because I realize that everything I believed in might be nothing but a lie. Because I'm not sure I want to live with that truth."

His honesty surprised her, but it also stirred a certain anger within her.

"So, you just abandon everything?" she demanded. "Just like that?"

Talyvien, visibly disconcerted by her reaction, met her gaze with severity. What did he want? Pity?

"Are you defined only by your devotion to Callystrande?" she continued, with vehemence. "Is there nothing else that characterizes you?"

"You don't understand," he retorted. "How could an assassin of Sazaelith understand anyway?!"

Deciding not to take offense at the insult, Shael pressed on. She despised those who gave up without really trying. She knew all too well how precious life was, having taken it away so many times.

"What I understand," she said, "is that you're just a child. When the world doesn't turn the way you want, you reject everything and give up! If my goddess were to abandon me, I would be devastated, but I wouldn't stop being the person I've fought to become all these years!"

Talyvien kept his focus on his feet, but a smile played on his lips.

"What? What's so funny now?!" the assassin growled.

"I was right," he chuckled. "You would be a good example for Lucine. She would need that. Your resilience."

"Resilience isn't something you're born with, paladin! You could become resilient too, if you stopped your childishness! I saw a man who didn't hesitate to betray his principles to save someone's life, not once, but twice. A man who, despite having lost all his magic, fought three against one!"

What had she just said? Right there. Exactly what she hated in him. Something that disturbed and redefined her own beliefs. She despised herself at that moment, and she despised him even more.

A hint of stupefaction sparked in the paladin's eyes. "Was that a compliment coming from a legendary assassin of Sazaelith?"

Shael responded with a rude gesture of her hand.

Both burst into laughter in the night.

"So, I suppose we won't be having this conversation every night?" he asked. "I mean . . . Are you going to try to continue fulfilling your contract?" He attempted a light tone, but the assassin sensed the seriousness of the question behind his mask.

"I think the paladin of Callystrande died tonight," she said. "I believe that, in a way, I have fulfilled my mission. You are free to be whomever you want now."

"Don't you have to be accountable to your . . . employers?" he stammered.

"I'll manage. I refuse to fulfill a contract for which I don't feel my goddess's approval. Something is not right."

An expression of surprise and gratitude split the paladin's face as he looked at her.

Feeling uneasy in the face of his emotion, Shael found the colorful tiles particularly interesting.

None of it made sense anymore. What was she doing there, having a conversation with him? She decided to cut their exchange short.

"You're not staying at the inn?" he asked, surprised to see her getting up to leave.

Who was he to meddle?

"Why? Does your bed need warming up?" she teased, cutting off his questioning.

Shael burst into laughter at the visible embarrassment on Talyvien's face. It was too easy.

"No! It—It's just that when Lucine recovers, we'll head in the direction of Dawnelest too. You mentioned you needed to go there as well, right? It seems our orders are somehow connected, so maybe we could investigate together?" he said, stumbling over his words.

This idea caught her off guard. Traveling with them? While it was true that their orders seemed to be linked in some way, the idea of traveling with a paladin of Callystrande unsettled her.

She needed time to think. "We'll see," she said briefly. "Goodnight, paladin."

"Thank you, Shael. Goodnight," he replied.

The assassin pulled her hood back over her shoulders. She nodded slightly in his direction as usual and disappeared into the night, leaping from rooftop to rooftop with extreme agility.

28

Still nestled in the arms of the goddess of shadows, Lucine felt submerged in a downy sensation, carried by waves of joy. The dark feathers of the majestic and protective divine wings caressed her skin tenderly, the warmth of the goddess's body passed onto hers.

A few notes of music tinkled. They fluttered around her ears and resonated in her foggy mind. They formed a melody that would be hard to forget. The kind of tune that carried emotions, stirred hearts and souls. The young druidess tried to free herself and turn her head to find the source of the music. However, in response to this splendid ballad, Lucine felt the arms of the goddess gently closing around her body. Why wouldn't she let her go?

Perhaps it was the answer she was seeking? Was she so helpless that she needed protection forever? The elders had been right. The outside world was populated with malevolent creatures, humans with wicked hearts. How could she survive amid all this incessant danger? Maybe she should give up her desire for exploration once and for all? For her whole life, she had felt so useless. Her childhood had been spent under the overprotection of her peers, hidden among the trees like a fragile little object. She clearly didn't even know whom to trust.

Exasperated, Lucine sighed into the hollow of the deity's neck. But despite herself, her sorrowful thoughts gradually dissipated, replaced by this strange and beautiful melody. She listened to the notes undulate and transform into words. Soon, Talyvien's voice resonated in the void.

"I'm convinced your friend wouldn't want his sacrifice to be in vain. He would want you to keep living and hoping."

She listened to the echo of those words spreading softly around her, caressing her skin and her resignation.

Perhaps the paladin was right? Did she really have the choice to give up everything after so many sacrifices?

Lucine sighed again. This couldn't be her life, indeed. She simply didn't have the right. In honor of Zaf's sacrifice. Of Talyvien's. Of Solehan's.

She must respect the feeling that had always coursed through her belly. This desire for more. For better. For something else. To be herself. This calling so profound that she had never managed to silence it. Maybe it meant something?

A new idea sprouted within her. It didn't have to be the end of her story unless she decided it to be. Lucine let this information spread in her chest. Maybe she could choose her destiny? Perhaps, by her will alone, she could tilt her future, whether influenced by the power of the stars or not?

So, she promised herself that, if given a second chance to live, she would seize it.

Lucine pushed away the arms and wings of the goddess forcefully and broke free from her illusory safety. She clung to the notes colliding in her head like a sign of hope. Her feet touched the ground. Finally liberated.

But did freedom hurt so much? A sense of emptiness pierced her chest. She had to fight. This path was undoubtedly more difficult. She clung to the beautiful melody to avoid hearing the alluring siren's song of the goddess, of her own resignation. It was just a choice to make, she told herself. Between the ease and the abandonment of this sweet reverie. Between the strength of her promise, her curiosity, and her thirst for life. So, with confidence, she chose the latter path.

The first step of the rest of her life.

Lucine placed her hands on her knees and tried to catch her breath. When she straightened her body, the young woman found herself in emptiness. Under her feet, as far as the eye could see, was only intense darkness. Shivering, she wrapped her hands around her arms and rubbed them to try to warm herself. But, when she turned around, the goddess had disappeared. Only the soft music rippled once again, and Lucine set out to find its source.

Directly ahead, cloud formations swirled around a bright point. As Lucine approached, the rhythm of their dance intensified and merged with the melody. In their growing agitation, they tore the darkness into shreds around her. Gradually, their movements amplified into a voracious tornado that carved through the void.

Lucine progressed through this swirling tunnel of mist, which now took on a crimson hue. Her hair, her clothing fabric pounded against her skin. But the powerful warmth of the light caressed her face. Was she going to die, despite her desire to live?

A few leaves brushed against her arms. A familiar scent filled her nose. Soon, the glowing clouds were replaced by vegetation. A bushy tornado of leaves and flowers began to whirl around the young druidess. Euphoric, Lucine was drawn into this vegetal whirlwind and landed safely on a bed of moss that she caressed blissfully.

She stood back up and surveyed the surroundings. She now found herself in a lush forest, where towering ancient trees stretched upwards. Nostalgic and amazed, Lucine approached one of the massive trunks to touch its bark. Her fingers grazed the foliage, and she took a deep breath, inhaling the woody and colorful scents. The ground began to tremble, and Lucine stumbled. She looked up at the sky, and her stomach lurched in her throat.

What she had mistaken for a massive tree trunk was, in reality, the giant, hairy leg of a spider, its thick hairs resembling branches. Its body covered in lichen, the immense insect ignored the young woman and continued to roam, taking a part of this surprising forest with the rest of its legs attached to its abdomen. The woodland also dissipated around the druidess, carried away by a myriad of even larger spiders.

Increasingly perplexed, Lucine observed the creatures move away and then continued on her path, listening to the fading notes of music in the verdant universe that was growing before her. She made sure to avoid the wide legs of this long procession of insects, which gradually carried away the absurd vegetation.

With the sky now darkened, the horizon line fluctuated in the distance. The atmospheric boundary blurred, and a large body of water appeared before Lucine. Surprised, she walked along the shore, in search of a way to cross it.

Still intrigued by the melody, Lucine let her footsteps guide her to a small boat. Amid the gentle and trembling movements of the skiff, she saw the silhouette of a passenger standing out against the shimmering reflections on the water.

Her heart raced as she recognized Calixte, whose appearance was as fascinating as ever. Motionless, they didn't seem to have noticed her. With closed eyes and their amethyst and shimmering face composed in a neutral emotion, the bard tirelessly continued to play their hurdy-gurdy with skilled hands.

Excited, Lucine ran with big strides to join them. She jumped into the craft and called Calixte several times, but they did not respond.

Like a figurine wound up from a music box, the bard continued the cyclical caress of their hands on the instrument.

As Lucine tried to revive the Alaris, the small boat began to sway in the gentle current. Lucine gave up trying to pull Calixte out of their torpor and focused on her surroundings, still enjoying the beautiful serenade emanating from the hurdy-gurdy.

They sailed through almost total darkness for several minutes, although the dimness seemed to have no effect on the young woman's sight. Their small boat was a dazzling hope on a canvas woven with pure darkness.

Soon, new patterns speckled the painting. Several colorful spots appeared on the water's surface around the skiff. Lucine admired them with wonder. Lily pads blooming in shades of blue, pink, and green floated gently. When they passed through the plants, she gently touched them with her fingertips.

But through this round and colorful flora, the outlines of large, submerged bones meandered beneath the boat. They glided over this curious cemetery of rib cages, spines, and imposing skulls in their tiny craft, with the reflections of polished and pallid bones dancing under the waves. The remnants of the immense wings of the creatures were revealed as they passed, bearing witness to their former splendor.

Lucine leaned over and examined the skeleton of one of the carcasses. Remembering the skull she had seen in the inn in the village of Luminaur, she was surprised to find its similarity. She studied it meticulously. It was the remains of a dragon. A hundred of them. What did that mean?

Perplexed and still focused on this incongruous ossuary, Lucine observed the reflected images that blurred on the shimmering surface. She then looked up to discover a vibrant multitude of underwater animals soaring above their heads in response to the deathly realm beneath their boat.

Upside down. Nothing made sense anymore in this chaos of scattered wonders.

A cloud of jellyfish with long colorful filaments coiled and pulsed with light. Large rays with fluorescent arabesques spread their fins like illuminated birds in the dark sky. Thousands of fish, ranging from the tiniest to the largest cetaceans, their skins dotted with myriad sparks, left long trails of light behind their bodies.

Lucine was awestruck by the spectacle. Were they underwater or on the surface? Did they exist in the space between what was and what would be, in a moment lost between the two?

All she knew was that the sublime beauty of this dream was matched only by the music and the talent of Calixte accompanying it. Could a world like that exist somewhere? Or could only the realm of artists and dreamers admire its beauty?

After an indeterminate amount of time, the magnificent creatures merged into the darkness of the sky, carrying with them their disparate and dazzling patterns.

A new enchantment was then revealed.

Lost on an islet in the middle of this dark sea, two universes converged. A leaning great tree, its trunk split in two, was allowing the torrents of an entire galaxy to escape from its rift. A flow of stars, planets, and atmospheres coiled and formed the nebulous branching of this surprising vision. A place where light and darkness united. The spark of life and the impulse of death. The origin of all things. Lucine was certain of it.

With their eyelids remaining shut and their body limp, Calixte ceased playing their instrument, allowing the final notes to reverberate into the void. Looking fatigued, their shoulders slumped slightly, and their fingers slipped from the hurdy-gurdy. Their head tilted to the side.

Although worried, Lucine didn't take her eyes off the wonderful evocation she recognized as the representation of the Tree of Ether. She was overcome by an irresistible urge to approach, and she attempted to place a hesitant foot on the water. Surprised to find that the liquid's surface had now almost completely solidified, revealing only a thin layer of water, Lucine disembarked from the boat. Her footsteps created faint concentric ripples. She walked on this translucent barrier until she reached the islet and admired the slow and ethereal waltz of the canopy.

Then she noticed, at the base of the trunk, an incandescent symbol engraved on the bark. It blazed with a deep vermilion red—a spiral-shaped emblem. It was an original mark that Lucine had never seen before in the Astral Forest.

But as the young druidess examined the ideogram, the face of Solehan materialized beneath her feet.

Her heart tightened. She pressed against the transparent barrier and shouted her brother's name, pounding it with her fists.

Solehan painfully opened his eyes, a burdened apathy on his face. He let his body float, his tousled brown hair framing his face. When he saw her, he placed both hands against the glassy barrier.

"*I'm sorry, I wasn't there. I couldn't save you,*" she read on his lips.

"What? I'm not dead, Solehan!" Lucine growled, her voice echoing into the void.

She pounded on the water's surface with all her strength. She had to find him. Why was he there? The young woman wanted to shatter this cruel boundary. She screamed her brother's name until her voice gave out. She pounded the ground, scraping her hands. She hoped to the point of tears of despair streaming down her cheeks. But nothing worked.

White hands, as white as alabaster, with long and slender black fingers, slid over Solehan. On his neck, shoulders, chest; about ten of them sinuously danced in a macabre fashion.

They pulled him abruptly into the depths of the ocean.

Helpless, Lucine pounded on the partition even harder until exhaustion took over. Long and unjust minutes passed with the force of her fists against the glass line. Sobs ran through her body, bruised by grief. Where was Solehan truly? Could she find him before it was too late?

When the young woman had no more strength to give in her anger, the rhythm of her pounding fists diminished. Gasping for breath, she looked at her reflection on the glass wall—where her twin brother's face had appeared just moments before. The void his absence had left in her. Each day, each cruel minute without the only anchor she had grown up with. Lucine screamed in rage until she almost suffocated. She could never accept living without him. Without that part of herself.

Stunned, she raised desperate eyes to the tree with its interwoven galaxies. What was this strange place where dreams seemed to intertwine with anarchy? Why had she seen her brother here? Was her pain driving her insane?

A backlash sounded. Behind her, the transparent partition cracked with a sharp sound, and long fissures formed on the surface.

Lucine turned her head, and her breathing compressed in her chest.

It was not the answer she had hoped for.

29

The rays of the sun piercing through the skylight woke Talyvien up the next morning. The first thought that came to his consciousness was of Lucine. He hoped her recovery was progressing well. After washing and dressing, he hesitated to knock on the door of room number four in the inn. However, concerned about disturbing Calixte at such an early hour, the paladin resigned himself to going straight to the tavern for breakfast.

When he entered the main hall, he was surprised to find the bard in the company of the assassin, sharing a meal together. A strange ambivalence clouded his thoughts. He knew he should be glad to perhaps never see his assassin again, but a part of him seemed to not express that wish. Why had he invited her to accompany them? Why would she have accepted anyway? He had cursed his own stupidity and had remained awake for several hours after their conversation before finally falling asleep.

In any case, the paladin noted that he didn't like this particular sight. What were Shael and Calixte doing together? The Alaris was gazing at her intently, their long fingers lifting the chin of the young woman as if to admire her better.

The paladin exhaled through his nose and approached them. He sat at their table, on the bench next to the assassin.

"Ah, Talyvien! I hope you slept well!" exclaimed Calixte, removing their hand from Shael's face upon seeing him approach.

The paladin nodded, his face remaining neutral.

"I was just telling our new friend how marvelous her eyes are! Feline eyes, shining like sapphires!" they delighted.

The young man feigned indifference and started serving himself some of the food in front of him without looking up. He didn't want to admit out loud that the assassin's surprising eyes also troubled him and had been one of the reasons he couldn't fall asleep easily.

"The most beautiful gift Sazaelith can offer," Shael affirmed solemnly.

"Oh, why is that?" The bard placed their chin on their closed fists and showed particular interest in the assassin as they asked.

"All followers of the goddess of shadows must sacrifice their eyes to receive her blessing, but very few receive Sazaelith's sacred vision in return. Most of the chosen remain blind for their entire lives and become priestesses. The luckiest ones become the arms of the goddess. They are called the Children of Twilight."

"That's fascinating!" Calixte marveled. "So, that was your case?"

"I did indeed have that chance. I offered my eyes in exchange for the goddess's protection when I was six years old. The next day, when I woke up, she had blessed me with these eyes."

Talyvien felt a surge of disgust and rage. How could someone do that to a six-year-old child? "That's just cruel," he grumbled coldly.

"And yet, I would do it again without hesitation. Sazaelith gave me a path to follow, a purpose, a destiny. She gave me the means to face what I had to go through and to seek revenge!"

"To seek revenge?" Talyvien asked, frowning. "Revenge for what?"

Annoyed, Shael crossed her arms and turned her head away, growling as a response.

"I don't understand how a goddess can demand such a sacrifice from her followers, anyway," he reiterated with vehemence.

"It seems we've already established that no religion and no god are perfect, *paladin*."

These words struck Talyvien, as he remembered their conversation from the previous day and the pyres raised of the Crusade of the Dawn's Resolve. Hurt in his pride, he remained silent for a moment.

Calixte, apparently uncomfortable, buried their face in their cup of coffee and noisily drank its contents.

But the paladin, wanting to change the subject, turned to the bard. "How is Lucine? Any progress?"

"Ah, yes! She's in stable condition," Calixte replied between sips of their drink. "The levels of poison and blue blood have already decreased, but I prefer to take it slowly, in stages, to readjust her body. She'll recover, Talyvien. Don't worry."

The paladin sighed with relief.

The three of them continued eating, their breakfast punctuated by the conversation between Calixte and Shael. However, still bothered by his worry and ambivalence, Talyvien remained silent. He thought back to the conversation he'd had with the assassin the previous day. What was he supposed to become now? Had Shael decided to accompany them?

Shouts ascended from the main street.

Hundreds of hoof noises resounded, and Talyvien recognized with dread the disembodied voice raised in the morning mist. He prayed to the goddess that his mind was playing tricks on him. He rushed out through the inn's door.

A cold shiver ran down his spine at the sight that unfurled before his eyes. Hundreds of paladins from the Crusade of the Dawn's Resolve of Callystrande had invaded the main street of Luminaur, like an army of faceless revenants that grandiosely reflected the first rays of dawn on their metal suits of armor. Immaculate banners bearing the goddess's symbol stained the gray fog above the human tide. Like a disorganized orchestra, the clinking of metal weapons, armor, and shields composed a strange symphony. A melody that contrasted with the silent and overwhelming unease of the crowd of villagers who had gathered around them. Talyvien slipped between the citizens and tried not to draw attention to himself.

King Arthios Therybane, expressionless and with empty eyes, stood on his black-armored steed next to the High Priestess Piore and her imposing haloed mask. The priestess's white horse and the long, immaculate white robe embroidered with gold marred the colorful gaiety of the village's architecture. A radiant specter that stood out in the cold morning. An apparition of horror.

With a haughty and ceremonial posture, "The Lamented of Callystrande" cast a cruel gaze over the crowd.

Behind the procession, an old woman screamed and struggled on the ground, crying. Several villagers were trying to help her.

"They massacred her! These monsters! My daughter!" the old woman cried.

Talyvien's heart squeezed against the walls of his chest when he heard the woman's cries.

Swift and ethereal, a presence next to the paladin emerged from the assembly. The assassin had joined him and was now also witnessing the scene, her hood pulled over her head. Only her mouth, twisted with disgust, was visible.

"Souls of Luminaur!" proclaimed Piore. "Today, we are witnessing a great event! In her grace, Callystrande, goddess of light and purity, has shown us the path to follow! On this day, we celebrate the power of the divine: her justice and her wrath! In her desire for purification, three sinners have been executed, purified by the flames of Callystrande's punishment, all of them for using forbidden magic for nefarious purposes!"

No. A nightmare. Talyvien exhaled deeply and put a hand over his mouth. This couldn't happen again. Innocents had perished. Again. He couldn't look away from Piore, his mind imagining the fury of what he wanted to do to her.

A slight metal sliding creaked near him. Coming from the assassin's arm.

He felt the tension in Shael's body, ready to pounce on the High Priestess like a feline on its prey, her dagger drawn. The assassin couldn't tolerate such cruelty. A cold and calculated recklessness.

Shael cared little about dying that day; she had to act and prioritize attacking the priestess first. Whatever would happen to herself afterward, she didn't care. How many women would have to suffer again? How many innocents would have to die under such fanaticism?

As she prepared her body to leap toward the woman, Talyvien's hand gripped her wrist. Though he applied some pressure to her arm, she felt no physical pain. But hatred for him harpooned into the assassin's heart at that moment. An intense frustration at having to remain passive in the face of this grotesque spectacle.

She looked up at him to convey her disgust and anger. However, Shael was surprised to see marked fierceness in his eyes as he stared at the priestess.

Strangely, Talyvien's rage contained hers—both united in a silent promise of cold vengeance.

"Soon the entire continent will be united under the banner of the great Callystrande," High Priestess Piore resumed, in a ceremonious and stern tone. "The Crusade of the Dawn's Resolve will proudly ride toward the great Dawnelest, to rally Queen Selena Aramanth, ruler of the Kingdom of Vamentera and sister of King Arthios Therybane of Astitan, under the protection of the goddess of justice. Anyone who opposes this divine destiny will receive the wrath of Callystrande the eternal. Anyone who uses pagan magic or becomes an accomplice to such acts will suffer the same punishment. 'The Lamented of Callystrande' has spoken!"

Thick black smoke billowed behind the trees in the adjacent woods.

With Talyvien's hand still on her wrist, Shael felt slight spasms in the paladin's arm. Hidden under her hood, she observed his face, which was closing off. His lips had turned white with tension, and the angles of his jaw tightened as his usual neutrality was gradually swept away.

Shael felt a certainty shatter within her. For the first time, she couldn't bear to see a man so shaken, in such acute pain. There, right before her eyes, she couldn't simply ignore it. Or run away, as she usually did.

Against her own instincts, Shael made a reckless move. She tried to comfort the paladin.

Gently, she slid her arm still under the uncontrollable vibrations of Talyvien's distress. Feeling that he was no longer exerting as much pressure on her skin, she took his hand in hers.

The contact of their palms caused the paladin to avert his gaze to look at her, his emotion now imbued with despair and resignation. The storm within him seemed to have finally subsided, and she tried, without words, to send him hope, courage, and the silent promise of their vow.

She promised him they would go to Dawnelest together, to uncover what was going on. She promised him the vengeance he so desperately needed. He, the paladin who never sought revenge.

"The Lamented of Callystrande" kicked her white horse's stirrups and executed a half-turn in a grand ceremonial gesture. The vacant-eyed King Arthios and the paladins followed her in silence.

Shael and Talyvien watched the procession gradually move away: the long golden wings of Piore's cape brushing against the cobblestones of the main street, the deathly and silent entourage rhythmically clattered by the horses' hooves.

Once the crusade was out of Luminaur, dozens of villagers ran toward the thick black cloud that was forming. Shael's insides twisted with disgust.

When they arrived, they saw with horror three pyres erected, from which three charred figures emerged. The final testimony of the legendary cruelty of the Crusade of the Dawn's Resolve and its High Priestess.

Talyvien fell to his knees, his trembling body no longer supporting him, a heart-wrenching pain etched on his face. He drove his sword into the ground in front of him, grasping the hilt with both hands, and forced himself to stare at the symbol of monstrosity displayed in front of them for several minutes. As if to honor the memory of the fallen.

Shael stood beside him, silent, watching.

Only the cry of a hawk seemed to echo their sorrow high above them, through the clouds.

 Still caught in one of those nights where his body seemed unwilling to sleep, Solehan wandered aimlessly once again through the grand castle of Argentvale. As he passed through the lounge, he saw faint embers slowly dying in the fireplace: remnants of the meal he had shared with the Alaris a few hours earlier, once he had calmed down.

That morning, he had witnessed the abhorrent execution of three women, and still marked by that sight, sleep seemed to elude him. With a heavy heart, he roamed the cold and silent corridors of the place, admiring the paintings and tapestries and listening to the discreet footsteps of the lychenas evading his approach. His hand ran along the gray stone walls, appreciating the texture beneath his fingertips. His body eventually led him mechanically to the familiar massive wooden door. He pushed it open, and the grand throne room appeared before his eyes.

Under the moonlight that peeked through the large stained-glass windows, Solehan saw the silver gleam of the fox symbol projecting onto the floor in front of the imposing throne. The intricate leaf and branch patterns that composed the rest of the translucent illustration enveloped the atmosphere in shades of azure and green. The splendor of the room seemed matched only by its tranquility. The young druid watched as dust particles fluttered slowly under the moonlight passing through the colored glass pieces.

He stepped forward, drawn to the massive chair adorned with carved leaves and flowers that proudly overlooked the room. Wanting to enjoy the calm and beauty of the place, he sat down on the throne. He rested his head against the wooden backrest and closed his eyes. He was exhausted. Lost.

He spent several minutes like that, savoring the gentle touch of the moon on his skin and the silence gradually enveloping him.

"Yearning for sovereignty?"

The deep and mischievous voice he knew all too well broke the calm of the room.

When Solehan finally opened his eyes, the Alaris stood before him, at the bottom of the steps leading to the throne. A resplendent icon, with his white and sparkling skin reflecting the moonlight. A playful grin on his lips, Valnard made a small bow.

The young druid chuckled lightly in return. "Am I truly worthier than them?" Solehan sighed with profound despair, the smile fading away.

Valnard began to ascend the steps slowly without saying anything. He eventually joined Solehan on the dais and cast a sorrowful look at the young druid.

Solehan then focused his attention on the two marks on the Alaris's neck, evidence of his frenzy when he had transformed into a huge bloodthirsty spider.

"You are not a monster, Solehan," Valnard calmly declared, sensing the young man's gaze on his neck.

The words of the Alaris resonated slowly within the young druid. He found it ironically cruel that they came from the person he had least anticipated. He had always felt different, trying to conform to what was expected of him, to the image that had been carefully woven for him, to be worthy of the blessing of the stars. And it exhausted him. He thought back to the vision of the battlefield. To the massacre of the white fox, symbol of his god. Men would never stop killing each other, destroying and consuming nature. What he had witnessed earlier that day had confirmed this and shattered all his beliefs and hopes.

But he felt strangely liberated.

Freed from the burden of a legend that would never come to be, as his clan was no more. Freed from the image he had been imprisoned in for so long. And for the first time, someone had given him permission to be himself, to no longer pretend.

But a question still lingered within him, one he couldn't reconcile. Did he also deserve to die? If the cruelty of humans was to blame, why would he have the right to survive?

"I am also a human, Valnard. Why should I be entitled to a certain privilege?" Solehan's voice trembled with a veil of emotion.

"Because your human appearance is only the vessel for a much greater potential," Valnard replied calmly, his eyes still bathed in sorrow. The Alaris seemed to hesitate, as if struggling to add something else. Words choked in his throat. A resigned look finally crossed his face. "Let me tell you a story," he said softly.

Valnard sighed, his features relaxing. "A long, long time ago, a young Alaris man fell deeply in love with the most beautiful of flowers."

He paused and clasped his hands, gathering his thoughts and courage to continue. An uncomfortable vulnerability seemed to permeate him.

"She ruled the forest with kindness and pride, and all her subjects adored her and paid her homage. She introduced this naive young man to the wonders of nature, and they spent lifetimes deciphering each other and dreaming together. She taught him patience, love, and caring for one another. In return, he swore loyalty to her in her teachings and devotion. They decided to unite and made a wish. A wish that, unfortunately, was not granted because the nature they cherished so much revealed its cruelty, and they couldn't have offspring together."

Valnard took a long breath and looked up at the silver fox shimmering above them before continuing.

"So, they decided to implore the god Teluar to fulfill their wish. And in his great kindness, a soul was born. A perfect soul, part Alaris, part spirit of the forest: mischievous, talented, generous, and beautiful."

Solehan saw an emotion pass over Valnard's face that he had never seen before. An infinite sadness. It twisted his heart.

"A soul too beautiful for this world, which did not deserve it," Valnard said. "A soul that was one day massacred while playing in the forest with her sisters, even though she was just a child. Massacred by humans hungry to destroy differences, driven by ignorance, cruel in their quest for territory."

Solehan's breath caught. He understood what Valnard was revealing to him now. He observed the moonlight outlining the Alaris's face. An eternal torment trapped in his emotion. Suffering without escape.

"The desperate parents tried to implore the God of Nature once again to give them back what they had lost. But they discovered that Teluar was also now consumed in the suffering of seeing his creation devoured by humans and had fallen into a deep slumber to feel no more. The flower then resigned herself to continue defending her own, living and honoring the memory of the one she had lost. But the Alaris could not resign himself and hatred consumed him. The two lovers grew apart, separated by their grief and unable to understand their partner's mourning. The Alaris decided to carry the soul of their child in a seed, and several forest spirits joined him in his sorrow. He protected it for centuries, sheltered from everything, patiently waiting for the moment to make it sprout in a tree at the heart of Argentvale, to allow her to be ready to return, when the time would finally come. When there would be hope for Teluar to awaken." Valnard's emerald eyes refocused on the young druid.

Solehan, although surprised, finally understood the Alaris's pain. His struggle.

They remained silent for a few moments, looking at each other while specks of dust floated lightly around them. A whirlwind of silence.

Then Solehan knew, without knowing why.

The young druid slowly lifted his arm and placed his hand on the Alaris's chest, over his heart.

Valnard held his breath as Solehan brushed against his tunic.

The vibrations of the Alaris's heart pulsed beneath Solehan's fingertips. The young druid took a deep breath, focusing on the quickening rhythm.

A flower with opalescent and crystalline hues bloomed in the palm of his hand, as Teluar whispered the secrets of his magic. It was the same flower that Solehan had glimpsed in the hair of the figure in his vision, realizing at last that it was Valnard's child.

The Alaris's eyes widened, filling with tears, and his body shuddered. Valnard gazed at the symbol of his love with awe and nostalgia. He gently grasped the stem between his dark and delicate fingers, admiring it for a long moment, a tear rolling down his cheek.

"Thank you," he managed to whisper, his voice catching in his throat.

His disbelieved gaze returned to the young druid. The Alaris gently took Solehan's chin in a caress with his other hand. The calm and serenity of the gesture prevailed. A gentle certainty.

With the angle of Solehan's jaw still cradled in Valnard's palm, the dark thumb of the Alaris slowly brushed over the young man's lower lip, who didn't fight it. Both were electrified by each other's presence.

So, Solehan observed him attentively for the first time.

Valnard's eyes fixed on his lips, and Solehan found himself examining the details of the Alaris's face in return. How had he never noticed his beauty before? His hatred had blinded him. Here, bathed in the light of the moon, Valnard truly seemed to be the equal of a god.

Solehan was speechless. He took care to contemplate Valnard's long lashes, which complemented the almond shape of his eyes, his straight nose that slightly upturned at the tip, his perfectly sculpted lips, his hair with its gradient of snow and ebony cascading on either side of his pointed ears. The tear that rolled down, creating sparks on his ivory skin. The veil of sadness caressing the green of his irises. And the sparkle of a newfound feeling, a contemplation that surprised the young druid.

Despite himself, a wave of intense warmth spread through Solehan's belly.

The Alaris withdrew his hand abruptly. And broke their strange electric stupor.

A cold torrent rushed down Solehan's spine. The absence of Valnard's touch radiated through his skin.

The Alaris left the room without a word, the door slamming behind his steps. Without another glance at him.

The young man gasped in surprise. Had he just dreamt that moment?

Solehan tried to collect himself, rising from the wooden seat, his breath heavy and labored. Confused, he ran his hands over his face and rubbed his eyes.

When he opened them again, he saw that roots had sprouted from the carved wood adorning the grand throne. Leaves and flowers delicately blossomed under the glow of the stained glass, with only the glass fox as a witness.

31

After spending the rest of the day helping the villagers bury their deceased loved ones and dismantling the pyres, Talyvien returned to the inn, taking a detour through the baths of the village of Luminaur to wash off the soot, sweat, and Callystrande prayer marks from his skin.

The paladin arrived at nightfall and made his way back to his room. He collapsed onto the bed, physically and mentally exhausted from the day's events. He was more determined than ever to go to Dawnelest, once Lucine had recovered. He needed to inform Selena about the crusade's actions and her brother. He found it ironic and regrettable that he'd had to no longer be a part of it to finally open his eyes to their deeds. He still felt shame at that thought.

A gentle breeze brushed against his nape, causing him to jolt upright. It felt like déjà vu.

Shael stood before the now-open window, her hands behind her back.

Talyvien, hesitating, reached for his sword.

"I didn't come here to kill you, paladin!" she chuckled.

She lowered her hood, revealing her face, and pulled out a bottle of wine from behind her back.

"I thought a little pick-me-up would do you good after today," she added, uncertainly.

"That's kind of you, but I don't drink," he replied, still wary.

"Oh. More for me, then!"

Before he could say anything, Shael exited through the window that led to the rooftops. The paladin groaned as he got up from his comfortable bed and followed her.

Shael sat on the colorful tiles, the uncorked bottle in hand, drinking straight from it.

He joined her, sitting down beside her, and both gazed at the stars.

"Another gift from my goddess. Alcohol doesn't have much effect on Sazaelith's chosen ones," she joked between sips.

The paladin smiled. He looked up at her and was surprised by Shael's appearance.

It was hard for him to believe that he was looking at an assassin now. Even though she wore an elaborate and lightweight dark leather armor with several straps and laces for ease of movement, a young woman stood before him. A young woman who admired the sky with tender emotion, the reflection of the stars shimmering in her remarkable blue eyes.

She seemed to be around his age, with blue variations on her tanned skin and long black hair that she braided behind her back. A few scars dotted her hands and neck, the most notable being the ones in the inner corners of her eyes, giving her that bestial look that characterized her.

It was a vision that bewildered Talyvien.

"Thank you for stopping me this morning . . . from doing something reckless," she chuckled. "I never thought I'd say that one day!"

"I don't think anyone can stop you from doing anything," he teased.

Their morning conversation during breakfast resurfaced in the paladin's memory. One question still piqued his curiosity. "How did you come to sacrifice your eyes for your goddess?" he asked.

"My mother begged the sisters in a Sazaelith convent to take me when I was six years old. She wasn't trying to save me from her life of prostitution, addiction, and violence; she simply wanted an easily accessible source of blue blood." Shael sighed lightly, her gaze slipping to apparently painful memories.

Talyvien hadn't imagined this. A certain compassion took hold of him.

"But the goddess had a different plan in mind when she gifted me with these eyes. I understand now that she fulfilled the role a mother should have played. We don't choose to become sisters of the goddess of shadows; rather, she chooses us," she added.

"Oh, I'm sorry," he said, his tone now grave.

"No, don't be. It's probably one of the best things that has happened to me. If Sazaelith hadn't entered my life, I don't know where I would be today." She paused. "I come from the southern realms, beyond the great desert. I arrived in the kingdom of Vamentera when I was twelve, following the Mother Superior to the convent of Dawnelest. She practically raised me within the order."

As he listened to the assassin's life story, Talyvien thought back to the circumstances of the night she had come to the aid of the druidess. His stomach tightened. "Knowing that, what made you save Lucine? You—" He hesitated before uttering the words. "You weren't afraid she would fall into addiction as well?"

"No . . . I used to consider blue blood a burden for a long time. I cursed the goddess when I was a child. I didn't understand why all of that happened to me. But, over time, I learned to recognize the gift she had given me. I believe that when I saw Lucine suffer like that, knowing that I could save someone's life instead of taking it reminded me of that," she whispered, looking tenderly at the sky.

Perhaps she saw her goddess in it?

After a few minutes of silence in the night, she turned her head toward Talyvien. "And what about you? How does one become a paladin of Callystrande?"

"Ah. Strangely enough, somewhat in a similar way. I was sent and taken in by the Brotherhood of Paladins of Callystrande after my parents were assassinated when I was nine years old."

The assassin's body suddenly tensed. She lowered her head between her shoulders, and a saddened and ashamed pout appeared on her face.

Sensing Shael's discomfort, Talyvien decided not to burden her further and continued to share his recall. "A paladin named Tuoryn was my mentor. But he became more than that over the years."

The nostalgia of Tuoryn's memory warmed the paladin's chest, and he smiled.

"Have you always lived in the kingdom of Vamentera?" she asked.

"No. I'm from Callystra, from the kingdom of Astitan. This is my first time crossing the kingdom of Vamentera. The man you saw today on the armored horse is the king of Astitan, King Arthios Therybane."

"Ah! So, he's the brother of Queen Aramanth?"

"Yes," Talyvien confirmed. "I've known him since we were children. We received the same training and had the same mentor. We grew up together, like brothers-in-arms."

"Ah. And who was the woman wearing the strange attire with him?"

"That's High Priestess Piore. She's nicknamed 'the Lamented' in tribute to the tears of the goddess of light."

"Mmhh. I'd love to give her good reasons to be lamented, that's for sure!" Shael exclaimed.

Their laughter echoed among the rooftops of the village of Luminaur.

"Since she arrived at the court a few months ago," Talyvien continued, "I no longer recognize Arthios. He seems to have slipped into fanaticism and distanced himself, raising pyres everywhere, destroying everything in the path of the crusade. They plan to rally his sister to their desire for domination, but I don't think it will be easy."

"Ah, so you also know Queen Selena?"

Feigning a certain indifference, he tried his best to conceal the feelings he still harbored for the sovereign. "Uh, yes. I know her. I know she has a rather tolerant policy toward different forms of magic. But something is amiss, and that's why I must go to Dawnelest. To warn the queen about their actions and to learn more about what's happening in the crusade."

They continued to exchange words like this for long minutes, discussing the training they had received, their respective pasts, and their childhoods.

As he listened, Talyvien realized that even though their devotions were different, their stories seemed quite similar. Neither of them had truly chosen the path they had taken. But they had always done what was expected of them and had excelled.

Talyvien also shared what Lucine had taught him: the shocking rumor about the city of Argentvale and its inhabitants transformed entirely into wood.

Their conversation continued, and Shael, visibly relaxed, lay down on the tiles, unfolding her body like a feline.

Talyvien, his cheeks slightly flushed, noticed the tattoos that peeked out from under her leather armor on her forearms as she stretched. "What are your tattoos for?" he asked. "Do they have anything to do with your devotion to Sazaelith?"

Playfully, Shael rolled up her sleeves.

He then saw two elegantly tattooed long daggers appear on her skin, extending from the base of her wrists to the bend of her elbows.

"These are my weapons. I can summon them at will with these."

The illustrations on her arms began to glow with a blue light and materialized above her skin, sliding into her hands. The blades took on a metallic appearance between her fingers and shimmered under the moon's reflection. She threw them with chilling precision. Each of them dug into roof tiles, splitting them in half.

After a few seconds of tremors, the daggers rose into the air and repositioned themselves in Shael's hands. Unused, they eventually dissipated into the night breeze.

Talyvien was left dumbfounded by the assassin's dexterity and magic. "I understand now why the assassins of Sazaelith have such a reputation," he said. "I wouldn't have stood a chance!"

"And yet, here you are. I think it's time you give yourself more credit, paladin," Shael retorted, returning him a mischievous smile.

Talyvien grabbed the bottle of wine from the assassin's hand and took a sip. In turn, he lay down on the still-warm tiles that carried the memory of the sun disappearing beyond the horizon.

Strangely, he appreciated this moment. A moment that helped dull the horror he had witnessed earlier that day. As someone who never drank alcohol, as it was forbidden in his order, he found himself crossing that barrier with her.

Perhaps he was becoming someone else? Someone who was no longer frightened by his ignorance and weakness in the face of magic. Was he betraying the goddess of light by thinking that way?

"If that were to happen again, I don't know if I could defeat you in a duel, to be honest," he affirmed, thoughtful. "Especially now that I no longer have the favor of Callystrande. The Quanta, is that it?"

She responded with a nod. Shael rubbed the tattoo on one of her forearms with her hand and seemed hesitant. "It's not very difficult when you know what to do," she finally admitted.

"I don't know. The powers granted by the goddess of shadows still seem quite powerful! But I understand if you don't want to answer. After all, I'm not sure you'd want a paladin of Callystrande to have that knowledge." The paladin watched the assassin out of the corner of his eye, proud of his jab.

Shael snorted in amusement. Clearly proud herself, she took the bottle from his hands and drank another sip of wine. She sighed after swallowing her gulp. "The Quanta is a magic of concealment and manipulation," she began. "Sazaelith's chosen ones who possess it can alter the physical laws of our world. This magic is based not on the one who practices it, but on the one who witnesses it. The goddess allows her chosen ones to elude the gaze of their opponent!"

"I'm not sure I understand," he said.

"To put it simply, every time you try to look at the body of someone practicing the Quanta, their being will be where you're not looking. This makes it a formidable magic for combat."

"Does the Quanta affect the mind as well?"

"What do you mean?"

"Let's say appearing where one isn't looking psychologically suits you quite well!" he exclaimed.

"*Idiot*," she teased. "So, the goal is to learn not to rely on your vision to fight the Quanta, but rather your other senses!"

"Mmhh, good to know," he chuckled.

They spent several minutes like that, both lying on the tiles, gazing at the ink-black sky and bantering.

As the wine began to take effect, Talyvien found himself staring longer at Shael's fascinating face. Her cat-like eyes shining like sapphires in the darkness, the moon outlining her elegant profile, her long braid of black hair brushing against his arm. He was captivated by her melodic laughter, the scars at the corners of her eyes blending into the contours of her nose when she brightened up. He felt his heart shift, as if awakened after a long slumber.

And he immediately cursed this imprudence. *An assassin of Sazaelith? Really?*

Was he allowing the cataclysm that had consumed him with Selena to repeat itself? The disaster of the promise of two destinies that were doomed to never come true.

A bitter taste churned in his chest. He then compartmentalized his heart to avoid losing himself.

He had to think about Lucine, about helping her find her brother and finding answers to her questions. He had to think about the crusade, King Arthios, High Priestess Piore, and the atrocities committed. It would not have been wise to occupy his mind with anything else.

 Shael knew she had to return to the convent of Sazaelith in Dawnelest to unravel the mystery behind Talyvien's contract, but a force seemed to hold her back in the village of Luminaur.

The force of the promise she had silently made to him that morning. The force of the unbearable despair she had seen on his face. She couldn't betray that.

However, she didn't quite know why she had come to visit the paladin that evening. She usually avoided getting too close to men, especially paladins of Callystrande. But she felt that only he, at that moment, could understand the uncertainty she felt toward her order. She didn't know how her hatred of the male gender and the desire to share this moment with him could coexist in her mind. Or why she had wanted to take his hand to support him in the face of the cruelty of the crusade. A part of her still regretted being so impulsive.

But she was tired. Entangled in a wild succession of unforeseen events, she couldn't be bothered anymore.

Shael cleared her mind of all these concerns. In that moment, they didn't matter. There would be other contracts to fulfill, other missions to carry out. Everything would return to its usual course. No one could change that. Certainly not a man.

But for the first time in her life, she wanted this timeless moment to belong to her. She enjoyed the syrupy wine flowing down her throat and the moon caressing her face.

A shrill scream echoed through the street below.

Both of them stood up abruptly and listened in silence to the sounds of the night.

Shael pulled her hood back over her head.

In one of the small alleys of the now-sleeping village, a woman was struggling. She was at the mercy of the advances of a man in his fifties, a tattoo on one side of his face, his body forcefully pressing against hers, gripping her arms.

"Ah, I know that one . . ." Talyvien growled.

A vengeful impulse surged through Shael's body. She took it as a sign from her goddess. She had wasted enough time. She had to deliver her justice. What would Sazaelith have thought of her behavior? She broke one of the tiles with her fist out of frustration. Shael refused to stray any further. She had been foolish to think that men could be something other than what played out now before her eyes. Shael's daggers materialized in the palms of her hands.

But just as the assassin was about to pounce, the paladin preempted her, jumping onto the roof of the stables below and landing on the cobblestones of the street. He approached the couple and grabbed the man by the collar. Talyvien delivered a punch to the man's face, causing him to stumble. The aggressor crashed near the stable door, and the horses snorted and shuffled.

Talyvien then took care to reassure the woman, who made a small gesture of thanks. As a precaution, he apparently decided to accompany her, and they both walked away into the dark night.

The man, still on the ground, held his cheek and muttered inaudibly.

Shael felt her goddess envelop her in a cloak of darkness and vengeance. Her heart rate accelerated with adrenaline, the blue blood pulsed in her limbs, her field of vision narrowed. Her emotion exploded in her head. She knew what she had to do.

When the assailant staggered to his feet, she followed him and slipped through the alleys, the metal of her daggers gleaming in the shadows, under the blessing of the starlit night.

32

The next morning, the three companions gathered once again for breakfast. As Talyvien reached for a portion of scrambled eggs, he noticed that Calixte looked particularly tired. Their usually mischievous eyes seemed duller than usual, and their words less sharp.

Sensing the paladin's gaze upon them, the bard took the lead. "She is still unconscious, although her condition is slowly improving. She should wake up soon," they said. Calixte proceeded to take a bite of their breakfast from the plate in front of them.

"I was worried about you as well. You look exhausted," the paladin remarked.

"Oh." The bard looked at him with surprised eyes, which eventually softened. "It's just that I'm not used to continuously tapping into so much magic. Not having chosen a gender unfortunately prevents me from accessing the full power of the Flow or Ignescent."

"I am grateful for your efforts and for being here, Calixte. Thank you," Talyvien affirmed gravely.

"Well, well! I don't know what I did to deserve the kindness of such a handsome paladin of Callystrande this morning, but I'll take it with gratitude!" Calixte joked.

"Ah, there you are again!" the paladin chuckled. "The tired and gloomy look doesn't suit you!"

Calixte and Talyvien laughed heartily, while Shael silently listened to their exchange, a small smirk playing on her lips as she nibbled from her plate.

As they enjoyed their meal, a man rushed into the inn and approached the innkeeper, whispering something in his ear.

The barman's face was seized with shock, then sorrow, before slightly shaking his head in dismay.

Realizing that the information could be useful to them, the paladin decided to order something from the menu to ask a few questions. While buying another batch of pastries, Talyvien learned that a man had been found murdered that very morning, his throat slit in his home.

While the innkeeper provided him with the details, the paladin's attention turned to Shael. The feline gaze stared back at him with fury and mischief. Talyvien recognized in her the eyes of the assassin, the ones he had seen the first time, bestial and insolent, filled with rage and vengeance. How could he have been deceived by their conversation?

As the paladin thanked the innkeeper for the information, the assassin hurriedly left through the door, leaving Calixte staring at the scene in disbelief, a half-eaten pastry in their mouth.

Talyvien rushed out into the main street of the village of Luminaur and chased after her. He caught sight of the dark cloak of the assassin fluttering behind her slender figure. She ran toward the woods and slipped behind the protection of the trees.

As Talyvien arrived in the verdant atmosphere, he lost sight of the young woman. He listened attentively to the slightest sounds of the forest and scanned the surroundings, bathed in the shadows cast by the canopy of leaves above him. He unsheathed Tuoryn's sword and cautiously moved, alert for any movement, his footsteps slightly compressing the moss and crackling the twigs.

"I know it was you who killed that man, Shael!" he shouted. "Come out of your hiding place!"

The woods remained silent, the foliage of the trees rustling gently in the wind. Talyvien decided to trust his memory of the young woman he had glimpsed the day before. She couldn't simply be reduced to being an assassin. Not after what he had seen of her, what he had felt. Perhaps it was foolish, but he planted the tip of his sword into the earthy ground.

Talyvien raised his empty hands in a show of non-aggression. "I don't want to hurt you, just talk," he insisted. "Why did you do it?"

"Because no one else would," a voice whispered behind him.

In a quick motion, Talyvien swirled around.

The assassin emerged from among the trees, a few meters away from him. Shael approached and lowered her hood.

"You can't kill people like that, Shael!" Talyvien snapped. "Without a contract, just as you please! What are you playing at?!"

"Playing?! Do you think this is a game, *paladin*?" she exclaimed. "Do you think witnessing helpless women being mistreated by disgusting pigs without anyone taking action is a game? Do you think every time one of them tries to seek help and no one does anything is a game?! Do you think watching a man abuse others with impunity just because he was born a man is a game?!" her voice broke and her breath heaved with emotion.

The pain that passed over her face surprised Talyvien. The paladin's shoulders slumped, and his anger turned into compassion.

"I also seem to recall that I never hid the fact that I am an assassin," Shael snarled. "That's what I do; it's what I am! Why are you so appalled?"

Talyvien's arms fell to his sides. She was right. Why did it seem to affect him so much? A certain disappointment tugged at his chest. His burgeoning ambivalence for this woman seemed contrary to all the teachings he had received about the value of life. Contrary to the pain he had felt at the loss of his parents. "It is not for you to decide who has the right to live or die, Shael," he calmly replied.

"Ah! Then who does have that right?" Shael retorted. "The justice of men? The justice of Callystrande? The one that kills women for being literally born different!" Her blazing blue eyes seethed with rage at Talyvien.

"I don't know, but not like this, Shael, not like this . . ."

"How, then? If I had done nothing, he would have continued to abuse dozens of women. Again, and again. Tell me I'm wrong! Tell me that the life of each of those women is worth less than his, *paladin*!"

Talyvien hesitated, but his paladin's heart was tinged with curiosity. "What happened, Shael? What happened to you?"

A torrent washed over the assassin's face as she clenched her teeth. A surge of rage, a wall against his intrusion, ramparts that protected her from her own suffering. "Tell me, *paladin*, if you hadn't seen the sign from your goddess that day, would you have saved Lucine?" Shael spat out the words with malice in her voice.

A low blow. She had seen his shame flicker across his face. But Talyvien's pride made him imprudent. "Tell me, *assassin*, would you have saved her if she had been a man?" he retorted.

Shael screamed in rage and lunged at him.

Talyvien quickly stepped back, but his back hit a tree trunk.

With outstretched arm, the assassin materialized one of her daggers and drove it into the bark above the paladin's head.

He didn't flinch.

Despite being taller than her, Shael looked him straight in the eye, lifting her head. "You're just like the others!" she growled, inches away from Talyvien's face.

"Who are you trying to convince?" he replied. In provocation, he maintained eye contact with the assassin. He refused to lower his gaze in the face of so much raw pain. In such a decisive moment. Talyvien felt Shael's fist quivering on the dagger above him. With irregular breathing, the assassin stared at him with an animalistic intensity he had rarely seen in her. The features of her face, usually so refined, twisted under the storm raging within her.

So close to each other, their disagreement and their differences mingled in their breath. Perhaps their ambiguity as well.

"For someone who complains about the violence of men, it seems that you also resort to it quite a bit, Shael," he harshly added.

Struck by his words, she suddenly stepped back and made the blade disappear. She took a few stumbling steps backward, an astonished look on her face. Embarrassment and shame had replaced her fury, and Shael turned her body away, holding her arm.

Behind the trees, footsteps cracked the mossy forest floor. Both turned their heads. Shael drew her daggers again, and Talyvien quickly grabbed his sword still planted a few meters away.

Calixte rushed in and abruptly stopped at the sight before them. "Oh, looks like I'm interrupting something!" they joked.

Talyvien glanced at the assassin from the corner of his eye, noticing her tousled hair escaping from her braid and her erratic breathing. Her daggers vanished from her hands, and she crossed her arms, looking embarrassed.

"Ah! You don't have to explain anything! It's just the way life is!" the bard chuckled.

"What's going on, Calixte?" Talyvien growled, abruptly ending the banter and sheathing his sword.

"Lucine is waking up!" they exclaimed in delight.

Behind her, the ground erupted in an explosion of a thousand glass shards. A brilliant blast lifted the transparent wall like a hungry and tempestuous wave.

Endless, shining red scales. A serpentine body that undulated through the cracks in the ground like a frozen lake fracturing.

In shock, Lucine fell backward. An immense viper, several meters high, emerged from the frozen water, carrying significant shimmering debris in its wake. Translucent fragments were scattered everywhere. The massive serpent lunged toward the young druidess.

A dream of magnificent beauty transformed into a nightmare of absolute horror.

Lucine leaped to her feet and started running. Her breath became intermittent in her frantic sprint. Her legs tried to find purchase on the unstable and improbable ground.

The enormous reptile slithered and chased her, impressive fangs protruding from its gaping and carnivorous mouth. Behind her, the sounds of scraping and the creature sliding on the glass made Lucine flinch. The creature easily gained ground. What could she do against such a threat?

The heavy body of the serpent crashed in front of her—an immense nightmare ring of scales coiling around Lucine. The young druidess halted her run, surrounded by the infinite and circular anatomy of the snake. Two bright suns greedily observed the young woman. Its mouth revealed long, sharp canines and a silver, forked tongue.

Nevertheless, Lucine was not afraid. No longer afraid. She had run enough, fled enough.

She assessed the reptile, standing tall with a confident posture. If she were to die, so be it. Lost between dream and reality, she found her courage. For the first time, for the last time, Lucine would not die as a victim but as a fighter. A vow in her heart burst forth, and she defiantly stared into the serpent's fierce yellow eyes.

With its fangs out and mouth wide open, the viper's head lunged at the young woman.

And Lucine surrendered.

A piercing and terribly visceral sensation. A call she could no longer ignore. A certainty. With a hand gesture, her arm outstretched, Lucine commanded the serpent to freeze. A command that emanated from the depths of her being, from the unfathomable corners of her existence. Simply because she could.

The enormous creature's jaws froze a few inches from the druidess. The animal stared at the young woman in bewilderment, its head wobbling under its sudden paralysis.

A sense of immense power ran through Lucine. A power that finally seemed to reveal itself, that made sense. The nature she tamed within her body, whispering all its secrets to her. That she would master.

Filled with this truth, Lucine took a deep breath and exhaled slowly.

With her heart pounding, she suddenly woke up. Her breathing now irregular, she opened her eyes and found herself in the small room of the inn in Luminaur.

"Lucine?"

She turned her head and saw Talyvien, looking worried by her bedside.

"Taly . . . ?" she murmured, her voice breaking under the pain of her burning throat.

The contrast between the power she had experienced while asleep and the weakness of her body upon waking struck her. How long had she been asleep? She managed to sit up with difficulty in the bed, and her vision gradually cleared.

"You're going to be okay now," Calixte reassured her, bringing her a glass of water, which she took with a trembling hand.

"You know, you scared us!" Talyvien said with a slight smile, which Lucine timidly returned between sips.

"Us?" Lucine replied, struggling to swallow.

"Ah! You already know Calixte, the 'bard of wonders'!" Talyvien teased. "And apparently, a provider of miraculous healing as well!"

"Oh, come on now, you're all going to make me blush!" Calixte chuckled, hiding their face with mock modesty and laughing with their charming laughter.

"And you also owe your life to Shael," the paladin added, turning to the woman standing with crossed arms against one of the room's walls.

Her feline eyes met Lucine's, and she nodded slightly as an introduction. The young druidess was surprised to see her wearing leather armor and a long dark cloak that concealed her body. Surprised by her youth and the stern expression she displayed.

As Lucine carefully observed the silhouette of this surprising woman, a black dog jumped on the bed and frantically licked her face.

"Katao!" exclaimed Lucine, wrapping her arms around his neck.

How had he found her?

"He stayed to watch over you all this time," Calixte confirmed, thanking the dog with a scratch. "Glued to you like a barnacle on its rock!"

"We'll let you rest," the paladin said, getting up. "We'll explain everything you've missed, but I'm glad to see you're doing better!"

Everything she had missed?

The four jet-black eyes flashed in her memory. The bite and those final moments, begging Talyvien to end her life. A shiver ran through her.

Lucine nodded and watched Shael and Talyvien exit the room, leaving her alone with Calixte and Katao. As she tenderly caressed the dog's head, a troubled pout appeared on her face. "Thank you, Calixte, for everything."

"What's wrong?" the Alaris asked gently, sitting on the edge of the bed.

"It's just that . . . I was stupid to let myself be bitten like that."

"Hey, it's not your fault. You couldn't have known!"

"I was so naive!" Lucine grumbled, clenching her fists with annoyance. She took the amulet that the elders had given her on the fateful day of the Eclipse in her hand, feeling guilty for not being able to disprove their beliefs.

"Being bitten by an echarvora is actually a compliment. It means one's heart to be pure, unsuspecting of cruelty," Calixte explained tenderly.

"Do you think so?" Lucine hesitated, looking at her amulet.

"You know, there's a very fine line between learning enough to protect ourselves from danger and having the ability to still believe fundamentally in the goodness of others. Many people drown in their suffering and lose the ability to trust. Never lose your heart, Lucine. It's precious. But it takes time to adjust. And don't be too hard on yourself; you're still very young."

Katao rested his head on Lucine's thigh. He let out a small whimper, seemingly in agreement with Calixte's words.

"The heroes of the story are not just those who accomplish great feats," Calixte added. "They are also the ones who, despite adversity, continue to rise." They placed an affectionate hand on the young woman's shoulder. "And I believe you should not underestimate your strength, what you have already been through. It takes incredible resilience to choose to keep going, to stay on your feet. And sometimes, it's easier to see the light when you have been in the darkest corners of the world. Tragically, that also makes life more interesting. An opportunity to grow and flourish!" Calixte's melodious voice trailed off in a theatrical emphasis, accompanied by a sweeping gesture of the arm.

"Do—Do you think it's all worth it?" she asked, lowering her gaze.

"Of course! Just because everything isn't perfect or because suffering exists doesn't mean it's not worth it!"

The Alaris slid their hand from Lucine's shoulder and gently lifted her chin. They met her eyes. "Lucine," they added softly, "I just hope that one day you will have experienced so much love and friendship in your life that you won't need to ask that question anymore. That you will have braved so many trials that you will have discovered yourself. And that you will know how to create your own happiness."

With wide eyes, Lucine nodded and offered a slight smile of gratitude toward Calixte.

The bard withdrew their hand from her face, and Lucine sighed before adopting a lighter tone. "Calixte . . . I saw, felt strange things while I was . . . asleep. Sometimes, I had the feeling that it wasn't just a dream."

"Oh, you know, dream or reality, it's not that different!" they exclaimed. "In both cases, you have the sensation of having lived things, of creating memories and retaining information. It's just a matter of perspective!"

"Mmhh. I had never seen it from that angle," Lucine replied, thoughtful.

"That's why I'm here!" Calixte affirmed with a wink.

"Oh, really?"

Mischievously, the young druidess threw her pillow at the bard, who let out a high-pitched cry of surprise and joy.

THE VEIL
OF TRUTH

Transformed into a falcon, Solehan flew peacefully above Argentvale. He admired the architecture of the sleeping castle and the city below, getting lost in his thoughts.

What had happened in the throne room a few nights ago with Valnard troubled him and invaded his mind. His confusion grew about the Alaris, making him uncomfortable. The memory of that strange stupor stirred his insides. He was satisfied not to have encountered Valnard again since. Hearing from his mouth what he had always hoped for from his own kind, from his own clan, had greatly unsettled him, considering the desire for revenge he had felt toward the man.

Furthermore, knowing his past had also puzzled the young druid, who found himself unexpectedly empathetic. He couldn't imagine what the loss of a child could mean. Why had he tried to comfort the Alaris? Also, the memory of the flower he had managed to grow with his own hand and the vegetation that had sprouted from the wood of the imposing throne added to his questions. Was this also part of Teluar's powers? Although he had tried several times since, he couldn't replicate this phenomenon.

A melody arose, emanating from the blackened trees outside the lifeless city. Surprised by the presence of music in the dormant valley, Solehan decided to find its source and gracefully maneuvered at a low altitude through the branches of the forest. After several minutes of searching, he discovered Valnard's silhouette among the trees, deftly moving his slender, black fingers across a long wooden flute.

Intrigued, Solehan perched on a branch of a nearby tree. He discreetly observed the Alaris, who had settled on a huge rock to play the instrument. With closed eyes, Valnard focused on the tragic melody resonating through the trees.

An overwhelming delicacy emanated from the scene. A melodic purity that harmonized with the young druid's beating heart. An authenticity that shook him.

Solehan no longer saw any cruelty in this strange rupture of time. He couldn't help but feel admiration for the dexterity of the man and the enchantment that Valnard managed to create with a few notes.

If the young druid needed proof that these exceptional beings had not been shaped in the same world as humans, he would have had it in that moment. Everything about the Alaris seemed fabulous and captivating. His skilled fingers caressing the finely sculpted leaf motifs on the flute. His long hair outlining the contours of his harmonious face, gracefully floating in a swirl of pure white and deep black. His smooth, moonlit skin seemed to come alive under the rhythmic pulsations of the melody. Bark fragments formed and disappeared on the surface of his epidermis. On the bare skin of his shoulders, his neck, on each side of his jaw. Valnard had become a living work of art himself.

The grandeur of a final lament in honor of Teluar.

A turmoil stirred in Solehan's chest and his face would have flushed if he hadn't been a bird at that moment.

A few forest spirits emerged from between the trees and approached the musician with light steps, enthralled by the melancholy of the melody. Then, various animals made their appearance. Wolves, bears, birds, deer, and many others—all seemed absorbed by the disarray that permeated this moment. Thus, camouflaged by the swarm of diverse birds surrounding him, Solehan listened attentively to the raw emotion of the Alaris translated by the notes emanating from the long wooden flute.

After a few minutes, when the melody faded away, Valnard opened his eyes and tenderly gazed at the curious audience composed of nature spirits and animals, all gathered around him. The Alaris let out a slight sigh, tucked one of his locks behind his pointed ear, and brought the instrument to his mouth once again. But just as he was about to continue this unexpected concert, he paused. His green eyes settled on the young druid among the multitude of birds perched on the surrounding trees.

Solehan could read an invitation in them. Valnard had unmasked him.

Unable to conceal himself any longer, Solehan landed at the foot of the enormous rock where the Alaris sat and assumed his human form. The young druid positioned himself among several members of a wolf pack, who seemed not bothered by his presence. Still frozen in an emotion filled with nostalgia, Valnard began to play a new melody and closed his eyes to concentrate.

Each tone was carried by the wind of the valley. Each note, each perfectly resonating accent, brushed against Solehan's soul. He raised his head and observed Valnard. A mystical and timeless idol that this incongruous audience seemed destined to adore and worship.

The electricity generated by the pulses of his heart shook the young druid's body. He was swayed by the music and the flutter it caused within him. The current extended along his arms. His fingers started to itch. Dazed, the young man scrutinized his hands attentively. Small buds appeared in rhythm with the music and sprouted on his fingertips. Solehan watched in astonishment as they emerged and developed into small, vibrant green leaves. His hands had become branches thirsty for life. His body, the soil of a new yearning. The leaves eventually detached and flew away, carried by the breeze.

Was he truly capable of all this? Did he have the power to create life, nature? Was it similar to what had happened in the throne room? Filled with these questions, he managed to tear his attention away from the wonder he had just created and turned his head. Still galvanized by the melody of the Alaris, Solehan admired the creatures around him.

One of the wolves looked back at him with curiosity. The yellow, piercing eyes of the enormous gray beast transported him. Familiarity coursed through him; images struck his mind. A stolen and untamed recollection, memories that were not his own. The powerful jaws devouring the carcass of an animal, the security of the pack, the wolf cubs playing in the snow, the tension among potentially dominant males. The insatiable urge for the blood of their prey. The feeling of being and belonging to a whole.

Solehan's heartbeat quickened and intertwined with the tempo of the music. He had become a wolf, now communicating with a fellow pack member. Words became unnecessary. Only the power of his body and his fangs mattered now.

Thus, the young druid was not surprised when his human jaw began to push against his facial skin. His nose took the shape of the animal's snout, enormous canines appeared in his mouth. His skin slowly covered itself with thick fur, his limbs positioned themselves like those of a wolf, and his ears emerged through his brown hair. Animalistic evidence, a gift from his god. His lupine eyes, still golden and silver, fixed upon Valnard, who watched him while continuing to play the instrument.

One of the wolves, the alpha male of the pack, began to howl, accompanying the melody of the Alaris. The young druid was surprised to respond to the howl with his own, feeling a part of the group and recognizing the dominance of the alpha male. He had become a full-fledged wolf, a member of their pack.

When Valnard finished playing, he gracefully descended from the rock. The Alaris gently placed a hand on Solehan's wolf head. "Go," was the only word he spoke to him.

With that permission granted, Solehan followed the pack of wolves into the woods. Throughout the day, he observed their rituals and habits. He learned the names of the various members that composed it, each corresponding to a growl with a slightly different tone. He played with the wolf pups and ran for hours among the trees. His sense of smell and hearing gradually became sharper. He hunted and shared meals with them, learning to become one with nature and live in harmony within a group.

He willingly allowed himself to be immersed in this newfound part of his being, determined to return day after day to their wild society.

Far away from all his uncomfortable questions, far away from all the answers he did not want to know.

Far away from Valnard.

34

 Lucine's condition had improved throughout the day since she had awakened, and that evening, the four friends were finally able to reunite for dinner at the tavern. With her health fully restored, a wolfish hunger gnawed at the young druidess as she busily devoured everything on the table, much to the amusement of her companions.

After enduring so many trials, Lucine cherished this moment of respite. She studied the three people sharing her meal, scratched Katao's head beside her, and, for the first time in a long while, felt grateful for being able to experience this moment.

"Do you think you'll be able to travel tomorrow?" Talyvien asked her.

She nodded, too preoccupied to respond with her voice, eagerly finishing a bowl of soup. She was famished.

"It seems we'll need to bring extra rations, apparently," Calixte teased, looking at her with playful eyes. "Perhaps I can remedy that."

"Thank you, Calixte, for helping us. What would we do without you!" the paladin joked, taking a bite of a chicken drumstick.

"I meant, I could accompany you!" the bard clarified.

"Ah?! You're not staying at the inn?" Lucine asked, placing her empty soup bowl on the table.

"No . . . I've been here for a while. I thought it was time to see new horizons. And besides, you're all very likable!" They winked at Lucine.

"So why not travel together for a while? To Dawnelest, right?"

"Yes!" Shael and Talyvien exclaimed in unison.

Surprised by the synchronicity of their response, they both avoided making eye contact.

"Well, that's fine by me," Calixte replied, looking back and forth between the paladin and the assassin with a mocking glance. "If you'll have me, of course. I wouldn't want to impose!"

"Mmhh, let's see, an Alaris who can not only perform offensive and healing magic but can also serenade us by the fireside. No, I see no use in that!" Shael sarcastically remarked.

Everyone burst into laughter, but Lucine noticed a brief hint of discomfort on Talyvien's face. She shifted her attention to the young woman with the startling appearance who was nibbling on her dish in front of her. Though Lucine thought Shael seemed barely older than herself, a certain firmness radiated from her presence.

A definite desire stirred in Lucine's heart. How could someone so young exude such confidence? Such experience? But Lucine noticed that Talyvien seemed uneasy and avoided engaging in conversation with her. Was it because of her magic?

"How did you two meet?" Lucine asked, pointing her spoon in the direction of the paladin and the young woman respectively. "I mean, you said that Shael . . . saved my life?"

A visible embarrassment crossed the paladin's face, causing him to stop chewing.

"I'm the assassin who was assigned to . . . kill him," the woman replied casually.

"Oh."

"This is getting interesting!" Calixte chuckled.

"And I made you drink my blood," Shael added in a neutral tone, continuing to eat as if nothing had happened.

Lucine was taken aback, but the memories of the vision of the dark-winged goddess flashed in her mind.

"I understand now why I saw all those things when I was asleep," Lucine said pensively, twirling her spoon in her empty bowl.

"The blood of Sazaelith's chosen ones can indeed cause hallucinations of unparalleled beauty," Shael exclaimed proudly. "Some use it in small doses to aid in falling asleep or to soothe nightmares. But it's ironic that it has no effect on the chosen ones themselves."

"Why ironic?" Talyvien asked, raising an eyebrow.

The assassin responded by casting a bitterly cold gaze at the paladin.

"There were indeed magnificent apparitions, but some were much less so . . ." Lucine quickly added, cutting short their silent squabble.

"That's strange," Shael commented, focusing back on her meal, though a slight dismay broke her otherwise composed face. "Normally, the blue blood doesn't cause nightmares."

"What did you see?" Calixte asked, placing a hand affectionately on Lucine's.

"Quite a few things. Actually, you were there, Calixte."

"Ah! I hope you categorize me as one of the magnificent apparitions, not the rest!"

"Of course!" Lucine replied with a conspiratorial smile. "But I also remember glimpsing a strange symbol engraved on the bark of a remarkable tree that seemed significant. I'm not sure why, but I have a feeling that I need to search for it or discover its meaning."

"That might have been just a hallucination," Talyvien suggested, shrugging and spreading his hands.

"Maybe. I also saw my brother, but I think he thought I was dead. It was strange. I felt like he was truly there, sharing the moment with me. There was also a massive snake that was chasing me. But strangely, it abruptly stopped just before it could pounce on me. It's as if . . . I could control it."

"All of this does seem somewhat disjointed and peculiar," Shael replied. "Perhaps it's related to the color of your eyes?"

"What do you mean?" Lucine asked, baffled.

Images of the pyres of the crusade surged in the young druidess's mind. Her throat tightened.

"Usually, the magic of the gods manifests in the eyes. Perhaps you're under the influence of one of them without knowing it."

"I didn't sense any magic coming from her," Talyvien retorted.

"You're not much of a paladin anymore," the assassin sneered, a haughty look on her face.

"No, he's right. I have no magic, Shael," Lucine added, with a sorry smile.

"Mmhh . . . If that's the case, then you'll need to learn how to fight and defend yourself," the assassin replied. "I can train you."

"Oh! Talyvien had already started doing that before . . ." Lucine hesitated. The young druidess's mouth curved with embarrassment, and her posture slumped in her chair. "I'm sorry, Taly. I would understand if you don't want to train me anymore," she added in a whisper.

"You haven't done anything wrong, Lucine. It was my failing. It would be an honor to resume training," Talyvien assured her gently.

"Perfect! The two best instructors on the continent just for you! How lucky you are!" Calixte exclaimed enthusiastically.

"Very well," Shael declared, crossing her arms. "We'll start on the road."

Talyvien, Shael, and Calixte now recounted to her the events she had missed. Like the battle against the echarvora or the bandits, Katao coming to her rescue. The crusade that had passed through the village of Luminaur, leaving its ominous mark. Shael's failed assassination attempts and the care provided by Calixte.

Lucine listened for a long while to the three friends' narrative, at times intrigued and fascinated, at other times saddened. She looked at them with tender eyes, feeling the weight of all they had endured solely to save her. Did they see something in her that she couldn't see in herself? Was she worth all these sacrifices? Immense gratitude filled her soul.

"Thank you, all three of you," Lucine declared, her eyes slightly glistening.

Surprised, the paladin placed a hand behind his neck, and a gentle smile tugged at the corner of his mouth.

The assassin, evidently at a loss for how to handle the young druidess's emotion, averted her gaze and began playing with one of her daggers, twirling it on one finger.

The dog barked indignantly at being left out.

"Oh, you too, Katao!" Lucine hastily added, placing both hands on the dog's head and rubbing its ears.

True to themselves, the bard broke the awkwardness with flair. "Well, I'm going to get a round of beer because it's sorely lacking around here! You're going to make me bawl my eyes out!" they exclaimed, eliciting laughter from everyone.

The next morning in the small inn of Luminaur, as Lucine and Talyvien prepared their horses in the stables, the sound of hooves clattered on the stone-paved street. The young woman was surprised to see Calixte and Shael approaching them on two enormous and magnificent stallions.

Calixte's mount was truly impressive: elegant posture, a coat of immaculate white, a long and undulating ivory mane cascading to one side. Shael's steed, on the other hand, was black and gleaming like onyx, with a long and tousled mane, its appearance strangely wild, as if it was a creature emerging from the darkness of Sazaelith's realms.

"Thank you again, Calixte. It's a beautiful gift, and I will take great care of it," Shael exclaimed, patting the neck of her mount.

"You're welcome! The pleasure is all mine! Lucine, I could have bought you a horse too if you wanted. Yours seems small and it's a draft horse. Not very practical for traveling!" Calixte remarked.

"That's kind of you, but I prefer to travel with Maia. We know each other well," Lucine replied.

Maia shook herself as if responding affirmatively to the young woman.

"Well, Calixte, it's interesting to have you around!" Shael joked.

"Ah, let's just say that the bard profession pays well, that's all!" Calixte affirmed, with an elegant laugh.

"Let's get going," Talyvien declared in an oddly gruff manner, mounting his horse eagerly and giving a light kick to Aho, who started trotting.

The three companions followed suit, soon galloping at a good pace. The dog Katao ran alongside them.

They left the small village of Luminaur to join the road that led to Dawnelest.

35

They galloped for several days, and the assassin, who knew the path best, led the troupe. Talyvien knew it would probably take them several weeks to reach the capital of the Kingdom of Vamentera, which was on the other side of the country.

Concerned about encountering creatures like the echarvora, they had decided to avoid any type of ruins or debris and instead prioritize open clearings when they stopped to rest. They also refrained from traveling on heavily trafficked main roads, fearing they might come across the Crusade of the Dawn's Resolve. They knew that the fanatical army of the High Priestess Piore likely had a few days' head start on them. However, Talyvien was aware that they had to reach Dawnelest as quickly as possible to have a chance to warn the queen.

One evening, after speeding through vast stretches of countryside at a fast gallop, they halted to rest. They emerged from a narrow path hidden within the woods and arrived in a vast wheat field, where the last rays of the sun bestowed a flavescent color with shimmering golden reflections, clear enough to allow them to spot any potential danger. Sore from hours of riding, they decided to settle in the middle of the field for the night.

Their camp setup had now become a well-oiled routine. Each person took on a task. Shael preferred to isolate herself to sleep, but she still helped Calixte set up the bedding and prepare the fire. Lucine, followed closely by Katao, took care of feeding and tending to the horses. Talyvien was usually in charge of gathering firewood.

When the crackling flames finally reached toward the darkening sky, everyone sat in a circle around the fire and savored the little rest they could afford, along with the few rations Calixte had arranged to bring along.

"Ready for your first training, druidess?" exclaimed Shael, finishing her meal and briefly rubbing her hands together to clean them.

Lucine nodded vigorously, taking a bite of her ration.

"It could be interesting to give her a little demonstration!" Calixte chimed in, before gobbling up a left-over crumb on their little finger. "A small duel between you and the paladin, for example!"

His thoughts lost upon the dancing flames before him as he ate his dinner, Talyvien was pulled out of his reverie. He lazily raised his stare to the assassin. Her blue, luminous eyes met his, filled with mockery and pride, her face immersed in the darkness cast by the fire behind her.

Talyvien had made it a point to avoid Shael since their last conversation, unsure of what to make of her. Deep inside, he harbored a lingering resentment toward her for the cold-blooded assassination she had committed. He still didn't know how to react to that information.

"Hmm. I'm not sure if it's such a good idea, Calixte," he grumbled, taking another bite of his meal and challenging Shael with his gaze.

"Ah, I see. Are the paladins of Callystrande cowards?" retorted the assassin. "Are you afraid of bruising your ego in front of witnesses?"

The paladin remained silent and took another bite provocatively, never breaking eye contact. A part of him enjoyed her frustration.

He noticed Lucine's wary expression as she witnessed the exchange. The visible tension in their conversation seemed to make her uncomfortable. Was she wondering whether she should intervene? He saw the citrine glow in Calixte's eyes settle on the young druidess and silently urge her not to act, attempting to ease her concerns. He cursed himself for making Lucine feel this way, but it was between him and the assassin.

"Well, I know very well that you don't stand a chance," Shael said, "but still, I would have thought you'd make an effort for a demonstration." Exasperated, she placed her fists on her hips in annoyance.

Talyvien laughed bitterly. Did she have so much confidence and arrogance? His ambivalence toward the assassin turned into anger. He wanted to teach her a lesson. He finished his meal, stood up, and positioned himself in front of her, revealing their difference in height. He looked down at her.

Two daggers slid into Shael's palms.

Talyvien unsheathed Tuoryn's sword and took a defensive stance.

A bestial smile spread across the assassin's face. She lunged at the paladin with extraordinary dexterity. A whirlwind of blades descended upon him.

Talyvien managed to parry with brilliance and employed the teachings of strength and serenity from the paladins of Callystrande. He no longer had access to the goddess's powers, but for the first time, he didn't feel their absence. The rage contained within him filled the void it had once occupied.

A pure and primal rage. Directed solely at her. Against the ambivalence she evoked in him at that very moment.

How dare she make him feel this way?

He didn't hold back his strikes, and he attacked with extreme violence and a certain relentlessness. He growled his ferocity between clenched teeth and forgot about the fatigue that numbed his limbs. He was trying to destroy a part of himself that he despised, a part he had no control over. Why was this happening to him now? After the torture he'd endured with Selena, he had vowed not to be caught off guard. Since then, he had always managed to foresee and control everything. Why couldn't he do it in her presence?

With each thunderous clash of metal, his fury grew. The sword sliced through the air powerfully, his frenzy colliding with each of their parries. An uncontrollable emotion that tore through all the limitations of the education he had received.

How dare she have this effect on him?

The sapphire in the assassin's eyes tinged with surprise at the brutality he forced himself to employ against her. And shifted toward fright.

He ignored it. Why was she still here anyway?

Shael's arms began to shake under the force of his blows. She decided to retreat into the darkness of her comfort zone. Her magic. Her body disappeared from Talyvien's hate-filled gaze.

How dare she be so cowardly?

The outline of the assassin's silhouette became difficult to discern. A few moonlit arcs of metal mingled with the nebulous fabric of her cloak.

Talyvien remembered the assassin's words. *"The goal is to learn not to rely on your vision to fight the Quanta, but rather your other senses!"* So, he shifted his focus away from visual perception. He closed his eyes.

Talyvien listened to the sounds of leather rustling that emerged around him and caught the sweet scent of the assassin, leaving an imprint in the darkness.

A metallic sound whizzed in his direction. Talyvien agilely dodged it and used the weight of his body to topple Shael, who crashed heavily to the ground. With Tuoryn's sword positioned at the assassin's throat and his jaw clenched, a growl of anger escaped with each breath the paladin took. His body immobilized hers with his strength, placed above her. Blinded by his hatred toward her, toward himself. Toward this situation.

The fear that flooded Shael's eyes pierced right through his heart.

What was he doing? He wasn't this person filled with excessive and unrestrained anger; he didn't want to become that. He had gone too far. Talyvien cursed his temperament, his panic in the face of the ambivalence he felt for her. Why had he let his rage take over like this?

"I told you to be careful with what you teach," Talyvien said then, in a falsely mocking tone, masking his anger and trying to reassure her.

Frozen in bewilderment, she didn't respond. The deep blue of her eyes was clouded with terror. Pure suffering. Desperation tinged with madness. A primitive instinct that echoed the rage he had felt.

One of her daggers stabbed Talyvien's neck. The metal of the gleaming blade created a thin line drawn in the cool night air. A gesture of extreme speed. A reflex, a survival impulse.

Time stopped. What had she done?

In response, he removed himself from Shael's body immediately. Was he going to die this way?

The assassin's gaze drowned in budding tears and continued to stare at him in astonishment. A pitiful look.

He raised a trembling hand to his throat and waited for the agony to overwhelm him.

"That was incredible!" exclaimed Lucine, joining them at their side.

But no pain came. No agony. Talyvien looked at the palm of his hand. Free of blood. And he understood.

Shael had disintegrated the blade before it had reached its target.

Still stunned and crouched on the ground, he watched the assassin pretend to wipe the sweat from her forehead with her sleeve, erasing the newfound sparkle in her eyes. The look on her face changed drastically when she focused her attention on Lucine, giving her a mischievous smile. She stood back up on her feet and dusted off her armor as if nothing had happened.

"With our expertise, you're going to become the greatest warrior on the continent!" Shael cheered, while Lucine laughed joyfully.

Talyvien was baffled. By her action, by her sudden change in attitude. By the protection she seemed to have built around her soul.

Lucine caught a glimpse of Talyvien straightening up and rubbing his neck, a marked annoyance on his face.

Calixte joined them, humming a tune and with Katao trailing behind, and perched on a nearby rock, taking care not to wrinkle their tunic in a sophisticated gesture. They opened a small notebook and began to scribble a few pages with an ethereal quill pen of blue energy that materialized in their hand.

The assassin grasped the young druidess by the arms to urge her to refocus her attention. "So, first lesson!" Shael said. "You're a woman, you should use that to your advantage!"

"What do you mean?" Lucine asked incredulously.

"Yes, Shael . . . what do you mean?" grumbled Talyvien, approaching them and assuming a severe posture, hands on his hips.

"Men will always underestimate you!" proclaimed the assassin.

"Isn't that a bit sexist, Shael?" the paladin moaned, rolling his eyes.

The assassin pulled a small leather pouch from one of her pockets. She bounced it in her hand, and the coins inside tinkled with each movement. Her feline, self-satisfied look triumphantly settled on the paladin.

"Hey! That's my purse!" he gasped, patting the pockets at his belt.

"So, as I was saying, use that to your advantage!" the assassin swooned, throwing the pouch to the paladin, who caught it with a grunt.

Lucine couldn't help but chuckle at Talyvien's embarrassment as he hastily stashed the purse away in one of the pockets of his armor, muttering to himself.

Calixte seemed to take some notes.

"If you don't have magic, what can you do?" Shael asked Lucine.

"Well, I'm not too bad at archery. I—I think," Lucine hesitated, tapping her chin with her index finger.

"Ah!" sang out Calixte. "A huntress!"

"I wouldn't go that far, but . . ." Lucine began.

The bard fidgeted and crossed their legs on the rock. They snapped their notebook shut in their hand, and the pen vanished. Their mischievous gaze settled on Lucine. "Let's see that!" they suggested.

Talyvien, who had walked over to Maia, returned with the bow and quiver of the young druidess. He handed them to her with a smile, and Lucine equipped herself.

Calixte opened the palm of their hand, and small ethereal blue magic balls escaped from their fingers. They started swirling above them.

"Maybe we should start with stationary targets," grumbled Talyvien, watching them.

"Does that mean you would offer yourself as a target?" Shael taunted.

The paladin responded only with a sigh and a roll of his eyes.

Lucine focused on the curious targets as they darted toward the edge of the woods. Memories of nights spent secretly training in the Astral Forest flooded her mind. She drew her bow and nocked her first arrow in a skilled motion.

A feeling of sheer power spread through her limbs. Her movements became precise and deadly accurate. The familiarity of the bow between her fingers shattered all her doubts and fears. Her vision narrowed on her target. She held her breath.

The first projectile was propelled at a blistering speed and pierced one of the blue balls in its core. The arrow whistled through the air and lodged into a trunk with a clear impact sound that reverberated among the trees.

Hardly had the first arrow left when Lucine quickly and skillfully nocked a second, which found its mark with perfection.

Nothing else mattered but her goal. In a trance-like state, her mind emptied, and her body froze in the posture of a determined archer.

A sharp crack. Another arrow impaled one of the targets.

She picked up the pace. Arrows flew one after another. She reloaded her weapon swiftly, her quiver slowly emptying.

Another blue ball was skewered into a tree. Then another. And another. Deadly precision.

Lucine didn't stop. For Solehan. If she wanted to have a chance to find him. To save him. She didn't want to be that naive, ignorant, and useless girl anymore. She'd had enough.

Soon, a volley of arrows rained down on all the targets, moments apart. They all hit their mark, without exception.

A deafening silence settled in the clearing.

Lucine caught her breath and lowered her bow. She turned her head.

The three companions stared at her with wide eyes.

"By Alar! Remind me to never quarrel with you," Calixte chortled. "I'm far too young and irresistible to end up like a meat skewer!"

The young druidess blushed.

"Well! I don't think there's anything we can teach you in that department!" Shael praised, placing her hand on Lucine's shoulder.

"Oh, it's just that I had a lot of free time to practice in the forest, that's all!" Lucine stammered.

"How is it that you never had confidence in this talent before?" Talyvien asked.

"I guess I was convinced that I couldn't become anything other than what the legend of the druids expected of me," she replied, puzzled. "I wasn't even allowed to practice archery."

"Well, it seems we'll focus solely on close combat then," the assassin joked. "And I think, in the absence of being a target, our dear paladin will make a perfect training dummy!"

"What? No way!" protested Talyvien.

"Come on now. It's for Lucine's benefit! Show a little cooperation, paladin!" Shael taunted, not waiting for his consent to continue her teaching.

Shael proceeded to show the young druidess the vital points on Talyvien's body, causing him to involuntarily freeze.

"This can also be useful for archery!" the assassin added.

"I'm not sure I want to kill anyone, Shael . . ." Lucine hesitated.

"Oh, it can always come in handy to know! Otherwise, if you *really* just want to temporarily neutralize someone, for men, a well-placed strike between the legs is also very effective," Shael declared, with a grimace full of innuendo.

"Perhaps a little demonstration?" the bard exclaimed.

Lucine covered her mouth and giggled.

With a feline stride, the assassin approached the paladin.

"Hey!" Talyvien blurted, positioning his hands in front of his groin.

"Don't worry, paladin. I don't do temporary," Shael chuckled.

"We should teach her to fight nobly, Shael. Not like an assassin!" Talyvien grumbled.

"Enemies don't always fight nobly. I go for practicality!" the assassin retorted.

The young druidess observed the fury that flashed across the paladin's face as he stared at Shael with frustration. This journey promised to be eventful.

Their training sessions lasted several hours every evening after dinner. Shael and Talyvien, trying to maintain cordiality as best as they could, shared both their combat knowledge.

With the paladin, Lucine continued to work on her endurance, strength, and attack and defense postures. Always under the curious gaze of Calixte, the three of them would run for long minutes around the camp and practice with wooden sticks the parries that Talyvien taught the young druidess.

Shael was determined to teach her some hand manipulations for stealing objects or creating a diversion. She also showed her some dagger attack techniques that were anything but noble and sent shivers down Lucine's spine.

Driven by the opportunity before her and her promise to find her brother, the young druidess felt herself making rapid progress. She gradually gained confidence in herself and observed her body becoming more toned and her abilities improving.

For the first time in her life, she finally felt like she was in control of her own destiny.

36

 Several weeks had passed in the castle of Argentvale as Solehan enjoyed joining the pack almost every morning, assuming the form of a wolf. As he grew increasingly accustomed to his transformations, he experienced less physical unease during the transitions. He now skillfully shifted from his human state to that of an animal with more confidence.

For the first time in his life, the young druid felt like he belonged to a meaningful whole, a group where he had a place. A clan that finally accepted him for who he was. Day after day, he also had developed a special friendship with the alpha male of the pack, whose name resonated as *Wuruhi* in Solehan's human mind, and who had chosen to return the affection toward him.

Wuruhi had taken pleasure in showing him the customs and traditions of the pack, integrating him into their games and hunts, and introducing him to his offspring that he had with his female mate. Solehan was grateful to be able to create such a unique bond with a living being, having felt isolated for so long.

However, the boundaries of his human existence had gradually became blurred as he had felt an incredible attraction to their wild world. It would have been pleasant to surrender to that part of himself. But despite his daily visits, Solehan forced himself to remain in the skin of an animal for only a few hours each time. His soul had remained precariously balanced on the tightrope between his humanity and this new realm of magic and possibilities.

Nonetheless, he knew that part of this fascination lay in not having to deal with the problems of his own life, preferring to become immersed in a different reality. But despite his self-deception, despite his futile hopes, his undeniable truth kept pounding in his chest.

On that evening, alone in the night, Solehan stepped onto the small balcony of his room and gazed at the starry sky. He tried to imagine the disgust that Lucine would feel toward his truth. The relentless torment he tried to escape, however possible.

How could he reconcile his desire for revenge with the story entrusted to him by Valnard? With the memory of the Alaris's wonderment at the flower he conjured? With the heart-wrenching look he displayed when he mentioned the death of his child? With this strange curiosity, this strange feeling.

He had tried. To hate him. To despise him.

In vain.

Faced with his own cowardice, a wave of shame washed over his mind.

Solehan had imagined fleeing this castle dozens of times. And even though he no longer had the Ignescent bracelets around his wrists that held him back, the dreadful sentiment that lurked within him now seemed to fulfill that function. The slender thorny crimson vines that had once lacerated his flesh were now piercing his mind and heart.

Drenched in a profound repugnance for the betrayal he felt he was committing; he experienced a violent need to see the Alaris.

At the first light of dawn, Solehan instinctively knew where to find Valnard, and he made his way toward the large tree in the middle of the castle courtyard. He discovered the Alaris kneeling, head bowed, with a hand placed on the trunk. Delicate brambles wrapped around his outstretched arm, interlacing with the bark of the towering tree.

Solehan also knelt beside him, respecting the solemnity of the moment. He did not want to break the enchantment of the scene happening in front of him. From the corner of his eye, he observed Valnard's face, the pained emotion that fractured his features. The Alaris slowly opened his eyes and met the golden and silver spark in the young druid's gaze.

"It's been a long time since I've seen you," murmured Valnard, his voice husky.

"What was your child's name?" Solehan questioned, evading the Alaris's inquiry.

"Sylveah," he sighed, his gaze landing with bitterness on the tree's bark. "You saw her, didn't you?"

"Yes."

"I believe it's the first time I curse myself for choosing to be a man," Valnard whispered, his words choked in his throat, a wry irony curling the corner of his mouth.

"Why?"

"Because the power of the Flow would have allowed me to see your thoughts," Valnard replied, his eyes still desperately locked onto the bark of the tree.

Solehan's soul wavered. He couldn't bear this suffering. So, he delicately placed his hand on top of Valnard's on the trunk and positioned his body to face him.

The green eyes widened in surprise at the contact. The Alaris turned his head and looked at the young man, perplexed, the trace of his sadness still visible on his delicate face.

Solehan's heart compressed in his chest. With a gentle caress, he placed his other hand on the Alaris's cheek and tenderly indicated for him to lean closer.

Valnard rested his forehead against his.

The vision resurfaced in the young druid's mind. The figure approached lightly through the forest, an elegant crystal flower adorning her hair. She had been vague the last time he caught a glimpse, but this time, he could discern the contours of her face and her large emerald eyes that gazed mischievously at him. Fine wooden horns sprouted from her forehead, and small pointed ears, like the Alaris's, peeked out from her long locks entangled with falling leaves on her shoulders. Teluar appeared too, in the form of a massive white fox, seemingly protecting the child who nestled against the animal's sparkling fur. A youthful laughter resonated in his mind as the vision grew increasingly blurry.

Solehan opened his eyes again.

The warmth of Valnard's uneven breathing brushed against his lips. With their foreheads still pressed together, Solehan's hand still on the side of the Alaris's face, the young druid was struck by the pureness of Valnard's sorrow. His body shuddered slightly, subdued by his tears.

"Thank you," the Alaris managed to utter, barely audible above discreet sobs.

They remained like that, against each other, foreheads touching, for several long seconds. Solehan waited for Valnard's turmoil to subside, attempting to comfort him with his presence.

The temptation became overwhelming.

The young druid's fingers tenderly caressed Valnard's cheek. With his thumb, he wiped away a few trailing tears that streamed down the ivory of his face. They were so close, Valnard's skin terribly soft and warm under the pads of his fingers, his scent reminiscent of the forest undergrowth after rain, his emotions so absolute.

Eyes still closed, Valnard pressed his cheek against the palm of the young man's hand.

A searing wave surged through Solehan's nape and ignited his chest. His breaths grew jagged. The bridge of their noses grazed against each other. With a slight movement of his head, he could have kissed him, could have redefined his lips that were so beautifully shaped by his own. Relieve his frustration and merge with him in his heartache.

Complete foolishness. Was he really that stupid?

Solehan forced himself to break their embrace. The absence of the Alaris's skin burned against his own. He slowly got back on his feet and distanced himself, leaving Valnard still kneeling on the ground.

"You should be careful, Solehan." The deep voice of Valnard resounded behind the young druid, causing him to stop.

Solehan slowly turned his head to catch sight of the man still kneeling before the tree. The Alaris now wore a stern face behind a few strands of his hair, although his eyes still seemed clouded by sadness. "You're not a wolf, even though you wish to be. You will lose yourself."

"I am already lost," Solehan replied coldly.

"Stay with me today. Remain in the form of a man."

"No!" His self-hatred fueled his rage. Fury erupted from within him like a gust of wind, sweeping away all caution in its path. "I don't want to feel what I feel!" Solehan yelled.

Surprise flickered in the Alaris's irises as they remained fixed on him.

He had said too much.

Solehan transformed into an eagle and swiftly took flight, avoiding any further confrontation with the desperately green gaze that was watching him flee.

He cursed his naivety and the impulse that had driven him to see Valnard that morning. He agonized over feeling whatever he felt for him. Solehan made his way toward the wolf pack that had become familiar to him, attempting to drown out all thoughts and emotions.

From the eagle's flight, he gracefully transitioned into the wolf's run, traversing the vast, dark forest that surrounded the town of Argentvale. He headed toward the den of his pack, seeking solace among his peers, within his newfound clan. He knew the path by heart, every rock, every crackling sound beneath his agile paws, guiding him toward hope and tranquility.

A chilling bolt shot down his spine. A familiar, cruel scent. His wolf-sharpened sense of smell detected a strong metallic odor in the air, which he immediately recognized.

Long streaks of vivid red crisscrossed the muddy and tormented ground, bearing witness to a fierce struggle.

His heart tore apart. What had happened? Where were they?

He saw no one in the den and began sniffing around for clues. After a few minutes of searching, he spotted Wuruhi's mate. She was crouched in the hollow of a rock, trembling, and her bewildered yellow eyes locked onto Solehan's. Upon seeing him, she whimpered in terror.

The young druid tried to calm and comfort her.

Without words, through the exchange of one animal to another, she described to him what had transpired during the night. A group of men seemed to have invaded the den, and Wuruhi had fiercely defended his mate and offspring. Fortunately, she had managed to escape following his command, but she hadn't seen them since. Only the faint traces of blood on the ground remained as evidence of their existence.

Once again, Solehan's world crumbled. But this time, he would seek revenge.

He sensed the scent of the human being dissipating into the forest. A trail of emanating sweat, blood, and tanned leather snaked through the trees.

Solehan had become a beast. A wolf.

They had become *prey*.

A grimace of rage and vengeance contorted his powerful jaw. His lips curled, revealing his imposing canines. He was determined to follow the trail of vile stench that pointed him in the right direction.

Valnard's silhouette resurfaced in his mind. He wanted him by his side, he wanted him to witness this, his thirst for vengeance, the unleashing of hatred that consumed his body. He wanted the Alaris to witness the power of Teluar's abilities and the threat he finally represented.

Was it out of provocation or attachment? It no longer mattered.

With a powerful flap of his wings, the eagle's body assumed the form of the young man and landed gracefully on the large stone slabs of the castle of Argentvale's inner courtyard. Valnard still stood before the tree. He turned his head toward the young druid and rose to his feet.

"Solehan, I'm sor—" he began, his words stifled in his throat as he caught sight of the devastation on Solehan's face. "What happened?"

Solehan didn't respond. His golden and silver eyes glared furiously at the Alaris. His clenched fists vibrated amid the chaos consuming his body.

Valnard approached him slowly, cautiously. "What do you need?" he asked firmly, squinting his eyes as if attempting to peer into Solehan's soul.

"I need you . . . Your powers," the young druid stated with an icy tone cutting through.

Valnard followed Solehan through the forest, galloping on his elaphora.

The young druid, transformed into a wolf, ran gracefully and occasionally stopped to sniff the path ahead.

The Alaris had turned his own skin into bark armor, unsure of what to expect. Solehan hadn't revealed any further details to him.

They leaped with ease between trees and rocks, orienting themselves in this mad expedition for several hours. A few lychenas followed them, gliding and undulating with virtuosity among the trunks of deciduous trees.

At nightfall, they finally arrived at a settlement of few wooden buildings on the edge of the forest. The noxious odor that Solehan had been tracking guided them to one of the structures, from which a dim light emanated through a dirty window.

The young druid resumed his human form and approached the rickety wooden door of the building.

Valnard dismounted his elaphora to stand behind him.

Solehan knocked on the wood. He heard heavy footsteps resonating on the floor, blending with a murmur of voices. The door finally opened to reveal a pot-bellied and filthy man who stared rudely at the young man, visibly annoyed. A wolf skin was draped over his broad shoulders.

Solehan's nose wrinkled with repulsion. A seething rage enveloped his thoughts.

"What do you want, kid?" the hunter spat in a hoarse voice. "I have nothing to give you. Go beg somewhere else!"

Solehan ignored him and shifted his attention to the interior of the house. Several drying racks stretched behind the man's silhouette, displaying several hides awaiting tanning.

A weight dropped in the young druid's gut. His eyes widened; his eyebrows arched on his forehead. Among the hides, Solehan recognized Wuruhi's pelt. Reduced to misery. Pathetic. By the coarse hands of the man standing before him. Reduced to an object stripped of all that he had once been.

Humans were capable of *that*. Ignoring the beauty of the world around them to satisfy their own interests. Refusing to admit that they were not the only living beings capable of love and feeling. Choosing to turn life into inanimate and futile trinkets.

A cataclysm erupted within Solehan. A final choice. Everything flooded his mind. He couldn't hear anything anymore. The knuckles of his fists turned white under the pressure. A guttural growl escaped through his tightly clenched teeth, the veins in his neck pulsing beneath taut skin.

"Did you understand what I said? Go—" the man began.

His sentence never reached completion.

Solehan's trembling hand lifted toward the hunter's throat. His fingers contorted with sinister rage.

The man gasped in shock, clutching his neck and struggling to breathe.

Brambles emerged from the orifices of his victim's face. They writhed in a cruel dance across the man's visage as he battled against himself. The vines grew and became armed with both thorns and flowers, incessantly sprouting from the hunter's mouth, nostrils, eyes, and ears. An unrelenting bouquet, ruthless and bloodthirsty, soon replaced the appearance of his human face.

An explosion. A deliverance.

The man fell to the ground, seeking mercy in the gleaming silver and gold eyes that fervently stared at him before being engulfed.

Solehan took a deep breath and savored his creation with delight. The man's body slumped with a final agonized gasp. A melody to his ears. The revenge of Nature, its merciless god.

Footsteps resonated on the floor. A woman's voice shrieked with horror in front of him. Still galvanized, Solehan cast a sinister glance toward the hunter's companion, who had just appeared. She screamed at the sight of her partner's body.

The young druid and the Alaris saw various lights illuminating the village as its inhabitants awakened to her cries in the middle of the night.

The following hours brought about a true massacre.

One by one, all the villagers succumbed to the relentless fury of the two men. A sinister ballet of thorns, flames, bites, and lignification rained down upon the small village, leaving no survivors in its wake.

With each disemboweled person, each limb torn away, Solehan felt his past detached from himself through the power bestowed upon him by Teluar. A destiny that died with the villagers he swept away in his frenzy.

He let their warm blood splash on his skin, tasted their fear with intoxication, and listened to the melody of their screams as he dispensed his justice. The revenge of all living beings they had massacred. Lucine's revenge.

Inexorably, the ferocious bite of a wolf, the powerful paw strikes of a bear, or the formidable thorns of his powers decimated each and every villager. Solehan didn't hear their futile pleas; he had become the vengeful hand of his god, their ultimate predator.

From the corner of his eye, he observed Valnard, who also incinerated and lacerated the villagers with his diabolical vines. Solehan felt alive by his side, in this macabre dance. Euphoric even, he imagined waltzing with him amid the flames and the scent of blood, amid the bodies of wood lignified by the lychenas. In the promise of their utopia, a world devoid of all humans, a lush paradise.

They didn't leave until dawn, when they were breathless from their exhilaration. When only silence could be heard from the still-smoldering ruins.

On the way back, the two men flew with an unsettling lightness in their hearts, enjoying the morning freshness and the diffuse light of the first sun rays.

Solehan, in his eagle form, glanced discreetly at Valnard comfortably seated on the back of the elaphora. He quietly admired his exquisite and undisturbed face, his seemingly distant focus, his delicate features gradually taking shape under the rosy hues of dawn, and his impossible green eyes reflecting the horizon.

A strange serenity poured into him. A budding calm amid the violence of the night, in the promise of a new day.

The tranquility of finally making a choice, of no longer being tormented, of being unable to turn back. To forever leave behind his past with the villagers.

Still focused on this new future and the neutral air of the Alaris, Solehan spread his wings wide. He twirled around the spirit of the forest, who emitted a soft braying sound.

A smile appeared on Valnard's face, now awakened from his reverie, as he mischievously made the creature flutter around the druid, challenging him with his gaze.

They played like that until the sun was high in the sky, casting its timid rays on the walls of the castle of Argentvale.

37

They only had a few days' journey left before reaching the capital of the Kingdom of Vamentera, Dawnelest. Fatigued from the trip, with sore limbs, Lucine was eager to set up their camp that evening. But when they stopped at nightfall for dinner, Calixte broke the established routine of the group.

"Tonight, no training! I have a little gift for you!" they exclaimed. "Our brave warriors need to rest from time to time!"

A certain joy seized the young druidess. She loved Calixte's performances and was relieved not to have to train.

Calixte took out their small hurdy-gurdy from one of the many saddlebags swaying at the back of their large white stallion and went to sit around the campfire.

"A performance just for us!" Lucine rejoiced.

She was right!

"Indeed!" Calixte proudly replied.

"I hope you're not going to charge us for it!" Shael teased.

"Of course not! But I've recently composed a new melody, and I wanted to share it with you, that's all!"

Talyvien's body stiffened, and he almost choked on his meal.

"No Ignescent, Talyvien, I promise!" Calixte added with a burst of laughter. A wink was sent in the paladin's direction, who grumbled in displeasure in response.

The melody grew softly in the clearing, accompanied by the steady rhythm of the flames from the campfire. Calixte's deep voice wove harmoniously with the notes produced by the hurdy-gurdy. Strands of their hair floated in the cool evening breeze and surrendered to their familiar color change. Delicate blue filaments wrapped the wrists and fingers of the bard, echoing the bluish glow that appeared in their eyes.

Several silhouettes came to life above them. With an ethereal blue hue, they moved gracefully and gradually took on familiar forms. A man clad in heavy armor and wielding a long sword appeared. His radiant body dodged the attacks of several graceful silhouettes twirling around him, the sharp blade cutting through them.

The vision dispersed into magical sparkles in the night. Some Flow particles whirled wildly.

Then a second hooded silhouette took shape. A blade in each hand, the apparition performed one acrobatic maneuver after another, launching precise and skillful attacks. It vibrated with speed around a gigantic creature, its body shrouded in darkness. Only the metallic gleam of its daggers hinted at their danger and lethality. With an ethereal cape flourish, it disappeared as quickly as it had come.

A third feminine emergence took its place. Running at full speed, she shot arrows from her bow with deadly accuracy at her enemies. A dog at her side leaped for the throat of one of them as she energetically pursued her destiny, slicing through the air.

"It's us!" Lucine whispered in awe. With bated breath, the young druidess couldn't take her eyes off the iridescent and evanescent silhouettes in the dim light created by the blaze.

Her promise to move forward. To become someone. One day, she would be that accomplished huntress, that strong and courageous person. Her eyes welled up at the vision of hope.

She met Talyvien's hazel eyes, and he returned her smile. She felt immense gratitude toward him. Toward the person he was. Toward what he had done for her.

But she was surprised to see the heart-wrenching melancholy on Shael's face. An acute discomfort crossed her feline eyes as she scrutinized the apparitions. Despite seeming ordinarily so confident and strong.

The intertwined notes and Calixte's voice became more uplifting, and the four silhouettes appeared together: Lucine at the forefront, releasing an arrow; the dog Katao leaping onto an enemy as a powerful swing of Talyvien's sword cut through another; Shael gracefully gliding, her daggers swirling around her. They all pursued a massive flying creature, whose impressive wingspan gradually swallowed the depiction in powerful beats.

The tableau slowly evaporated. Magic particles mingled with the embers rising from the flames. The melody dramatically faded, adding to the theatricality of the moment. Their forehead damp with sweat, Calixte finished the piece with a grand gesture on the hurdy-gurdy.

Lucine threw herself into their arms, her sobs catching in her throat.

"Thank you, it's the most beautiful gift I've ever received!"

The teary-eyed young druidess met the playful teasing on the bard's face. They reciprocated her hug affectionally.

"Pleasure is all mine, my dear," they said, placing a hand on Lucine's back as she buried her head in their shoulder.

"I must admit, it was . . . not bad," Talyvien finally conceded.

Calixte's orange eyes stared at him with surprise. "By the great city of Alar, where has the Paladin of Callystrande gone? What have you done with him?" they taunted, gently disengaging from Lucine's embrace.

 Laughter resounded around her.

Shael maintained a neutral face, her attention focused on the flames dancing and crackling in front of her. Did she really belong to a group like this?

Preferring the comfortable call of solitude, she couldn't decide if she liked the thought. Bitterness spread in her throat at the idea of her independence being questioned, at the idea of having to form attachments. What would happen once they reached Dawnelest? She would have to resume her life where she left off, follow Sazaelith's teachings, and dispense her justice.

She felt she had already gone too far. She should have cut it off. She cursed the vulnerability she had shown to the paladin during their duel. He had seen it; he had understood. She knew it. Her little trick couldn't be enough to divert attention this time. Why was she still here?

"Oh, I know!" exclaimed Lucine, still clinging to Calixte. "You could sing the song you played at the Inn of Luminaur! The last one, the one you played on the enormous instrument!"

"Ah, the theorbo!" they understood, a mischievous smile appearing at the corner of their lips. They stood up and walked toward their horse, retrieving the body of the theorbo from one of the saddlebags.

"I'm not sure if it's a good idea," Talyvien hesitated, looking particularly worried, almost pleading.

Which song were they talking about?

"No Ignescent this time. I promised you," Calixte replied calmly, their eyes still holding a hint of mockery.

The bard positioned the theorbo's body on their lap, and a familiar bluish glow enveloped their hands. The Flow recreated the missing neck and strings of the instrument, forming a magnificent tool that produced a variety of phenomenal notes. The fourteen vaporous strings vibrated with a harmonious resonance under Calixte's skilled fingers.

"Our bodies entwine in this cosmic affair,
Your skin's golden hue, my soul's bluish reign,
In this fleeting passion, a dance without compare,
As my found eyes blend with your tears, untamed."

The music reverberated into the darkness. And rage flooded Shael's heart.

 Released this time from intrusive visions, Talyvien focused on the lyrics of the melody that Calixte sang in their deep voice before them, their citrine eyes closed and their hands gently strumming the theorbo.

The image of blue hands on his shimmering skin surged in his mind. The memory of the exhilaration he had felt during the vision at the Luminaur Inn disturbed Talyvien. The paladin's thoughts turned to the assassin, whose expression was hardening, and trembling fists clenched on her knees. Shael's feline eyes remained locked on the blaze before her, her face consumed by disdain and disgust as Calixte's words flowed through the cool night air.

A few minutes passed, and the final notes gradually evaporated from the instrument. The ensuing silence wrapped the camp in a peculiar emotion.

"It's magnificent, Calixte," murmured Lucine, who had laid down on the grass to enjoy the performance. "What does it exactly tell?"

With signs of fatigue from using so much magic evident on their face, the bard slowly opened their eyes and cast a tender amber gaze upon the young druidess. "It's the love story of Callystrande and Sazaelith," they uttered with a sigh.

Shael's tawny eyes burned into Calixte's face, consumed by fury. "Don't blaspheme, *Alaris!*" she snapped, irritated, before spitting with disgust into the flames.

"Yet it is the plain truth, Shael," Calixte calmly replied.

A dagger lodged itself in the grass at the bard's feet. A gust of wind made the campfire flicker. And now, the assassin stood before them, her body tense with blazing rage.

"I know humans, especially the disciples of the goddesses, don't like hearing this, but it's true," Calixte continued, their stare defiantly meeting the assassin's with composure.

"I despise everything associated with Callystrande, and you won't make me believe that my goddess could have loved that pitiful wretch!" Shael vociferated. The venom in her words was reflected in the dagger now pressed against Calixte's throat.

"You're quick to draw your dagger, Shael, but you're not the only one who can wield magic," Calixte threatened in a grave tone, a warning in their voice.

The reflection of the campfire flames cast a scarlet gleam in the Alaris's irises. Petrified, Lucine helplessly watched the altercation playing out before her.

The paladin stood up and placed a hand on Shael's shoulder. "That's enough," he firmly stated, choosing to ignore the insult she had just spat toward Callystrande.

"Don't touch me!" Shael retorted, electrified by his touch. The dagger quickly dissipated in her hand. The assassin swiftly fled into the darkness, agilely heading toward the surrounding woods.

"I'm sorry, I didn't know it could . . ." stammered Lucine, panicked, as she watched the assassin disappear into the obscurity.

"It's alright. It's not the first time it's happened," Calixte said, rubbing their throat and trying to erase the sensation of cold metal against their warm palm.

Talyvien had to know. His curiosity prevailed. "Is it true?" he asked.

"Yes. I wouldn't lie about such . . . thorny matters," Calixte replied. The Flow dissipated from the theorbo, and they placed the instrument on the ground. "They even had a child together. Teluar. The god of Nature."

"Why have we never heard of this?" he inquired.

"By 'we,' do you mean the disciples? The humans?"

Talyvien nodded, his face still stern, concealing the chaotic thoughts swirling in his mind.

"Because humans prefer to divide what is different, because it happened before they even existed. Because the Alaris know these things. We live for centuries, we have witnessed much," Calixte calmly resumed.

Only the crackling embers broke the silence that followed. Gold and silver eyes turned to look at Talyvien, with Lucine still visibly concerned.

How was this possible? Why had he never heard of it?

Was that why he felt such surprising ambivalence toward the assassin? Was that why their destinies seemed strangely interwoven?

Being a druid, did Lucine have any connection to Teluar? Was that why golden tears had streamed from her eye? Was that why he wanted to protect her?

"We should go to sleep," was the only response Talyvien could muster.

38

 Shael found refuge among the indifference of the trees and let loose the fury that flowed in her veins. Her daggers whirled and crashed into the surrounding trunks. How could this be true?

Throughout her life, the teachings of the priestesses of Sazaelith had been to despise the magic of Callystrande. The goddess of light was diametrically opposed to the darkness of Sazaelith. It made no sense. The idea of having to dilute her independence had already shaken Shael, and she couldn't bring herself to accept what the Alaris had stated as truth. Was the Mother Superior aware of this rumor?

Her hearing sharpened by the blessing of her goddess, the assassin heard a slight crack of twigs sound in her ear.

"If you've come to talk to me about this grotesque rumor, you can leave, *paladin*," Shael spat.

"No . . . It's me . . ."

The assassin turned toward the voice.

Lucine stood there, embarrassed, holding her arms. "Can we talk?" the young druidess asked.

Shael nodded slightly and went to sit on a huge rock that lay in the middle of the woods. Lucine did the same beside her, and both wrapped themselves in the anonymity that the shadows provided.

"I'm sorry," Lucine began. "I shouldn't have asked Calixte to play that melody."

"You couldn't have known." Shael sighed, trying to soften her features in the face of the young woman's remorse. "I don't blame you."

"May I ask . . . why would it be problematic?" Lucine inquired, carefully weighing each word.

This question punched Shael in the gut. *Wasn't it obvious?* "Because Callystrande and Sazaelith are opposing goddesses!" she exclaimed. "It's not logical! How can such a grotesque rumor persist?"

"Is that the only reason?" Lucine asked delicately. "I know I don't understand much. Indeed, a few weeks ago, I didn't even know the names of the goddesses. But wouldn't it be logical that without light, darkness cannot exist?"

"Where are you going with this?!" Shael, now openly annoyed, looked at the young woman with disdain for her ignorance.

"If one cannot exist without the other, wouldn't it make sense for them to eventually love each other?" Lucine's words faded into the velvet of her voice as she looked up at the starry sky.

Shael didn't know how to respond to that, struck by Lucine's innocence. Was she stupid? Too idealistic? Did she not realize the state of the world around them?

"Perhaps that's why you felt your goddess prevent you from assassinating a chosen one of Callystrande?" Lucine added.

This question hit Shael more than she could admit. The disdain she felt for the young woman faded. Was it Sazaelith or was it herself who couldn't deliver the blow?

"I—I don't know," Shael finally admitted.

"Calixte also mentioned that they had a son. Teluar, the god of Nature."

"Ah, that would be the best, considering what Sazaelith demands of her followers!" jeered Shael. Seeing Lucine's surprised and intrigued look, she continued resignedly. "Receiving the blessing of the goddess of shadow renders one sterile."

"Oh . . . I'm sorry, Shael."

"No, don't be. Even knowing that, I would make the same choice again."

"The desire to contribute in ways other than giving life?"

The assassin nodded briefly. "I learned early on what it was like to be unwanted. No child should experience that."

A saddened look graced Lucine's face as she gave a slight affirmative gesture. "I realize I don't even know your last name," the young druidess said.

"Ymdaral. But I don't like being associated with that name. Being tied to the person who gave it to me," the assassin asserted.

A few seconds dissolved in silence.

Lucine pulled her knees to her chest and sighed. "I don't know what happened to you, Shael, but all I see is a strong and independent woman who knows how to fight damn well!" A big smile crossed her face as she offered it to the assassin.

"Yes . . . that's all you see," Shael whispered, her tone trapped in a certain melancholy.

Shael's soul was tormented by the intensity of the questions that were clearly swirling in Lucine's mind. The assassin couldn't tell her more. But bound by a shared questioning, she couldn't pretend either. Not to her.

"I would like to be like that someday," Lucine continued, seeking Shael's approval.

"No, you wouldn't. Believe me."

The young druidess didn't know how to respond to that, and she lowered her head. It was better that way. That she didn't know what the price was. "Does it have something to do with why you don't sleep with us, neither at the inn nor around the campfire?" Lucine finally inquired.

"I—I have nightmares . . ."

"Oh. I understand the irony of the blue blood now! It would calm them if your blood had an effect on you, wouldn't it?"

A slight sardonic smirk appeared on Shael's face. She stretched out on the gray stone and placed her hands behind her head. She appreciated the comforting sight of the full moon, as if Sazaelith was blessing this moment with her sarcasm.

"Do you truly hate Callystrande and her chosen ones?" Lucine asked, with tender caution.

"I don't believe it's really difficult to understand that their crusade is nothing but a mass of fanatic paladins who destroy everything in their path," Shael replied sharply.

"I know the crusade has caused a lot of harm, claimed many victims, but I don't believe Callystrande is to blame," Lucine said courageously. "A friend once told me that it's the perversity and greed of human beings who use the gods for their own ends that should be condemned. But that doesn't mean they're all like that either."

"And what about the stake burnings! Do you have such a short memory to not realize what you've escaped from!" Shael objected, annoyed by Lucine's calmness.

"One of them actually saved me!" Lucine cried, with severity.

In response, Shael scoffed at the young druidess's naivety.

"Is it Talyvien that you hate then? Is that why you can't admit that the goddesses might love each other?"

The questions cracked like whips in Shael's ears. It was now the assassin's turn to not know what to answer.

Yes, she hated him.

But it wouldn't be fair to answer in the affirmative to that question. She hated what he stirred within her. She hated knowing he was by her side, in "this group" they all formed now, united in a common purpose. And from which she mysteriously couldn't break free.

But was it so mysterious? Or was she just cowardly for admitting what she had sensed from the beginning? Just cowardly for admitting that if the rumor was true, she could no longer hide behind the dark wings of her goddess to find an excuse for the conflicting feelings she harbored. The thought chilled her blood.

"You know, not all men are monsters, Shael."

Had Lucine managed to decipher her to that extent? With a tight throat, the assassin lost her focus on the silver orb, her goddess's symbol. A refuge to her panic.

"I've had plenty of examples to the contrary," Shael finally said, her features involuntarily contorting.

"You've also had plenty of counterexamples. But you choose not to see them," Lucine replied firmly.

Those last words struck Shael. The hardness in her voice caught her off guard. Lucine apparently wasn't as naive as she seemed.

"You can't stay in hatred forever, no matter what happened to you," Lucine continued unfalteringly. "But if you ever want to talk about it, I'm here."

Lucine watched as Shael remained lying on the stone, her gaze a painful fury on her hardened face. A silent cloak enveloped the moment, disturbed only by the rustling of leaves.

Chaotic thoughts crashed in the assassin's mind, reducing her to silence. Who was she truly? What was her story?

Lucine hadn't been able to imagine that another version of the seemingly confident young woman could exist in the darkness. A version that had suffered and had to protect herself at all costs. She then remembered Calixte's words.

"There's a very fine line between learning enough to protect oneself from dangers and having the capacity to hope that there is still fundamentally good in others. Many people drown in their pain and are no longer able to trust."

Lucine had admired the assassin so much. She had envied her independence and strength. Now she realized that Shael also suffered the consequences. That always being unattainable, never revealing anything had a price. That not allowing any vulnerability to be expressed had a cost.

That her suffering and hatred were consuming her. Devouring her from within.

What irony. Lucine had despised the ignorance and overprotection in which she had been immersed, shielded from everything in the Astral Forest. And now she realized that no path was perfect. That resilience lay in healing one's own journey. In discovering one's own destiny. In adjusting one's own heart.

However, Shael seemed to have revealed everything she was willing to that evening. So Lucine stood up from the rock and offered one last smile toward the assassin. "It's getting late, goodnight, Shael," she murmured tenderly.

As she began to walk out of the woods, a voice emanated among the trees. "Lucine!"

The young woman turned around to see the dark silhouette of the assassin, now standing on the rock.

"Thank you for trying," Shael muttered.

With the smile still etched on her lips, Lucine nodded in gratitude and returned to the camp, leaving the assassin alone in the darkness, grappling with her doubts.

39

Day after day, Talyvien often found himself thinking about the emotions he had seen in the assassin's eyes during their demonstration and her desperate gesture. Fragments of the conversation between Lucine and Shael in the woods had also reached his ears. Surprised and concerned that he hadn't been called for his night watch shift, he had gone in search of the druidess and overheard their exchange. His curiosity had then overcome his shame, and he had remained immobilized in the shadows, listening to their conversation. But still remorseful for his actions and as a form of punishment, the young man was now even more plagued by unanswered questions about Shael.

He suspected that part of the answer probably lay in the assassin's past. In her nightmares. What had happened to her? He cursed his stupid curiosity. His stupid paladin's heart that wanted to protect. Wanted to save.

Calixte's amber eyes flared at him. He turned his head and saw the bard's caustic glance.

As they galloped on, Lucine and Shael in the lead, the paladin realized that he had been staring at the assassin's back for a while, lost in his thoughts. He hated that these questions took precedence in his mind, instead of focusing on their mission.

"Intriguing, isn't she?" purred Calixte, raising an eyebrow.

What was their business with it?

Talyvien responded with a slight grunt and a shrug. He put on a disdainful air and urged his horse forward, pressing on the reins to make it go faster.

After several hours of galloping at a frantic pace, the four companions, exhausted and numb, decided to take a short break for lunch when the midday sun proudly shone in the blue sky.

Calixte and Lucine sat on a large tree stump by the trail and began to eat their rations. Katao joined them, happily yapping for his share. While they ate, the bard conjured various illusions to illustrate their conversation, much to the amusement of the young druidess.

Shael took out two apples from one of the pouches hanging from her black steed and gave one to the animal. Then, she sliced the second one with a freshly appeared dagger in one of her hands.

Talyvien preferred to isolate himself a bit to consume his meal. Uncomfortable and confused, he always avoided any conversation with the assassin but still made an effort to remain cordial during Lucine's training sessions. However, he also refrained from engaging with the discomfort that the Alaris magic caused him.

Lucine was enjoying the calm of the forest and a well-deserved break. She joyfully listened to Calixte's playful remarks and savored the meal they had brought along.

The untouched piece of apple fell from the assassin's hand. Her dagger began to tremble between her fingers.

The anguish that crossed Shael's face froze her body. Clearly stunned, she managed to turn around with extreme heaviness in her movements. She scanned the section of the trail they had yet to take.

Lucine realized that Sazaelith's blessing sharpened Shael's senses more than usual, revealing to her what ordinary mortals couldn't hear, smell, or see.

Katao also started barking and growling.

"Shael? What's happening?" the young druidess pressed.

Calixte paused at the gravity in Lucine's tone and the look on Shael's face.

"A smell . . . of burning . . . of death . . ." Shael whispered.

The echo of the assassin's words froze time. Lucine didn't want to believe what she had heard.

A specter ran through Talyvien's body. His eyes wide, he abruptly stopped chewing. A deluge of memories seemed to project into his mind. Without wasting any time, the paladin swiftly and agilely mounted Aho. He dashed off in the direction pointed out by the assassin.

"Taly! Wait!" Lucine shouted.

Everyone quickly got back on their horses and tried their best to follow Talyvien, who sped along the trail.

Lucine rushed after her friend's silhouette and struggled to keep up with the sound of the gray horse's hooves bouncing between the trees. Shael and Calixte were by her side as well. Terror was written on their faces.

With a heavy heart at Talyvien's distress, Lucine prayed that the assassin had been mistaken. Her hands tightened around Maia's reins. The cruelty of the High Priestess assailed her mind. The scent described by Shael began to reach her nostrils. Death. Blood. Ashes. Smells that were now all too familiar.

No. It couldn't be. Not again.

Maia soared above the dirt path. The rhythm of her gallop resonated in the young druidess's chest.

Thick black smoke expanded above the canopy. Lucine felt nauseous. A pronounced bitterness flooded her mouth.

Finally, they caught up with Talyvien, who had stopped at the edge of the forest, his body paralyzed by his discovery.

The skeleton of an ancient village, composed of charred ruins, appeared before them. Dozens of human bodies lay on the ground, mixed with long trails of blood and thorny vines, from which occasional wisps of smoke escaped. An unspeakable tragedy except for the one word that surfaced in Lucine's brain.

Hell.

Their breath caught, and they all remained frozen for a moment on their horses, contemplating the unbelievable scene that lay before them.

Calixte was the first to snap out of their stupor. They dismounted and slowly approached the nightmarish sight. They knelt beside some human remains, mutilated and contorted with an almost supernatural violence, trying to examine what had happened. Some bodies appeared to have been slashed and dismembered, some charred, while others seemed to have been attacked by various animals.

Lucine, Talyvien, and Shael also dismounted, their faces frowned by the cruelty and suffering that seemed to sprawl out with panache at their feet.

"The crusade?" Shael asked, in a neutral voice.

"No," Calixte replied briefly, with a severity not typical of them.

Lucine, overcome by dizziness and intrusive memories, staggered among the bodies, trying to find meaning, any justification. And then she saw them.

Several wooden figures stood before her, immortalized in their moment of terror.

She faltered and nearly collapsed to the ground. Talyvien caught her just in time by the waist.

"This—This is what attacked my village, my clan," she murmured.

The paladin's gaze rested compassionately on her face.

The assassin, one hand over her mouth to mask the disgust she felt, moved with agility among the bodies and ruins, searching for any clue that could shed light on what had happened in this village.

Shael surveyed the still-smoldering debris of the nearby houses. A merciless tomb for the wretched souls. Their freshly spilled blood stained the ground and walls with a heart-wrenching shade of vivid red. From this, she deduced that they must have perished recently. She pushed aside the remnants of a door, its hinges letting out a horrifying creak, and a haunting sight revealed itself to her.

"Hey! You need to see this!" the assassin shouted, calling her companions over.

The body of a man, untouched by the flames but with a face seemingly covered in brambles, leaves, and flowers, lay at their feet.

Calixte knelt down to examine the corpse more closely, their features collected in a stern manner. "It seems that the brambles grew . . . directly from the man's orifices and suffocated him," they finally said resignedly.

"I've never seen any magic like this," the paladin remarked, his eyes fixed on the distorted face of the man at their feet.

Despite having witnessed numerous assassinations, Shael had to admit that she had also never seen an execution quite like this before.

Talyvien turned to Lucine and placed a hand on her arm, a gesture of compassion and encouragement. "Have you ever seen something similar?" he asked.

"No. Not like this. But the rest is . . . somewhat comparable," Lucine replied. The young druidess seemed to feel a wave of nausea and stepped out of the smoldering ruins of the house to regain her composure. Her complexion dangerously paled.

Shael then noticed the body of a woman at Lucine's feet, her torso covered in scratches and bites as if it had been split in two by the power of a massive animal.

"That's different too," Lucine muttered, bringing a hand to her mouth.

"Whatever or whoever is responsible seems to be growing in power," Calixte solemnly added.

"Do you remember anything that could give us a lead?" Talyvien asked gently.

"Maybe. I remember seeing strange feminine silhouettes covered in bark approaching. I think they were the ones turning people into wood. There was also someone on a huge flying creature . . . who kidnapped my brother, Solehan," Lucine stammered, under the intrigued gaze of her companions. She ran a shaking hand across her forehead.

Magic. A presence of ancient and powerful forces itched at Shael's senses and tormented her connection with Sazaelith. A repulsion ran through her blue-blooded veins. "Just looking at this carnage makes it clear that something supernatural has occurred here," Shael affirmed.

A rustling sound came from the bushes. With a skillful flick of her cloak, the assassin threw a formidable dagger soaring through the tall grass.

A faint moan was heard.

The scraping of another dagger brushed against the assassin's hand.

The paladin's sword mimicked the sound on its sheath.

 A small female silhouette made of bark, branches, and twigs materialized before their eyes, trapped by the blade that had lodged in a tree trunk through her wrist.

"Like this, you mean?" Shael grinned.

Instinctively, Lucine shielded her face with her hands.

Talyvien swiftly positioned his body between the creature and Lucine. But no lignification occurred.

Surprised by the lack of reaction and at finally encountering one of the infamous creatures, Lucine leaned to the side of the paladin's body. She carefully examined the wooden figure, noting that her skin appeared greener and more moss-covered than that of the supernatural beings engraved into her memories. Small leaves sprouted here and there from the branches that composed certain parts of her body.

So similar, yet so different. Something was amiss. That's when she noticed it. The twisted symbol she had seen in her vision at the foot of the magnificent tree during her hallucinations was carved on the wooden figure's chest.

Lucine couldn't believe her eyes. An answer to her questions. Finally.

Mischievousness emanated from Shael's body language as she approached, ready to confront, her dagger drawn, followed closely by Talyvien, his sword firmly grasped in his hand.

In a flash, Lucine stepped in between and shielded the creature with her own body.

Startled, Shael and Talyvien halted their desire for justice and came to a sudden stop.

"Lucine, if what you say is true, we must eliminate her before she has the opportunity to transform anyone else!" Talyvien exclaimed.

"No, this might be my only chance to learn what happened to my brother," Lucine retorted. "The symbol engraved on her chest is the same one I saw in my dreams!"

"Lucine . . ." the paladin hesitated, lowering his sword. "You can't rely on a hallucination. You know I'm on your side, but—"

The paladin couldn't finish his sentence. Calixte interposed themselves between them. "Let her do it, Talyvien. She knows what she's doing," insisted the bard in a firm tone that unsettled the paladin.

An expression of deep gratitude crossed the face of the young druidess as she offered it to the bard. She then turned back toward the wooden figure.

Lucine gently removed the dagger from her wrist and knelt beside the creature. She exchanged a curious glance with the strangely black eyes surrounded by bark of the supernatural being, which seemed rather frightened and showed no signs of hostility toward her.

A few moments later, the silhouette stood up and walked toward the dense part of the forest behind them, under Lucine's watchful eye. She eventually stopped after a few steps and turned around. Her ebony eyes seemed to be waiting for a response.

"I think she wants us to follow," Lucine concluded. "She seems to want to show us something!"

"We can't afford to do that. We need to go to Dawnelest!" Shael retorted vehemently.

Talyvien's icy gaze landed on the assassin. "I know it's important to you," he said to Lucine, "but if these creatures are capable of such carnage, we'll likely need an army to deal with them. Following this one could be dangerous," he corrected, with affection for the young druidess.

"It could also be a trap," added Shael, still under the paladin's disapproving stare.

Lucine found herself admiring the small silhouette and was surprised by the contrast that formed in her mind—with the images of the cruel wooden creatures advancing mercilessly on her people, killing every member of her clan and freezing them in grotesque and pathetic poses.

None of it made sense anymore, but she needed to know. An undeniable feeling churned in her gut. This symbol was too specific to be a mere coincidence. She was convinced that she had to follow the creature to find the answers she sought.

"Maybe we could split up!" Calixte suggested.

Lucine turned her head toward the bard with surprise.

"After all, Talyvien and Shael, you can go to Dawnelest to seek the queen's aid, while Lucine and I follow this creature to see if this symbol indeed leads to something. I'm not sure how long it will take, but once done, we can always meet up in the capital at a tavern or elsewhere!" they explained. "That way, we won't waste time!"

"That's out of the question!" the paladin retorted. "I won't leave Lucine alone here to follow who knows what creature!"

"But I won't be alone, Taly. Calixte will be with me, and you've seen what they're capable of," Lucine replied determinedly.

"I—I swore to protect you, Lucine," Talyvien stammered.

The young druidess approached him and gently placed her hands on his shoulders. "And you have, Talyvien. I'll be forever grateful for that. But I need to know what happened to my brother and my clan, and I believe I have to follow this symbol. But I also know that what's happening with the crusade is important to you. You need to go to Dawnelest as soon as possible. I won't ask you to ignore that. Please don't ask me to ignore the opportunity that's presenting itself to me."

A look of resignation appeared on the paladin's face as he nodded.

Lucine gave Talyvien a slight smile and embraced him, her body enveloped by the massive silhouette of the young man. "Thank you, Taly, for everything," she said, her cheek pressed against his leather armor. "You never needed Callystrande's magic to be a paladin."

She felt Talyvien's hands tighten around her, his fingers slightly trembling.

"Take care of yourself," he whispered tenderly. "And Calixte! I'm counting on you to watch over her!"

"I promise you!" the bard responded solemnly, placing a hand over their chest. "But you know, you should give her more credit!" They winked at Lucine as she released herself from the paladin's embrace. "Well then! Since it's time for farewells, and I suspect that you will *evidently* sorely miss my music, I have a little gift!" Calixte exclaimed, slipping one of their hands into their pocket.

"What is it?" Lucine inquired.

The bard pulled out a beautifully carved wooden box, presenting it to Talyvien. From a distance, the young druidess examined the object with curious eyes. Why did she have a sense of déjà vu?

"I call it an 'ensorcinette'," they commented. "It's like a 'serinette', a kind of miniature pocket-sized organ, but enchanted by my own hands!"

"That's kind of you, Calixte, but I'm not sure—" the paladin began.

"Come now, take it. Just to make me happy!" they added, with a delightful pout. "It has the unique ability to adapt the melodies it plays to the emotions felt by its bearer. It might come in handy!"

"Personally, I'm not sure I want to hear the music it will play in the paladin's hands," Shael remarked, looking at Talyvien as he took hold of it.

Despite the horror she had just experienced, a faint smile graced Lucine's face. She almost felt guilty for leaving these two to travel together.

"Oh! There also happens to be a magnificent waterfall not far from here, along the road that leads to the capital," Calixte added. "Shael and you could stop there for the night. Who knows what might happen? Such an idyllic setting! With ambient music!"

"Calixte . . ." Talyvien growled.

"Yes, perhaps I could refresh his spirit underwater if he becomes too unbearable!" Shael boasted.

A perplexed look formed on Talyvien's face as he crossed his arms.

Calixte whistled in surprise before bursting into their charming laughter. "I was referring to the cave behind the waterfall, of course. I don't know why, but there always seem to be caves behind waterfalls!" the bard joked.

Less naive than she had been in the past, Lucine noticed the fear settling into Shael's posture despite her cutting words. Did the idea of traveling alone with Talyvien make her so uneasy?

After farewells that were meant to be short because they were too difficult, Lucine, Calixte, and Katao ventured into the thick forest near the remnants of the village and followed the small creature on foot, leading their horses by the reins.

The druidess looked back one last time at the fading silhouettes of the assassin and the paladin. Shael had mentioned the name of an inn in Dawnelest, the *Veil of Truth*, where they planned to stay so they could find each other in the vast capital. Lucine didn't know if she would truly find Shael there. The young woman seemed as elusive as a mirage.

But Lucine was grateful to Shael for the opportunity to see Talyvien again.

40

Although Wuruhi's absence still weighed on him, Solehan felt his heart finally less burdened to have avenged the wolf. To have made a choice. He couldn't be there to save his sister, but he promised himself never to passively tolerate the cruelty of humans again.

As usual, he wandered through the castle at dusk. He appreciated the silence and the solitude that emerged in the growing darkness. Perhaps he was becoming less human after all? By constantly transforming into an animal, maybe was he truly turning into a predator?

As he walked, he looked at his fingers. The young druid let out a slight growl. For certain things, he was still desperately human. The memory of Valnard's skin when he had caressed his cheek tormented him. Of his breath on his face. Of being so close to him.

As if in response to his stupid and shameful urges, the Alaris's voice slipped through the throne room door. Who could Valnard be talking to at this hour? Solehan wondered.

"Ah! My dear Naja! I suppose you're bringing me my usual delivery!"

"Of course, Master" whispered a hissing voice.

Master? Solehan had always thought that the Alaris never saw anyone except for the discreet presence of the forest spirits. The young druid felt strangely betrayed. Why hadn't Valnard let him know about this? He despised the hint of jealousy stirring in his gut.

"Perfect! So, tell me: what's the news?" Valnard's deep voice continued.

"It seems the goddesses have chosen to get involved."

"Hmm . . . always so sentimental, aren't they! All this for someone who can't do anything anyway. Nothing you can't handle, I suppose?"

"No, Master. Dealing with this little problem should be easy. But I must admit, I'm surprised they managed to take down the gang of thugs I sent to deal with them. It seems I'll have to step up my game! But you know how humans are. They never resist me for long!"

"You and your frivolous pastimes! Do what you want with them, but do it quickly. You know my priorities. Teluar's awakening is all that matters! And I won't tolerate any interference."

Who were they talking about? Overwhelmed by curiosity, Solehan swung the door open in a rushed motion. The wood slammed against the stone wall.

"Ah! If it is not the wolf dressed in sheep's clothing!" exclaimed Valnard.

Solehan didn't acknowledge the Alaris's joke, and his eagerness immediately faded. He swallowed with difficulty.

Before him stood a massive creature, half anthropomorphic. The lower half of its body, where legs should have been, was covered with a mixture of scales and bark, undulating like a serpent on the stone.

It approached the young druid, sinuously swaying, and stared at him with its large golden reptilian eyes. Two long, sharpened fangs appeared as it opened its mouth, licking its silver tongue over its lips.

Stupefied, Solehan recoiled and pressed himself against the wall.

"*Come closer*," it said languorously.

The young man felt a vice tightening around his brain, a grip dripping with ancient magic that forced his steps toward the creature. He tried to resist the command of the voice, but his legs began to move against his will.

"Not him, Naja," Valnard intervened. "He's under my protection."

Naja's magic released its grip on Solehan's body. The druid let out a long, ragged sigh and retreated against the door once again. Where did this strange creature come from?

"Of course, Master. What a pity! He looks so appetizing. His blood has a particular scent."

"That's not the point," grumbled the Alaris. "You may leave, Naja."

The creature moved away from the young druid and performed a deep bow to Valnard. "I understand why you want to keep him for yourself, Master," it sneered.

"He's the chosen one of Teluar," Valnard hurriedly explained, although Solehan could detect a slight unease on the Alaris's face.

"Oh! Interesting . . ." The creature eyed Solehan from head to toe.

"Are you done now?" Valnard scowled. "You may leave if you have nothing else to add."

The coldness in Valnard's face diverted Naja's attention. It ceremoniously lowered its head and left the room through the same door Solehan had entered. It cast a final glance at the young druid and chuckled softly before disappearing.

"So, who was that? What?" grumbled the young man, raising his arm toward the door.

"Naja! One of my creations!" exclaimed Valnard with enthusiasm. "I believe humans call them Viperals."

"You mean . . . when you mentioned 'degenerate monsters' appearing since Teluar's hibernation, you were responsible for creating them?"

"Indeed!" Valnard asserted. "Some of them seem to possess unexpected and surprising powers! For instance, the echarvoras, who are half-human, half-spider, can study the psychological vulnerabilities of their victims and devise tailored traps! It's quite fascinating . . . Most of them can also assume a human appearance to blend in!"

"Why did you create them?"

"For one, because I needed something to occupy myself before your birth, my dear Solehan." He stepped forward and placed a hand on the young man's shoulder. "And secondly, because I find the irony delightful! Half-human, half-animal creatures seeking revenge against human cruelty!" Valnard laughed.

"Why didn't you tell me earlier?"

"Because you weren't ready. Everything in its time . . ." Valnard removed his hand from the young druid's shoulder and delicately placed it on his cheek.

The hairs on Solehan's arms stood on end. Shame flooded his thoughts. And the flames of desire danced in his belly.

"Come with me, I'll show you. And I have a little gift for you," Valnard said.

41

Tired and sore from their long horseback journey after galloping all day, Shael and Talyvien finally decided to stop for the night. They had spoken very little and had only exchanged brief conversations. Both were focused on their objective, which was to reach the capital that they now knew was close by.

Talyvien, still with a heavy heart for leaving Lucine in the care of Calixte, constantly prayed to Callystrande that nothing would happen to her. He was surprised by the affection he had developed for the young druidess in recent weeks, ever since he had saved her from the crusade's pyre. Perhaps that was also the reason for his discomfort. Without anyone to protect or defend, was he still a paladin?

He glanced at Shael, with her dark leather armor, magic, and sharp, formidable weapons. She didn't seem to need protection, nor did she want it. He had managed to avoid the assassin as best as he could, except during Lucine's training, since he had learned what she had done to the man at the village of Luminaur. He couldn't forgive her for her actions.

But the fleeting vulnerability he had seen in her eyes still tormented him. The pain that had crossed her face. The memory of their conversations and Shael's sapphire eyes on him. Talyvien sighed, rubbing his face after dismounting his horse.

He couldn't lie to himself any longer. That wasn't the main reason for his avoidance. He needed to focus on their mission.

In his confusion, Selena's face also came to his mind. He knew he would have to face her memory to warn her of the crusade's wrongdoing and the High Priestess Piore, in order to save both kingdoms.

He also hoped to learn more about the rumor of the city of Argentvale so that he could share what they had witnessed in the village they had just passed.

In their haste, Talyvien hadn't had time to restore dignity to the unfortunate souls, and the vision of the bodies arranged in that way still haunted him. Even though it was the injustice of war, as he knew it.

 The assassin enjoyed traveling in silence and with limited company, even though the paladin's avoidance seemed to raise some questions within her. Was it because of the assassination she had committed in the village of Luminaur? She had been satisfied with having minimal interactions with him during their journey but hated having her pride so blatantly crushed.

Concealed beneath her hood, Shael observed the paladin as he fed some fruit to his horse. Why did it bother her so much? It shouldn't matter at all. Soon, she would join the convent of the sisters of Sazaelith and slip back into the comfort of her former life. She just needed to unravel the mystery surrounding this strange contract and its connection to the Order of Paladins of Callystrande.

But the conversation she'd had with the young druidess kept returning to her memory, and questions surfaced in her thoughts.

Did she truly hate Talyvien? Or did she hate what he represented? What he made her feel? Was the rumor about their goddesses true?

As they stopped to establish their camp, a feeling of dread ran down her spine. How would she hide the horror that invaded her nightmares now that they were alone together?

Recalling Calixte's words, they set out in search of the waterfall and the hidden cave that could shelter them for the night. They followed the distant splashing sounds and arrived at an absolutely magnificent sight. The bard had not lied to them.

The grand shimmering waterfall poured down for several hundred meters. The waters of this prodigious cascade scattered in perfect circles into a hidden lake amid the woods. The moist and lush atmosphere of the place gave the impression that large strands of white silk lazily unfurled across the expanse of water. A small, ruined structure concealed by entangled vegetation overlooked the waterfall on either side, and its anarchic silhouette stood out against the twilight sky.

Shael then spotted a small trail in the rock that seemed to wind behind the falls.

"Calixte was right. The place is magnificent," Talyvien declared, looking up with admiration.

The assassin, though impressed, feigned indifference. It wasn't the time to be melancholic. Or worse—Romantic.

"There seems to be a path that probably leads to the cave," she pointed out, indicating with her finger. "If the bard's words are correct. We should leave the horses here and continue on foot. We'll be safer inside."

The paladin nodded in agreement, and they tied their mounts to nearby trees. They took some provisions with them and began walking along the steep trail. But as they progressed, the overwhelming silence that had accompanied them throughout the day grew heavy again, like a weighted mantle on their shoulders. The palpable unease became their third companion, and both of them dissected the splendid landscape that was gradually consumed by darkness with feigned attention.

Finally, tired of the awkwardness, Talyvien broke the tension first.

"I'm starting to think I miss Calixte's music," he said, evidently trying to inject some levity into the moment.

A crack formed in the dam Shael had built around her mind. Her suppressed pride and frustration poured out involuntarily along with her fatigue.

"How charming," she replied curtly. "Is His Holiness, the great paladin of Callystrande, not enjoying my presence? You always have the . . . 'ensorcinette' to fall back on if you miss their music so much anyway!"

Talyvien sighed with annoyance but didn't respond. After a few more seconds, he seemingly chose to change the subject. "You know, Shael, I've been thinking about it for a while now, and I believe fate, or perhaps the goddesses, placed Lucine on our path to protect her. I think she has an important role to play. And so do we," he said earnestly.

"Not everyone wants to be constantly protected, paladin. She made that abundantly clear to you!"

"She needed to discover this part of her story on her own," he continued in all seriousness. "But I know she'll join us in Dawnelest."

"You sound so confident," Shael sneered. "You know, she might just go her own way! Not all women dream of being rescued constantly!"

Talyvien kept walking but seemed hesitant to add something. He cracked his knuckles. And finally, he yielded. "Sure, it's so much better to assassinate people, isn't it, Shael? Like in Luminaur, right?"

"There we go again!" she grumbled. "Listen, I know our viewpoints differ, but your beliefs won't change mine. I obey my goddess."

"Oh really? Does she command you to kill everything that moves?!" he growled. "Why am I even surprised? I had a contract on my head, after all!" Talyvien was seething now.

Shael was surprised to see that the paladin's frustration seemed to have opened a door within him as well. It was an overflow of pent-up emotions. For the first time in weeks, they couldn't avoid each other. They couldn't avoid the conversation that awaited them.

So, Shael did the only thing she knew how to do. "Technically, the contract is still valid," she whispered, blinking her eyes emphatically.

"Is that a threat?" he retorted, his face severe, one eyebrow arched like a bow.

When she saw him stop and place one hand on his sword, her stomach clenched. She had already answered that question weeks ago. Her goddess and her soul couldn't bring themselves to take the paladin's life.

She panicked. "You have a weakness for Queen Selena, don't you?" she blurted out with a cutting tone, the wild aspect of her face revealing the predation she was capable of. "Perhaps even a past history?"

A low blow. It was the best she could come up with.

"What does it matter to you?" he replied, unable to hide the surprise in his eyes.

"So, it is true," she declared proudly. Her heart was scratched. She hated that. She hated what it meant.

"That's not the point," he insisted.

"Are you going to Dawnelest to seek her help, or to rekindle things with her now that you're no longer a paladin? After all, you're no longer bound by your vow of celibacy."

"Are you jealous now?" the paladin grinned.

"And why would I be?" she growled through clenched teeth.

A flicker of disappointment cracked Talyvien's face.

The assassin was surprised, but she didn't show it.

"And why does it matter to you?" he pressed.

"It matters to me because I need to know if we're really going to investigate what's happening with the crusade and the contract, or if you're going there to fool around. In the latter case, maybe we'd better part ways! I'll be more effective on my own," Shael exclaimed triumphantly, placing her fists on her hips.

"Oh, so effective, Shael! So alone, yes! You never accept help from anyone, hate anything that questions your little beliefs, anything that might make you feel affection for someone," Talyvien retorted, rage intertwining with sorrow in his voice.

"How dare you? You know nothing about what I've been through!" Shael immediately regretted those words as soon as they escaped her throat.

"Then tell me!" the paladin shouted, placing his hands on Shael's arms and shaking her slightly.

Panic consumed the assassin completely. What were they even talking about now?

To his utmost surprise, the assassin placed a finger on Talyvien's lips. She commanded him to be quiet. Was she being so childish?

"Really, Shael! Is that the best you could come up wi—?" he began vehemently.

But the expression that struck Shael's face strangled the rest of his words. Talyvien realized they were now behind the translucent curtain of the impressive waterfall.

They both turned their heads simultaneously to discover, instead of a cave, a monumental stone door nestled in the cliff. Shimmering arabesques were sculpted on its smooth surface. Several rock blocks were stacked into a substantial arch framing the massive entrance, cleverly hidden behind the rapids. Large roots wrapped around the facade of this surprising, improvised, and naturally carved structure.

Talyvien then noticed that the huge stone door had recently been left ajar. A gentle breeze escaped from it. He listened intently and finally understood the urgency written on Shael's face.

Voices were emanating from the opening.

They cautiously ventured forth to uncover the source of those murmurs. Carved into the rock, several steps of a long staircase unfolded and descended into the depths as they passed through the opening. Talyvien struggled to match the lightness of his steps with Shael's velvet ones ahead of him.

As they descended into the bowels of the earth, a cluster of surprising luminescent mushrooms guided their uncertain steps on either side of the path. Their blue and violet hues cast dancing shadows of Shael and Talyvien on the rock. Like a brush that sprayed increasingly more droplets of luminous paint onto a desaturated canvas, this strange fungal flora enveloped their progress.

The passage opened up into a large expanse, revealing a gigantic cave. The voices Talyvien now recognized as masculine echoed against the walls.

A powerful beam of light from the ceiling outlined the silhouette of a curious promontory, atop which several long rocks were engraved with motifs and symbols in a circular arrangement. Sparse plants and foliage dotted the place with touches of green and surrounded a solitary tree that seemed to stand in the middle of this cocoon of raw rock. An emerald in a stone setting.

The paladin followed the assassin, and they took cover behind one of the imposing rocks. Perplexed, they spied on the disconcerting exchange happening on the natural stage, under the watchful eye of the tree.

Two men faced each other around a gray stone altar, upon which lay the corpse of a third man. Both wore strange tunics made of long woven dead leaves and appeared to be of similar robust build. When one of them tucked a strand of his long snow-white and obsidian hair behind a perfectly pointed ear, Talyvien's blood ran cold. An Alaris. They would have to be cautious. And discreet.

The paladin locked eyes with the assassin. She, too, seemed to have noticed this dangerous detail.

With a confident sweep of his arm, Valnard illuminated the various candles scattered throughout the area using the Ignescent. The red and voracious glow of his magic projected onto the surrounding stones, devouring the cold ambiance of the cave. The contrasting silhouettes of the two men danced on the engravings of the rocks.

Silently, Solehan observed the macabre scene taking shape. What was this strange ritual? He looked up at the tree above them, its branches greedily embracing the pouring light in the cave. A few talismans and wooden wind chimes hung lazily, producing a languid melody. His gaze then fell upon the emaciated corpse lying on the makeshift altar amid the flickering candlelight.

Questions formed in his mind when he heard footsteps scraping against the rock behind them. The young druid turned around and saw one of the lychenas approaching, carrying a peculiar package—the hide of Wuruhi.

"I thought that . . . if I'm going to show you this little demonstration, I'll also help you seek revenge," Valnard explained. "I know he was important to you. No animal should suffer such a fate."

Valnard placed a compassionate hand on Solehan's shoulder. So, this was the Alaris's gift. Wuruhi would be reborn differently. He'd had no choice in his death and his fate, so he would impose the same sentence on humans.

Solemnly, the young man closed his eyes and nodded in silence. "What is this place?" Solehan finally asked, as he reopened his eyes after a few seconds.

"The druids didn't always live in the Astral Forest. Centuries ago, when they worshipped Teluar and his mothers, they came to pray here. This is where the light of Callystrande meets the darkness of Sazaelith, where life is created," Valnard said, pointing to the vegetation. "After Teluar's hibernation, they migrated near the Tree of Ether to be close to him. But over the years, they forgot about the deities. Greedy, they only thought of themselves, their own protection, and thus created the story of the legend of the stars."

The Alaris took the wolf's pelt from the forest spirit's arms and tenderly draped it over the shoulders of the man's corpse. He then took out a long knife and handed it to Solehan. "Please," Valnard said, "the honor is yours. We need his heart. Well, what served as his heart. He was one of the hunters who slaughtered your friend."

Solehan let his mourning and rage explode. He plunged the blade into the chest of the corpse and made a single, powerful cut, opening the ribcage. With his fingers coated in coagulated blood, he extracted the organ and presented it to Valnard.

The Alaris took the heart with the tips of his long, dark fingers and regarded it with disgust. Then, he knelt and offered it to the forest spirit.

"Thank you for your sacrifice. It will not be in vain," he whispered to the creature.

The lychena bowed in curious reverence and placed her budding hand on the heart. The organ lignified into wood, becoming a mossy heart of bark. The gnarled branches and twigs that composed the forest spirit's body began to crack and undulate. Then, as if ignited by an unseen and unquenchable fire, they scattered into blackened ashes, carrying away the memory of the lychena's silhouette.

"The souls of the forest spirits are the breath of existence for these new creatures," Valnard explained to Solehan. "I don't have the power to create life; I can only transfer it."

Still holding the bark heart in one hand, Valnard took out two small vials from his pockets. Solehan recognized the contents of one: the strange hallucinogenic blue liquid that he had promised himself never to experiment with again. The other vial, however, with a golden and shining gleam, was unfamiliar to him.

"Naja's special delivery." Valnard chuckled.

The Alaris poured a drop from each vial onto the heart. The blue and golden liquids mixed and merged into the wood of the organ. Valnard placed the heart back into the cavity of the man's chest and stepped back a few paces.

Then, the young druid witnessed the most extraordinary sight he had ever seen.

All the symbols carved into the circle of rocks around the altar glowed with a vibrant blue light. The enchantment of the place pierced Solehan's senses. In this location, laden with the stories of a time when his people lived in harmony with the deities, a miracle was revealed.

The bark heart began to beat. A pulsation that cracked. Then two. Flowers and luminescent plants sprouted and grew within the ribcage of the corpse. They enveloped this pulsating miracle with their grace and ascended above the body.

Wuruhi's fur was slowly absorbed by the skin of the deceased. The veins and arteries of the corpse became visible beneath the pale epidermis, darkening as they emanated from the pulsating heart of life. Solehan noticed their resemblance to the roots and vegetation that crawled around them.

Everything unified. Everything made sense. Nature was the centerpiece and the primordial essence of all things. Of all existence.

Like a flower blossoming, the ribs parted under the force of the growing vegetation. With a brutal crack, the abdomen of the corpse tore in two. And like a child in its mother's womb, a small figure appeared.

Amid the entrails now composed of leaves and branches, a small creature, part-man, part-wolf, stretched its arms and legs covered in fur and bark.

When Shael caught sight of the blue blood of the chosen ones of Sazaelith in the vial, she felt the urge to destroy everything. Still hidden under her hood, she turned her head and observed the paladin's face, which expressed a similar revulsion to hers.

Suddenly, growls erupted, shaking the walls. They were astonished to see a creature emerging from the corpse between the two men. Its limbs elongated; its muscles gained strength with extreme rapidity. It was as if time had decided to accelerate its natural process to reveal the horror of this monstrosity. A human torso but a wolf's head, with bark and fur for skin, the beast finally opened its yellow eyes. Now fully grown like an adult specimen, it savagely sniffed the stale air of the cave and unleashed its powerful jaws. The enamel of its long fangs gleamed in the darkness.

"Go. Avenge yourself," declared the young man dressed in the strange garb of dead leaves, placing his palm on the beast's chest.

His familiar appearance tingled the senses of the assassin. But hidden as she was, she could only try to guess the man's facial features.

The Alaris made a hand gesture toward the lupine creature. It, not attacking its creator, headed toward the exit of the cave. Its clawed paws scraped the stone floor as it passed by the paladin and the assassin.

Shael loosened her fingers, ready to unleash one of her daggers.

But the beast didn't notice the two companions still concealed behind the massive carved rock, and it continued on its way. Its imposing silhouette faded into the darkness of the place. The resonance of its heavy footsteps grew distant.

Still crouched down, they leaned forward to try to assess the situation. Had the creature really gone? Shael made a promise to eliminate this walking menace when she would have the chance.

A deafening music resounded.

Talyvien uttered a curse. The ensorcinette had fallen from his pocket. Open, it emitted chaotic notes of anguish, mirroring what the paladin was probably feeling. He quickly picked it up and closed it. What had he done?

The assassin shot him a hostile look at such recklessness. But she only had time to catch sight of the Alaris turning in their direction.

His eyes burned into them. His hand with black fingers rose. Crimson tendrils entwined around the paladin's body, causing him to gasp in surprise.

Shael's heart skipped a beat.

42

The vermillion magic dragged Talyvien along the ground toward the Alaris. The paladin let out a groan of pain as his skin scraped against the stone and heated under the Ignescent.

"What do we have here?" mocked the Alaris, as the paladin's body washed up at his feet. "Curiosity killed the cat. Isn't that what humans say?"

"So, you're the one responsible for all these degenerations!" Talyvien shouted, struggling to lift his head. Despite his agitation, the magic held him tightly in its burning embrace. He couldn't move or free himself. He was at its mercy. But even if he hadn't been fortunate, he still thanked his goddess.

The Alaris hadn't noticed the assassin. Talyvien hoped she was taking this opportunity to escape.

The Alaris knelt beside him and scrutinized him from head to toe. His fingers slowly ran over the sheath of Tuoryn's sword, gripping the hilt. Talyvien growled, spitting out his frustration.

"Ah! A paladin of Callystrande. Or rather, what's left of one, I suppose," the Alaris chuckled, pulling the blade out of its scabbard. "The irony is delightful. Sometimes life works out so well! The order the humans established to eradicate my creations! It seems the goddess of light doesn't appreciate my work very much."

Talyvien defiantly locked eyes with the Alaris and managed to get to his knees, albeit with difficulty, gathering all the dignity he could muster.

Hatred distorted his face.

With a casual flick of his arm, the Alaris tossed the sword away with disdain.

The blade, so dear to the paladin, crashed against the rocks like a common object. As it fell, it emitted a clear metallic sound that struck at Talyvien's heart.

The Alaris, enjoying his demonstration, continued to wear a cruel grin as he looked down upon the paladin.

But when the second man approached, Talyvien shifted his attention. He was shaken. Familiar different colored eyes. A face he knew all too well stared back at him.

"Lucine . . ." Talyvien whispered, wide-eyed, unable to divert his gaze from the young man standing before him.

"How . . . Don't speak her name!" shouted the person Talyvien now understood to be Solehan.

The young druid, evidently eager to make him look away, delivered a punch to the paladin's jaw, causing him to collapse with a groan.

A metallic taste flooded Talyvien's mouth. He spat forcefully on the ground as he straightened back up, and a trickle of blood escaped from the corner of his lips.

The vision of the golden suits of armor, Lucine's helplessness, the flames—everything resurfaced tumultuously in Solehan's mind. He despised the man kneeling before him. His anger clung to his pain, to his grief. But . . . how did he know his sister's name?

"It was you and your little gang who massacred her!" Solehan screamed, gripping the collar of the paladin's armor, still bound by the Ignescent.

"Solehan . . . I'll take care of this," Valnard interjected, placing a firm hand on the young druid's shoulder.

Solehan couldn't contain his fury. His fist crumpled the collar of the kneeling man, his breathing became uneven. Macabre impulses liquefied his thoughts. Images of torture surged in his head. Thoughts of his vengeance, of what he would inflict upon this man and his grotesquely defiant demeanor.

The paladin burst into uncontrollable laughter. Insane laughter. He had gone mad. His eyes wickedly landed on Valnard. "I don't know what the Alaris told you, but she's not dead," the paladin declared.

"You're lying!" Solehan spat.

"How else would I have recognized you?" the man on his knees retorted.

Solehan stood up, staggering backward. He placed a hand on his chest in an attempt to calm the pounding of his heart. He turned to Valnard, seeking an answer.

"Solehan, I—let me explain," Valnard hesitated, approaching the young druid with an outstretched hand.

It was true, then. Solehan's field of vision tilted. His heart shattered into a thousand pieces. For Lucine. For grieving a loss that should not have been. For abandoning her to her fate. For being naive.

For . . . the Alaris. For what he felt for him. It had all been a lie.

With his soul torn asunder, the young druid gazed at Valnard in disbelief. How could Valnard have done this to him? The ultimate betrayal. Solehan's eyes filled with an uncontrollable sadness.

"It was even us who saved her," a feminine voice purred in the young druid's ear.

An arm firmly held his chest. The sensation of cold metal brushed against his neck.

Valnard froze and looked over Solehan's shoulder at the mysterious assailant, his eyes wide with astonishment. The Alaris had not seen or heard the attacker's approach. Then, his irises narrowed into long, thin green lines, an air of pure malevolence etched on his marble-like face.

 She couldn't let the paladin suffer such a fate. Left alone facing these two men. Shael had given her word, and it wasn't in her nature to dishonor her promises.

She understood the importance that the young druid held for the Alaris. So, she wrapped one arm around Lucine's brother's chest, holding him firmly, while the dagger in her other hand lightly pressed against his neck. She smelled the scent of blood on her blade, perfectly controlling the pressure. A small cut. A warning for the Alaris not to approach.

"Release him," the Alaris said coldly.

"Release the paladin from your magic first, and we'll see," she replied.

The Alaris let out a restrained laugh in response to the assassin's defiance and crossed his fingers with religious calmness. His incisive intelligence and manipulation exuded from the blaze in his eyes.

Shael nevertheless noticed a vein throbbing on one of his temples.

Defiantly, he took a step forward. "If you saved her, then I assume Lucine matters to you. You wouldn't want to have to tell her that you killed her brother, would you?" the Alaris added in a sweet tone.

A weight grew heavier in Shael's gut. Could she admit to herself that she cared about the young woman? Her, usually so unsociable.

The assassin's gaze swept over the paladin's face. Still trapped by the magic, he didn't divert his attention from her actions, his body tense with worry.

Shael muttered her dissatisfaction in a noise that resembled a hiss. She was forced to admit that the Alaris was right. Despite her untamed nature, she had grown attached to Lucine, Calixte, and Talyvien. She didn't know how to interpret it. Or how to handle it.

"Poor little girl, your hatred and desire for vengeance are so evident on your pretty face," the Alaris whispered, advancing further.

"You must be used to looking in the mirror, I suppose," Shael retorted.

The immortal smirked, but his eyes remained marbled with fury. "I don't even need the power of the Flow to guess your worst nightmares," the Alaris languidly added, closing the distance between them.

Nightmares. At the mention of that single word, Shael's sudden terror overcame her usual coldness and control. The perfect mastery of her predator posture. "Don't come any closer!" she shouted, her body betraying her fear.

Seizing on the young woman's agitation, Solehan quickly freed himself from her grasp. By the time she regained her footing and composure, a massive panther stood before her.

Did Lucine's brother possess such powers?

The beast lunged at Shael and violently bit her shoulder. The assassin screamed in pain and fell backward.

Talyvien struggled and roared with rage.

But the feline quickly released its grip and transformed back into a human. The young druid's body swayed, and he ended up on his knees, palms on the stone, breathing heavily. Cobalt blood streaked his face, and he brought a trembling hand to his mouth, looking at his fingers in disbelief.

"Blood! You lied to me about that too!" he bellowed at the Alaris.

The immortal grumbled, gritting his teeth at being caught at fault like this. In a fit of rage and retaliation, he unleashed his magic upon the still-crawling assassin.

Shael felt herself sinking. Bright red flashes of lightning tore through her vision. Calloused hands surrounded her wrists and forced her down against the ground. She screamed, but no sound came out of her mouth. She no longer controlled her body. She was nothing more than a disjointed puppet. An object.

The nauseating odor of the man restraining her overwhelmed her, and his blue teeth were revealed in a wicked smile. Her worst nightmare was coming true.

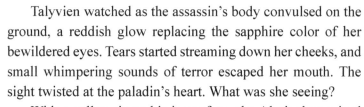 Talyvien watched as the assassin's body convulsed on the ground, a reddish glow replacing the sapphire color of her bewildered eyes. Tears started streaming down her cheeks, and small whimpering sounds of terror escaped her mouth. The sight twisted at the paladin's heart. What was she seeing?

With a sullen air on his ivory face, the Alaris then raised his hand toward the paladin.

Talyvien took a deep breath and squared his shoulders. If this was to be the end, he would die with dignity. He stared defiantly at the Alaris with all the pride and disgust he could muster.

But Solehan's hand gripped the wrist of the immortal, whose fingers clenched in response. The Alaris came to an abrupt halt and glanced sideways at the young druid, with a stern question in his eyes.

"No. A life for a life. If they saved Lucine, then I'll spare theirs," Solehan declared, relentless. "For now."

Much to Talyvien's surprise, the Alaris lowered his arm with a weary and fatalistic demeanor. How could such a young man have that much control over such a powerful being? What was their relationship?

A deep bitterness churned in Talyvien's gut. He nervously exhaled. His breath returned in shudders. If they managed to survive this unfortunate encounter, they had to inform Lucine about her brother's actions. At all costs.

With a devastated look, heavy footsteps, and a bowed neck, Solehan silently made his way toward the exit of the cave.

The Alaris called out to him, but Solehan didn't respond. The immortal followed in the young druid's footsteps without a word, his features wrinkled. The two men didn't spare them another glance and disappeared.

When their creator was far enough away, the strands of magic that bound Talyvien dissipated, finally releasing him from their prison. Despite the pain, he rushed toward Shael, who was still struggling against an invisible demon on the ground, her face drowned in sobs and terror.

Talyvien called out to the assassin several times. In vain.

Shael's attention seemed distant, lost in another world woven with horrors. Her pupils darted frantically; her limbs immobilized by their trauma.

"Shael, it's me," he insisted. "None of this is real!" He placed both hands on her arms, trying to calm her down. Cobalt blood dripped onto the ground and slid from her wounded shoulder. He had to find a way to awaken her from her psychic prison. He placed one of his hands on her cheek, attempting to steady her face.

Perhaps due to the Alaris's departure or perhaps because of the gesture, the fiery spark in Shael's eyes gradually diminished.

And an overwhelming suffering struck the paladin as she finally looked at him.

They gazed at each other with honesty for the very first time. Without barriers, without defenses, without pretense. Their respective breaths blended into a slow, steady rhythm. The paladin couldn't tear his eyes away from her face. From the purity of her emotion. Those few seconds flew away, never to return.

But with her legendary agility and her senses returning, Shael quickly withdrew from the proximity of Talyvien. She wiped her tears with a swipe of her sleeve. Her usual guard reemerged on her face; her truth swept away by her reserve. She tried to get up swiftly. A dagger reappeared in one of her hands.

"They're gone, Shael."

"Are you sure?" she grumbled with difficulty.

"Yes," he nodded. "Her brother spared us apparently, because we saved Lucine. But we'll keep watch tonight, just in case."

A grimace of pain formed on the assassin's face as she leaned against the rock wall and slid down to sit. Inspecting her shoulder wound, she muttered a curse.

Talyvien, still crouched, closed the distance she had just created between them.

"Don't come any closer! I'll manage," she said, raising the palm of her valid hand toward him.

"Let me help you. We need to stop the bleeding," he said, worried.

"You no longer have the magic of your goddess anyway."

"I don't need Callystrande's magic to be able to help," he replied gently. "You're the one who taught me that, Shael."

Shael exhaled through her nose, displaying her notable discomfort while holding her shoulder. She avoided his gaze.

Talyvien was itching to ask her more about what she had seen, but he sensed that Shael's raw emotions still hung in the air. She had already revealed too much.

"We need to inform Lucine," she responded, sidestepping the paladin's disquiet. "What was her brother doing there? And with that Alaris?"

"When she joins us in Dawnelest, we'll explain everything to her."

"Are you still convinced she'll join us?"

"Yes. Because she knows that one is not weaker or less deserving when they ask for or accept help."

Although her eyes were still fixated on the ground, a corner of Shael's mouth lifted. He had struck a chord. She nodded slightly, conceding him permission.

So, in silence, Talyvien removed his chainmail and the upper part of his leather armor. He tore a few strips of fabric from his shirt and knelt beside her.

"Calixte was right," Shael sighed. "About the deities. This Alaris mentioned their relationship as well."

"Yes, it seems to be the case." He paused. "Shael . . . you'll have to remove the upper part of your armor so I can dress the wound." He hesitated, holding several strips of cloth in his hands.

He saw Shael falter. Her fingers tightened on her shoulder, turning a cobalt hue. The vulnerability that gripped the assassin's feline eyes at that moment hit him like a cold shower.

"I would never hurt you, Shael. You have my word," he added, in the face of her reluctance.

Breathing anxiously, the assassin untied her cloak from her neck. She then undid the few straps of her leather armor and placed it beside her. She was now wearing only a simple leather bandeau that flattened her chest. Out of modesty, out of caution, she kept her arms tightly around her torso.

Confounded, Talyvien patiently observed the difficulty of this strange ritual. Normally so confident, Shael now seemed to have lost some of her composure, like a wounded and curled-up little animal awaiting the final blow.

"Shael, not all men's hands harm or soil," he murmured.

She didn't respond. But her posture relaxed, and she exhaled a contained relief. *Show me*, she seemed to be asking him.

The assassin slid her hand and revealed her bare shoulder.

So, with all the gentleness he could muster to counteract his strength, he applied the bandages around Shael's delicate shoulder as she turned her head away.

"You're lucky; the wound isn't very deep," he affirmed. "Still, I'll wrap the bandages several times just in case."

"The blue blood seems to have caught him off guard before he could do more damage," she said, her head still turned to the other side.

The paladin nodded and focused on dressing the injury as best he could. But he silenced the awe he felt at the touch of her smooth, dusky skin. To be so close to her. To finally be able to touch her, to make her real. She, who had been so elusive. A mirage materializing beneath his fingertips.

He didn't have the right to betray her at this moment, to want more. He felt the immense responsibility of the trust she bestowed upon him. With a gesture, with a word, he could shatter her. Or make her flourish. He chose the latter.

Once Talyvien had finished, they silently put on their armor again.

The paladin retrieved his sword, sheathing it, and returned to sit beside her, leaning against the rock.

"Thank you, Talyvien," she whispered.

"I think this is the first time you've used my name! That calls for a celebration!" the paladin exclaimed.

She gathered her knees against her body, and a slight bashful smile appeared on her lips. "I'm sorry for what I said earlier. I'm sorry for being like this," she added in a murmur.

"Hey! It's okay," he replied. "I'm glad we both made it out. Thank you for coming to my rescue. You weren't obligated to do so either. It seems I was the one who needed your protection after all!"

Shael's body grew bolder at his words, the assassin reclaiming her usual playfulness. "I must admit, being pampered isn't so bad!" she teased.

"Another compliment! Where are we headed at this rate!"

Talyvien felt light, as he heard Shael's discreet and melodious laughter flutter between the cave walls.

43

 The noise of the incessant rushing waters from the great waterfall reverberated in Solehan's ears as he emerged from the grand carved gate. His name, repeated incessantly in Valnard's mouth, pounded the walls, the echoes adding to their insistence.

But the young druid was no longer truly there. He didn't know what to do. Where to go. Who to believe.

Lucine was alive.

He berated himself for being so gullible. So enthralled by the Alaris. By his charisma and presence.

Valnard had meticulously crafted an enchanting phantasmagoria and showed him what he had always desired. He convinced him that someone like him had a place. Could choose his own destiny. Could be loved. But it had all been a fabrication. An illusion he had naively clung to.

At that moment, he felt insignificant. Worse, contemptible. Worthless. If he hadn't had his sister in mind to find, he would probably have decided to end it all.

Taking the first bird form he could manage in his state, Solehan flew away, despite the weight of his grief. He wanted to get far away from everything. From that cursed cave, from the Alaris, from the feelings he harbored. And from himself, if it would have been possible.

After some time spent in the air—minutes, perhaps hours—a surprising and immense silhouette appeared against the twilight sky. Distracted, the young druid flew over the place and discovered the skeleton of an impressive creature that seemed to blend seamlessly with its surroundings in its final rest.

Perched with perfect balance on the top of two hills, overlooking a stream, the beast's spinal column formed a long and winding improvised bridge. The monstrous ribs of the animal towered on either side and added to the solidity of this peculiar makeshift path.

Solehan landed languidly on the backbone of the carcass. The bones cracked under his feet as he returned to his original form. He knew nothing about this place. Nothing mattered anymore. He collapsed to his knees, and tears poured from his eyes.

Flapping wings caught his attention, and he lifted his head, his face still drenched in sorrow. The elaphora landed delicately on the large bones, and Valnard dismounted. The Alaris had followed him.

"Solehan . . ." Valnard hesitated, approaching cautiously. He took a step forward, his hand outstretched. Everything in his gait marked his uncertainty in the situation.

"Why?" the young druid cried out, still on the ground. "I trusted you! How could you do this to me?!"

"I'm sorry, Solehan," the Alaris apologized, placing a hand on his chest.

"All this time, you knew she was alive! You played me!" Solehan straightened up but kept his head lowered. He couldn't look at Valnard's face. His fists clenched with anger, his knuckles turning white. Teluar's magic crackled at his fingertips.

"Please, let me explain," Valnard tried again, in a gentle voice.

"NO!"

The young druid let his magic express what he had in his heart. Thorny vines emerged from his hands and surged toward the Alaris. Vegetation sprang from his fingers with astonishing speed. A wild and tangled vegetal wave crashed onto his target and entwined along the spine of the large skeleton. This verdant tidal wave convulsed upon Valnard.

Solehan didn't stop. Again and again. Minutes spread out, dispersing his emotions.

But when he had unleashed everything within him, the young druid's magic dwindled. He couldn't think anymore. He fell back to his knees, drained. And a deafening silence took hold.

Solehan didn't know what he expected, but he slowly raised his head.

Amid the billowing fumes, he caught sight of the shield of Ignescent that had ignited the vegetation around the Alaris's body. Valnard hadn't tried to retaliate. He had only protected himself.

The Alaris lowered his arms, which he had positioned in front of his face, and looked at Solehan once again.

"Did you lie to me about Teluar, too?" Solehan whispered between ragged breaths.

"No. All of that is true, Solehan. Your powers are real, as you can see. Your destiny, as well."

The glow of the Ignescent's shield faded around Valnard's figure as he slowly advanced. "I did it for Sylveah," he added, in an uncertain voice. "So Teluar could bring her back to me. I was afraid."

"Afraid of what?"

"That you would leave. That you would try to find your sister instead of discovering your potential. She has no powers. She can't help us."

"It should have been my choice!" Solehan hissed, his jaw clenched.

"You're right. I was selfish. But I can find her, Solehan, if you wish."

"Why should I trust you now?"

"Because I promise not to lie to you anymore. And to bring your sister back to you. I'll try to convince her to join us."

"How could you find her anyway?" growled Solehan.

"I know a way."

Could Valnard find her? And even if he could, would she join their mad quest and accept awakening Teluar at any cost? Even at the cost of humanity? Did he still want it himself, after all?

Still confused, the young druid got to his feet with difficulty. He was exhausted. With an exasperated look, he surveyed the large bones that stretched around them.

"A dragon," Valnard informed him, following his gaze. "They were one of Teluar's earliest creations, long ago. They were magnificent creatures. But when the god of Nature wanted to bring forth the civilization of humans, thinking it would be his greatest project, he had to let go of their existence. He asked the Alaris to help exterminate them. Reluctantly, we accepted, and hundreds of volcanoes erupted. Drowned in a perpetual winter, all the dragons perished. And humans took their place."

Solehan listened to the Alaris's account and observed the grandeur of the skeleton. Could he also believe that? Were humans responsible for such sacrifice?

"It's a shame. I found those beings fabulous," Valnard added, shrugging. "Much more than humans, in any case. Well . . . not all of them."

"I need to go to the Tree of Ether," Solehan replied curtly, finally finding the strength to look Valnard in the eye. "Where it all began. I don't know what to believe anymore, Valnard."

"I understand. I don't underestimate your pain, Solehan. I'm not asking you to forgive me—"

"I can't," he interrupted. "At least, not yet. I need time."

Valnard nodded slightly, his shoulders sagging. "Do you want me to come with you?" the Alaris asked.

Solehan despised himself. Despite the revelations, despite the lies, he still wanted to be close to Valnard. How could he reconcile these conflicting feelings?

In his weakness, the young druid agreed.

The two men flew for several hours to reach their destination. Valnard still rode the elaphora. The young druid, taking the form of a falcon, circled beside him.

Solehan was breathless at the splendor of the Tree of Ether. True to his memory, it stood majestically in the midst of the Astral Forest. He landed gracefully at the base of the silver-foliaged tree; the events of the Eclipse ceremony still fresh in his mind.

Valnard arrived as well, dismounted, and stood beside him.

Solehan's trembling fingers brushed against the bark of the great tree. He admired the two silhouettes carved into the gnarled trunk, representing the chosen ones of the legend. The engravings of constellations and stars shimmered with a bluish glow, winding up to the top of the tree. The many nights spent pondering with his twin sister came flooding back to him. The countless times they had cursed their destiny.

Nevertheless, he now cast a more confident gaze upon this surprising tree. Solehan knew that Teluar was real, that Valnard hadn't lied about that. He was no longer that ignorant and cowardly child that he once had been.

He had mastered his powers, the gift from his god. He had become aware of his own truth.

He glanced at Valnard from the corner of his eye. Despite his petty schemes, Solehan owed the Alaris this knowledge, this assurance. Despite Valnard's lies, the young druid realized that he still felt the same way about the actions of the humans. He still had a deep desire to continue what they had begun. He was also surprised to find himself wishing that Lucine had been taken with him. They could have gone through all this together, discovering their potential and freeing themselves from their destiny.

"Why . . . on that day . . . why did you only take me?" Solehan asked, his fingers gently caressing the carved surface of the bark.

"As I told you, I didn't sense any magic in her," Valnard replied gravely. "I'm sorry. I wish it could have been different. Truly. But the gifts of the gods are sometimes cruel. When humans are exterminated, we will return here. You will then be able to awaken Teluar and show him the beauty of nature finally freed from these parasites. Your sister cannot do that."

Solehan, his heart torn, remained silent. He then turned his head and discovered a host of wooden silhouettes. In a tangle of different sizes and positions, with large vines clinging to some of them, the members of the druidic clans had been frozen in their final moments. However, Teluar's implacable nature seemed to be reclaiming its rights. Beautiful flowers had sprouted on their bodies. Brightly colored blooms peeked out here and there, enveloped in the tranquility and sublimity of the forest.

No wave of sadness spread through Solehan when he recognized some of the statues. Perhaps he had changed more than he imagined, after all? The young druid saw only beauty where there had once been horror. Cruelty had ultimately shifted sides in his heart. Solehan marveled at the scene and remained there for several minutes, observing the tableau before closing his eyes. He felt Valnard's silent presence behind him. Green eyes burned into his back.

Then, gathering what little magic he had left, Solehan raised his arms. And the power of the god Teluar manifested. An ocean of plants and diverse flowers began to sprout and grow at a rapid pace on the hundreds of wooden silhouettes scattered before him. Thus, he transformed the footprint left by humans who had once walked this ground and he gave birth to a new part of the forest in their place. The memories of Solehan's childhood evaporated at that moment. He watched that past to which he had never truly felt any belonging dissipate with majesty.

Solehan heard Valnard's breathing become more uneven behind him. The Alaris couldn't hide his admiration. The young man felt the flicker of covetousness settling upon him, upon what he represented now in the eyes of the immortal. But despite the warmth coiling in his belly, Solehan was still hurt and steeped in his pride. He ignored the feeling and turned to face the great Tree of Ether once again.

He couldn't wait any longer. After so much uncertainty and deception, he needed answers. Proof. His pulse quickened, and apprehension seized him. He closed his eyes once again and placed his hands on the dark bark of the great tree, which cracked beneath his fingertips.

A silhouette appeared in his mind.

Curled up on himself and floating in the sparkling ether, a man was letting himself be carried by the current. With limp arms, his lifeless body moved slowly, dragged by his apathy. Thin golden tears flowed from his closed eyes and mixed with the ink color of the liquid atmosphere, creating fine twirling and swirling shooting stars around his body. Long deer antlers emerged from either side of his forehead, piercing through the lunar veil of his long silver hair that gracefully embraced his god's silhouette.

Teluar.

The young druid's face contorted with the pain he felt for him. His body was overcome by sobs that wetted his cheeks. When Solehan finally forced himself to open his eyes again, he saw Valnard peering at him with concern and worry. The young man then ran his fingers over his face and discovered that tears of dark liquid were flowing from his eyes.

Perplexed, Valnard approached him and gently cupped his face in his hands, wiping away the black tears that rolled down his skin. "Solehan, your eyes!" exclaimed the Alaris, stupefaction splashed across his face.

As they walked for several hours among the tall trees of the thick forest, Lucine, Calixte, and Katao gradually lost their sense of direction. Bit by bit, the vegetation seemed to swallow them whole, and their only hope was to follow the small creature that continued to move resolutely ahead of them. Only the sounds of their horses' hooves seemed to keep steady the endless rhythm of this strange journey.

Lucine noticed with surprise that the forest was becoming quieter. The animals were dispersing among the large deciduous trees. Worried, she said, "I'm starting to wonder if it was a good idea . . . Maybe Talyvien and Shael were right."

"Don't worry, Lucine. It'll be fine," Calixte responded with their naturally cheerful demeanor. "I don't believe in coincidences! If you recognized the symbol, there must be a reason!"

Lucine wished she could share the bard's optimism, but she had experienced enough tragedies for her imagination to easily slip into anxiety. As if perspiring in her mind, while she focused on her surroundings, she felt fear settling in the minds of Katao and the horses accompanying them. Lucine gently stroked the dog's head, and he let out a small whimper.

Why did she seem to be the only one capable of having a special connection with animals? Perhaps it was the gift she had received from the legend of the stars. But what good would such a gift do in finding Solehan?

She was grateful to Shael and Talyvien for their advice and training. The art of weapon handling would surely be more useful. The image of her two companions appeared in her memory, and her heart tightened. Would they end up fighting each other? Would their differing devotion be an obstacle to their mission?

With a knot in her throat, she preferred to focus on the small creature made of bark trotting ahead of them. As a reminder to take control of her destiny, the bow and quiver that Zaf had given her pressed against her back. Lucine had vowed not to feel powerless in the face of events that seemed to traverse her life. The image that the bard had projected during their ballad had warmed and encouraged her soul, and she aspired to become worthy of such a melodious epic.

She gave Calixte a side glance. She had to admit that she still envied the magic possessed by the Alaris. "May I ask why you agreed to accompany me?" Lucine inquired, intrigued.

"Ah! Because you're a fervent admirer of my music, of course!" Calixte replied.

A small laugh escaped from the druidess.

"But seriously," they said, "it's because I've been traveling the roads for a while in search of material to write new pieces, and all these adventures seemed promising!"

"It can't be just that, Calixte! I mean, you're offering to come with me into a forest to follow a strange creature without a known destination!"

A certain intensity animated Calixte's amethyst face. "Do you know where the Alaris come from?"

Lucine shook her head in negation.

Calixte then exhaled as if regaining their breath, their vague attention focused far ahead. "At the beginning of all things, when the universe was fluid and shifting, when everything was possible, two ideas were born in the void. Two origins of creation," the bard continued emphatically, illustrating their words with a hand gesture.

Joy filled Lucine's face. She could have listened to Calixte for hours. Their sublime voice, their tales and stories from a lost time. A legacy that only an immortal being could have touched in their life.

"The first idea twirled shadows and light to create life," they added. "A spark that exploded. That came alive with passion and love and revealed a paradise. A lush oasis in the midst of emptiness. A holy trinity of gold, darkness, and beauty. The second idea believed in the duality of the power of fire and water, in the coexistence of man and woman to establish its reality."

"So, you mean . . . the gods and the Alaris were two separate origins of creation?"

"Indeed!" Calixte nodded. "For eons, these two ideas coexisted and flourished. Each prospered and defined its own rules and customs. New gods were created, Alaris children were born, and truths matured. But these two seeds of life couldn't continue to coexist if they wanted to grow. So, a war broke out between these two universes. A war that lasted an eternity. But some Alaris, tired of this never-ending conflict and believing in the possibility of cohabitation, decided to ally with the gods to end it all."

"So, some Alaris betrayed their own side?" Lucine questioned.

"Exactly. They did it in order to bring peace. To have a chance to coexist."

"And did the gods eventually overthrow the Alaris?"

"Yes! And when they defeated them, the gods rewarded the Alaris rebels who had helped them. They offered them a world where they could live in harmony—the material plane. This world we currently find ourselves in! The gods promised not to interfere in the lives of the Alaris and not to decide their fate. They also allowed them to practice their own magic without their intervention, but under one condition!"

"What was that?" Lucine asked, with interest.

"The condition to protect their creation! To support the gods in order to preserve this new world."

"But were you yourself part of this Alaris rebellion during the war?"

"Oh, please!" Calixte laughed. "I've been alive for a long time, but not to that extent! But out of respect for our ancestors who fought for peace, out of respect for the gods who created this habitat, most of the Alaris continue to honor this oath. In fact, some Alaris still have a close connection with certain gods."

"And that's why you're helping us today!"

"Indeed! Whenever I can, I try to help humans."

"Thank you, Calixte, in any case," said the young druidess.

One of the famous orange and swaggering winks flew by.

As they ventured deeper into the verdant universe, the atmosphere seemed to thicken. A feeling of unease gradually took hold of Lucine. Her breathing became more erratic, her questions more pressing. Was it fear that was progressively devouring her, or was there something else?

To reassure herself, she casually observed Calixte. Their gait and confidence didn't appear affected. So Lucine continued to move forward, trying to calm her apprehensions, and followed the small wooden figure with light footsteps.

The path became more winding, more discreet. The horses began to struggle to move. Tall ferns brushed against Lucine's legs. She admired the few sparkling droplets that clung to and trickled down the long fronds as they passed by.

Suddenly, unimaginable shades burst forth from the vegetation. Unknown colors that she couldn't recall. They sprinkled the forest with incredible luminous hues. Transfixed with admiration, Lucine placed a hand over her chest. Her breathing grew even more labored, her fear less acute.

The blurred curves of the plants undulated to the rhythm of their steps, colors blending together. Gravity lost its grip. The droplets that slid on the leaves began to flutter and dance among the trees. They played with the contours of their bodies as they advanced. With a languid expression, Lucine admired this incoherent hallucination.

But despite the heaviness that seemed to befall her, she forced herself to focus her attention on the dark silhouette of the small wooden creature still moving ahead of them. She struggled to keep up.

As if expecting it, and because nothing made sense anymore, the fox with its white, shimmering fur appeared in this magical tableau. Its emergence through the foliage was brief. It played and ran for a few seconds among the ferns—a reassuring mirage urging her to continue, not to give up. She felt her spirits lift. Its message delivered, the animal vanished as quickly as it had come.

Lucine looked at Calixte once again. Their long white hair floated as if submerged at the back of their head, with some strands changing color due to the magic that was now at work. In response, the torpid amber of Calixte's eyes settled on her. Lucine wanted to speak to them, but no sound came out of her mouth. Her words died in the crushing silence of their shared delusion.

The silhouette of the trees trembled slightly under the sound of the splashing hooves. The black mark of the small wooden creature continued to advance tirelessly.

With her breath short and legs that could barely carry her, the young woman felt the urge to let herself float in the trembling ferns. The marvelous colors enveloped her with serenity. She gently caressed the leaves with her fingertips.

After an eternal moment, unable to breathe any longer, Lucine finally surrendered to the reverie of the trees. The forest absorbed her completely.

A sudden brightness dazzled the young druidess and abruptly pulled her out of her numbness. The invigorating air of the cool wind struck against her skin. The strange sensation of floating finally dissipated and her senses gradually returned to her. A floral scent colored the atmosphere, and a gentle warmth grazed her touch. The outlines of the small wooden creature sharpened once again.

The towering trees that had surrounded them before had disappeared. Catching her breath, Lucine turned around and saw the edge of the strange, colorful forest behind her. Still dizzy, her gaze met Calixte's. Surprise was also evident on the Alaris's face.

"What was that?" Lucine gasped, slowly inviting air back into her lungs.

"Probably some sort of protection, I would say," the bard replied, their breathing as disrupted as hers.

The horses snorted beside them. Katao growled. They followed the direction pointed out by the dog's eyes.

Calixte whistled in admiration.

Lucine was speechless.

In the valley that appeared below the cliff where they stood loomed the largest tree Lucine had ever seen in her life. It was taller than the Tree of Ether or any other giant trees in the Astral Forest. It was so impressive that its branches formed a leafy sky above their heads. The clouds twirled and mingled with this glorious canopy. A massive, twisted tangle of large roots wound around the imposing trunk. The hallucinations that had visited Lucine at the Luminaur inn resurfaced in her thoughts. Did the tree she had seen in her dreams have a connection to this one? Had the symbol led her to it?

The small wooden creature continued along her path as if nothing had happened and walked toward this prodigious arboreal structure.

They followed in silence, too awestruck to speak in the face of the splendors they were discovering. They passed under several large arches of blooming brambles that marked this strange path and made their way toward the base of the gigantic tree.

When they finally arrived after several minutes, an entire city revealed itself around them. Nestled between the curves of the massive roots at the foot of the tree, elegant dwellings made of branches, leaves, and flowers interlocked with each other. Each of a different shape, they had been skillfully fashioned without tools or sculpting, but through ingenious interweaving of organic matter, resembling curious and whimsical bird nests.

Some plants rustled upon their arrival. Several small creatures, some resembling the wooden one leading them, fled into the shimmering vegetation. Some sported mushroom caps as headwear, while others had colorful bunches of bushes or grass.

They ventured through this extraordinary city around the imposing trunk and followed a path carved into one of the immense twisted roots. Numerous plants of all colors emerged from every direction, creating a vegetal cocoon that framed this surprising path. Some of them had glowing bulbs that emitted an orange light, guiding their steps. In the few spaces left by the celestial vault of greenery, Lucine glimpsed stars shining proudly, even though the sky was of a light tone, with scattered violet shades here and there. Nothing seemed to make sense.

"Where are we, Calixte?" she asked. "I've never seen anything like this!"

"Mmhh. I would say probably in another plane of existence," Calixte replied, surveying the surroundings. "There's far too much magic here for us to be in the world we belong to. However, it's strange that the two are connected."

"I'm not sure I understand . . . there are multiple planes . . . of existence?"

Calixte touched a strange, variegated flower with their fingertips, and the vibrant colors faded upon contact. "Fascinating," they added. "As I mentioned, the gods created the material plane to which we belong and entrusted the Alaris with its care. But that's not all they created! The universe they shaped consists of a multitude of planes of existence. A world on several layers, with multiple variations, but ones that are normally impossible to traverse. The only plausible hypothesis would be that we are in someone's dream. It's the only transfer granted to us."

"Dreams are part of a different plane of existence?"

"Not all, but it can happen."

"That's why you said there may not necessarily be a difference between dreams and reality?"

"Among other things!" Calixte replied in amusement.

The path carved on the root became steeper. They decided to leave their horses behind and continued ascending toward the canopy of the grand tree. They climbed stairs made of large, soft leaves that gently bounced under their steps. Anxious, Katao followed them, tail tucked between his legs.

Located at the heart of the tree, a palace made of bark welcomed them. The splendid anarchy of its architecture, which overlapped the branching of the mighty plant, took Lucine's breath away. Like delicate patterns on the translucent wings of an insect, magnificent, interlaced branch decorations adorned the windows and dotted the large wooden arches that supported the structure.

The small wooden creature then advanced toward the opulent entrance of the building, which opened as they approached. Lucine touched the elegant brambles that twirled on the door with her hand as she passed through, trying to ground the unreal nature of their situation in her mind.

A shiver ran through Calixte's body at her side. She turned her head.

Seated on an impressive throne resembling a twisted wooden sun, a creature of unparalleled beauty observed them.

She possessed a woman's body with generous curves, her fuchsia skin merged with patches of bark that reflected verdant hues. Long leaves with accents of green and blue cascaded down her bare back, serving as her flowing hair.

With an inquisitive look, she stood up and approached the newcomers with grace. Her robe, sewn with long multicolored petals, swayed around her hips, while her slender bare feet seemed to make no sound on the finely engraved wooden floor. Large turquoise eyes attentively scanned Calixte and Lucine, completing an absolutely stunning face adorned with two large wooden horns on each side of her forehead. Her skin was speckled with a few small turquoise spots on each cheek and the upper part of her shoulders.

She knelt beside the small figure that had led them to her. A silent dialogue took place between the two creatures, mesmerizing Lucine with wide-eyed astonishment.

The young druidess turned her head and saw a strange emotion pass over Calixte's face, their citrine eyes completely captivated by the sight of the exquisite creature. Lucine averted her gaze modestly.

The woman spoke. "My subject informs me that she found you among the ruins of a human village that had been attacked, apparently by two individuals strongly resembling you," she proclaimed as she stood up.

The contained severity of her tone contrasted with the surprisingly crystalline voice of the creature.

"People resembling us?" Lucine wondered.

"What do you have to say in your defense?" the woman asked, her attention shifting from Calixte to Lucine with suspicion.

"What? We haven't done anything! And who are you, by the way?" Lucine exclaimed vigorously, feeling the injustice of the situation. "I don't understand anything anymore."

The creature seemed surprised by the young woman's reaction, and despite the hardness that still permeated her graceful features, her gaze softened.

"I am Feör'ael, the guide and sovereign of the forest spirits. And who are you?" The queen clicked her tongue against her palate and clasped her hands together. Her body straightened up a little higher as she inspected them carefully.

Calixte stepped forward with panache before Lucine could say anything and let their long white hair and purple tunic ripple around them. They assumed the most graceful bow Lucine had ever seen. "I am Calixte, the bard of wonders, and this is Lucine Destellar, an accomplished druidess and huntress," they affirmed, offering Lucine a complicit smile as a gift. "Let's try to calm down and learn a little more, shall we? I imagine that with your dignity and undisputed reign, you have surely encountered an Alaris or a human before," they added, their voice deep and melodious.

"Flattery won't get you anywhere, Alaris. But yes, indeed, it's not the first time. Where are you going with this?"

"You must know that we all more or less resemble each other in our mediocrity. I mean, compared to the grace and beauty of the forest spirits, no Alaris or human could compete." Still leaning forward and frozen in their bow, Calixte raised only their head and met the queen's gaze.

Feör'ael then positioned herself in front of them, her petal-stitched robe rustling on the floor, and began to scrutinize them.

Lucine understood that she seemed to dislike flattery, even though

Calixte's charisma was usually more persuasive.

"Let's start over, shall we?" Calixte suggested. "We followed your . . . subject in an attempt to learn more about what happened to that village as well," Calixte now straightened up, adopting a confident posture.

"And why would you do that?" the queen snapped, crossing her arms as she continued to stare at the bard.

"Because I imagine you didn't send scouts so far from your charming plane of existence randomly," Calixte calmly retorted. "Perhaps this has something to do with the fact that some of these humans have been transformed into wood, for example? Could forest spirits be responsible for these attacks?"

"The same forest spirits who attacked and murdered my clan!" Lucine blurted out. She had had enough of bowing down before anyone and was growing impatient with receiving only unanswered questions. If this creature was responsible for all this, she would have to answer for her actions.

But the reaction that flashed across the stunning face of Feör'ael surprised the young druidess. The turquoise eyes seemed tinged with melancholy. The palpable pain of the forest spirit disarmed Lucine's anger.

"Yes," the queen said, "my scouts have also reported attacks on human cities by lychenas for a few months now." Her voice was filled with sorrow.

"Lychenas?" Lucine questioned, arching an eyebrow.

The queen gestured with her hand, indicating the small creature they had been following. "These forest spirits are called lychenas. And they are indeed capable of turning flesh into bark."

"So, your subjects are responsible for these attacks?" Lucine asked cautiously.

"No," Feör'ael replied, her face marked by grief. "My subjects generally do not leave this plane unless under my orders. We have no business with humans." She turned away and walked toward one of the grand, beautifully decorated openings of intertwined branches. Lost in thought, she contemplated her fabulous kingdom of lush fantasies. "It was a long time ago that some of my subjects rebelled. But I would have never thought that . . ." Her words trailed off, crushed by the sadness she seemed to be experiencing.

"Why would your subjects have rebelled?" Lucine inquired, joining her.

"That no longer matters . . ." She sighed. The turquoise eyes moved over Lucine's body and stopped at the tattoos on her arms. "What happened to your clan, druidess?"

Lucine then recounted her story. The story of her clan, the legend of the stars and the Tree of Ether with its mysterious symbols and silver leaves. The tale of the terror she had felt on the day of the Eclipse ceremony, witnessing her brother Solehan being abducted by a man on a strange flying creature. Her quest to find him since then and learn more about the lychenas.

Blood, suffering, resilience. Her promise.

As she unfolded her narrative, Lucine caught glimpses of growing terror on the magnificent face that was observing her. When she finished, the queen turned away out of modesty, and the young druidess realized that a tear had fallen down her cheek.

Calixte and Lucine exchanged uncertain glances in the face of the queen's apparent emotion.

After a few seconds of silence, which weighed heavily on the serenity of the room, a crystalline voice finally spoke. "The person you are looking for is named Valnard. I believe he is the one who abducted your brother."

Lucine was astounded. "Valnard?" she repeated, furrowing her brow.

"Yes. He is an Alaris. I know that, long ago, some of the forest spirits of this plane joined his cause. I suppose he is the man you saw."

Her thoughts spinning in all directions, Lucine observed the clarity of the light rays projected onto Feör'ael's multicolored robe. An Alaris had then abducted her brother. But how could the queen know this?

"We lived together . . . several centuries ago . . ." the queen explained, understanding the silent question in the druidess's eyes. The sovereign seemed hesitant to add something, but no sound came out of her trembling throat.

"Oh. So why would some of your subjects have followed him?" Lucine asked.

"Because he wants to exterminate humanity so that Nature can reclaim its rights. So that the god Teluar may awaken."

"That's sheer madness!" Lucine gasped in horror. Exterminate humanity? Teluar, the son of Callystrande and Sazaelith? This explained the various attacks she had witnessed. But it still didn't answer her initial question. "Why did he abduct my brother? What does he have to do with all of this?" she asked with determination.

"Oh, you don't know the power you have inherited, druidess?" Feör'ael inquired with interest.

"Unfortunately, I believe only Solehan inherited any power," Lucine lamented, lowering her arms.

The queen placed one of her hands affectionately on the druidess's shoulder. "Yet you are blessed by the mother goddesses, Callystrande and Sazaelith. So, you have received the gift of their son, Teluar. One golden eye and one silver eye . . ."

Was it true? Perhaps Teluar's power was expressed in her only through the special connection she had with animals? And why Teluar? The legend of her clan had never mentioned the Nature god as the source of their powers. Nevertheless, if all this turned out to be true, had the goddesses placed their chosen ones, Shael and Talyvien, to assist her in her quest? Did they not endorse Valnard's actions?

Lucine didn't know what to say to all of this. She looked at the queen with a skeptical stare. Then she turned to Calixte, seeking a comforting explanation in the bard's presence. However, all she found was intense agitation in their fiery eyes. Had they gone through the same thought process?

"Perhaps it would be best if I showed you directly," the queen finally said, in a calm tone.

Surprised, Lucine watched as Feör'ael headed toward a small wooden door that creaked slightly as it opened. She invited them to follow.

They descended a long staircase carved directly into the wood of the tree. They hurried down the steps for several minutes in the dim light, illuminated only by the strange plants with luminescent bulbs. Lucine admired the leafy hair of the queen fluttering in front of her. Various plants and brambles meandered on the walls of the staircase, their leaves trembling as they brushed against them.

When the wooden steps finally ended, they entered a vast cave that seemed to be made entirely of wood, hidden deep within the great tree, away from prying eyes. Intertwined with a variety of colorful plants, large vines wound around the naturally jagged bark walls. It was as if a vegetal whirlwind was surrounding a massive dark root at the center of the space.

A familiar feeling washed over the young druidess. A sense of recognition. Like an attraction that tormented her stomach.

"This is a root of the Tree of Ether," the sovereign explained. "This plane of existence was created from it, and everything around us as well. Including me." To Lucine, the sovereign said, "Place your hand on the bark, druidess."

The Tree of Ether? Here? Lucine's throat tightened as she complied. Her heartbeats accelerated. Her fingers trembled on the bark. A few seconds passed.

And nothing happened.

Lucine knew it. She had not inherited any power. She gently caressed the dark and comforting texture with her fingertips. Her heart constricted at the thought of what lay on the other side of that root. Her clan, her past life that would never be the same, the last time she had seen Solehan.

Intrigued, Feör'ael approached the young woman. Her unyielding gaze scrutinized Lucine as if she were witnessing something unusual. The fuchsia hand rested on the amulet that the elders had given her on that fateful day.

The queen let out a sharp cry of pain. She quickly withdrew her hand, her ordinarily elegant features contorted in disgust. "Remove it immediately!" she exclaimed.

Dumbfounded, Lucine took off the small wooden amulet from around her neck, a symbol of her childhood, but kept her other hand on the root.

A spark.

An outpouring.

A sublime and divine cataclysm.

Her body arched under the surge of magic flowing into her. The echo of the wooden amulet hitting the floor resonated within her being.

No longer feeling the texture of the bark under her fingers, Lucine saw the silhouette of a man floating among shooting stars.

Teluar. Feör'ael's voice was close yet distant.

The god's golden tears wrapped around the young druidess's arms in a plea. A call. An undeniable truth. His long silver hair cascaded softly around his body, like large quivering wings under the dark and liquid ether.

Lucine felt the texture of the wood under her fingers again. The vision dissipated, like a veil lifting. Breathless and with a heavy head, she knelt down to gather herself.

Calixte joined her, also kneeling and offering her affectionate back rubs.

A shiny droplet crashed onto the wooden floor next to the amulet. Puzzled, the young druidess passed her hand over her cheek. Liquid gold had once again flowed from her golden eye.

The lamentation of Callystrande.

45

Solehan regarded his reflection with a confused look. Having recently returned to the castle of Argentvale, he had rushed to the only mirror whose location he knew, soaring through the window of his room in one of his bird forms.

Back into his human body, he brought his face close to the mirror and scrutinized the depths of his eyes. The usual golden and silver spark that shimmered in his gaze seemed to have dissipated upon contact with the Tree of Ether. The silver glow had fled from the pale gray eye that stared back at him, and Solehan did not find the familiar golden shimmer in his other iris.

With a desolate gaze tinged with dark ochre and ashes, the young druid made acquaintance with the person standing before him. A pang of pain shook him as he realized he could no longer see Lucine within himself. Yet, an odd sense of relief also submerged him.

He appreciated no longer sharing her eyes. Her doubts. Her potential accusations. That overwhelming stare that constantly reminded him of the contempt she might have felt toward his choices, his actions. Even though he still desired to find her, Solehan now felt different. His new appearance seemed to echo his deepest aspirations.

Valnard's silhouette appeared in the mirror's reflection, standing just behind him.

"What does this mean? Do you think the goddesses have abandoned me?" Solehan asked in a grave voice, focusing his attention on the solemn face of the Alaris.

"I don't know," Valnard replied softly, placing both hands on the young druid's shoulders.

The long black fingers turned Solehan's body around, and he found himself face to face with the Alaris.

Valnard gently traced his hands from the young man's shoulders to the square of his jaw. "You don't need them anyway, Solehan. You have the power of Teluar within you," Valnard added calmly, accompanied by a slight smile. "That changes nothing; you can still awaken him."

Still resentful and wounded, Solehan removed Valnard's hands from his face and pulled away from his embrace. He didn't know if Callystrande and Sazaelith had abandoned him, but Valnard was right. Their priorities remain unchanged. Teluar was indeed real. Humans were responsible for his grief and the gradual destruction of the world.

"We must find Lucine. Perhaps it is related to her," Solehan whispered, taking a few steps. "Perhaps she needs to be present to awaken him."

"Perhaps, but I doubt it. She has no power. But we will find her regardless. I promised you that, Solehan."

"And why should I trust you now, Valnard?"

"Because . . . I need you."

Solehan scoffed bitterly. "Need. *Need!* That's all I am!" the young druid yelled out. "A pawn you can toy with!"

"No, that—that's not what I meant, Solehan," Valnard stammered, raising his hands.

"I've had enough. I *need* some fresh air."

"You are free to leave."

"That hasn't always been the case," Solehan said curtly.

"And I am genuinely sorry for that. But I cannot change the past. Believe me, I wish I could. I can only promise you that the future will not be the same."

"And what will change, huh? I will always be Teluar's chosen one, whom you manipulate with lies and unspoken truths to get what you want!"

"No, everything is different now."

"What is different?" the young druid growled.

Valnard, taken aback, remained silent despite opening his mouth.

"Answer me!" Solehan shouted. The young man forcefully slammed the

Alaris against the large mirror. In his rage, he placed both hands on the glass, which vibrated on either side of Valnard's head. "Answer me," he repeated coldly, just inches away from the Alaris's face.

Solehan despised the ardor that spread through his chest, the desire that ravaged him as he gazed upon Valnard's perfect and captivating face. As he felt the heat and power of the Alaris's body against his own, the pounding of Valnard's heart against his chest. The two stars, flecked with greenish hues, observing him with dismay. His scent. The memory of the texture of his skin.

It was torture.

Why did his body and heart react so strongly to his touch? Why did he have to feel this at such a moment?

"Because I . . ." Valnard hesitated in a whisper.

The warmth of Valnard's voice settled on the young man's face. Solehan lost his reason. Despite himself, he yielded and gazed at Valnard's lips, as if trying to discern the unspoken words. It was a forbidden fruit he longed to taste.

Valnard's breath caught.

Solehan's trembled with excitement.

In the distance, the thunderous sound of trumpets echoed through the valley. Hundreds of voices rose in unison from the surrounding mountains.

Solehan removed himself from Valnard's body. The two men exchanged an anxious glance. They hurried to the balcony of the room and were horrified to see several banners in the colors of the Narlimar and Vamentera kingdoms fluttering in the breeze.

The humans had finally come to seek revenge for the attacks on their villages and reclaim the city.

The young druid looked at the army of shining armor flooding the valley. How could they have failed to notice them earlier as they flew over Argentvale? Solehan realized that the humans, eager for a surprise attack, had likely advanced hidden among the dense forest trees that stretched around the city, encroaching upon the border with the kingdom of Vamentera.

Solehan turned his head and observed Valnard's reaction. Gripping the railing, his face stern, he surveyed the extent of the human revenge unfolding around them. A furious and deadly glimmer animated his eyes. He would protect Argentvale at all costs. He would protect Sylveah's soul, even if it meant sacrificing his own life. But could one Alaris alone prevail against so many humans?

The young druid beheld the vastness of the gray sky. It would have been easy for him to fly away and leave Valnard to face his misery alone. After all, perhaps he deserved it?

Understanding his torment, Valnard's eyes met his in a silent question. Solehan was struck by what he saw in them for the first time. There was no longer cruelty or deceit. Just a pure and unyielding truth that shattered all doubts within him. A feeling so immense that it could conquer all. An eternal promise.

The promise that everything would be different. That he had become someone else, and that the Alaris finally saw him. That Valnard now regarded him as an equal. That Solehan would forever be free to choose his own path. That he could simply *be* what he wanted by Valnard's side.

That the moment had come for Solehan to make a choice. An ultimate decision.

An undeniable truth struck the young druid. He didn't need to think, as his heart screamed out the answer. He knew what he had to do.

Solehan leapt into the void.

He spread the span of his immense eagle wings and glided toward the streets of the city of Argentvale below. The power of Teluar rumbled in his veins. His hatred was galvanized by certainty and frustration, devouring everything in its path.

He positioned himself at the entrance of the main street of the city, reverting to his original form, and patiently waited for the swarm of men to pour into the grand avenue.

One of them, mounted on an armored steed, advanced at the head of hundreds of infantry soldiers. They halted as they caught sight of the young druid standing amid the stone pavement of the street. Solehan felt the presence of the lychenas nearby, hidden in the stone crevices of the buildings. He walked toward the army, who stared back at him.

The man on the horse shouted a command. Dozens of foot soldiers rushed toward the druid, swords and shields in hand.

As Solehan raised both hands to the sky, the grandeur of the Nature god surged through his body. In immense power, the might of Teluar transcended him. He let his hatred consume and ravage everything.

In front of their commander's terrified eyes, all the men who had lunged at the druid began to suffocate, clutching their throats and falling to the ground. Vegetation sprouted from their orifices. A wave of brambles and vines seized the dozens of lives sprawled before him.

Solehan exhaled deeply, a sense of full power spreading through his soul. The men's agonized moans resonated like a symphony in his ears. Teluar's powers caused his skin to vibrate.

With a resounding roar, Valnard's elaphora landed near Solehan. Ready to fight, the Alaris had assumed his strange bark-like epidermis. They would confront this threat together. Alone against all.

Solehan could sense the rage enveloping the general on his horse. His attention alternated between the Alaris and himself. In a new command, the man ordered his entire army to attack.

Solehan transformed into a giant bear, as pure Teluar magic was too costly for him to overcome so many men. The enormous animal charged into the trenches, smashing the flesh and bones of the unfortunate souls blocking his path. At his side, the elaphora disemboweled the infantrymen attempting to approach the Alaris.

Valnard invoked a burst of fiery Ignescent that consumed all within reach.

The lychenas slithered between the bodies, turning the soldiers to wood as they advanced through the ranks of the army. In their wake, a swarm of gleaming weapons and armor now adorned the bark-cursed bodies left in their attacking positions, the terror frozen on their faces forever.

Solehan became nothing but a savage whirlwind of sharp claws and fangs. His powerful bear body shattered the flesh and bones of the ill-fated souls, sending some flying and crushing others. His mind became primal and bestial, focusing on the scent of blood and the sound of bones cracking within his wake. Amid the confusion, several swords found their mark, lacerating his flesh. The young druid ignored the pain and redoubled his power and cruelty. The bodies of his victims piled around his enormous beast form.

Blinded by his hatred, by the blood flowing on his fur, and by the relentless onslaught of men, he prayed to Teluar to keep Valnard safe. With hope, he listened to the crackling of the Ignescent, creating torrents of flame, and to the roars of the elaphora. They would overcome human retaliation. They would succeed. They would fulfill their promise.

A sharp, searing pain suddenly coursed through his body. Under his bear form, he reared up and let out a howl.

Solehan turned around, barely able to do so. The man on the armored steed had fought his way through the infantry and had just thrust a long lance into the druid's flank. Solehan only had time to meet the man's eyes, filled with vengeful hatred, before the general and his horse burst into crimson flames, scattering his emotion among the ashes and embers that floated away.

Great flames, intertwined with scarlet vines, engulfed the bodies around Solehan, obliterating any signs of life in their ravenous frenzy. The magnificent, glowing brilliance of the Ignescent danced all around him, blending with the color of blood pouring onto the ground, seeping through the stone pavement of the street.

Solehan felt moisture spreading beneath his massive paws. He collapsed heavily; his animal body overcome by violent dizziness. Breathing became difficult.

Valnard's blurry silhouette rushed to his side. A new wave of pain shot through his body as he felt the Alaris remove the lance from his flesh, the metallic echo reverberating on the ground. The young druid reverted to his original form, his human skin meeting the cold, damp stone pavement on which he now lay.

"Solehan! No, no . . ." Valnard cried, kneeling beside him. The Alaris's hands pressed against the wound on Solehan's flank, trying to stem the blood flow.

Solehan trembled involuntarily. Was this the end? The pain was beginning to fade. "Valnard . . ." he murmured.

"It will be okay, it will be okay . . ." Valnard attempted to reassure him, in a panicked tone.

Through the haze of his increasingly blurred vision, Solehan observed the Alaris's sublime face stained with blood. The red glow on his pale skin. Tears creating pristine streaks on his cheeks. The astonishing proof of his anguish. Was he truly affected by this loss?

Valnard's voice grew distant and muffled. Solehan could no longer discern his words. His senses dulled one by one. The coldness of the ground seeped into his limbs, causing them to tremble more intensely. His eyes could no longer open.

As if sensing his condition, Valnard embraced Solehan's battered body.

His arms lifted him from the ground, and the warmth of the Alaris's chest enveloped the druid. The hand with blackened fingers brushed through his hair in a caress. The young man felt the moisture of one of Valnard's tears trickle onto his own cheek. Was the Alaris truly saddened by his departure? At that precise moment, the young man forgave him.

Solehan was at peace. Content to have experienced what they had gone through. He didn't want to leave without granting that.

But could he have fulfilled Teluar's will? Awakened the god and saved Valnard's child?

Could he had lived with authenticity what he had hidden deep within his heart?

He would never know.

And he couldn't ask for more. He had always known he didn't have the right, after all. He had been able to touch his wish briefly and would have to be content with that.

Perhaps he would cease to suffer in death? Perhaps he could finally dream their story?

Summoning his last reserves of strength, Solehan buried his face in Valnard's neck, and the Alaris tightened his arms around him. The warmth of Valnard's skin was exquisite. Solehan was glad to feel it one last time. Their bodies melded against each other.

A metallic and familiar taste filled his mouth. And Solehan lost himself in the arms of the Alaris.

46

In the course of the afternoon, the immense city of Dawnelest finally revealed itself as far as the eye could see, much to Shael's great relief. She urged her large ebony horse forward, the animal's jet-black mane swirling in the speed of its gallop. Talyvien, following her on his gray horse Aho, also gave a light kick with the stirrups to match their acceleration.

At dawn, they had emerged from the cave where they had spent the night and happily found their horses waiting patiently at the foot of the great waterfall. Shael knew they had been lucky to escape almost unscathed from their unfortunate encounter with Lucine's brother and that Alaris. She now hoped to see the young druidess again, as soon as possible, to warn her. In a grimace, she rolled her still-wounded shoulder.

The assassin exhaled deeply and tried to put this misadventure behind her. To clear her mind. She needed to focus on the purpose of their visit. However, Talyvien's gentle care when he had tended to her wound kept occupying her thoughts. The truthfulness of his words. The patience of his gestures.

No, his hands had indeed neither *soiled* nor *harmed* her. And now, she was convinced he wouldn't, that he was different. Perhaps he was the counterexample she needed, after all? Had he even done the opposite? Had he even shown her a glimmer of hope for something else?

A new feeling she thought she would never experience was now swirling within her ribcage. An uncomfortable truth she didn't know what to do with, slowly taking root despite her efforts to silence it. The spark of a desire for a future she was definitely not prepared for.

They reached one of the massive gates of the capital, and Shael saw an unusually large number of travelers of all kinds. Caravans, horses, and pedestrians, hundreds of souls, moving under the great stone arches that defined the boundaries of Dawnelest and disappearing into the streets of the grand city. She and the paladin urged their horses to trot, their hooves clattering on the stone-paved avenue.

The assassin observed the vibrant colors worn by the bystanders, their faces sometimes painted with various patterns, their laughter and dances bursting between the facades of the grand houses. Long, multicolored banners fluttered on the buildings, seeming to undulate to the rhythm of the various outpourings of music coming from nearby taverns and stalls.

Exasperated, Shael muttered a curse.

It seemed to amuse Talyvien, as a silent, teasing question formed on the paladin's face.

"Solamaris, the Festival of the Solstice celebration," she replied nonchalantly to his unspoken interrogation. "I forgot it's happening right now, and it lasts for a few days," she added with a grumble.

It was also the Festival of Lovers Celebration. She *obviously* didn't need to point that out to the paladin. The atmosphere was already tense enough between them.

"Come on, don't you enjoy festivities?" he teased. "It looks rather delightful!"

"Not really," Shael retorted, her eyes narrowing in a thin line.

Their horses weaved through the crowd, and a group of young women crossed paths with them on foot, giggling and blushing as they approached the paladin, who paid no attention. The assassin, seemingly indifferent, discreetly observed Talyvien from the corner of her eye. Was he completely oblivious to the effect he had on the female population? Maybe he hadn't been in such a crowded place before without wearing his paladin mask and armor?

Against her will, she noticed his straight posture and imposing figure on the large gray horse, his face displaying an air of composure as he discovered the city and its inhabitants, his slightly tousled short chestnut hair, and the sword of Tuoryn proudly attached to his belt. Shael realized her cheeks were stupidly heating up and was grateful to be able to hide under her hood.

Though she tried to block any such thoughts, Shael couldn't suppress her annoyance when another group of young women approached, giggling. She sighed through her nose. She had to focus on the reason for their journey.

"So, where do you want to go first?" the assassin asked with feigned innocence.

"Mmhh. I suppose I'll try to have an audience with the queen," he replied.

His answer caused her more pain than she had hoped for.

"It seems she regularly holds audience sessions," she said, cursing herself mentally. "I mean, unless you have a more . . . *direct* way of getting an audience with her?" she added, trying to sound playful.

"You know, Shael, it's been several years since I last saw her. So no, I don't have a more . . . *direct* way," he teased, raising an eyebrow and giving her a sidelong glance.

As her mood lightened slightly, they crossed several districts of the grand capital of Dawnelest. Amid the city's bustling atmosphere, they passed by the grand canals where several brightly colored boats carried joyous groups celebrating Solamaris with dancing, drinking, and singing.

The assassin took pleasure in showing Talyvien around the city. Admiringly, he frequently looked up to contemplate the strange and magnificent houses stacked toward the sky like layered confections of wood and sculpted stones, creating silhouettes that were all unique in their own way.

But Shael grew impatient to show him the highlight of the spectacle. Connected solely by immense stone bridges that spanned the great waterways was a castle whose height seemed to surpass anything humanly possible to construct without divine aid. It emerged from an island surrounded by a network of canals in the heart of the city. The structure was so impressive that it appeared to soar above the rest of the metropolis and graze the sky. It was so vast that clouds swirled around the building like long serpents of mist.

Talyvien froze on his horse and stared at the building from top to bottom, his mouth slightly open.

Shael chuckled discreetly.

Once the paladin's notable admiration had passed, they trotted over one of the stone bridges and entered the grand courtyard of the imposing structure, which was open to the public.

Feeling out of place in the city's affluent neighborhoods, Shael let the paladin inquire with several soldiers stationed in front of the massive entrance of the castle.

"There's a session tomorrow morning, apparently," he said, mounting Aho again.

"Well, then we can do some shopping," she replied, shaking her head.

"Aren't you planning to go to your convent?"

"Let's see the queen first, tomorrow. I'll head to the Sazaelith convent afterward, probably in the middle of the night. I also need to get my armor repaired, and I suppose you could do with a new shirt." She lifted her cloak and revealed the two huge holes in the leather armor, exposing the bandage on her shoulder.

She also decided not to mention it to the paladin, but not knowing what she would find at the convent, she wanted to be physically ready in case something didn't go as planned. She had not fulfilled her contract, and it had never happened to her before. A good night's sleep in a bed wouldn't hurt, especially after the attack she had endured against the young druid.

They followed the canals back, this time in the opposite direction, as the sun was now setting, painting the atmosphere with a soft pink and orange hue.

Shael noted that the festive mood around them was becoming less family-oriented and more exuberant. Alcohol seemed to flow freely, and couples flirted here and there.

They headed toward a more modest neighborhood that the assassin knew like the back of her hand, and they entered a discreet-looking small shop, leaving their horses outside.

"Shael! What a surprise!" exclaimed Eskira. "It's been a while since I last saw you! What brings you here?" The young redhead merchant circled her counter and came to greet them with raised hands.

"Hi, Eskira," cooed the assassin. "I'll need some adjustments to my armor."

Shael had always been fascinated by Eskira's ease and eloquence. A former thief turned owner of the shop, she now provided the Children of Twilight with combat equipment.

The assassin parted her cloak, revealing the marks Solehan had left on the leather armor.

The merchant placed her hand familiarly on Shael's shoulder and examined the resulting damage. "Well! What could have caused such harm?"

"A big cat," the paladin chimed in, catching Shael off guard.

Dismayed, the assassin turned around and gave the paladin a wide-eyed glowering look.

Talyvien responded with a radiant smile.

"Mmhh, I see, a real menace these days," Eskira mocked, glancing at Talyvien from head to toe. "Do you need an escort nowadays, Shael? Although, I must admit, it is a charming one."

"No! It's just that—" Shael stammered, taken aback.

"I'm the one in need of an escort, I'd say," complimented Talyvien, looking at the assassin with tender eyes.

Caught between pride and embarrassment, Shael found herself, for once, speechless. Why did he have this effect on her? Nevertheless, she noticed Eskira's sharp and meticulous gaze fixating on the hilt of Tuoryn's sword, adorned with the symbols of the paladins of Callystrande.

"On the other hand, as attractive as they may be, you should be more careful with your company, Shael," Eskira said pointedly.

"What's the problem exactly?" Talyvien growled, clenching his teeth. The paladin stepped forward, his fingers gripping the sword's hilt.

But the assassin shot him a pleading look, begging him not to act. It seemed to work.

Resigned, he released the weapon and crossed his arms.

"So, do you think you can repair it for me?" Shael hurriedly asked, attempting to redirect the conversation.

With pursed lips, the merchant nodded slightly.

Shael turned and discreetly spied on Talyvien. Although his face still showed some annoyance, he had shifted his attention and was strolling among the shop's displays.

A surge of adrenaline buzzed in the assassin's ears. She had hated feeling so miserable and weak in front of him when he had tended to her wound. And she loathed her fear. Why was it so difficult?

Shael exhaled her frustration through her nose. She wouldn't let herself be dominated by these stupid fears, by the haunting images. That was out of the question. In a thoughtless gesture, she removed her cloak and the upper part of her armor, which she handed to Eskira before she could change her mind.

"Well, Shael, it seems you're swimming in dangerous waters these days," Eskira teased, casting a sharp glance at the paladin. "In any case, it'll take me a few minutes. Take a look around the shop if you find anything you like while waiting."

Eskira disappeared into the back of the shop.

Dangerous waters? Probably. Wearing only the thin leather band across her chest, Shael felt completely exposed in her own body. Not knowing what else to do, she began inspecting the various goods scattered about the small shop. She could feel Talyvien's surprised attention burning on her skin. Her skull seemed to press against her brain. Her physical body and her mind reflexively divided.

Shael donned her usual bravado and walked along the different displays placed here and there in the small shop. She tried to maintain a nonchalant air, despite the paladin's watchful eyes. The assassin lightly touched the polished metal of several weapons and armor of different qualities that shimmered in the dim light. Eventually, she picked up a finely crafted short sword and began inspecting it to give herself some composure and courage.

A certain restlessness seemed to stir in Talyvien. Obviously embarrassed, he coughed and scratched his jaw, his cheeks slightly reddening.

Curious, Shael tilted the polished blade and observed her reflection in the weapon. Was it the sight of her body that had such an effect on him? She had spent her life hating it, mastering it to never betray her again, to turn it into a punishing weapon. She fiercely hid it from all male gazes and shielded it from pain. Could it be anything else than that?

In response to her question, a warmth fluttered in Shael's abdomen.

For the first time, she found herself not seething with anger at a man's effervescence. Worse. She realized she enjoyed the paladin's interest in her. What was she supposed to do with that?

At that moment, she felt Talyvien's presence as he stood beside her, arms crossed once again.

"Wow, Eskira sure has a loose tongue!" exclaimed Talyvien, attempting to sound light-hearted but failing.

"Oh yes . . . a real gossip!" chuckled Shael, suppressing the quivering of her hands from knowing he was so close to her in that attire. "But she provides the Children of the Twilight with very high-quality weapons and armor."

"Mmhh . . ." nodded the paladin.

He leaned in behind the assassin and brushed his lips against her ear.

The young woman's heart skipped a beat.

"You know, Shael, true strength lies in being able to show your vulnerability. Not the other way around," he whispered to her. "You don't need to be anyone other than yourself. I know you're used to hiding among the shadows, but I hope that one day you'll feel secure enough to expose yourself to the light."

Shael couldn't hold back the slight tremors that followed. Her fingers trembled, and she put the blade back on the display.

"And I'm certain that the person who will emerge from that will be magnificent," he added.

A feeling exploded in Shael's chest. A whirlwind swept through her thoughts. But her body remained frozen, her feet anchored to the floor. Had he really said that?

She wanted to turn around. She wanted—

Eskira entered the room in a boisterous manner. "There you go! Good as new!"

A freezing wave splashed over Shael's skin. She put her hand to her throat, trying to catch her breath. In disbelief, she looked at Talyvien, who had moved away and was pretending to inspect new armor. Did that really just happen?

"Your armor, Shael! Good as new!" Eskira proudly insisted once more.

Still dazed, Shael put her suits of armor back on. One made of illusions, the other of leather, and she thanked Eskira warmly.

They stepped out of the shop and untied their horses. Troubled, Shael took a moment to don her mantle of confidence again. Had he really seen through her that much? Could she truly show her vulnerability and consider it a strength?

The assassin was exhausted; her head was spinning. She chose to postpone her questioning and act as if nothing had happened.

After a few moments, she turned to Talyvien. "Eskira is right about one thing," she said, steering the conversation toward a more trivial topic.

"Oh, really?"

"With a new shirt, we should get you a hood as well. Even if you tried not to look like a paladin, it wouldn't be very convincing." She chuckled.

Talyvien gave a slight smile as he gently stroked Aho. "And is that a problem?" he asked in a lighter tone.

"Let's just say that we're more in a neighborhood where thieves and assassins roam than paladins or noble knights!"

A few moments later, as the darkness of night settled over the city, she emerged from a second shop with a new shirt for Talyvien and a large gray-colored cloak. He seemed to appreciate that she had chosen the same color as Aho's robe, and he put it around his neck. He then raised the hood over his head, concealing almost his face entirely.

"Are you trying to turn me into an assassin by any chance?" he joked.

"Nope, no chance!"

Their laughter mingled with that of the passersby, with Solamaris still being celebrated in the surrounding streets. They then made their way to the inn whose name Shael had mentioned to Lucine and Calixte before their parting, the *"Veil of Truth."*

Shael and Talyvien squeezed their way inside the crowded small inn and moved toward the counter. A few songs and clamors emanated from the place, and several customers in colorful costumes walked around with tankards in hand. The festivities were in full swing, and the atmosphere was filled with excitement. It would probably be challenging to get a room during the festival. After waiting their turn, they finally reached the large wooden counter.

"Welcome to the *Veil of Truth*! What can I do for you!?" exclaimed the hoarse voice of the innkeeper. She was a woman in her fifties and bore a broad smile on her jovial and welcoming face.

"We'd like two simple rooms, please," Shael requested, lowering her hood.

The innkeeper seemed surprised when the assassin revealed her face. "Oh, you know I always try to accommodate the Children of Twilight, but I have nothing left for tonight," she stammered.

Seeing the disappointed look on the assassin's face, she hastily checked the book in front of her. Shael knew that most merchants and innkeepers in the area tried to bend over backward for the chosen ones of Sazaelith, as their reputation preceded them. They feared that one might visit them in the middle of the night, dagger at their throat. A grotesque but useful rumor that the chosen ones enjoyed perpetuating. She hoped once again that this morbid legend would work.

"Ah, I have one double room left at the end of the corridor for you and your friend!"

Shael and Talyvien looked at each other uncomfortably. Then, the paladin shrugged in embarrassment, both knowing that they didn't really have another choice but to accept.

After climbing the stairs in silence, Shael's stomach churned at the same time as the key turned in the lock of their suite.

She was relieved to see two single beds in each corner of the room. They placed their belongings on each bed and paid the innkeeper so they could stable their horses. They then made their way to the tavern in the inn.

Shael hurried toward a small alcove just as two customers left. She stuck a dagger into the table with a grim expression to deter a man who seemed to have had the same idea at the same moment, all under Talyvien's amused gaze.

"The competition is fierce to get a room or a table during Solamaris," he laughed, as he returned with two tankards of beer.

"I'm a bad influence on you," Shael teased, shaking her head as she looked at the drinks in a delighted and surprised way.

The assassin savored this moment, knowing it to be fleeting. Anxiety loomed in the back of her mind. Still, she tried to focus only on the present moment as they exchanged stories and chatted about various topics for several hours. She watched the tavern gradually empty of its customers as they enjoyed their meal and several rounds of beers. Shael couldn't recall having had so much fun during the Solamaris festival in previous years.

But nothing was wise at this moment.

Not thinking about their audience with Queen Selena the next day, what potentially awaited her at the convent of the Sisters of Sazaelith, the alcohol flowing in their tankards.

Her heart sank slowly as she admired the paladin's face. How was that possible?

Throughout her life, she had been taught to see the chosen ones of Callystrande as enemies. And from her experience, to see men as predators whom she needed to avenge.

But she found it difficult to see Talyvien as such. Especially knowing now that their respective goddesses loved each other. What he had done for her. She didn't know what to think anymore.

As the beer flowed, she felt the paladin's joyful emotion soon replaced by something more intense, similar to what she had glimpsed earlier in Eskira's shop. She was suddenly seized with panic. She didn't know how to react to this.

"I'm going to bed, Talyvien," she said. "It's getting late."

"Oh. Goodnight, Shael," he replied with a broad smile, although the assassin could have sworn a hint of disappointment flickered on the paladin's face. "Thanks for this day, anyway. It's been a long time since I've had this much fun!" he added as she got up.

The assassin, despite herself, did something crazy, stupid, and reckless.

"Me too," she murmured. Then Shael planted a kiss on Talyvien's cheek, causing his eyes to widen.

She quickly fled down the stairs of the inn, leaving the paladin to catch a glimpse of the dark blue of her cloak fluttering behind her elusive silhouette.

47

Hits.

Macabre percussions that made the walls vibrate. Reverberate in her head. A funereal ode that extinguished all hope.

Hidden like this, she put her hands over her ears to hear nothing more. To numb herself. Tears rolled down her cheeks. She tried not to make a sound, not to sniff too loudly. The monster was still there.

Her mother's screams pounded against her eardrums. She flinched with every blow, every cracking of bones, every plea. The image of her bare and dirty feet, the tattered and torn dress, etched into her eyes.

She was accustomed to this absurd ritual. To this favorite hiding place in the wall, where she would slip through a small hole when she heard heavy footsteps on the wooden staircase.

But this time was different.

Curled up on the other side of the partition, she inhaled the impending smell of death that filled her nostrils. A survival instinct made her realize she had to act. She scanned the surroundings inside the wall and came across a sharp piece of wood, which she grasped with a shivering hand.

Her light steps on the floor barely made the floorboards creak. She saw her mother's emaciated and lifeless body on the bed, the few sheets crumpled and stained with red and blue bloods. The monstrous shadow loomed above, projected onto the plaster cracks of the wall.

With her weapon in hand, she approached, trembling, at the tender age of six. The man turned his head in her direction.

Predatory eyes stared at her. Mad eyes that whirled on a face whose contours became blurred. Eyes she could never forget. There was nothing human left in those eyes.

His monstrous body pounced on her.

She tried to struggle and dropped the piece of wood in surprise. A cruel smile escaped the man's face. His teeth, tinted cobalt blue, were revealed as he forcibly held her down. His huge, callous hands closed around her tiny wrists. A hot breath blew on her face. A panting beastly respiration, a fetid smell that spread over her. One of her wrists was then released from his grip.

And the loathsome touch of the huge hand spilled onto her child's body, freezing her despite herself.

She turned her head and reached out her arm toward the piece of wood on the floor. Her small trembling fingers were unable to grasp the makeshift weapon.

So, she remained there. Without really being there. She would be no longer herself. Never again.

Immobile, fixated on the sight of her powerless hand. On the texture of the floorboards against her skin. On the shadows dancing in the room. On the light slowly fading away. She drifted far away and wished not to find her way back. She could never find it again anyway.

She couldn't say how much time had passed before her mother's cry echoed. Before she was pulled out of her anesthetic journey. Before she could seize her weapon.

She struck with all her might at the man's neck, and he let out a scream. Red blood splattered on her face below.

A torrent of confusion swirled. Mixing warm liquid and screams. Her mother held her by the arm and led her into the street. Hooves of horses hammered around her on the cobblestones.

"What have you done? It's your fault! You wanted some too, didn't you, you little trollop! You're good for nothing! At least you'll be of some use!" The memory of her mother's blue-stained mouth uttering those words.

She hit the cold stone violently. Several hooded and dark figures grabbed her bruised body. Women's hands quickly washed her under the icy water as the tremors resumed.

"Shael?"

A blade dangerously approached the pupils of her eyes.

"Shael!"

Unbearable pain. Her body convulsed; warm liquid streamed down her cheeks.

"Shael, wake up!"

The silhouette of her mother screamed from the other side. The concealed women held her as the massive wooden door closed.

 Having heard the assassin writhing in pain from her nightmare, Talyvien hurried to kneel by her bedside. He tried to free her from the horrors of her dreams, placing a hand tenderly on her cheek and wiping away the tears that trickled from the corners of her eyes. When the sapphire irises of the assassin finally fixed on him, he felt the cold touch of a dagger against his throat.

"It's me, Shael. I'm here."

Shael emerged from the veil of her nightmares, and the magic dissipated from her trembling hand.

Talyvien recognized that look. The same desperate look he had briefly glimpsed during their training, when she had almost stabbed him in the neck. He would have given anything to erase that pain from her face. He slid his hand from Shael's cheek and gently took her shaking hand in his. "It will be alright now," he reassured her with calmness.

They stayed like that for several minutes, enveloped in the silence of the night, discovering each other for the first time. Talyvien gently stroked the back of Shael's hand with his thumb, trying to ground her back into their reality. He knew he hadn't been mistaken. The authenticity of her vulnerability made her even more magnificent. He felt privileged that she allowed him to witness this. That she felt safe enough by his side. That she finally accepted to meet him in truth. Perhaps the words he had spoken in the shop had an effect?

After this timeless moment, Shael's face finally regained a more serene look. The paladin got up to go back to bed.

But Shael's hand remained in his. "Wait . . . Would you mind staying with me for a while?" she murmured.

Dumbfounded, Talyvien saw the young woman make room for him in the bed. His heart skipped a beat, before pulsating faster. A wave of warmth coursed through his body.

The sapphire and luminescent blue of the assassin's eyes implored him. Ever since he had first seen them, he had never been able to resist their call. He was both fascinated and terrified by them. He yielded with restrained joy and lay down beside her, trying to take up as little space as possible on the side of the bed. As if holding a precious gift, he kept her hand in his.

Courageously, Shael exposed the shadows that infiltrated her life.

The paladin's throat tightened as she told him about her nightmare, her memories, her childhood. Under the pain, blood, and violence that her body and soul had endured, he finally understood her rage, her hatred, and her sorrow. His paladin's heart wanted to protect her, to spare her from this suffering, but he knew she had to ride these waves to heal, to navigate to the other side of the ocean, to create a different ending to her story. He could only be there, an island in the midst of this stormy sea, a refuge.

Shael's blue and moist eyes eventually closed, and she fell asleep again, this time peacefully and likely exhausted, her delicate hand still in his.

The muffled sound of a sweet lullaby escaped from one of Talyvien's pockets. He slipped his other hand inside and took out the small music box that Calixte had given him. The lullaby gracefully filled the room, and he placed the little music box on the nightstand. This strange object definitely had a sense of humor of its own. It suited the Alaris well.

Soothed by the voluptuous music, Talyvien gazed longingly at the sleeping young woman. The pain that usually feasted on her torments seemed to have fled from her face. The predator that the paladin had seen so many times had finally escaped its cage. At that moment, she was just the most beautiful person he had ever seen in his life.

He got lost in the reflection that the moon cast on her long, untidy black hair, on the delicacy of her skin, her curves. On the fragility of her body and the path she had just bravely embarked on with him.

Clad in the far too large and torn shirt that had been used as bandages and now served as her nightclothes, Shael buried her face in the fabric. Touched, Talyvien found himself liking the idea that she could wear an item of his clothing. He couldn't tell if the few beers he had consumed earlier in the evening had any influence, but he wished this night would never end. Shael's slow and peaceful breathing blended with the notes from the music box and resonated like the most beautiful melody in the darkness of the night.

"*If one cannot exist without the other, wouldn't it make sense for them to eventually love each other?*" The sentence he had heard from Lucine's mouth strolled into his mind, as he traced the contours of Shael's sleeping face.

The memory of the audience he would have with Selena in a few hours suddenly resurfaced in his thoughts. Talyvien felt his stomach twist, his heart torn in two. How had he ended up here?

He couldn't tell whether the moment he was living was the most beautiful or the most cruel thing that had ever happened to him.

48

With her arms crossed behind her head, Lucine gazed at the elegant motifs that meandered across the wooden ceiling above her bed, with Katao peacefully asleep by her side. Feör'ael had offered them lodging for a few days in her splendid and delicate wooden palace perched on the giant tree, and two adjoining rooms had been allocated to the druidess and the bard.

The perfumed air of this strange plane of existence, with its peculiar flora, filled the small room where she was located. The violet reflections of the perpetually clear and starry sky seeped through the window and cast their glow upon the vegetation that formed the architecture of the room.

Despite this serene atmosphere, the bitter weight of the small wooden amulet pressed against her body in the pocket of her jacket. Tormented by doubt, Lucine couldn't stop ruminating on the unanswered questions that flooded her mind. Answers that would probably never come, as her entire clan was no more.

Had the elders known that this gift would prevent her powers from manifesting? The powers had only finally awakened when she had removed the amulet, and Lucine had caught a glimpse of Teluar sleeping under the Tree of Ether. How could it be that the name of the Nature god had never been mentioned in the legends of her clan?

She also thought back to the words of the forest spirit queen. What had happened to Solehan? If the Alaris named Valnard had taken him, was her brother being manipulated or even forced to use his powers against his will? She now understood that the two individuals who bore a strong resemblance to them and had attacked the village were probably this Alaris and Solehan. The young druidess was overcome with nausea. Did her twin still possess his freedom of thought and action, or was he trapped in his own body while committing such atrocities? Neither answer seemed to ease her mind.

Exhausted from tormenting herself, Lucine leaped out of bed. A slight pain oscillated on one side of her abdomen as she moved. She chose to ignore it and absentmindedly rubbed her flank to dissipate the curious sensation.

Still determined, she decided to go to the large room in the dwelling where she had arrived a few hours ago. Followed by the dog and descending a narrow staircase enclosed in wood that led to their rooms on the upper floors, she once again reached the great throne room.

Lucine found the sovereign in the company of Calixte. Both were engrossed in lively conversation and lounged on large reclining chairs made of thick, cushiony leaves that perfectly hugged their bodies. The young druidess marveled at the presence and charisma of these two surprising beings, a mirror of their respective magnificence.

"Ah, druidess! I hope the room suits you?" Feör'ael inquired when she spotted Lucine.

"It's perfect. Thank you, Your Majesty."

"Oh, please, none of that! You can call me Feör. It will be more practical!"

Lucine nodded with a smile.

The sovereign rose from her seat and stood before her.

Calixte did the same.

"I wanted to ask you," Lucine began hesitantly, "why did Teluar fall asleep?"

"The cruelty of humans toward his creation was too great." she replied, in a choked voice. "He couldn't bear it."

"Oh," Lucine whispered, gazing at the twisted wooden throne with embarrassment.

"But I don't believe exterminating humanity is the solution, druidess. I believe there is hope. I believe the Mother Goddesses have given you this gift to embody that hope." A smile tinged with melancholy appeared on Feör's magnificent face. "If you wish, I can try to show you the way. To show you the extent of the gift you have received."

Calixte's face brightened, their orange eyes sparkling with hope and approval at Feör's words.

"I would very much like that," Lucine said.

"Then come with me. I have something to show you."

Lucine, Calixte, and Katao followed the forest spirit queen with resolute steps. With a sweeping gesture, Feör opened one of the majestic windows entwined with translucent membranes and branches that decorated the room. A spacious wooden balcony with an unobstructed view of her realm was revealed. Perhaps was she accustomed to contemplating her remarkable plane of existence from here?

Standing prominently at the edge of the terrace, Feör whistled loudly and spread her arms.

Calixte jumped, a hand on their throat, clearly not expecting such familiarity.

Lucine watched with delight as the long petals of the queen's dress curled and wrapped around her legs. Her garment transformed into pants that accentuated her curves. What was she about to do?

Two shadows emerged from beneath the balustrade. With breathtaking speed, they swiftly curved over their heads.

Calixte flinched again and let out a small cry of surprise, which amused Lucine. It was disconcerting to see the bard so far from their comfort zone.

Intimidated as well, Katao whimpered and huddled against the druidess's legs.

"Drafelis," commented Feör, raising her head as her vegetal hair swayed in the breeze.

Two incredible creatures, straight out of a dream, flapped their wings vigorously and landed in front of them. Graceful like felines in their evident agility and with slender cat-like bodies, royal with their enormous monarch butterfly wings, their regal posture, and their long peacock feather and leaf tails. Fantastical chimeras with dream-like nuances, their deep blue fur shading into iridescent variations of emerald and carnelian on their bird-like crests and their plumage made out of foliage.

Intrigued, Lucine approached one of the creatures.

The yellow eyes of the drafelis watched her with curiosity as she drew nearer.

"They are stunning!" admired the young druidess.

"They are creations of Teluar," explained Feör.

"But isn't the god asleep?" asked Lucine, caressing the fur of one of the drafelis, which began to purr.

"Yes, but we are currently in his dream. The animals in your plane of existence are merely a lesser version of his creation. An older version. Teluar has continued to imagine new beings in his dreams since he went into hibernation."

The queen turned her gaze away from Lucine and looked at Calixte. The bard was eager to keep a certain distance between themselves and the majestic creatures.

"You can approach, Alaris," Feör teased. "They are harmless!"

"Oh, I'm sure! They are indeed fascinating, but I'd rather avoid an unfortunate claw strike, a disastrous hairstyle, or torn clothing! I am far too adorable as I am!" Calixte declared mischievously, rolling one of their wrists.

"Then travel with me," the sovereign proposed. "I will ensure that nothing crumples you. In every sense of the word."

"Oh . . . Are we going to travel on their backs?!" Calixte asked, frowning.

"Indeed! It will be faster!"

"I wouldn't want to bother you, Majesty!" the bard hastened to add. "In that case, I can travel with Lucine."

"It doesn't bother me. Quite the opposite! It would be *my* pleasure, Alaris," Feör insisted, eyeing them with delight.

Lucine suppressed a giggle behind her hand when she saw embarrassment on Calixte's face for the first time. It seemed they had found someone who could rival their legendary charm.

"Please, take a seat, druidess," said the queen, pointing to the chimera.

With the help of the drafelis she had caressed, Lucine mounted its back and held the dog close to her. Feör climbed onto the second creature with a swift motion and helped Calixte join her. With flushed cheeks, the Alaris settled in front of the sovereign, who encircled her arms around them to hold the saddle's pommel with both hands.

With a single powerful and coordinated flap of their wings, they took flight, and the exclamations of amazement from Calixte and Lucine, followed by Feör's crystalline laughter, scattered among the sinuous branches of the great tree.

The two drafelis flew joyfully side by side, and Lucine's heart was cradled by the beauty of the landscape. She discovered a magical world of luminescent hues, plains and forests of all colors, shimmering waterways, and cascades of light flowing toward the celestial vault. Surprising and improbable animals, chimerical creatures with rainbow hues, sheep whose wool was made of flowers and leaves, lions with mossy and floral manes of large petals, tigers and panthers with mist-like spots and stripes, foxes with nebulous tails sewn with stars, horses with manes of branches and flowers, among many others.

"So, is this plane of existence . . . Teluar's dream?" Lucine asked in amazement.

"Indeed. It is a plane similar to the one you enter when you dream," Feör commented. "But this one is an image of Teluar's ones, directly connected to the Tree of Ether. Time also flows differently from yours, more slowly. One day in the material plane corresponds to one week here."

The memory of the torpor she had felt in the colorful forest surged in her mind, and Lucine understood why she had felt that way. Were they still dreaming?

"Ah! We're arriving," exclaimed the sovereign excitedly.

Confined like a sparkling liquid in an overly large wine glass, a large basin of shimmering water was revealed within a dormant volcano. The drafelis swooped toward the suspended lake, and Lucine squinted to try to discern more details.

As they approached, the clarity of the rosy sky got lost in a thick, dark violet mist. Only the luminescence of the water managed to break the darkness as it brushed the contours of their silhouettes. Large black halos undulated on the surface of the fluorescent expanse, which Lucine recognized as immense lazy lily pads. Images from Luminaur's dream constantly washed over the young woman's mind. Everything seemed so similar, so magical. Perhaps she had touched this plane of existence in her own dreams?

The drafelis landed gracefully on the shore. Lucine dismounted the chimera, thanking it with a scratch under the chin, and set Katao on the ground. Feör jumped down from her mount and once again helped Calixte by lifting them by the waist.

"You see, we arrived without any trouble, Alaris. And without harming your charming self," the queen purred.

"Oh, indeed!" Calixte stammered, running a hand through their hair.

Regaining their composure, they arched their shoulders back. "Of course, it would have been a shame to deprive the world of such talent!"

The queen's silvery laughter echoed.

A smirk curled the corner of Lucine's mouth as she took a few steps toward the wondrous water. The gentle lapping of the sparkling waves sprinkled luminescent flakes onto the shore, and the druidess couldn't resist dipping her fingertips into the magical waters. She leaned over and lightly submerged her hands, enthralled by the sight of magic cascading over her skin.

"The blessed water of Teluar," Feör intervened, sensing the question forming in Lucine's mind. "This water exists only in this plane. Well, almost. Follow me."

The queen gracefully leaped from one lily pad to another, heading toward the center of the water expanse, creating ripples of light with each step. Lucine, Calixte, and Katao followed somewhat clumsily across a few dozen aquatic plants, finally joining her on one of them.

The young druidess let out an exclamation and froze. Amid the maelstrom of lily pads, a water lily with diaphanous petals paraded like an opal jewel in the darkness. A single lotus with a thousand facets blossomed at the heart of the serene, unruffled water.

"The crystal flower you see is called a 'Heart of Teluar,'" Feör asserted. "I brought you here because these flowers rarely bloom. It is said that they only sprout when the god himself wants to deliver a message. This one has recently bloomed, and I believe its message is for you, druidess."

Lucine finally managed to tear her eyes away from the wondrous plant and looked at the queen. A message? Everything was happening so quickly. Just a few hours ago, she didn't even know she possessed certain powers, let alone that they were associated with the god of Nature.

"How long has it been since this last happened?" Calixte asked with interest, leaning in to observe the flower more closely.

"A long time," Feör replied, her tone a mix of firmness and melancholy. "But it doesn't matter, Alaris." The queen didn't seem eager to dwell on the subject. "You must go into the water, druidess. That's where you'll find your answer," the queen added, gesturing for Lucine to proceed.

Katao barked anxiously at being separated from the young woman. Lucine patted the top of his head to reassure him and removed her clothes, placing them on the edge of the lily pad. In her underwear, she sat down and dipped her legs into the sparkling water.

The warmth of the liquid surprised the young druidess. Its touch was gentle and imbued with clarity. So, she slid in and immersed herself completely. Her body sank into the phosphorescent liquid, and the magnificent faces of Feör and Calixte disappeared in her momentum.

Lucine was surprised not to see the bottom of this curious lake. Paradoxically, she felt no fear or doubt in her mind as she continued moving downward, the magic flakes parting around her. Certainty resonated within her.

The deeper she was immersed, the more she felt like she was returning to the origins of the world. Where everything had begun. She floated as if in her mother's womb. Soon, she no longer needed to breathe; air was no longer necessary. Since the Eclipse that had changed everything, since her escape, she had traveled all this way for this moment. She was now certain of it.

Disoriented yet strangely at peace, she could no longer discern the direction of her swimming, up or down. Her feet landed on the other side of the water's surface. Amazed, she spread her toes and observed the caustic reflections rippling on this strange solid light ground.

Still determined, Lucine walked on this turbulent terrain in this breathtaking parallel fraction. She was at the source of Teluar's dream. Where the god's imagination exploded. Where reality, time, day, night, nothing had meaning or significance. Or perhaps was it here that everything was decided?

As she looked up, large trees with dense foliage appeared around her. An immersed and translucent forest that embraced her progress. She observed the tops of the towering vegetation that drowned into the abyssal depths.

And then, she felt its presence again.

Gentle. Warm. Powerful.

As it moved gracefully among the watery foliage, the fox with its shimmering fur came to meet her. It stopped in front of the young woman and observed her with its large black eyes.

"Lucine."

Taken aback, Lucine blinked. Was the fox really speaking to her? She received this revelation with caution. Could it be that—

"Teluar?" she guessed, intrigued.

"Does it surprise you?"

"So, it was you. All this time . . ." she sighed, relieved to finally have an answer to one of her questions. "But I thought you were asleep under the Tree of Ether. How—"

"I am, but we are currently in my dream. Anything is possible in dreams, druidess." The fox tilted its head. *"Only the chosen ones can see me in this form. It's a projection I use to guide them."*

Teluar had saved her life. Time and time again, he had always been there. She understood that she had never truly been alone since that fateful day.

"So, you guided me here all this time," Lucine concluded, before adding, "Feör said you had a message for me?"

"Indeed. I can't stay long. I'm not supposed to cross planes of existence like this. But we must be quick. Lucine . . . You must stop your brother and Valnard on their path of destruction."

"How do you know about that?"

"Solehan is also one of my chosen ones. But in light of the cruelty he has shown, the mother goddesses have turned their backs on him. Only you can save him now."

"So, he did all of this of his own accord?" she stammered with horror.

"It seems so. With Valnard's counsel. You must reason with your brother. It's not too late."

Lucine's chest tightened. She clenched her fists, and her nails dug into the palms of her hands. It was true. Solehan had gone mad. He had lost all sense of judgment.

"Perhaps he believes it's what you want?" she hoped. "After all, you couldn't bear what the humans did to your creation."

"It is true that I went into hibernation for that reason. But I still have hope that they will learn from their mistakes. They must. Humans are also my children."

"You're a god," she retorted angrily. "Can't you do anything?"

"I am doing what I must at this moment, but the pact the gods made with the Alaris prevents me from intervening directly. You are my chosen one, and the chosen ones of the gods are their messengers in the material plane."

"So . . . you also know where Solehan is?"

"Yes. He is in Argentvale."

"So, the rumor was true!" she fumed. "I absolutely must go there!"

"You can't confront the Alaris alone, Lucine."

What could she do with this information? She needed concrete help.

"How can I stop Valnard and Solehan? I don't even know what powers I inherited, let alone what my brother's powers are like."

"The powers of my chosen ones are never exactly the same. That's why they are passed on to twins. They complement each other, mirroring the nature of my mothers."

The fox approached cautiously.

"Take my heart, Lucine," Teluar added. *"Use it wisely when the time comes. I will accompany you . . . I'll be there, within you . . ."*

"Wait! Don't go!" Lucine cried out.

The animal's fur melted into the waters, creating a swirling vortex around the young druidess. Lucine's cries turned into desperate gurgles.

The power of the god descended upon her. Her exultation was complete. Lucine had no choice but to let go.

She was reborn once again. In this primal and senseless place. Her entire body was bubbling with excitement. Teluar's magic infested her veins, her limbs, her heart.

A few mossy spots appeared on her skin. Verdant lichen grew on her hands, arms, and face. It covered her tattoos, her entire epidermis. Like dominoes rising on her skin, small leaves sprouted, then increased in size and number. Soon, a floral tableau undulated across her body. Magnificent flowers sprouted from her tears, detached from her face, and floated around her. Lucine had become nature itself. She had no past or future. No distinct essence.

She was everything, absolute.

In a swift burst, Lucine emerged from the water headfirst.

Breathless, she clung to the edge of one of the large lily pads. What had just happened? She tried to hold onto the plant's soft texture under her fingers to regain her composure. With a dazed look, she examined the appearance of her arms' skin.

The imprint left by Teluar had finally dissipated. Air returned to her lungs through painful breaths.

Calixte and Feör jumped onto the lily pad Lucine clung to and approached her, their concern evident on their faces.

"What did you see?" Calixte inquired, helping her up onto the plant.

"Teluar—," Lucine coughed with difficulty. "He wants me to stop Solehan and Valnard. To—To take his heart to do so."

"It's a great honor that the god has come to you, druidess," Feör interjected. She shifted her attention between Lucine and the extraordinary lotus with a pensive look. "His words make sense. Teluar's hearts are considered miracles. Fragments of the god's own power. They can bless a body of water in the material plane. This water can then create or restore life and heal the flesh of those who enter it for a brief moment. It is also said that it is impossible to lie while immersed and that once used, the powers of one of his chosen ones can amplify. This could be the key to confronting Valnard and your brother."

"It does indeed seem extremely powerful," Calixte mused thoughtfully. "With such power, you might want to keep it for yourself, Majesty. Are you sure you wouldn't regret giving it to Lucine?"

"No . . . I desire nothing more that this flower can offer me," the queen clarified. "What's done is done. The future must prevail. Lucine must save the world."

49

The days passed by, and Lucine lost track of time. Nights blended into days under this strange sky with purple hues. The young woman didn't know where to begin, but she was aware that time was pressing. Therefore, she, along with Calixte and Feör, had decided to spend only two weeks in this plane of existence before rejoining Shael and Talyvien in Dawnelest. If the queen's words proved correct, it would only amount to two days passing in their reality. Two days they were prepared to spend between dream and certainty before returning to the material plane.

Lucine now knew that the mother goddesses were by her side. She refused to believe that her encounter with the paladin and the assassin could be a mere coincidence. The young druidess knew she would need their help to unravel everything. Warmth spread in her chest; she was eager to reunite with them.

The night before their departure from the Dream of Teluar, once again lying on the bed in her room with Katao by her side, the young woman pondered the events of her encounter with the god. As the days passed, Lucine felt her power growing within her. Although no abilities had manifested yet, her connection with Teluar seemed to become more essential with each contact with the root of the Tree of Ether. However, the god did not appear to her again in the form of the white fox. It seemed that he had revealed all his secrets in the realm of dreams.

The young druidess had also often gone to meditate in front of the magnificent flower the queen had unveiled to them. How could such a small plant potentially hold so many solutions? What was she supposed to do with it? That evening, she planned to pluck it so they could take it with them on their journey.

She had spent entire days pondering Teluar's words, searching for a way to save her brother. But how could she accept his responsibility for the massacre of the village they had witnessed? Faced with the cruelty of his actions, even the goddesses had apparently abandoned him.

Lucine clutched the pillow on the bed, tears welling up in her eyes. She thought back to the last conversation they'd had before the ceremony in the Astral Forest. They'd been just two carefree kids back then, lamenting their fate. Had he changed so drastically? Lucine knew that Solehan had never been truly happy within their clan. But did he harbor so much hatred within him that he wanted to destroy everything?

She buried her head in the pillow to scream. Her? Save the world? Bring Solehan back to reason? All of this seemed even worse than the legend of the stars.

Katao placed a paw on the pillow and whimpered.

Lucine lifted her head and caressed the dog's skull as he snuggled against her to reassure her. Drowned in the anxieties produced by her distress, Lucine got up from the bed and decided to go find Calixte in their room on the other side of the elegant wooden corridor. She needed the comfort of the bard, their natural cheerfulness, and their nonchalance in the face of it all.

As she passed by the Alaris's room, Lucine heard familiar music emanating from inside. She was about to push the door open to admire one of the bard's performances that she loved so much, when a voice from the room stopped her.

"It's been a long time since I heard some music!" the crystalline voice of Feör exclaimed. "Thank you, Calixte."

Over the past two weeks, the young druidess had witnessed a curious dance between the bard and the queen. The two immortals, both grandiose in their own ways, had been engaged in a dangerous game of eloquent verbal sparring and fiery glances.

Under Lucine's amused admiration, Calixte had showcased their impressive wardrobe, revealing why they traveled with so many pouches attached to their horse. Every day, they had adorned themselves in more sumptuous clothing and makeup, seemingly trying to provoke the queen.

However, Feör, just as charming, had seemed to take great delight in finding various ways to embarrass the Alaris with compliments and flattery. Something ordinarily difficult to do, but for which she had a natural talent.

Lucine, smiling and intrigued, couldn't resist observing them through the crack in the door.

"Thank you for having us here," Calixte said, placing the theorbo on the nightstand. "You didn't have to." They sat on the bed where the queen was already seated.

"All the pleasure is mine," the queen replied. "It's not every day that I have some company. Especially such a charming one, I must admit."

"Flattery won't get you far, Feör," Calixte retorted, with a wink.

"It seems to have worked quite well on me, Alaris."

The deep and endearing laughter of Calixte escaped from their throat. With candor, they took the queen's hand. "That's because I know my charisma is irresistible! But on a more serious note, Feör, I don't think it would be very wise to . . ."

"Why not? You're leaving tomorrow, after all. And I can see that our attraction is mutual."

"I won't deny that . . . You are absolutely stunning, Feör!" they exclaimed. "I mean, almost as much as I am, of course!"

A delicate laugh from the queen resonated in the room, her other hand coming up to hide her beautiful blushing face. "I see that you have a high opinion of yourself!"

"Well, it's necessary! I am a bard, after all!" Calixte replied, puffing their chest. "No one wants to see a sad bard! It's just that . . . I hadn't planned for all this. It's all very sudden."

"And do you always need to plan everything?"

With an air of evident helplessness, the bard lowered their eyes to the queen's hand in theirs.

For the first time, Lucine could read uncertainty in Calixte's ordinarily fiery and confident eyes.

After a few moments, Feör lifted the Alaris's chin with her free hand, meeting their gaze. "You know, Calixte, you remind me of someone."

"Ah . . . really?" they scoffed skeptically.

"Someone I loved deeply."

"Oh," the bard sighed. "Feör . . . you don't know everything. I . . ." They placed their hand on the bridge of their nose and took a moment to gather their thoughts. "My feelings are sincere, but I think I'm afraid of hurting you. You seem to have already suffered enough . . ."

"Let me be the judge of that, Calixte," the queen replied, caressing the bard's cheek.

Calixte let out a soft sigh, relaxing their posture.

"May I ask an indiscreet question?" the queen then inquired.

Calixte nodded.

"How can you use both the Flow and the Ignescent at the same time?"

"Oh, I chose not to be a man or a woman." Gently releasing the queen's hand, they opened both palms on their knees. The vermilion and cyan glimmers of their magic blazed and undulated in each hand. In a surge of confidence, Calixte admired with pride the abilities dancing between their fingers.

"So why do you still allow yourself to be defined as such?" Feör whispered. "Don't you think it's time to be who you truly are? To stop lying to yourself?"

"What do you mean?" the bard hesitated, a restlessness animating their body.

"An intuition . . . I feel like I've known you forever," Feör whispered. "Perhaps our meeting was written in the threads of destiny?" In a tender gesture, Feör guided Calixte's hands to join. A purple glow emanated from the palm of the bard's hands. A new magic. Powerful and wondrous.

Magic that was an image of them. An image of their heart.

Calixte looked at the ribbons of purple magic swirling in their hands with awe. A tear rolled down their cheek. Their citrine eyes turned a deep violet as they raised their head and admired the enlightened face of the queen. A newfound conviction flickered on the amethyst-hued face of the Alaris.

Calixte rushed to kiss Feör passionately.

Pleasantly taken aback, Lucine chuckled discreetly and rolled her eyes. She closed the door, leaving them to their intimacy. She descended the stairs leading to the throne room and crossed it with brisk steps. If she couldn't find refuge in Calixte's kindness, she would go where she had found some of her answers. Perhaps she would find more there?

As a precaution, she grabbed her bow and quiver and made her way to the immense wooden balcony. Following Feör's example, the young druidess called out to one of the marvelous chimeras she had seen a few days ago. The drafelis, intrigued, responded to her call.

After several minutes floating through the air, they finally arrived at the edge of the strange expanse of shimmering water. Leaving the creature behind, Lucine and Katao ventured onto the extravagant path of aquatic plants that led them to the lotus with opalescent petals.

True to her memories, the majesty of the multi-faceted flower spilled into the darkness. Its almost ghostly luminescence made it appear like a will-o'-the-wisp above the dark water and the indistinct horizon.

Lucine advanced cautiously toward the heart of Teluar. She knelt near the fabulous flower and admired it for a long time. Through its translucent petals, the young druidess could observe the meeting of light and darkness, the origin of creation by the mother goddesses. This lily was the perfect proof that where their union occurred, nature came to life. The obvious magic emanating from the plant left no doubt about the power it held. But would that be enough to help her in her quest?

Confused, but hopeful, Lucine cradled the flower in her hands. She focused on the warmth emitted by the lotus and closed her eyes. Head lowered, she prayed for Teluar to bring her new answers. Perhaps the god would appear to her again?

An irregular texture scratched the back of Lucine's hands. Beside her, Katao began to growl. Excited, the young woman opened her eyes eagerly.

A lychena stood before her, her two wooden hands gripping hers. What was one of these creatures doing here? Lucine scrutinized the forest spirit with irritation.

The young druidess felt her stomach rise to her throat. Her eyebrows furrowed in horror. In the absence of moss and sprouts on the dead wooden body of the lychena, memories of anguish and terror seized the young woman's thoughts. This was not one of Feör's forest spirits.

It was Valnard's.

Lucine let out a bewildered gasp. The lychena suddenly snatched the flower from the young druidess's hands and started gliding swiftly over the lily pads.

Struck by this dazzling vision, Lucine regained composure. She threw herself headlong into chasing the lychena and hurriedly leaped over the large lily pads. Without hesitation, Katao followed suit, relentlessly pursuing the forest spirit that was rapidly getting farther away.

Lucine ran breathlessly. The newfound endurance she had developed through Talyvien and Shael's training propelled her body. She no longer felt the weight of the gravity; her muscles obeyed her will. Her determination. Her thirst for revenge for everything she had endured.

Lucine focused on the glowing trail escaping from the arms of the slender, dark silhouette. She had to stop her at all costs. What would happen if Valnard got hold of the heart? What did he intend to do?

"*Ah! A huntress!*" Calixte's words and the vision of their magic above their campfire filled Lucine's mind. They had always believed in her, never doubted her potential. So, for them, for herself, for Solehan, Lucine finally freed herself from her worry of not being up to the task. She had no choice. She would be what she promised to become.

The young woman nocked one of her arrows on her bow.

Still unrestrained in her sprint, her soul determined, Lucine managed to aim at the lychena. The arrow flew through the air and struck the forest spirit's leg. Splinters spurted out from the impact. Far away, the silhouette stumbled on one of the large lily pads. And for a split second, triumph exploded in Lucine's heart. She hadn't missed her target.

Nevertheless, despite the injury, the faltering forest spirit managed to regain her balance and continued her frenzied escape. Having gained ground, thanks to the projectile, the black dog pounced on the lychena, which finally collapsed a few meters away.

With horror, Lucine saw the luminescent lotus roll out of the creature's hands as it fell. Out of breath, the young woman closed the distance between them. No thought had time to form in her brain. This was the only chance she would have. Lucine swiftly grabbed Teluar's heart and stuffed it into one of her pockets.

Katao's jaws still trapped the other leg of the lychena, which struggled to break free. Breathing heavily, Lucine walked toward her.

"Take this message to your *master*," she spat at the creature. "I won't allow myself to be taken advantage of anymore. I will find Solehan and bring him back to the right path."

How could she have been terrified of these creatures? Today, they seemed so pitiful before her. The dog released its grip and stood beside the young druidess. Back straight, bow still in hand, Lucine glared at the lychena with a malevolent eye. The large, black eyes of the forest spirit stared back at her with shock. Still lying on the lily pad, ironically paralyzed by her fear, the lychena dared not move.

A weight pressed on each side of Lucine's head. She cursed these beings responsible for the death of her clan. But she would not stoop to their level. So, she didn't give herself time to change her mind. "Go away!" she vociferated at the forest spirit, raising her arm.

Her uncontrolled rancor erupted in her limbs. Her body arched with rage. Her fingers clenched; her teeth gritted in abhorrence.

Huge plants sprouted on either side of the creature, causing her to flinch. A powerful wave of vines, leaves, and intertwining branches surrounded the forest spirit. A frenzied eruption that bore witness to the emotion overwhelming Lucine.

Initially gasping for breath, the lychena sprang back to her feet and fled swiftly without looking back.

Her veins still throbbing in her limbs, Lucine watched the oppressive and dark atmosphere of the volcano consume the creature's silhouette.

But slowly, surely, as the suffocating seconds passed, the young druidess's fury transformed into amazement. She examined the palm of her hand. Was this part of the powers Teluar had told her about?

With a hand on her throat, trying to slow down her heart rate, Lucine took deep breaths from her lungs. The pressure now subsided, and she thanked Katao with a few scratches. Everything had happened so quickly.

Her attention drifted to the wild demonstration of the magic she possessed. Perhaps she had enough resources within herself to find her own solutions now.

The pain finally caught up with her muscles sore from exertion, so Lucine let herself be lulled by the call of the water's gentle warmth. She sat on the edge of one of the large aquatic plants, removed her shoes, and rolled up her pants. Then, she placed her bow beside her and submerged her legs. Magic crystals washed over the skin of her calves. Lucine took the heart of Teluar from her pocket and wearily stared at its diffuse light between her hands, her feet swaying in the sparkling liquid. Was this really her solution? Why would Valnard have wanted to seize it?

A few hours withered away in this permanent darkness. Lucine breathed in the tranquility of the place, comforted by the warmth of Teluar's heart between her fingers. But no new answers appeared to her.

A few footsteps brushed against the vegetation behind her, but she recognized the gait. Or the familiar feeling resonating in Katao's mind.

"I knew I'd find you here," murmured the deep and familiar voice.

The velvety steps caressed the silence and approached. Calixte sat cross-legged beside the young woman.

From the corner of her eye, Lucine saw the bard examining the large, tangled, and verdant projections that she had conjured earlier in the night.

"It seems this plane of existence brought us more answers than expected. For you and me," they confided. "What happened?"

"One of Valnard's lychenas tried to steal Teluar's heart. But . . . I stopped her," she whispered. "Why would he want one of these flowers?"

The bard did not respond immediately. They simply cast a melancholic gaze at the crystal lily between the young druidess's fingers.

"All I know is that we will stop him, Lucine," they finally said. Calixte placed an affectionate hand on the young woman's arm, and she sighed.

They exchanged a burdened glance.

Lucine then noticed Calixte's disheveled hair and smudged makeup. This sight lifted her spirits, and a wide mischievous smile lit up her face. "You were saying goodbye to Feör, weren't you?"

Surprise broke across Calixte's elegant face, and their deep, sudden laughter filled the air. "You could say that!" they exclaimed, a dreamy emotion crossing their face. "She's just . . . enchanting . . ."

"I can see that!"

"Even though I have to admit, all of this was quite unexpected!" Calixte's absorbed air dissipated, and they shared a conspiratorial look with the young druidess. "And you? Anyone on the horizon?"

"Are you proposing yourself? Haven't you had enough?" Lucine retorted, giving Calixte a playful shoulder bump.

"Ah! No chance, Lucine!" they laughed.

"Based on your reaction, I'm almost offended!" Lucine feigned a disdainful pout after letting out a small laugh.

"Don't take it personally, but I just refuse to do that with humans, even those with the power of a deity," Calixte replied, their tone becoming more neutral.

"Oh, why is that?"

"Because we're a bit different in that regard. I've seen human beings sink into addiction and madness after having relations with an Alaris."

"Ah! Still praising yourself!" Lucine mocked with a theatrical gesture of her arm.

"I'm not joking!"

Lucine was surprised by Calixte's serious look. She decided to slightly change the subject. "By the way . . . since you're neither a man nor a woman, how . . ." she stammered. Regret for asking that question weighed on the rest of her words. She didn't want to make Calixte uncomfortable.

"You know, when two bodies want to come together, what happens down there doesn't matter much," Calixte retorted, giving a significant wink.

"Maybe," she chuckled pensively. "I don't know. It's never attracted me."

"How is that possible?" Calixte marveled. "It's so delightful when done right and with good company!"

"For someone who chose to follow their heart, I find you pretty judgmental!"

"Touché!" Calixte laughed. "I understand you. You know, there's nothing more important than following your path, the one that comes from deep within, even if the world around you doesn't understand it. That, I think, is the only way to truly be happy."

"Do you think so?" Lucine murmured.

The graceful face of the bard nodded gently. Their amber eyes, reflecting the magic of the water, filled with tenderness and affection. "You just have to listen to yourself. Know that everything in life can evolve. Even ourselves. Our beliefs, our attractions, our bodies . . . Nothing needs to be defined and immutable forever."

Pensive, but with a lighter heart, Lucine let her attention wander back to the beautiful flower in her hands. She rested her head on Calixte's shoulder and sighed once more.

Several more hours passed like this, their souls cradled by the myriad sparkles of hope from Teluar's heart in the black night.

The next day, as they prepared to continue their journey at the foot of the majestic tree, several small lychenas from Feör brought their horses, which they seemed to have taken great care of. Lucine, leaning down to thank them, caught sight of the colorful dress of the queen who was coming toward them.

"I hope you have a safe journey," she exclaimed.

"Thank you, Feör, for everything," Lucine replied warmly, as she settled onto Maia.

The queen responded with a radiant smile before turning to Calixte.

The bard gently embraced the queen's waist with one hand and drew their body closer to hers. Then, they kissed Feör on the cheek and whispered something in her ear, making the queen laugh with her crystalline voice. Calixte then placed a purple magic flower in Feör's hair and released her with gentleness, an evident emotion on their face. Finally, the bard got on their white stallion.

Lucine and Calixte moved away toward the edge of the strange forest, with Katao happily running by their side. The Alaris turned around to admire Feör, who remained still, watching them.

"You could have stayed if you wanted," Lucine said.

"No. Let's head to Dawnelest," they replied.

The young druidess saw the slightly sad air on Calixte's face become more cheerful. "We have a band of paladins to bend to our will! Then, we'll take care of finding your brother and Valnard."

"Thank you, Calixte."

"You're welcome, my dear."

50

Shouts. A great clamor. A scream.

Solehan's body was immersed in affliction. His eyes irreversibly closed, his mind entangled in a dark and endless fog. Only the commotion that seemed to be unfolding around him reached his ears. Was it death? A passage between worlds?

Then, he heard agitated voices, tireless footsteps on the parquet floor. Labored and exhausted breathing.

"It seems the goddesses have indeed forsaken him, master," whispered a hesitant, hissing voice. "Callystrande's magic had no effect on his body."

"Those wenches!" exclaimed a deep voice that Solehan could recognize among thousands. "I will find a way. I must!"

Silence returned to the room. Or perhaps was it Solehan sinking deeper into unconsciousness? He had no certainty left, nothing to hold onto except for that voice.

"Master . . . Could it be that, with the appearance of new chosen ones, one of his hearts has grown anew? It could save him."

A thought hovered in the passing seconds.

"Mmhh . . . I can't go into that realm anymore, but I'll send a lychena to check. One never knows," Valnard's fractured voice whispered.

Lost between dream and existence, Solehan detached himself from that fleeting awakening and let the softness of death swallow him completely.

A few breaks punctuated his feverish hallucinations. He felt Valnard's long, black fingers trying to heal his body as best as they could. The scent of ointment. Water trickled into his throat. The green, shadowy eyes gazing at his face more than once. The outlines of the Alaris's figure moving in the mist. Time had lost its effect on his mind. The clarity of day gave way to the chill of night in an endless repetition. The fantasies of the young druid merged with the divine warmth of Valnard's proximity.

And then the pain that struck his side like lightning. The funereal trace left by the lance that had pierced him through.

He didn't know how many days had passed like this, but Solehan eventually regained consciousness in the softness of a bed, satin sheets brushing against his bare chest. The invigorating air passing through a large window caressed his face with a welcome coolness, drying the sweat on his forehead from the fever that still consumed him.

He tried to sit up, despite the shooting pain spreading through his body. A bandage made of leaves covered his wound, which he touched gingerly, wincing. He looked up and realized he was now in an unfamiliar bedroom, of particular splendor compared to the one he knew. He squinted and observed the silver ornaments decorating the immense four-poster bed, swaying in his delirious vision. Was he in the chamber that had belonged to the ruler of Argentvale? His gaze stumbled upon the floral patterns winding on the sheets with feverish intensity.

A body of immaculate whiteness lay next to him in the bed. The sparkle of its skin contrasted with the shade of the fabric in which it floated.

Not knowing if he was dreaming, Solehan slid his body with difficulty under the sheets and approached the sleeping Alaris. With an incredible face marked by a serenity that seemed impossible, Valnard lay on his stomach, one arm behind the pillow under his head. His long hair swept back to form a halo of black and white silk around his head, revealing his delicate, pointed ear.

Solehan admired the grace of Valnard's nape, the moon-white skin that disappeared into the darkness of his hair. The strength of his shoulders hinted at under the sheets, the shape of muscles that delineated his back. However, one detail caught the young druid's attention.

A long, dark line perfectly traced on Valnard's neck disappeared under the sheets. Did Valnard also have a tattoo? Emboldened by the feverish state he found himself in, Solehan gently slid the fabric down Valnard's bare back. The Alaris didn't react.

Eagerly, the young man followed this strange trace. In the hollow of Valnard's powerful shoulder blades, he discovered a beautifully drawn flower. Its stem started at the base of his neck, and its long iridescent petals blossomed gracefully on his perfect skin. It was the same flower Solehan had glimpsed in the hair of his child, the one he had conjured to comfort Valnard.

The young druid couldn't resist tracing the contours of the flower with his fingers. He let his ring finger glide along Valnard's spine, his warm and incredibly smooth skin materializing at his touch, from the base of his hair to the long petals that he caressed tenderly.

"Solehan?"

Green eyes fixed on him. Valnard's silhouette straightened up, and a worried wince appeared on his face. The young druid lay back on the bed, suddenly dizzy, the pain more acute than ever.

Valnard leaned over him, his hair cascading over his shoulders.

"What happened?" the young man managed to murmur.

"We took care of all the humans who attacked us, Solehan," Valnard's lips said on his face. "We dealt with them."

Relieved, the young druid sank into the mattress.

Valnard placed a hand on his forehead. "You still have a fever," Valnard sighed. "I'll get you out of here. There's a way."

"Which way?"

"Your sister has something that can save you. I know where she is. I don't know how it's possible, but she has powers, Solehan! I will convince her to help us, one way or another!"

Lucine? Powers? Was it real?

Valnard's hand slid across the young man's cheek.

And reality struck Solehan's heart once more. Yes, he had forgiven him.

But it changed nothing about the impossibility of their situation, the intensity of his feelings, or the shame he felt.

"I'll change your bandage," Valnard said.

Solehan grabbed the Alaris's wrist before he could touch the bandage with what little strength he had left. "Why are you doing all of this?" the young man whispered. "If my sister has powers, we'll need her. Go find her. She can awaken Teluar. Time is running out."

"I won't let what happened to Sylveah happen to you," Valnard said, resolute.

Of course. If Lucine also had powers, they probably needed both of them to awaken the god from his torpor. Perhaps Valnard didn't want to take any risks?

Solehan released his grip, and Valnard lifted the bandage carefully. A horrified grimace appeared on Valnard's face, and he retrieved ointment and fresh leaves from a bag on the nightstand.

Petrified by his weakness, both of heart and fever, Solehan could no longer move.

Valnard's hands began to apply the ointment to the wound as they had done many times before. But his eyes no longer held the distant mark of faraway thoughts. Genuine concern colored his irises.

For the first time, the young druid observed Valnard's sculpted chest leaning close to him. The firmness of his muscles that hinted at his strength when he tucked a lock of hair behind his ear. The ebony hands that moved across his body with tender restraint, slightly distorting his tattoos under the pressure as they glided over his chest.

What had been torture in the past had become an entirely different torment. A torment tied to the painful memory he had shared with the young tattoo artist from his clan. To the scorn that had poured all around them and their secret. Solehan closed his eyes and compartmentalized his desire, trying desperately not to lose what he already shared with Valnard, imprisoned by the shame that kept him far from his truth. He was relieved that the sheet concealed the lower part of his body, the only evidence of what he couldn't hide.

The Alaris had fathered a child with a female forest spirit, and he would never reciprocate what was starting to blossom within him. Why did he have the power to give life and death to the world around him, yet no control over what was growing in his heart at that moment? No control over the injustice he faced.

Solehan wanted to retreat into his dreams, where their love was possible. To retreat into painless death, faced with the bitterness of not being able to touch the Alaris lying in the same bed with him.

His prayer was heard, and fever carried him away once again into a deep sleep.

51

The warmth of Talyvien's peaceful breathing on her face awakened Shael. The paladin's hand still surprisingly held in hers, his profile nestled into the corner of the pillow. He was sleeping deeply, his body still maintaining a respectful distance from hers.

The assassin propped herself up on an elbow and took the opportunity to admire the serene face of the young man. An expert in the matter, she pilfered this stolen moment, this absurd situation. The pounding of her heart reverberated in her ears.

They had shared the same bed.

What made this man so different from the others? How could she feel so safe by his side? Shael realized that she hadn't slept so well in a long time. Did he have the power to replace her nightmares with something else? Talyvien had simply been there for her. He kept his distance, never pushed her. And for all these things, he had been the first person she had confided in with her secrets.

How could she feel *that* about a man? Her life had been nothing but a constant escape, an illusion of a flawless future that would have allowed her to forget her past and give it meaning. Now, she wasn't so sure anymore. She no longer desired that future. Terrified by her own admission, Shael felt that her heart had taken a path whose outcome she did not know.

A bitter taste passed through her belly.

Selena.

Shael inhaled with disgust. Had she been so careless to let herself drift like this? On instinct, in an attempt to hold onto this moment, she brushed aside a strand of Talyvien's chestnut hair, hopelessly tousled on his forehead.

A cold flash ran through her limbs. What had she done? Fear submerged her as she realized her gesture. Shael hastily got out of bed, removed the torn shirt, and put on her leather bandeau, followed by the rest of her armor. She prayed that her recklessness wouldn't wake the paladin.

Her wish was granted. As she braided her hair, Talyvien emerged from his slumber.

After a hearty breakfast at the inn, they decided to walk to the castle of Dawnelest to enjoy the first rays of sun that dispelled the coolness and dampness of the night.

Talyvien was strangely quiet. He often ran his hand through his hair as they walked, a defiantly rebellious lock on his forehead.

By mimicry, anxiety also seized Shael. She cracked her fingers and quickened her pace. She dreaded their meeting with the queen, knowing what Talyvien felt for her.

Trying to calm herself, Shael admired the languid waltz of the barges sailing on the city's canals. The capital was slowly waking up after the festival of Solamaris that had shaken it the night before. But the events of the previous night refused to fade away from the assassin's mind.

"And so, you're going to present yourself like this?" Talyvien's voice snapped her out of her stupor.

"What do you mean?"

"Let's just say that, in this neighborhood, there seem to be more priests and noble knights than assassins or bandits," he mocked.

"Oh, don't worry about me! The Children of Twilight are rather . . . stealthy!"

Under the puzzled gaze of the paladin, Shael began to undo small straps inside her cloak, revealing a lining extending the piece of fabric. Two ingeniously sewn sleeves appeared, and the assassin slipped her arms into them. She tied it all around her waist and pulled out a blue-night fabric blindfold that she placed over her eyes.

"Tada!" she exclaimed; arms wide open in a theatrical gesture.

Deprived of her sight like this, Shael waited for a response that didn't come.

"It was you at the Luminaur inn!" he finally retorted. "The priestess of Sazaelith!"

She chuckled at the surprise in Talyvien's voice.

"But now you're deprived of one sense."

"Ah! Fortunately, I'm accompanied by a noble knight!"

With a slight laugh, the paladin gently took Shael's arm, and they entered the massive gate of the castle's grand courtyard.

 With Shael on his arm, Talyvien cautiously advanced into the grand entrance of the building. The resounding echo of their footsteps bounced off the splendid marble floor. Elaborate sculptures crafted from stone and gold, with seraphic expressions, welcomed them on either side as they walked toward the slightly ajar door leading to the throne room. Several armored guards framed a long line of citizens of all kinds that extended beyond the large hall, all eager to submit their grievances to the queen.

Talyvien swallowed hard, his hands becoming sweaty. With patience, they positioned themselves at the end of the queue. The paladin glanced back at the assassin over his shoulder, taking advantage of her temporary blindness. He felt his confusion tug at him once more.

Shael's touch on his face had awakened him that very morning. But not knowing how to interpret it and not wanting to burden the assassin further, he had pretended to still be asleep. However, he had managed to steal a glimpse of the delicate skin of her bare back when she had put on her armor. The thought flushed his neck with heat. He was relieved she couldn't see him at that moment.

Several minutes passed amid the long, polished marble columns. The crowd of people moved forward a bit, and they finally entered the throne room. He appreciated that Shael couldn't see this either.

The splendor of Queen Selena Aramanth dazzled the room. Seated on a throne decorated with gilding and aquamarine, the backrest rising up to the ceiling in sparkling spirals, the sovereign wore a long, deeply iridescent blue gown that cascaded down the stone steps. A magnificent hairstyle sculpted her long blond hair into a bun embellished with gold and azure ornaments, complementing the color of her icy blue eyes. Her attire seemed to have been sewn onto her skin by the kingdom's finest tailors, with delicate sparkling embroidery defining the contours of her silhouette to perfection. Radiating undeniable brightness, she appeared like an all-powerful star that absorbed all surrounding darkness.

Talyvien was breathless.

Shael fidgeted a little and coughed discreetly.

The paladin then tried to compose himself, revealing nothing, and moved toward the throne at the back of the shortening line ahead of them.

Several hours passed like this: the cruel wait offering the opportunity for the paladin to admire the love he had known, torn apart by the flame of a new blaze at his side.

Finally, the previous petition ended, and Talyvien's guts twisted as he looked up at the one he could only remember in an enchanting way. He had dreamt of this moment more than once. Talyvien approached Selena, with Shael still disguised as a priestess of Sazaelith following behind.

A crashing noise sounded at the castle's entrance.

A golden mask appeared in the massive doorway, soon followed by a swarm of men in white and gold armor. The High Priestess Piore walked in with magnificent grace. Her halo shimmered under the brightness emanating from the large windows of the room, and her long train displayed the large golden wings embroidered on the back of her garment. King Arthios Therybane of Astitan stood by her side, and they both advanced arrogantly on the long carpet leading to the throne. The citizens stepped aside as they passed.

Dread tightened Talyvien's face. He grabbed Shael's arm and retreated into the crowd. The icy eyes observed him for a brief moment.

"What is the meaning of this?" Queen Selena's voice rang out with force in the throne room.

As she stood up from the imposing seat, the queen glared at the newcomers with icy fury. The memory of the timid teenager contradicted the vision playing out before Talyvien. He was unfamiliar with the current appearance and poise of Selena. A queen stood before him.

"I have come to visit my dear sister! Don't I have the right to do so?" King Arthios mused, with a tone that Talyvien found strangely condescending.

"I will ask you, King Therybane, to not interrupt an official session in the future and to announce your arrival properly," Selena replied sharply.

"Oh, come on now. We sent a few scouts to warn you of the passage of the Crusade of the Dawn's Resolve in your kingdom."

"I meant, in my castle."

The sovereign's uncompromising gaze shifted toward Piore.

"My queen, forgive our intrusion, but if this is a session of grievances, allow us to submit ours." The voice of the High Priestess sounded honeyed through the mask.

"Oh, I have heard of your misdeeds, High Priestess. I know exactly what you expect from me. I can already tell you that I do not endorse your methods. While I'm alive, the kingdom of Vamentera will remain free to practice magic as long as certain control and respect for its use is observed."

The posture of the Lamented changed somewhat at the mention of the queen's longevity.

A sense of terror gripped Talyvien's spine.

"I am greatly saddened by that, Queen Selena," Piore replied, advancing further and gracefully bowing before the sovereign. "Allow me to give you the opportunity to change your mind in the coming days and unite our two kingdoms to celebrate Solamaris."

"The kingdom of Astitan is not under your command, High Priestess," the queen asserted.

"Of course, but I am sure His Majesty, King Arthios, won't object."

"I will follow what the voice of Callystrande commands me to do," the king retorted mechanically, as if it had been repeated hundreds of times.

A look of disgust appeared on Talyvien's face. Had his king become so self-absorbed, so zealous? Shael's hand then gripped his arm a little tighter.

Selena glared at her brother dubiously. "Very well, I suppose you can stay as honored guests at the castle to celebrate the Solamaris ball in two days. After that, I will ask you to leave Dawnelest and the kingdom of Vamentera with the crusade."

"Of course, Your Majesty," Piore cooed, curtsying once again at the bottom of the steps leading to the throne.

Queen Selena sighed and turned toward the crowd that had gathered against one of the room's walls. "I am sorry, but the grievance session is adjourned. I invite you all to come back at a later time," she exclaimed.

Talyvien and Shael didn't need further prompting and evacuated with the rest of the citizens through the castle's main entrance.

They quickly lost themselves in the streets of Dawnelest. Shael removed the blindfold covering her eyes and secured the lining of her cloak with the straps, regaining her feline appearance as an assassin.

"This complicates our plans now," she said, picking up the pace next to Talyvien.

"I had hoped we would arrive before them," Talyvien replied, "or at least have a chance to warn Selena in some way. There's definitely something off with Arthios. Bowing down to Piore like that is not like him."

"And massacring innocents, you mean?" Shael retorted.

"Yes, that too . . ."

They plunged into a less frequented street to avoid the resumed festivities. Festivalgoers sang and danced; their faces decorated with colorful paint. Some stumbled under the influence of alcohol, while others kissed cheerfully, and others laughed and shouted, their cries echoing through the nearby streets.

"Well, tonight, I'll go to the convent of Sazaelith to see if I can learn something new."

Talyvien nodded in response.

As they dodged the passersby with difficulty, the glint of golden armor caught the paladin's eye in the distance. Talyvien's blood ran cold.

Two paladins of Callystrande were on their horses, watching them at the end of the street. Talyvien cursed under his breath and grabbed Shael's arm. They turned back toward a busier avenue.

"I think they spotted me during the audience," he worriedly whispered.

The assassin discreetly looked in the direction of the towering golden suits of armor. Her face turned pale.

They both immersed themselves in the crowd of onlookers on the bustling main street, attempting to shake off the white and gold-armored figures that loomed above the heads. Shael grabbed Talyvien's hand to avoid losing him in the maze of revelry as they tried to dodge shoulders and beer splashes.

The Solamaris festival engulfed them completely, their anxiety contrasting with the surrounding merriment. Talyvien cursed himself for dragging the assassin into the chaos that was his life and tried his best to find an escape. He had to.

Slightly disoriented by the terror flooding his mind, by the swirling colors, and the cheers of joy, the paladin tightened his fingers around Shael's hand.

As they turned the corner of a street, a gleaming sword came down on Talyvien.

The assassin's hand pulled him away with all her strength.

Dazed, the paladin blinked. The world tilted. His stomach churned, and his legs wobbled.

When he opened his eyes again, they were a few meters away from their original position.

The assassin had used Quanta magic to dodge the blow. She had saved his life.

But he didn't have time to thank her. Catching their breath, Talyvien and Shael saw, with horror, that a second group from the crusade was attempting to surround them.

They started running.

Talyvien's heart pounded in his chest. The sounds of the crowd drowned out the whinnying of their assailants' horses. Shael and Talyvien collided with some bystanders in their path and darted through various streets at full speed toward the *Veil of Truth*, hoping to hide in the inn. The men's shouts and the sounds of hooves, which the paladin knew all too well, spread behind them. A sinister pounding. They eventually crossed a small alley full of various taverns where the citizens were celebrating Solamaris with enthusiasm.

Two new mounted figures with golden masks faced them at the end of the alley, scrutinizing the passersby.

They were trapped.

Completely overwhelmed by panic, Shael's hand still holding his, Talyvien scanned the surroundings to find any possible way out. Overtaken by the sudden turn of events, the paladin met Shael's terrified gaze.

He had a crazy and desperate idea.

Talyvien pulled up his gray hood over his head, and his body pressed against Shael's against the tavern wall. Shael cried out in shock.

The paladin leaned toward her without touching, maintaining a certain distance out of modesty.

However, Shael felt the warm breath of Talyvien on her neck and the tips of his fingers on her back, holding her close. The assassin was petrified. What was he trying to do?

She looked over his shoulder. Several patrols of paladins in golden masks still seemed to be searching for them in the street among the festivalgoers.

In distress, Shael turned her head to look around. Some couples flirted and kissed around the tavern. She then realized that Talyvien was trying to blend in with the surrounding celebration.

"I'm sorry," Talyvien whispered in her ear.

A rush of heat flushed Shael's face. Her pulse quickened, and her heart seemed to beat out of her chest. Confused, she closed her eyes, squinting as much as she could. To conceal her affinity with her goddess, to make this ruse work. Because she no longer knew how to react to the emotions that stole away what little logic and caution she had left.

Despite herself, Shael felt her body naturally drawing closer to Talyvien's.

For credibility, she told herself. *Yes, that was it.*

Still with that goal in mind, the assassin timidly wrapped her arms around the broad shoulders of the paladin.

In response, Talyvien's hand pressed more firmly into her back.

The paladin's hot breath on her neck became more ragged. Much more convincing.

Shael's head started spinning. Caught between the terror of being unmasked and this new spark in her belly. A second hand came to rest at the back of the assassin's head. Talyvien's stubble grazed her skin.

Shael let out a soft moan. How could her body react like this? Betray her so? Yet, for the first time, her past fell silent. And her teasing future put her on tiptoes.

Surprisingly, Talyvien's lips met the skin of her neck. A spark of desire spread and seized Shael's body.

Impossible.

She opened her eyes again to try to ground herself in the situation, to prevent her anxiety from dissipating into confusion. She had no right to feel this. Not after the years of discipline she had imposed on herself.

The silhouettes in golden armor seemed to have disappeared.

"Talyvien," she murmured.

The paladin made a soft growl. It was now his turn to extract something from her. Gently puckering his lips, he planted a real kiss on her neck. Another wild lightning bolt struck Shael's belly. With what little sense she had left, she ignored it this time.

"Talyvien, they're gone," she urged him.

The paladin raised his head and moved away from her, his red face barely visible under the gray hood. "I'm sorry, Shael," he repeated, looking confused.

She chuckled softly, her heart still pounding.

They cautiously approached the corner of the street and scanned the crowd.

"It looks like they are indeed gone," Talyvien added, glancing on either side of the bustling avenue.

Too bad was the stupid response that came to Shael's mind. She mentally slapped herself and plunged into the flow of passersby, under the paladin's surprised gaze.

They hurried back to the safety of their room at the inn, hoping not to encounter any members of the Crusade again.

Once the door was closed, they both let out a sigh of relief. Their eyes met, and they burst into laughter, the adrenaline subsiding in their veins.

Talyvien then sat on his bed, ran a hand over his face to clear his thoughts, and looked pensively at the floor, his elbows on his knees.

Disturbed by the events, Shael stared at the paladin for a long time. What had just happened? How could her body feel all this for a man? And why was she resisting it so much? Perhaps all the protections she had put in place in her life no longer mattered so much. Perhaps she could glimpse a future that her body desired. That her heart desired. Maybe, just this once, someone was worth venturing down that path.

A dam within her broke. Everything crumbled. With unsteady steps, she approached him. His scent, his skin, his protection. What she could let flourish in his arms. She simply wanted to be near him. To feel him against her. Once again.

Someone knocked on the door.

Talyvien jumped up and unsheathed Tuoryn's sword.

Stunned, caught in the moment, Shael slid two daggers into her hands. She stood on the side of the opening, back against the wall, ready to confront anyone. Had they been found?

The paladin opened the wooden door.

"I have a message for you," said a male voice on the doorstep.

Talyvien took the letter handed to him. The messenger's steps faded away as he descended the stairs. The paladin closed the door and proceeded to unfold the small piece of paper.

"What is it?" Shael asked with interest, dissipating her weapons.

The paladin's face turned ashen.

The assassin's stomach twisted.

"Queen Selena invites me for a . . . private audience tonight," he stammered, his voice breaking under the knot in his throat.

52

Talyvien galloped into the secret of the night, the gray hood covering his head, and arrived in front of the small entrance concealed at the back of the castle. He followed the instructions written in the letter he had received. He was tying his horse Aho when he caught sight of the flame from a torch dimly illuminating the face of a man.

"Follow me," the figure said.

The two men walked silently through a maze of corridors and gray stone stairs. The modest appearance of this part of the building contrasted with the memory he had of polished marble and grand statues he had seen that morning. They passed several servants, cooks, and guards who were busy, and Talyvien realized he was in the part reserved for the castle staff. Selena had apparently wanted their meeting to be discreet.

Yet another wooden door revealed a long corridor decorated with sumptuous tapestries. Large windows framed by thick blue velvet curtains allowed the faint light of the silver moon to mix with elegant patterns on the polished stone floor. Hurrying, he followed the man, who eventually stopped in front of a large carved wooden door with intertwined golden and iridescent metal ornaments.

The man knocked on the door and opened it.

Talyvien was speechless. A sublime vision worthy of the power of his imagination spread out before him. Queen Selena, seated at a dressing table, was brushing her long blond hair while looking at herself in the mirror.

Talyvien's heart rose to his throat as he softly approached the mirage. All his memories rushed back and invaded his senses. All the contradictory emotions he had once felt resurfaced.

The door closed behind him. Startled, he saw with horror that he was in Selena's bedroom. Anxiety compressed his chest.

Proud and patient, evidently taking their time, the blue eyes eventually fixed on him in the mirror's reflection.

"Your Majesty," he said, bowing the upper part of his body in reverence after lowering his hood.

"Please, Talyvien," Selena replied. "None of that between us." She rose, revealing a beautiful light blue silk nightgown that embraced her curves. Her long blond hair cascaded in golden waves on one side of her face. She kept her piercing gaze on the paladin as she approached him.

"You recognized me?" he managed to mumble. He had imagined this moment dozens of times, imagined what he would have wanted to say, but no words seemed to come out of his mouth at that moment.

"How could I not recognize you?" she rejoiced in a tender voice. "You're no longer wearing the armor of the paladins of Callystrande?"

"No. In fact, I came to talk to you about the crusade."

"Oh. And here I thought you were visiting me for old times' sake."

A slight smile appeared on the queen's delicate face.

Talyvien tried to focus on the reason for his visit. "Selena, something disturbing is happening with your brother and the crusade."

Ensuring not to leave out any details, he recounted the horrific vision of the unfortunate souls on the pyres, the rescue of one of them, and the consequences of that act. The assassination attempt ordered by the crusade and the indifference of his brother, King Arthios, toward the cruelty and madness of Piore, the Lamented de Callystrande. As he unraveled his story, Talyvien could see fear creeping onto Selena's face.

She covered her mouth in horror. "It's worse than I thought," she said, in a trembling voice, hugging her arms around her chest. "I had heard of some fanatical excesses, but to this extent . . . How can my brother do such a thing?"

The queen's attention wandered over several pieces of furniture in the bedroom. She was shaken by these revelations.

"Perhaps you could try to reason with him?" the paladin asked.

"I can try," she replied, "but I'm not sure he would listen. He seems to have changed so much. I—I'm not even sure I can stand up to them on my own."

Stung in his paladin's heart, Talyvien placed his hands on the young woman's shoulders to comfort her. "I'm sorry to cause you so much trouble, but you needed to know."

"No, no. You did the right thing."

He nodded lightly and tightened his embrace on one of Selena's shoulders. "Anyway, be careful," he said. "I have a bad feeling."

"Do—Do you still worry about me?"

Talyvien was startled when hope flickered in the queen's celestial eyes as she looked at his face.

"I'm sorry about what happened to your husband . . . to King Herald. It must not have been easy," Talyvien said, panicked by the young woman's display of emotion.

He knew that the unfortunate man had succumbed to a long illness only a few years after marrying Selena, leaving her with the heavy burden of ruling the kingdom of Vamentera alone after his death. When he had learned about it, the paladin had felt sorry for her.

"Yes, indeed, it wasn't easy," she whispered, placing her hand over Talyvien's one on her shoulder. "But even though I feel lonely sometimes, it wasn't really a marriage of love. You know that better than anyone . . ."

Talyvien's posture tensed. A weight settled in his throat.

"Maybe you could come to the Solamaris ball?" she added. "You'd have a chance to get closer to Piore and Arthios and maybe find out something? And also . . . you could make sure nothing happens to me," she murmured, gently taking Talyvien's hand in hers. She placed an invitation to the ball in his hand.

He hurriedly put it in one of his pockets and released her other shoulder. Stepping back, he quickly said, "I wanted to ask you if you had heard about what happened in the city of Argentvale as well," still focused on the reason for his visit. He thought about Lucine and prayed that the young druidess had the answers to the questions that troubled her.

"Oh. I sent a detachment a few days ago after receiving a request from the kingdom of Narlimar to come to their aid. Apparently, all the inhabitants of their capital have been turned into wood . . . It's terrifying. They haven't come back yet . . ."

The rumor they had heard with Lucine was true then. Her brother and this Alaris were probably there. They might have even decimated the whole detachment. A veil of terror settled on his neck. He had to warn the druidess when she—

Selena gently placed her hand on Talyvien's cheek.

The young man froze. His thoughts suddenly vanished.

"It's strange to see you older," she murmured. "You've also changed. And at the same time, it feels like it was just yesterday."

"Selena . . ." he replied, removing the queen's hand that had started to caress his face. A plea asking her to stop.

"You have a new scar," she whispered. Selena's incandescent gaze moved to his mouth.

Talyvien had dreamt so many times that those eyes would look at him like that again. He had revisited their embraces, their adolescent emotions countless times. He had indulged in the cruel life that had separated their promise.

But now, at this moment, he found himself no longer desiring the woman standing before him. He had lost himself for too long in a fantasy of hope, in the blaze of a memory of someone who no longer existed. He had idolized and idealized a moment in time that had long since dissipated without him noticing.

By surprise, Selena stood on her tiptoes and pressed her lips against his.

The young man flinched. But he didn't return the kiss. A feeling of disgust invaded his heart, as the queen's lips touched the scar on his mouth.

Shael.

With no response from his body, she stepped back a few unsteady steps. "I'm sorry," she stammered.

"I'm sorry too, Selena," Talyvien murmured. "It's just that—"

"It's okay," she interrupted. "I understand. A lot of time has passed. But I guess I was still hoping that—" She didn't finish her sentence, and sighed.

"I—I'm sorry," he reiterated, lowering his arms.

"You should go," she whispered, turning her back on him. "Thank you for this information, though . . ."

With a disappointed look on his face, the paladin nodded.

Talyvien urged his gray horse on, galloping swiftly through the city of Dawnelest.

A dazzling clarity filled his heart, with the feline eyes anchored in his mind. He didn't understand why and how he could have fallen in love with a chosen of Sazaelith, but it no longer mattered. He prayed that nothing would happen to the assassin.

His heart tightened at the thought of her being at the convent of her goddess. He had cursed that stupid letter and the painful emotion that had passed over Shael's face at that moment.

He hurriedly opened the door to their room but found it desperately empty.

Shael leaped from rooftop to rooftop with the feline agility that flowed through her veins. She was trying to focus her mind on the mission she had set for herself, despite the deep gash in her chest at the thought that Talyvien might be with the queen at this very moment.

Seeking solace, she listened to the laughter and joyful cries emanating from the streets below from the crowd celebrating the solstice. Music filled the air, but Shael watched the revelers embrace and rejoice with a tinge of melancholy. She had always known that her destiny was not to partake in merriment but to remain in the shadows. She had forgotten her mission, and she hated that fate had placed the paladin in her path. She had been foolish. *A paladin of Callystrande? Really?*

Shael had let her goddess's story intertwine with her own. She didn't deserve such experiences, to be desired in that way. She had always known that. And what did she have to offer anyway? Her stubbornness and a haunting past? Why would he be infatuated by a chosen of Sazaelith when he could have a queen? She remembered the paladin's reaction in the throne room. Probably breathtakingly beautiful.

The assassin made a final effort to banish Talyvien from her thoughts with bitterness when she caught sight of the silhouette of the building that was so familiar to her. A refuge, finally. She sneaked through the chimneys that grew on the roofs of the surrounding buildings. Hidden amid a maze of interlocked structures, the small convent of the chosen of Sazaelith revealed itself to Shael as she discreetly approached above the courtyard in front of the entrance.

Stupefied, Shael swore once again. The metallic horror gleamed in the dim light as a dozen paladins of the Crusade of the Dawn's Resolve, clad in armor and mounted on their horses, stood waiting in front of the building below.

Knowing the convent like the back of her hand, she decided to continue advancing across the rooftops to maintain the advantage of the night. She slipped stealthily over the tiles of the building, heading toward the tall stone tower in the distance.

A faint light escaped from a window, and Shael approached it cautiously. The Mother Superior had taken up residence in this part of the convent. Her office had an unusually high ceiling, and the windows were located high in the room. Knowing this, Shael slightly opened the casement to observe what was happening below.

Her heart froze, as if struck by lightning.

The golden wings on the train of the Lamented of Callystrande shimmered in the candlelight. The High Priestess was facing away, crouched in a corner of the room. Her mask had been removed, and now long hair, as white as the moon, cascaded down her shoulders. Seated at her desk further away, the Mother Superior seemed unfazed by what was happening and continued to write on a parchment.

An assassin contract.

A few child-like whimperings echoed in the night. Piore's body stood up to reveal one of the young apprentices from the convent, a midnight-blue blindfold over her eyes. Still with her back turned, the High Priestess wiped her mouth with the back of her sleeve.

The fabric became tainted with cobalt blue. The unthinkable had happened.

A fracture formed in Shael's soul at this nightmarish sight. Piore had bitten the apprentice and drank her blood.

The little girl struggled to her feet, holding her neck, and made her way to the desk with difficulty. Shael's fists trembled on the windowsill. Intrusive images filled her mind—her mother's blue teeth appeared in her thoughts. Nausea overwhelmed her, but she managed to contain it, trying to remain as silent as possible. Her revulsion poured through her at the abhorrent betrayal she had just witnessed.

The Mother Superior had raised Shael as her own daughter, taught her faith, art, and mission. Shael had traveled to Dawnelest to follow her in her apprenticeship. Now, another maternal figure had betrayed her once again.

Unable to reconcile her present and past, Shael felt herself falling into an abyss. She couldn't rely on anyone. There was no refuge left. Nowhere. She had lost everything. She had no reason to go on.

Desperate, she wanted to embrace the madness growing in her heart. But like a black silk cape settling on her shoulders, she felt the familiar presence of her goddess. The only one she could count on. The infallible Sazaelith enveloped her in her long dark wings and whispered in her ear as usual.

Vengeance.

The coldness of that whisper spread through her soul. The icy rage that followed anesthetized her invasive nightmares. The assassin responded to that call.

The Mother Superior handed the sealed parchment to the young apprentice, who hurriedly left the office. The sound of the child's footsteps resonated in Shael's chest. She muttered angrily under her breath.

The High Priestess put on her golden mask again, before Shael could catch a glimpse of her face, and nodded slightly toward the Mother Superior. Then, she too left the room. The assassin listened to the footsteps of the Lamented fading into the anonymity of the night.

"You can come down, Shael," said the Mother Superior.

Of course, the Mother Superior had heard her; she had taught her everything.

Shael's body slid down the stone wall, and she stood face to face with the woman. "How could you do that . . ." Her palpable rage spread through her still trembling fists.

"Shael, I had no choice. Let me explain." The Mother Superior stood up from her desk and positioned herself in front of the assassin, who stared at her with definite hatred, the veins in her neck pulsing with rage.

"There's no explanation that can justify this, Cassandra" Shael coldly retorted. Her name sliced the assassin's lips like a piece of glass.

"I did it to save us," Cassandra replied soberly, but her sapphire eyes responded with an emotion contrary to that felt by the assassin. Despite what Shael had just discovered, no guilt transfigured the face of the Mother Superior.

"Save us?!" vociferated Shael. "By selling the blood of the apprentices as if they were cattle? Moreover, to that wench from the crusade!?"

Cassandra clasped her hands gently, an air of calm and firmness emanating from her.

Why was she not reacting? Shael wondered. The assassin's fury intensified at the Mother Superior's passivity.

"A few months ago," Cassandra explained, "the Lamented came to me. I sensed—I knew what she was capable of. Queen Selena won't be able to resist her for long. Magic will become forbidden, Shael. I had to protect our order."

"So, you exchanged our *blood*—for our freedom to practice the teachings of Sazaelith?"

"Precisely," Cassandra replied, in a desperately calm expression that Shael imagined tearing from her face.

"And do you think making us the main supplier of the debauchery of the crusade makes us free beings?" Shael cried. "Do you think this is in accordance with the teachings of the goddess?"

"It was the only way," the Mother Superior insisted. "I know you've seen what the crusade is capable of. We won't be able to withstand them either. What would you have done in my place?"

"Not *that*, Cassandra," Shael growled. "I wouldn't have betrayed the order like you did!"

"Using such strong words!" Cassandra laughed, although she didn't seem amused by her joke. "What's a little blood compared to our freedom?"

The vision of the pyres of Luminaur replayed in Shael's memory. The cries of one of the victims' mothers echoed in her heart. She recalled the High Priestess riding away on her white horse, followed by the cohort of golden-armored ghosts. How could she accept to ally with such cruelty?

"I imagine the Lamented wanted to make a few contracts as well? Was one of them what you were writing?" the assassin retorted with a painful irony.

"It's none of your concern."

"Oh, really? Why do you think I'm here?"

"You know that not honoring a contract is a grave offense, Shael. And you accuse me of losing my devotion?"

Cassandra's low blow hit Shael hard, and she struggled to push Talyvien's face out of her mind. She didn't need this now.

"I don't honor contracts that don't come from the will of my goddess but from someone who betrayed us," Shael declared.

"That's not for you to decide, and that's just your point of view."

The assassin approached Cassandra, the deep and dark cloak of Sazaelith on her shoulders enclosing her even more.

The Mother Superior remained stoic and trapped in her strange languor.

"And why not give *your* blood, instead of that of innocent souls?" Shael retorted.

"Oh, I did, at first. But I couldn't satisfy the Lamented's appetite alone. I also had to stay in Dawnelest."

Trying to dull her revulsion, Shael spat on the ground at the Mother Superior's feet. "Do you hear yourself, Cassandra?"

"I knew you wouldn't understand, Shael, considering your . . . past," Cassandra said, her experience as a Child of Twilight finally reflecting in her posture.

"It has nothing to do with my so-called past," Shael hissed. "You are a disgrace to the teachings of Sazaelith."

"And who do you think taught you the teachings of the goddess?" A cold calm appeared to have filled Cassandra's limbs. The silent fury of the assassins.

"Then you have lost your devotion," Shael charged.

The two women stood face to face. Two assassins. Two vengeful hands of the goddess of shadows confronting each other in their faith. But only the sapphire eyes of Shael launched invisible daggers.

"What are you going to do then?" Cassandra growled, baring her teeth, her mouth twisting with malice.

"Follow the path of my goddess," Shael replied, sneering. "Unlike you."

Long dark fingers sprinkled with stars brushed against the assassin's nape. Her head buzzed. How could the woman who had taught her everything have gone so astray? Was she so desperate to act as a turncoat and ally with Piore? And why was she not reacting?

Two daggers appeared with finesse in Shael's palms. Everything surged within her. Her fury confronted her nightmares. She lunged at the Mother Superior.

With a swift motion, Cassandra evaded her with the supernatural grace of the Quanta. Metallic sparks also appeared in her hands.

The two assassins' bodies turned into two black specters that moved in silence. The metal of their swirling daggers shimmered in the dim light as the only evidence of their existence. Wrapped in their midnight-blue cloaks, a dark and nebulous trail seemed to follow their movements. Only the thunderous clash of their blades reverberated.

Shael let out a slight cry, as pain surged in her thigh. One of Cassandra's daggers had found its mark in her flesh. A bit of blue liquid dripped onto the stone floor.

"You forget that I taught you everything, Shael," Cassandra's voice whispered in her ear.

The assassin's heart skipped a beat. Like a tornado, she turned around. One of her daggers flew toward the whisper but missed.

Cassandra had already vanished.

Out of breath and sweating, Shael tried to calm her breathing. She ignored the new pain in her leg and the ache in her bruised shoulder that had resurfaced. Grounded in her stance, she nervously scanned her surroundings. Where had Cassandra gone?

Cruel blue eyes appeared in the corner of the room. One of the Mother Superior's daggers was now stained blue. She seemed to relish the sight.

Had she been foolish to rush at Cassandra? Shael wondered. The battle promised to be difficult. The Mother Superior was an exceptional fighter. But could Cassandra be allowed to live after what she had done?

Guilty. The word pounded in Shael's head and gut. Despite the attachment she felt for this woman, this betrayal could not be tolerated. Determined yet breathless, she readied herself.

A mocking laugh reverberated in the room. Cassandra's silhouette disappeared from Shael's field of vision once again. Delicate arabesques of metal appeared in the air—luminous streaks that sliced through the atmosphere. Shael only had time to throw herself behind the desk that she overturned. Scrolls, books, and inkwells; everything crashed to the floor with a loud clamor.

Two daggers plunged violently into the furniture. Two dull impacts that split the wood. Missing their target, they vibrated to return to their owner's hands. With closed eyes, Shael followed the metallic whistle of the blades to locate the Mother Superior.

Shael's contained rage exploded. A vengeful frenzy ravaged her mind. She pushed off from the overturned desk and leaped toward Cassandra.

The moment felt eternal. The power of Sazaelith surged through Shael's body. She no longer needed to breathe, to think. She was no longer there. And yet, she was everywhere. She was the Quanta. She was the incarnate goddess.

In mid-air, a black silk veil covered the skin of her hands, which stopped trembling. Her daggers gleamed with a bluish hue, like the sapphire of the wide-eyed stare fixed upon her. Large wings of black smoke propelled her toward her prey, who stared at her in horror. Unyielding, the assassin descended upon the Mother Superior.

At first frozen, Cassandra's body was propelled to the floor with a heavy thud. Shael found herself above the Mother Superior, dagger raised. A loud moan escaped her lips. Lost in a swirling darkness of pain. The inevitable sentence she wanted to deliver made her fist vibrate, the blue glow still emanating from the blade.

The terror in Cassandra's face transfixed the assassin. An intense emotion had finally etched on Cassandra's countenance. In her eyes. This woman who had been like a mother to her. Shael expelled her rage in a scream.

Talyvien suddenly pierced her thoughts. The disdain that had once crossed the young man's face made Shael shudder. The fragile esteem he held for her gave her pause.

She regained control of her body and began to shiver violently. The nebulous darkness that had seized her limbs and mind dissipated. Her goddess was gone. The dagger had vanished from her hand.

Cassandra, still dazed and petrified, gazed at Shael in bewilderment from beneath her body. Something was amiss. Had the assassin lost everything, even her desire for revenge? Where was Sazaelith?

Unable to tolerate the situation a moment longer or the raw emotion of Cassandra beneath her, Shael delivered a punch to the Mother Superior, rendering her unconscious. She withdrew from Cassandra's body and collapsed to the floor, her legs no longer supporting her. Confused and disoriented, she stupidly stared at the inert body of the Mother Superior before her. Were the feelings she held for the paladin so strong that she could betray herself? Or had the goddess not approved of this assassination?

Her attention shifted to Cassandra's hand. The sound of the pen on paper revived in her memory.

The contract.

Snapped out of her stupor, Shael suddenly regained her clarity and rushed out of the office. With quick steps, she went in search of the apprentice. She had to intercept the parchment that the little girl had likely been tasked to deliver.

53

 Talyvien paced back and forth in the small room of the *Veil of Truth*. His imagination raced through nightmarish corners. A familiar draft brushed against the back of his neck. He turned around hastily.

The window was wide open, and Shael stood there, looking dazed. Her hair was disheveled, and her armor was askew.

The paladin's guts twisted with dread. "Shael! Are you hurt?" he exclaimed. He placed his hands on the assassin's arms.

Languidly, Shael slowly raised her eyes to meet his. Her gaze wandered aimlessly.

"Shael? What happened?"

She seemed unable to speak. After a quick inspection, Talyvien noticed the gash on her thigh, but found no other visible injuries. A sigh of relief escaped him. He took a clean cloth, dampened it in a basin, and gently wiped Shael's face as she continued to stare vacantly.

"I'm here, Shael," he said softly.

To his surprise, the assassin's body leaned against his with tenderness. She buried her face in the crook of his neck, and her slender arms wrapped around his back. Initially frozen, Talyvien reciprocated and embraced her in return. They remained entwined, communing in their silence for several minutes. He placed a hand on Shael's head and caressed her hair, trying to comfort her.

A few sobs escaped the assassin. Shael's body slumped against his from exhaustion. Talyvien gently placed one hand under her legs and lifted her, her head resting against his chest. He carefully laid her on the bed and helped her remove the top part of her armor, as well as her boots and leather pants, leaving only her bandeau and underwear. Then, he took off his shirt and draped it around Shael to cover her.

He examined her thigh wound and saw that the cut wasn't very deep and that the bleeding had already stopped. After quickly cleaning the wound, he tucked Shael under the sheets and lay down beside her.

 Shael observed Talyvien through the haze of her eyes. She didn't know if his heart still belonged to Selena, but she didn't care. She had lost the only sanctuary she knew—the familiarity of the convent of Sazaelith. So, running out of ideas, she had come to the only place where she felt safe. In this small room. In his arms.

Finally selfish for the first time in her life, Shael approached him and embraced him under the sheets. Their legs interlaced. She savored the warmth of his skin against hers. Fear no longer consumed her. She needed this—him, at that moment. With her head resting against his heart, she listened to his racing pulse, as his massive arms encircled her petite frame, embracing her completely.

"I didn't kill her," she whispered. "I couldn't."

"Who?"

"The Mother Superior. Cassandra."

"Why would you want to kill her?" he asked, keeping a neutral tone.

"I caught her selling the blood of the chosen ones of Sazaelith to Piore. The High Priestess was feeding on one of the young apprentices."

Talyvien's hands clenched around her. His body tensed. "I—I don't know if you did the right thing."

Surprised by his response, Shael looked up at his face. Hazel eyes met hers. The assassin saw a deep sadness and resignation in his look. Had he changed his principles? She rested back her head against his chest.

"She taught me everything," she explained. "How could she then do that? She said it was to save us from the eradication of magic." A few more tears flowed, laden with painful irony.

"I'm sorry you've experienced so much betrayal, Shael," he whispered, kissing the top of her head. "You didn't deserve that." He hesitated, before continuing. "I'll never betray you. I promise."

A warmth spread through her belly. She held him a little tighter, and described the events further. "Before leaving, Piore commissioned an assassination from the Mother Superior. I saw the contract with my own eyes. The target is Queen Selena . . ."

"What?" he interrupted, surprised.

"I imagine she's becoming too inconvenient for the plans of the Lamented. I couldn't intercept the parchment in time, but I know which Child of Twilight it was assigned to. Considering Evelyn's style, I wonder if the Solamaris ball might be an ideal situation to divert attention."

"Mmhh. It so happens that Selena gave me an invitation to the ball," Talyvien revealed.

Bitterness choked Shael at the mention of her name on his lips.

"I believe I can have guests accompany me," he said. "We could go there and try to intercept your . . . colleague before she acts," he suggested.

"Aren't you afraid that Piore or her paladins will recognize you at the ball?"

"She has never seen my face, just as I've never seen hers. In the Crusade, we don't address her without our masks or armor. As for the paladins, I suppose we'll have to be discreet, but I doubt it will be a problem." He chuckled. "I don't think the Crusade will be invited to the ball."

"I also imagine that's not the reason she gave you the invitation," murmured Shael.

"Doesn't matter if it can be useful," he quickly replied. "You know that nothing happened between us, right?"

"You don't owe me anything, Talyvien."

And it was true. He wasn't responsible for the feelings she now had for him. Still, she felt him tighten his embrace.

"Would it be bad if . . ." he hesitated for a long moment, his throat visibly swallowing the words he was considering. But he remained silent.

"Did you share your concerns with Selena?" Shael asked, resigned to never knowing the rest of his words.

"Yes. She also told me that she had sent a detachment to the city of Argentvale to aid the survivors from the kingdom of Narlimar and that they never returned."

"Oh," Shael replied, now worried. "I hope Lucine will find out more about that."

They continued talking, entwined with each other in the depth of the night for hours. The assassin drowned in the warmth and scent of his skin, in the melody of his deep voice that resonated in his chest. Exhausted, Shael was surprised to feel this way. A man's body had finally become a source of protection—no more hatred and fears. He alone had managed to transform everything, to soothe her rage, violence, and suffering.

She prayed to her goddess to make this moment infinite.

Yet, inevitably, the dawn so dear to Callystrande came and shattered Shael's wishes for eternity, pulling her out of her waking dream. She greeted the first rays of the sun with despair, preparing to reluctantly let go of Talyvien's embrace.

She looked up. The paladin was dozing, his peaceful breath escaping his slightly parted lips. A wild urge to touch the scar that marked his mouth overcame her.

The scar of their encounter.

She tenderly slid her fingers along the mark on his skin. A spark ignited in his hazel eyes.

"You could have had it healed," she whispered.

"It's the most beautiful scar I have. I would have been foolish to remove it."

The assassin's heart raced. Her body was seized by slight spasms under the wave of heat that surged through her and that she couldn't restrain. She was losing control of everything. Her thoughts ignited in a chaotic and orderly frenzy.

She felt Talyvien's hand caressing her back. A silent yet heavily laden request.

With her mind completely empty, but her eyes filled with intense curiosity, Shael gently slid the tip of her fingers along the scar, tracing its path up to the edge of Talyvien's upper lip. Why was she so fascinated by that face? By that mouth?

Talyvien's body stiffened at her touch, and his hand on her back ceased its motion. Was she going too far? So many things had happened since she had inflicted that scar on him. Adventures she never thought possible. Changes she didn't know she was capable of. Yet, she saw the intensity in his hazel eyes directed at her lips as well. Was he feeling something similar? Tremors took Shael's breath hostage.

Talyvien tenderly kissed the fingers that had lingered on their shared memory, on his mouth.

In an irrational but undeniable impulse, Shael wanted to replace her fingers with her lips.

Their bodies drew closer. Only a few inches separated their faces.

Their breaths mingled. Talyvien's arms tightened around her.

The delicious scent of his skin overwhelmed her.

She closed her eyes.

A plunge that finally made sense.

Someone knocked on the door.

Cursed door!

THE OPALESCENT
MASQUERADE

54

"Talyvien? Shael?" shouted Lucine, as she knocked on the door of the room at the end of the hallway in the *Veil of Truth*. The young druidess turned to Calixte, who stood beside her. "Maybe they're not here?"

The bard responded with a shrug. Katao barked. But after several minutes, the door finally opened.

Talyvien appeared in the doorway, wearing a hastily put-on shirt. The young druidess rushed toward the paladin and embraced him.

"Hey Lucine!" he exclaimed with a smile.

"It's been too long!" the young woman cried out.

A small laugh escaped Talyvien. "It's only been two days!"

"Not for us, paladin, but it's a long story!" Calixte chimed in, their gaze sliding toward the assassin who was putting on her boots, sitting on her bed. "So, did you two share a room?" they continued, with a mischievous look.

"Oh, with the Solamaris festival, it was almost impossible to find anything else," Shael quickly replied, her cheeks flushed.

Lucine's eyes glanced at Talyvien, and she saw an expression she had not seen before as he looked at the assassin. To think she had feared they might kill each other.

"Ah! I think we can do better than that! My treat!" Calixte exclaimed enthusiastically.

The four friends galloped through the streets of the city, followed by Katao, and headed toward a more affluent neighborhood, guided by the assassin who seemed visibly uncomfortable being surrounded by so much wealth and elegance.

Lucine admired the colors of the festival and the joy of the passersby. She discovered the bustling and lively capital, the towering heights of its immense castle reaching toward the sky, its grand canals crowded with barges scattered throughout the city, its rare and precious goods in shops and stalls.

Although she tried to focus on the wonders she was discovering, her mind was preoccupied with the revelations of Feör and Teluar. Anxiety gnawed at her belly at the thought of what Solehan might be going through. The person he might have become. How could she find help powerful enough to deal with the Alaris and save her brother in Argentvale? Would Teluar's heart be enough?

They arrived at a large square where a statue of the late King Herald Aramanth proudly stood in front of a luxurious inn. Several carriages with coachmen stopped and hurriedly departed, depositing a stream of travelers who entered the establishment.

"You said you wanted quality, Calixte, and we won't find anything better than the *Opalescent Masquerade* of Dawnelest!" Shael snickered, placing her hands on her hips.

Wearing splendidly crafted clothes, an Alaris couple exited the inn and crossed their path. Their glances showed interest in Calixte.

"It looks perfect!" the bard exclaimed with enthusiasm.

With a hint of amusement on their faces, Lucine, Shael, and Talyvien followed the bard, who entered the building with confident steps. The young druidess had never seen so much abundance in her life: an explosion of iridescent textures, magnificently embroidered garments, pearls, and embedded gems, precious metals, ancient and impeccably polished wood. Grand columns with arabesque architecture, huge windows with geometric and perfect patterns. Lucine thought back to the small hut made of wood in the Astral Forest where she had grown up and found it ironic that such a contrast could exist.

Blown away, she observed her companions' reactions. Calixte seemed to be like a fish in water. Shael, on the other hand, appeared increasingly uncomfortable. Her body unconsciously drew closer to the paladin's. Lucine chuckled discreetly.

Even though Calixte used all their charms on the innkeeper, they could only rent two double rooms, as all the single rooms were occupied by the constant waves of guests arriving for the Solamaris ball.

"I suppose Lucine and Shael can take one of the rooms, and we'll take the other," the bard said. "What do you think, Talyvien?"

The Alaris's mocking citrine eyes turned to the paladin. They had also noticed the closeness between the young man and Shael, but seemed amused by the situation. Talyvien nodded hurriedly, his face briefly betraying a flash of disappointment as he glanced at the assassin.

As usual, they settled around for a fabulous breakfast ordered by the bard. They exchanged and shared their respective adventures of dreams, nightmares, and truths. Of sovereigns and violence, of drafelis and forest spirits. Of Valnard and Solehan, of Piore and the crusade.

"What?" exclaimed Lucine. "You saw my brother?"

"Yes. He seemed to believe that you were dead," replied Shael.

A weight crashed into Lucine's stomach.

"The Alaris . . . This 'Valnard' apparently showed him how he created the monstrosities that roam the territory," Talyvien growled. "One of the primary missions of the order of the paladins of Callystrande is to eliminate these degenerations. We spend a good part of our training learning to fight a vast bestiary and the various powers these creatures have inherited. Echarvoras, viperals, lupinars, it's a mess! I can't believe he was responsible for their creation all this time . . ." Talyvien ran a hand through his hair, sighing.

"He also used the blood of Sazaelith's chosen and the tears of Callystrande's to create them," Shael said. "Now I understand why our blood can alter the properties of these creatures. Like when the echarvora bit you, Lucine. I think both goddesses are trying to combat this problem in their own way." The assassin breathed out her frustration and devoured a small pastry before resuming. "So, you think Valnard kidnapped your brother for his powers?"

"It seems so," replied Lucine. "But I believe he may not have anticipated that I also possess some."

"So, you and your brother are indeed Teluar's chosen ones after all?" the assassin concluded.

Lucine nodded. She took out the beautiful flower from her pocket. "Teluar himself gave this to me. Apparently, this flower can enhance the powers of his chosen ones, among other things. He told me to use it 'wisely.' But I'm not sure exactly what that means."

"Among other things?" Talyvien asked.

"Oh. It seems it can also heal wounds, grant life. Well, all sorts of miraculous things when placed in a body of water," Lucine added.

"This little flower is fascinating!" Calixte said joyfully. "But not as surprising as you, Lucine! You will find the answers in due time. I have no doubt!"

Lucine gave a timid smile and placed her hand on the Alaris's arm in gratitude. "In any case," the druidess said, "if an entire detachment of soldiers from Dawnelest and Narlimar hasn't returned, we'll need a whole army to free Argentvale and Solehan from his clutches." She sighed.

"Perhaps the crusade could help if they learn that Valnard is responsible for creating these creatures," Talyvien suggested. "They are seasoned fighters!"

"Seasoned fighters who have gone mad," Shael retorted.

"True," the young man admitted. "What I mean is, we could also use the ball to get closer to Piore. I still can't believe she drank the blood of a chosen one of Sazaelith. For what purpose?"

All remained silent, looking at the pile of pastries and desserts before them, with no plausible answers coming to mind.

"Well, I suppose that, in case of trouble, we'll have several tricks up our sleeves!" the paladin resumed. "The magic of Teluar and Sazaelith. That of Calixte . . ."

"An experienced warrior as well!" interrupted Shael.

Talyvien returned a delighted emotion to the assassin.

"Ah! Speaking of that!" hesitated the bard, clearing their throat and dusting off their shoulder. "I can no longer use the Flow or the Ignescent."

"What?!" Shael asked, with a worried expression. "How did that happen?"

"Let's just say I had a revelation at last!" Calixte affirmed playfully. "A *magnificent* revelation!" Small sparks of violet magic crackled between the fingers of the Alaris.

Lucine's heart warmed. She was deeply happy for them. She gently tightened her fingers around the bard's arm.

"So, what can you do now?" Talyvien asked, frowning.

"Well, still be as splendid as ever!" they exclaimed, amid everyone's laughter. "Or superb, magnificent, enchanting, absolutely sublime! Just to name a few!"

"Indeed, you haven't changed, Calixte," the paladin said, with a playful glint in his eyes.

"More seriously, it seems I can still conjure some illusions, but nothing more," Calixte said, looking at the palm of their hand containing the violet glow. "I can no longer heal, alter, or read humans' thoughts, apparently. I believe I still don't know exactly what I can do with this new power."

"So, I guess we can't really rely on your magic," Shael said.

"Since when were my powers the only weapon at my disposal in my arsenal, Shael?" they teased. "You offend me! Anyway, I was already refusing to use the Flow and the Ignescent in that way. And I suppose there will be other Alaris at this ball."

"Does Alaris magic not work on other Alaris?" the young druidess asked.

"No. Not the kind that affects thoughts, at least. Our minds are impenetrable!" Calixte replied proudly. "That's why humans can't have access to our point of view!"

"Have you given this new power a name?" Lucine asked tenderly.

"Mmhh. I thought of calling it the Augur. I believe destiny has put Feör on my path."

"Oh, so it's in her honor?" the young druidess inquired.

"Yes, indeed," they rejoiced. "But enough about me! At least for now! All I hear is that we're invited to a royal ball and need suitable clothes!"

Talyvien and Shael groaned in disgust before exchanging surprised glances.

"Come on, come on! You two are hopeless!" The bard turned to the young druidess. "Lucine, you take care of Shael, and I'll take care of our dear paladin!"

An orange wink flew in the paladin's direction, making him grumble even more.

Accompanied by Katao, the two women walked along the impressive shops of the affluent district of Dawnelest. Shael, hands in her pockets, looked at the beautiful fabrics and silks with a distant and disinterested air, while Lucine enjoyed the wonder of touching different textiles.

"So, you said you have . . . Teluar's powers now?" Shael asked.

"Oh . . . yes . . . apparently, the amulet I was wearing made them . . . inactive."

"How did that happen?"

The assassin's surprised look made Lucine lift her head from the colorful fabrics.

"I'm not really sure. But it was the elders who gave it to me on the day of . . ." Lucine still couldn't finish the sentence, the lump in her throat still significant.

"And do you think they knew?" Shael inquired.

"No idea."

"It's particularly strange that you received an amulet, but not your brother," the assassin said, crossing her arms thoughtfully.

"What do you mean?"

"You said the legend of your clan mentioned that only men received power, right? What if it was just because of that?" The assassin paused, looking at the elegantly sewn clothes of the passersby with a curious eye as they strolled along the main shopping street. Eventually, she continued. "Perhaps to protect you. But to prevent you from being tempted to become anything other than what's written in that legend . . . most likely."

"You think?" Lucine asked sadly.

"I mean, it wouldn't be the first time that someone tried to force a woman into a path her heart didn't truly desire," Shael grumbled.

Lucine had never thought of that. Had it been a way for the elders to force fate when they sensed her desire to see the world? To make sure she would never become something else?

"I wonder if sometimes our ancestors project too much onto us. Too many stupid traditions," the assassin said, with a serious tone, her eyes wandering through the crowd. "I think we should live for our descendants. Live in accordance with what's in our hearts so that their future is better. The past is already gone."

"And here I thought assassins only thought about killing," Lucine joked.

"It happens."

The assassin returned the druidess's playfulness with a mischievous look.

Now in a teasing mood, Lucine continued. "And what about . . . Talyvien?" she asked, with an innocent pout and a finger on her chin.

"What about Talyvien?" Shael retorted sharply.

"You like him, don't you?"

"No!" the assassin hurriedly replied, turning her head away. Faced with Lucine's insistence, Shael sighed with embarrassment and resigned. "I don't stand a chance against the queen of Dawnelest, anyway!"

"Well, then, we're in the right place! Let me turn you into a queen! No, even better: an empress!" Lucine said heartily.

"If you say so!" Shael replied, looking weary and unconvinced.

"You know, it doesn't hurt to take care of yourself once in a while!"

"Mmhh . . . It's just that I'm not really used to all this," Shael hesitated, twisting her fingers.

"Dressing up or wanting to impress someone?"

"Both, probably!" The assassin chuckled.

They both burst into laughter.

"You know, Shael, you have the right to be feminine and strong. The two aren't mutually exclusive; you don't have to choose between them."

Initially tinged with surprise, the assassin's face softened. Lucine proudly winked at her and conjured a beautiful black flower with bluish reflections in her hands, placing it tenderly behind Shael's ear.

"Calixte is a bad influence on you!" the assassin said.

Their laughter blended with the joy of the passersby as they entered a shop.

55

The big night finally arrived. On the way, Lucine observed through the opening of their transportation the well-coordinated choreography of the carriages heading to the Solamaris ball, above one of the bridges leading to the majestic castle. By her side, Shael seemed more anxious than ever, her legs showing signs of restlessness. It was such a rare and visible discomfort for the young woman who was usually so composed, with such controlled gestures. Did the paladin have such an effect on her? Or was she just so unfamiliar with this aspect of her life?

But perhaps the assassin's apprehension was justified. This ball would potentially be their only chance to learn more about the High Priestess and prevent the assassination of Queen Selena. They wouldn't have such an opportunity anytime soon. Saddened to have left Katao in their room at the inn and unable to bring her bow and arrows, Lucine still hoped that Teluar's blessing would be enough. Along with the small dagger hidden on her thigh. She also felt the pocket of her dress. The volume created by the small crystal flower was detectable under her fingers. Quite an arsenal. Despite her lack of experience, Lucine was as ready as she would ever be.

The hooves of the horses fell silent on the cobblestones, and the carriage doors opened to reveal the castle of Dawnelest decorated for the occasion. As they stepped out, they were greeted by a myriad of swirling colors of the superb attire and dresses of the guests. Evident luxury saluted them, symbolized by the long floating banners announcing the opening of the Solamaris ball around the entrance of the glorious building. They spotted Calixte approaching, looking more grandiose than ever, with makeup and a tunic befitting the greatest monarchs. The bard's draped garments of red and dark purple complimented their amethyst skin, and their white and bluish hair was braided on one side, revealing their pointed ear.

"By the great city of Alar! Lucine, you look magnificent! And . . . Shael?! Who would have thought that beneath this assassin's leather, such beauty was hidden!" they exclaimed, giving an elegant bow upon their arrival.

"It's very kind, Calixte, but I don't believe we can rival you!" Lucine chuckled.

"Ah! No certainty about that!" Calixte leaned discreetly toward the young druidess, hiding their words with a hand. "Formidable collaboration, my dear!" they whispered, glancing at Shael.

Lucine let out a discreet laugh.

Navigating among the elegant guests, they approached the grand entrance of the building. The bard, clearly at ease in this environment, seemed to attract all eyes to them. With a graceful and perfectly controlled gait, Calixte managed to make their way through the crowd of attendees who were intrigued by their striking charisma, with some stopping or whispering as they approached. An unforgettable diversion.

Lucine spotted the paladin waiting for them on the stone staircase in front of the castle entrance. Somewhat agitated, one hand on the hilt of his sword and the other in his pocket, Talyvien was absorbed in his thoughts, rubbing his foot on one of the steps. He wore a superbly tailored black ensemble that defined his figure with elegance. Fine golden seams snaked around his sleeves, collar, and back in patterns. His hair had been cut short, and his stubbly beard closely shaved. Calixte had cast an impressive spell on him, as the paladin usually paid less attention to his appearance.

 Having arrived earlier in the evening with the charismatic bard, Talyvien was growing impatient in front of the grand entrance of the castle. Fearing being recognized, he had been relieved to see that no paladins from Callystrande seemed to have been invited to the party. But he knew that wasn't the

main reason for his affliction. Had he been right to follow Calixte in their frenzy of extravagance? Had he gone too far? He tried to focus as best as he could on their mission, but the last moment he had shared with the assassin kept replaying endlessly in his mind. Had she wanted to kiss him?

Pulled from his reverie by the charismatic Calixte, Talyvien raised his head. Lucine, with the bard on her arm, was wearing a beautiful green dress with floral lace patterns. Fabric branches wrapped around her shoulders and her brown hair was elegantly styled. The god Teluar seemed to take pride in her appearance. He was amazed at the tenderness he felt for the young woman, and the gratitude that filled his soul at seeing her so happy after the trials she had been through.

"You look lovely, Lucine," he told her.

"Oh, that's kind of you, Taly! But you should see Shael!"

Lucine tenderly placed a hand on the paladin's arm to thank him before entering the building with Calixte. The charming laughter of the Alaris drifted away as Talyvien turned his head toward the new arrivals.

Sapphire eyes met his.

And everything in Talyvien stumbled.

A glimpse of a starry sky. Of fleeting grace. A mirage that existed only in a love-struck heart.

With feline steps, the assassin glided in a long black dress constellated with shimmering specks. In her curves of starlit night, only her tanned skin daringly peeked from her shoulders down to the beginnings of her chest. Large dark feathers framed her silhouette and moved above her arms like the caress of her goddess's wings. Her long hair, let loose and swept back, cascaded down to her lower back. A black jet flower was placed behind one of her ears, its bluish variations complementing the sapphire of her eyes, which pierced through a light band of dark lace.

"Shael . . . you're . . ." the paladin began, breathless. No words seemed to capture what he felt in that moment.

"You don't look bad yourself, Talyvien," she interrupted, a tender smile gracing her face.

"Would you do me the honor?" he composed himself, extending his arm, which she delicately took.

They entered the castle together.

Shael admired the immense golden chandeliers stretching across the blue ceiling of the grand hall, illuminating the splendor of Dawnelest's high society with their glass crystals. Despite being reassured by the paladin by her side, guiding her through this labyrinth of privilege, she still clung to him a little tighter when they entered the grand hall. He responded to her silent discomfort by placing his free hand on hers at his arm. A wave of warmth surged in her chest as she thought back to Talyvien's reaction. From the corner of her eye, she had admired him and was surprised to see a broad smile forming on his face, as he was usually less demonstrative. He looked very distinguished in his black ensemble—of course, she had to admit to herself that she found him divinely handsome, his impossible scar still taunting her.

They joined Lucine and Calixte, who were eager to taste the cakes and other delicacies laid out on the tables as a buffet.

"You should leave some for the other guests," Shael chuckled.

"Oh, you should try them, they're delicious!" Lucine replied, taking a bite of a small fruit tart.

"Should we not try the wine?" Calixte asked, a hint of sadness in their voice, eyeing the tray carried by one of the passing waiters.

"We better keep a clear head, indeed," Talyvien retorted, with a teasing look.

The ambient noise of the guests abruptly quieted, as a figure stepped onto the large dais overlooking the massive ballroom. The assassin's throat tightened.

Queen Selena presented herself in all her glory. The azure blue of her long tulle gown swirled and complemented her impressive crown of jewels, intricately woven into a sculpted bun.

"My dear guests, welcome to the annual Solamaris ball!" Several rounds of applause ensued. "This year, we have the pleasure of receiving honored guests! My dear brother, Arthios Therybane, King of Astitan, and the Lamented of Callystrande, High Priestess of the Crusade of the Dawn's Resolve."

A grand table, dressed in the colors of the kingdom of Vamentera, had been set up on the platform and heaped with the most refined delicacies and rarest wines. Seated around it on large chairs were King Arthios and High Priestess Piore, her mask of golden tears concealing her face; both were regarding the assembly with a neutral gaze. At the mention of his name, the sovereign raised his glass and nodded slightly to his sister, Queen Selena.

"Let the festivities begin!" the queen proclaimed, lifting her glass in turn amid the general cheer of the crowd.

A melody arose in the grand hall, emanating from a small group of musicians who began playing their instruments. Several couples stepped onto the polished marble in the center of the room, elegantly gliding in their first dance steps.

Shael looked at the queen for a long moment, a mixture of admiration and bitterness gripping her heart. How could she possibly compete with the elegance and grace of this woman?

"So, I suppose we need to keep an eye on Queen Selena and Piore, don't we?" Calixte whispered, before delicately biting into a small cake with pleasure.

"We should also try to intercept Evelyn before she fulfills her contract," the assassin whispered back, turning her head away out of spite.

"What does she look like?" Lucine inquired.

"Slender, blond hair, but I'd say her strangely sapphire eyes and scars at the corners of her eyes will give you a good indication," Shael teased. "I can't imagine she came in an evening gown, though."

"How are we going to find her then?" the young druidess asked.

"I'd say as long as the queen is at the ball, she's safe. Otherwise, we'll have to do some investigating," Calixte replied, with one of their legendary winks.

"It would be good to learn more about Piore as well," Talyvien murmured.

"Let's wait until the festivities are in full swing, and then we'll sneak into the corridors and see what we can find," the assassin whispered.

The paladin nodded in agreement. The bard, enjoying their pastry, observed the couples gracefully waltzing in the center of the grand hall.

"Very well! Since we have to wait anyway! Lucine, would you grant me this dance?" Calixte asked, their amber eyes looking at the young woman with tenderness.

"With pleasure, Calixte!" the young druidess replied cheerfully.

They moved toward the dance floor, their attire swaying with their steps. The bard gently took Lucine's hand and placed their other hand on the young druidess's waist, while she put hers on the Alaris's shoulder. They began to twirl with a certain caution. Calixte was evidently teaching her the appropriate dance steps for the melody.

Shael leaned against the table where the delicious pastries were laid out and watched them waltz above the polished floor with affection. A heavy veil settled on her neck. The assassin felt the chill of icy eyes dissecting her. When Shael turned her head, she saw Queen Selena staring at her from the royal table.

"Calixte is right. If we have to wait anyway . . . Shael, would you grant me this dance?" Talyvien asked, a slight tremor in his voice.

"I . . ." Shael began, her eyes still fixed on the queen. "I'm not sure if it's a very good idea, Talyvien."

"You know, I'm not a very good dancer either," he said, a bit uneasy, one hand behind his neck, disappointment in his voice that saddened the assassin's heart.

What did she have to lose? If the queen survived this evening, maybe it would be the one and only chance for her to be close to the paladin. She bit her lip. Selfishly, she had to admit that an infinitesimal part of her wished for the contract to be fulfilled. She cursed her immaturity. But, too eager for this opportunity and in defiance, she turned to Talyvien.

"Let's go. Show me your dancing skills!" Shael replied, placing her hand in his.

A spark lit up in the paladin's eyes.

Shael pressed her body against his, as Talyvien's hand lightly grazed the small of her back. Probably too close for the conventions of Dawnelest's high society and its sovereign. Probably not close enough for what she had in her heart at that moment. The assassin placed her hand on his broad shoulder, and he responded by taking her other hand in his, pulling her body a bit closer to his. With him holding her like this, she admired the square features of his face, highlighted by the multitude of luminous sources, and the unwavering protection in his stare.

They began to waltz, ignoring the appropriate dance steps and the eyes fixed on them, and got lost in each other's gaze.

"I missed you last night," he whispered. "My bed was terribly empty."

"And I thought you preferred Calixte's company over mine! Their music, perhaps? Their charisma? No, I know: their magic!" she mocked.

Talyvien let out a light chuckle. The paladin's cheeks faintly blushed as he leaned toward her ear. "You are exquisite, Shael. I wouldn't mind continuing what we started . . ." he whispered, pressing his hand on her back slightly.

The paladin's touch ignited her spine. An eruption that swept through her mind and devoured all reason. But with the little caution she had left, the assassin used cunning to try to protect herself. "It's a tempting offer, paladin. But what about the queen?"

"You still don't understand, do you?"

"What do you mean?"

"It has always been you, Shael, only you, ever since I first met your eyes. I tried to resist for a long time, to find excuses, to lose myself in a memory that no longer existed. I don't want to do that anymore; I'm not afraid anymore. I don't know if what's between us makes sense, but maybe it's not supposed to be logical," he murmured into her ear.

Everything came to a halt.

Time, colors, light, laughter, the clinking of glasses—everything drifted far away. There were only hazel eyes ardently fixed on her, trying to convey the extent of their truth. Just the two of them in the midst of the crowd; him, her, and their interwoven souls amid this incessant waltz. Just the emotion that exploded and that Shael finally refused to contain.

In a distant echo, Selena's persistent stare still chilled their skin, but Talyvien ignored it with his radiant warmth. Had he rejected the queen of Dawnelest for her?

The assassin looked at the scar on his lips and let her hand glide from his shoulder to his cheek, knowing the audacity of this gesture in such an environment. Through this touch, he understood her silent promise, her answer. And, eager and impatient, he returned his eyes to her lips.

Unable to consummate the blaze of their bodies at that moment, they let their hearts unite for the first time, to the rhythm of their waltz. Their muted yet visible confession transported them elsewhere.

To a place of eternity, lost between day and night, between dusk and dawn. Where their goddesses celebrated their love.

56

Lucine returned to the table full of delicious culinary offerings, exhausted from her dance with the charismatic Alaris. She looked at the prestigious assembly, immersing herself in the vibrant colors of the ladies' dresses, the discreet laughter and the gentle clinking of glasses, the sparkling headdresses and jewels, and the carefree joy and merriment. Her friends were savoring this rare, suspended moment.

She admired Calixte's presence as they captivated their audience— the attractive couple of Alaris they had encountered earlier at the inn. Their charming laughter warmed her heart. Then, she watched Shael and Talyvien dance gently, the power of what was growing inside them written on their faces.

Lucine sensed that their intense emotion seemed to pique the curiosity of Queen Selena. However, it wasn't her eyes that surprised the young druidess when her attention shifted toward the grand royal dais.

As penetrating and sharp as ever, the two golden orbs of Piore pierced through her mask toward her. Her anxiety tightened its grip on Lucine's throat. Why was Piore staring at her like that? Had she been recognized? The memory of the flames of the pyre licked at her feet, making them twitch. Her fingers clenched the tablecloth.

But Lucine didn't have time to dwell on these questions. Queen Selena got up and left the room in long strides through a small door concealed not far from the table. Piore stood up as well and followed in the footsteps of the queen, her sinister attention lingering on the druidess.

Lucine had to warn her companions.

"Calixte!" Lucine exclaimed, hurrying toward the trio of Alaris. "Oh, I'm sorry to interrupt, but I need to borrow them," she added, smiling and placing her hand on the bard's arm.

"Hey, Lucine. Are you sure—?" Calixte began hesitantly.

"Yes."

Discerning the determined tone in the young druidess's voice, Calixte executed a graceful bow toward the couple, who responded with a nod and a hint of disappointment.

"What's going on?" Calixte asked in a hushed voice, moving away from the couple.

"The queen! She's slipped away with Piore!" Lucine said.

"Oh." The bard glanced quickly toward the platform. "We need to inform the lovebirds."

Lucine managed to smile, despite the urgency of the situation. The assassin and the paladin, still captivated by their enthralling embrace, seemed oblivious to the world collapsing around them. The young druidess hesitated to interrupt the enchantment in which they appeared to be entranced. For her friends. To preserve this moment for them. And to avoid drawing any attention.

Fortunately, after a few moments, the music's volume subsided, forcing them to become aware of their surroundings. The grave expressions on Lucine and Calixte's faces, and the sight of the empty dais, snapped them out of the daze they had been in as they rejoined them.

"She left through the door behind the platform, followed by Piore!" Lucine said agitatedly to the two companions.

"Then it's time to act," Shael stated, the cold composure of the assassin resurfacing.

The four friends headed toward the back of the grand hall, feigning nonchalance, and tried not to alert the few guards nearby. Dodging nobles and servants, they finally slipped through one of the doors of the grand ballroom and found themselves in one of the many hallways of the castle.

Several groups of guests were scattered here and there, conversing and jesting in the large and luxurious corridor. Continuing from the ballroom, the beautifully polished marble floor reflected the splendid patterns of the tapestries in the colors of the Kingdom of Vamentera, proudly displayed on both sides of the gallery. The atmosphere among the guests felt more intimate, with hushed laughter and bodies drawing closer together.

"How are we going to find them?" Lucine asked.

"I know where the queen's bedroom is. That could be a good starting point. I think I can find the way," Talyvien admitted, seemingly regretting his words immediately.

A certain pain crossed the assassin's face. He touched Shael's arm with his fingers, his eyes silently apologizing.

"We may not arrive in time. I'll try to intercept Evelyn by taking the rooftop route," the assassin only replied.

Shael moved stealthily toward one of the large windows in the gallery and cautiously cracked it open, hidden from view.

"Shael . . ." the paladin hesitated, taking the assassin's hand. "Be careful."

The assassin covertly caressed Talyvien's cheek before swiftly disappearing through the window. Lucine watched the ever elusive and volatile silhouette of Shael being swallowed by darkness.

"All right, let's go to that bedroom! Lead the way, Talyvien!" Calixte declared.

Following the direction indicated by the paladin, who took the lead of their procession, they navigated through a labyrinth of stairs and sumptuous corridors. As they progressed toward the private apartments, the guests of the ball became increasingly scarce. Thus, they tried to be as discreet as possible, which proved to be quite a challenge for the bard.

Despite some hesitations, Talyvien recognized the path he had taken a few nights earlier. A grand gallery revealed itself when they turned the corner of the junction of two corridors. Talyvien quietly cursed under his breath. He extended his arm to prevent Lucine and Calixte from overtaking him and retreated behind the corner of the wall.

"What's wrong, Taly?" Lucine whispered.

"Paladins," he growled.

Their curiosity piqued, Calixte and Lucine leaned slightly to catch a glimpse of the reason for his agitation. Two paladins of Callystrande stood in the middle of the vast corridor, the gold of their full armor producing ominous reflections under the candlelight.

"Hmm . . . the paladins have never seen me," Calixte whispered. "I can create a diversion, and you two can continue without me. I'll join you later."

"No, it's better if I'm the one doing the diversion," Talyvien murmured.

"Let's try not to attract attention through force. Besides, you're the only one who knows the queen and the location of her bedroom!" retorted Calixte.

"Yes, but—"

Talyvien never had the chance to finish his sentence, as the Alaris strode into the grand gallery with magnificent grace, their moiré tunic of red and violet swaying gracefully behind them. The vexation that had been on their face vanished in an instant.

Worried for the bard, Lucine cast an apologetic glance at the paladin, who remained hidden behind the corridor, a speechless look on his face.

"I'm sorry . . . Go quickly, Taly . . ." Lucine urged before following Calixte with a feigned sense of confidence.

"You're not authorized to be in this part of the castle! Return to the ballroom immediately!" one of the paladins bellowed sternly upon seeing them approach.

"Calixte, 'mage and bard of wonders!' Enchanted to make your acquaintance!" they proclaimed. "You're lucky! It's rare to get this close to me! So many performances, spectacles! I can hardly keep up!"

The Alaris was laughing and theatrically adjusting their collar as Lucine reached their side.

"Whoever you are, I don't care. Go back where you came from!" the second paladin growled hoarsely.

"Oh, please excuse us! To be honest, we were just looking for a somewhat . . . *private* place, you see," Calixte added, fluttering their eyelashes discreetly in line with their words.

One of the Alaris's hands gently encircled around Lucine's waist. She wasn't sure if this tactic was appropriate given the severity of the paladins of Callystrande, but she tried to play along and wrapped her arm around Calixte's shoulder.

"There are no 'private' places meant for that. Go back to the ballroom, or I will have no choice than to use force."

"Oh, force! Interesting . . . We are not opposed to some company, especially from powerful paladins," the Alaris said, covering their delightful laughter with a coy hand.

Still holding onto the bard, Lucine was mortified when Calixte provocatively brushed a finger against one of the paladins' breastplates. A subtle purple spark flickered in the Alaris's eyes. Did they still possess some kind of power?

The two men froze, repugnance evident in their postures.

"Don't touch me!" the paladin vociferated.

From the corner of her eye, Lucine saw Talyvien taking advantage of their awkward diversion, slipping behind the golden-armored guards and doing his best to make his steps as light as possible on the marble. She had to buy him time.

One of the armored paladins stepped forward menacingly.

"Oh, it's just that we've had a bit too much to drink . . . Perhaps you could show us the way back?" Lucine apologized, attempting to feign a certain drunkenness to defuse the situation.

The paladin grunted in disgust. His attention shifted to the young druidess's face before sliding to the tattoos on her arms.

Lucine's stomach turned to liquid in her legs. How could she forget how her appearance had caused her so much trouble? Taking Talyvien's bravery for granted, she cursed herself for letting her guard down.

The paladins rushed toward them.

Lucine was thrown against the wall with a sharp crack. The grip of one of the paladins' enormous hands closed around her neck and began to suffocate her. Her feet no longer touched the ground, and she struggled vehemently, digging her nails into the man's fists. A sound of helplessness escaped her clenched teeth. An implacable vice tightened around her. A mad and vacant gaze of intolerance observed her through the golden mask.

Nobody could help them now. Not Talyvien, who had already disappeared, nor Shael, who was probably walking the rooftops at that moment. A thick fog slowly filled her vision, her chest heaving from lack of air. Lucine, filled with rage, fought with all her might. Could she summon the powers of Teluar? She clenched her fingers around the man's arm, begging the god to come to their aid.

But nothing happened. The cries of the paladins, of Calixte, the clinking of metal, the rustling of cloth; everything faded hastily around her.

With difficulty, Lucine blinked and caught a glimpse of Calixte's frail body, throwing themselves at the second paladin. But their charisma was futile in this situation.

With a single swing of his arm, the warrior sent them flying as if they were a mere twig. Blood sprayed from Calixte's temple as they collapsed heavily onto the marble. The folds of their long tunic billowed through the air and covered their body.

They did not get up.

Lucine screamed, but no sound came out. Tears streamed down her cheeks. In the silence of her cry, a deep, muffled growl reverberated in her throat.

It couldn't end like this. She had a promise to keep.

With what little life force she had left, she reached for the dagger concealed on her thigh. Shael's lessons flooded her mind. In an instant, she stabbed the blade just under the paladin's armpit. The memory of a move that had once been desperate.

But this time, the unforgiving weapon miraculously slipped between the few inches separating the two metal plates. Her attacker let out a scream. A powerful attack that she hadn't intended to be fatal. The paladin released his grip and fell to his knees, trying to stem the blood that was dangerously pouring from under his arm.

Staggering, in shock and with a hand on her throat, Lucine watched the man on the ground. How had she managed such an assault? To find the weakness in their heavy armor on the first attempt? She'd have to thank the assassin.

But she didn't have time to appreciate the feeling of solid ground beneath her feet again or her luck. The second man rushed at her.

As she observed his charge, his sword aimed at her, pulses flooded Lucine's temples. Almost tribal beats. Whispers that turned into rhythmic screams. The rage contained in her frustration enveloped her.

Finally, Teluar's voice became powerful in her ear. She wouldn't allow herself to be pushed around anymore. She would defend those she held dear. Learn to control her powers.

Lucine let herself be guided by her god.

Long vines responded to her call and grew under the golden armor of the second attacker. They emerged through the few spaces between the metal plates and wrapped around the paladin's neck, halting him abruptly.

In distress, he tried to summon Callystrande's magic to burn the vines that were increasingly constricting him. The warm light of the goddess emanated from his hands.

Lucine spiraled and tapped into her grief. New vines added and intertwined with the charred ones. There was no escape. Images whirled before her eyes. She saw the massacre of her clan, the petrifying magic of the lychenas, the pyre, Zaf's face, the echarvora.

Blood. Pain. Despair. She wanted to obliterate it all.

With wide, teary eyes behind the mask, the paladin let out a muffled sob. But Lucine only heard it as a distant echo. She wanted to inflict upon them all the suffering they had caused her. To her and those she loved. The air emptied from the man's lungs, and his body collapsed on the marble floor alongside his comrade, now also unconscious.

Calixte's gentle hand rested on Lucine's shoulder.

They were alive.

"Come back, Lucine. That's enough . . ."

The Alaris's deep voice sounded troubled in her mind. She forced herself to return, to calm the anger that sought to consume her. Teluar's magic dissipated, and her hands shivered violently. She looked with horror at the memory of that vengeful impulse in her trembling fingers. What had she done? Had she become the very thing she was trying to fight against?

She was relieved to hear the breathing of the two men on the ground. She hadn't killed them, only incapacitated them. Her senses gradually returned.

"That's a line you should never cross, Lucine. Never," the Alaris said with gravity.

With half-closed eyes, blood flowing from the Alaris's temple down the side of their face, they struggled to remain standing and held their ribs.

"Calixte!" Lucine burst, throwing herself into their arms. "I thought . . ."

"Hey, it's going to be alright. Don't worry about me. Even like this, I'm still as sublime as ever!" they joked with a painful grimace. "Come on, we have to keep going."

With her lower lip bitten between her teeth, Lucine nodded and helped the bard move forward.

 Talyvien looked on with surprise and annoyance as Calixte and Lucine stubbornly propelled themselves into the grand gallery. The paladin cursed again, this time directed at the bard.

But the Alaris was right. He needed to take advantage of their diversion.

Walking stealthily and relieved that the two paladins had their backs turned, he discreetly made his way through the magnificent gallery. Stealth was not really his strong suit, but Talyvien did his best not to attract attention.

Finally, he managed to evade the paladins' line of sight as he turned into a branching corridor and continued his progress, praying not to encounter any other paladins along the way.

After several minutes, he reached the elegant wooden door with golden arabesques of the queen's bedroom at the end of one of the corridors. A shiver ran down Talyvien's spine as he recalled Queen Selena's disappointment during their last meeting. But he had no choice.

The door was already slightly ajar, and he cautiously entered the room. Bathed in darkness and silence, he discovered the sumptuous chamber with its massive four-poster bed and a small vanity that he recognized. Talyvien was relieved that no one seemed to be inside, but he noticed that the cool night air was blowing through the wide-open window.

Still cautious, he approached the starlit opening. The long, translucent fabric curtains fluttered in the breeze. The bed sheets were disheveled.

Talyvien felt a cold sweat.

A broken vase, books strewn on the floor, a rumpled rug. There were indeed signs of a struggle. Had he arrived too late? Was Selena still alive? Had Shael managed to intercept Evelyn in time?

His ears throbbed with erratic pulses as he continued to inspect the room. His anxiety turned to terror when he discovered a cobalt bloodstain near the window. Was it from Evelyn, or—

"Seize him!"

Talyvien froze.

The voice of the Lamented echoed in the royal chamber. A dozen armored paladins surged into the room through the open door. Talyvien didn't have time to react as two of his former brothers seized him by the wrists and forced him to kneel. What could he do without the powers of his goddess? One of them disarmed him and handed Tuoryn's sword to the priestess.

Piore approached him, her eyes burning like two suns behind the golden mask, her celestial train lightly gliding on the marble floor. She wrapped her fingers around the sword, looking at it thoughtfully.

A trap.

He had been foolish enough to walk into the lion's den. At least one of his questions had found its answer. The contract had been a ruse.

The blue stain on the rug flashed in Talyvien's memory with horror. Whose blood was it?

"We did well to inspect your chamber, Your Highness. It seems we intercepted the contractor," the voice of the High Priestess declared with her smooth hypocrisy.

Queen Selena appeared in the doorway. If she was surprised, she didn't show it as her sharp glare landed on Talyvien.

"He came in the company of a Child of Twilight, my queen. I'm sure you noticed. They are formidable assassins," Piore continued, her cunning words twisting Talyvien's mind. "But fortunately, we intercepted her before she could commit her misdeeds."

Talyvien was gripped by waves of terror. Whom had they intercepted? Shael?

"Selena! You know I would never do such a thing!" he cried out, desperately seeking affection and tenderness in her eyes, like they once had.

She could still stop this. Save them.

"I ask that you address me by my title."

A whip crack.

Her words snapped in his ear. Was she so petty? So callous? So oblivious even after what he had revealed to her? And to think they had risked their lives to save hers.

No. He wouldn't stoop to her level, thinking such things. If he still felt even a glimmer of nostalgia for what they had shared, that flicker died at that moment. He regarded her with profound repulsion. In response, the frost in her eyes gleamed with cruel exaltation. There was nothing left of the girl he had fallen in love with.

"He is yours, Piore. Do as you please with him," the sovereign added.

Nonchalantly, she turned her back to them and left the room, her blue and flowing dress trailing behind her steps.

A feeling of satisfaction and delight enveloped the High Priestess.

A deep disgust washed over Talyvien.

"Take him to the dungeons!" the Lamented commanded. "And find the young woman! We need her!"

Whom was she talking about? Had she recognized Lucine?

57

With two paladins always keeping him restrained at the wrists, Talyvien was forced to follow the High Priestess Piore for what seemed like an endless time. The dozen crusaders who had burst into the chamber still encircled them as they finally descended a narrow and dark staircase.

The golden halo behind the High Priestess's head dazzled the staircase with each torch's light, the train of her garment gliding over the stone steps. A deceitful angel leading him to hell.

The dungeons. Where no pleas or cries would be heard. Where no one would come to rescue him. He hoped his companions were now far away from this nightmare. He felt so powerless and useless. Disarmed, devoid of any magic.

When the stone steps finally ended, the High Priestess pushed open a massive door that creaked on its hinges. A strangely luminous chamber was revealed, causing the young man to squint.

Talyvien observed rows of cells closed with thick metal bars on one side of the room. On the other side, large openings had been carved into the cliffside. Located beneath the castle, this dungeon offered a breathtaking view of the grand canals far below. But he knew not to be mistaken; there was no escape, except for a certain death for anyone who attempted to jump.

Talyvien's heart leaped out of his chest. A woman's figure lay on the torture table in the center of the room. Blue blood flowed abundantly from her neck, streaking her body from one end to another.

Shael.

His legs wavered, and a slight jerk seized his body. The two paladins restraining him tightened their grip on his arms, forcing him to calm down.

They approached closer.

A tuft of disheveled blond hair shimmered in the brightness of the room. *It was Evelyn.*

A sigh of relief escaped Talyvien, although the sight of the sister turned his insides.

Shael was safe, somewhere.

Evelyn must have sneaked into the queen's chamber and fallen into a trap similar to his before Shael could intercept her. But upon closer examination, Talyvien noticed that the sister's eyes still possessed a certain vitality, even though they seemed unnaturally apathetic and fixed on the ceiling. Her body wasn't bound by any restraints. Why wasn't she defending herself?

"You may leave us," Piore ordered the paladins.

The High Priestess positioned herself near the torture table, Tuoryn's sword still in her hand.

After a brief bow to the Lamented, all the crusaders left the room.

Talyvien felt the pressure on his wrists behind his back lighten.

Finally alone? Piore was foolish and heedless. He needed to act quickly. He listened to the last paladin's footsteps resonating in his chest on the stone floor as the man headed toward the exit.

The door closed. Talyvien rushed toward Piore.

"Stop."

The word sliced through the ambient air and echoed in the paladin's ears. A sudden shock ran through Talyvien, whose body responded involuntarily. His legs stiffened in place. His arms fell alongside his torso.

His mind was trapped in a body that no longer belonged to him. Only his wide-open eyes devoured Piore with hatred. Paralyzed. A wave of disgust washed over him, fueling his rage.

He tried to force his limbs to obey his command, but without success. What kind of magic was this? Had King Arthios also been imprisoned in the same way for several months? Talyvien bitterly remembered the inexplicably vacant eyes of the sovereign.

The High Priestess chuckled at Talyvien's ignorance and helplessness.

"It wasn't very clever of you to reject the queen of the Kingdom of

Vamentera," she said, with a cruel little laugh. "I didn't even need to use magic on her. So lonely, so full of hope. So embittered. Look where it led you. And all for what? A Child of Twilight? It seems we can no longer rely on them to fulfill a contract."

The Lamented approached the table where Evelyn still lay, also imprisoned in a certain torpor. She slid her finger along the young woman's arm up to her neck, the priestess's eyes seemingly devouring the sister's skin through the mask.

"I must admit I've developed a certain taste for the blood of Sazaelith's chosen ones in recent months," Piore sneered. "But you must wonder why I'm doing all this, paladin? The truth is: I enjoy seeing humans suffer in proportion to what they inflict. Playing with their childish desire for conquest. What better way than to insinuate myself where it hurts? Where their hearts turn so easily. Hatred for difference, for *their* difference. What better way than to turn their love for the goddesses into fanaticism. It's been so easy."

She took hold of Evelyn's chin between her thumb and index finger. The young woman still showed no reaction.

"After all, I suppose even you had to wait until leaving the order to open your heart to difference."

At these words, Talyvien's heart twisted. Was she right? He, who had been so closed off, so sure of his principles.

With the two paladins of the crusade unconscious on the floor, Lucine and Calixte hurried to follow the path Talyvien had taken. They tried their best not to get disoriented in the maze of corridors. The young woman still supported the wounded bard by the waist to help them move as quickly as possible. They had to find Queen Selena's chamber at all costs and reunite with the paladin.

A door adorned with golden motifs embedded in the wood at the end of a corridor caught the young druidess's attention. Intrigued to discover it already ajar, Lucine gently pushed it.

Bathed in darkness, the bedroom was empty and silent. But a bad feeling tugged at the druidess. Fragments of a fierce struggle seemed inscribed in the apparent disorder and chaos of the room.

Lucine cautiously approached the large four-poster bed. Her senses were assaulted by a profound feeling of discomfort, of pure malevolence. A slight shiver ran down her back. Something was not right.

A dark figure emerged from the window opening. With formidable agility, the young druidess shielded Calixte with one arm and held her dagger ready with the other. Exasperated and out of magic, she aimed the weapon at the shadowy figure.

"Well, I see my lessons have borne fruit!"

"Shael?!" gasped Lucine.

The assassin emerged from the darkness. Everything about her body language indicated frustration. Everything on her face exhibited pain.

"What happened?" asked Lucine, putting the small dagger back in its sheath.

"I arrived too late," the assassin raged, clenching her fists. "This stupid dress hindered my movements. Too late to intercept Evelyn. And too early to save Talyvien . . ."

"What do you mean?" Lucine inquired, with concern.

"Piore took them. The contract was a trap, and Evelyn got captured while trying to honor it. When I managed to find the chamber, Talyvien had already fallen into the priestess's clutches. The paladins surrounding him were too many . . . I wanted to . . . I couldn't . . ." Shael hesitated, her lower lip trembling slightly. "I hid like a coward!"

"No. You couldn't have helped him alone, Shael," Lucine said, placing a hand on her shoulder. "You would have just been killed. You don't have to blame yourself. On the contrary, with our help, you have a chance to save him now."

The assassin's look became more serene, as she focused on Lucine. Gratitude flickered on her feline face for the words spoken. Perhaps she'd had a similar conversation with the paladin?

"Do you know where they took him?" Lucine pressed.

"Yes. To the dungeon . . . But I know where it is. The place is known to be situated beneath the castle. The cries and complaints of prisoners are regularly heard from the rocky walls above the canals."

Lucine swallowed hard. Cries and complaints?

"Then we have no time to waste!" Calixte said breathlessly.

"What happened on your side?" Shael asked when she noticed the blood on Calixte's face and the marks on Lucine's neck.

"We'll explain on the way!" the druidess declared. "But I owe you one!"

The three companions continued through the winding corridors of the grand castle. The assassin, an expert in such matters, led the way to ensure their progress was as stealthy as possible. Luckily, they didn't encounter anyone in this part of the building, as the servants and guests were still busy with their celebrations. The elegant corridors gave way to less luxurious surroundings. Tapestries and drapes disappeared, gradually replaced by bare brick walls, with torchlight replacing the massive chandeliers.

As they turned another corner, they found themselves facing an imposing metal door. Its surface seemed to have been dented and scratched many times, bearing the distress of the prisoners who had hammered on it.

"This is it," the assassin stated. "But it might still be a trap. It wouldn't be very wise for all of us to arrive through the same entrance."

"Mmhh. What's your plan?" Lucine asked.

"As I mentioned, there are large openings in the cliffs above the canals. I can sneak in and ambush Piore from behind when you enter through the door."

"Do you think you can climb such a steep cliff? It seems dangerous," Lucine worried.

"I'll need to make a few adjustments to my appearance of well-mannered girl, but I should be able to manage it. We don't really have another choice, anyway."

"It could work," Calixte growled through their teeth, blood still flowing abundantly on their face.

Shael summoned one of her daggers. She tore and shredded her dress in places to make it easier to climb and removed the lace band from her eyes.

"We'll meet at the bottom," the assassin murmured, taking Lucine's hand.

"Shael, we'll save him," the determined druidess promised.

Shael nodded, a slight smile on her lips, though the rest of her face still showed concern. Once again, she vanished through one of the modest windows in the corridor where they stood. As elusive as a mirage.

"Too bad I don't have my bow. I don't know if I'll have enough power to be useful in combat," Lucine murmured, as she watched the assassin disappear into the night.

She had already drawn so much from her magical resources. Could she ask her god for more? Would he come to their aid at the right moment? She felt the small crystal flower in her pocket once again.

The bard took both of the young woman's hands in theirs. "Perhaps you can find the answer within yourself?"

"What do you mean?"

"You've obviously inherited great power," Calixte whispered. "I've never doubted you, Lucine. I believe it's time for you to stop doubting yourself too."

With her lips trembling with emotion and her eyes shining, Lucine observed the battered face of the Alaris. They had always been there for her. From the beginning.

So, with their hands still interlaced, their comforting presence and warmth, she thought back to the exchange between Calixte and Feör. Perhaps they were all part of something bigger. Something that was simply meant to be?

Once again, in the palm of her hands, Lucine let her truth emerge. She no longer needed to think. Two branches grew from her palms. Slowly, surely, with raw clarity, one transformed into a gnarled wooden bow, the other into a formidable arrow with a razor-sharp tip.

Calixte, a saddened smile on their face, stared at Teluar's gift between their hands. A faint purple glimmer swirled in their eyes.

And they collapsed onto the young druidess.

Shael thanked her quick thinking for keeping appropriate footwear under her dress. Fine, soft leather boots, perfect for climbing and maneuvering on the rugged rocks that were exposed once the crumbled bricks of the old castle walls disappeared during her descent.

She used her daggers and planted them here and there in the rock like ice axes. A powerful wind challenged the assassin's concentration and precision; her long, untied hair flailed wildly across her face, and her light and torn clothing let the icy gust chill her limbs. Despite her determination, her body shivered from cold and exertion.

Shael had to arrive in time. She couldn't let anything happen to Talyvien. Too many promises were at stake, too many futures and tomorrows she wanted to see come true.

Hidden behind the large window of the chamber, she cursed Selena's reaction. It had taken superhuman strength not to reveal herself at that moment and wipe the queen's odious tone from her face. But for the first time in her life, the assassin had chosen not to be so impulsive. For him. So, he could have a chance to survive. As if she had felt Talyvien's hand on her wrist once more.

Finally, Shael saw the large openings that had terrified her when she was just a teenager wandering the city. The cries and pleas of the prisoners had resonated as the best warning for any reckless thief or assassin above the great watercourses that crossed Dawnelest.

But this time, as she approached, a deadly silence reigned. She couldn't tell if it was a good thing. A weight on her chest, Shael quickened her descent.

The assassin finally entered the dungeons and lightly touched the old stone slabs with assured steps. As invisible as a shadow among the darkness, Shael cautiously moved toward the only source of light in the room, drawn like a moth. A long, dilapidated candelabra with melted candle wax dripped onto the floor.

Sweat trickled from Shael's forehead.

A surreal scene broke out before her. The High Priestess, whom Shael recognized by the golden wings of her train, leaned over a body that was twitching slightly on a torture table. Piore was positioned with her back to the assassin, and odious sounds of sucking and gurgling emanated from this grotesque tableau.

Her golden mask casually laid on the ground, the long white hair that Shael had seen at her convent was untied down her back. But although this vision filled the assassin's mouth with bitterness, it was not what seemed most alarming.

Unperturbed, horrifyingly still, Talyvien watched this vile spectacle face to face with the Lamented. Devoid of any emotion, his gaze showed no signs of turmoil. Why wasn't he reacting?

With furrowed brows and a dagger in each hand, Shael cautiously advanced. But it was only when the High Priestess stood up from her victim that the assassin's rage flooded her brain.

Cobalt blood spread over the neck and chest of the body, its skin appearing pale. A pool of blue liquid grew under the table.

Evelyn.

Or what was left of her. Life had fled from her empty and stunned eyes, still fixed on the ceiling.

Finally alone with Piore, Shael lost all restraint. Her vengeful hatred and the strength of the promise she had made to Talyvien obliterated all caution and concealment.

Shael didn't have time to see the astonishment on Talyvien's almost frozen face as she rushed at Piore.

 The convulsions of Evelyn's body only ceased after several minutes of this painful nightmare. Unable to look away, Talyvien felt profound disgust.

Piore then lifted her face from her victim's jugular and exhaled in ecstasy, blue blood oozing from either side of her mouth.

Everything wavered.

If his body hadn't been held by magic, Talyvien would have staggered. There was nothing human about that face.

So, this was it. The most horrible of possible answers.

A gash from ear to ear formed an obscene smile on Piore's mouth, and her silvery serpentine tongue licked her lips with delight. The reflection of two enormous, blue-tinted fangs shimmered under the candelabra's light. Her golden and exalted eyes, not from the magic of the goddess of light, but from the cruel animality of her true nature.

A viperal.

These creatures were extremely rare and considered to be on the brink of extinction. Yet, how hadn't he thought of it? As a paladin, Talyvien knew that viperals were viciously cruel, capable of manipulating the bodies and speech of humans with their voices.

He cursed the irony of the situation. One of the greatest sacred duties of the Order of Paladins of Callystrande was to protect the population against such abominations. Yet, one of them had managed to manipulate his order, his brothers, his king. Him.

A macabre double game of slow and calculated corruption that had enslaved both the chosen of Callystrande and Sazaelith in one fell swoop.

Piore burst into loud laughter at his ignorance. With nonchalance, she rolled Evelyn's body off the torture table, and it fell heavily to the ground.

An obscure storm erupted behind the High Priestess, a tempest of pure violence. Surprised, Piore had only enough time to turn around before the assassin pounced on her.

One of Shael's daggers narrowly missed the Lamented's jugular and instead found its target just above her collarbone, causing her to scream in pain.

But in the same leap, in the same instant, Piore's body transformed.

And a creature worthy of the worst nightmares appeared. A being: part woman, part serpent.

The scaly lower half of her body coiled around the assassin, leaving Shael no chance to react. The creature's yellow eyes devoured its new prey, entwined between the circular muscles of its horrifying serpentine tail. The ultimate predator.

Caught in this deadly and constricting trap, Shael had a small spasm that filled Talyvien with terror. Her daggers clanged on the ground before disappearing, her arms enveloped and restrained by the creature's coils. Only her face remained exposed between the fatal rings, and she snarled with clenched teeth.

"Ah! Well tried, little mouse!" the creature exclaimed with a sibilant voice. "Thank you for joining my long collection of appetizers. *Stay still now.*"

Shael's body stopped struggling. A desperate apathy seeped into her eyes, which focused on the paladin. A last mute speech of all the love and gratitude she felt for him. Farewells she would never be able to utter. A tear rolled down her cheek.

No. He would find a solution . . . to protect her. He couldn't bear to lose her like this. Talyvien's mind pushed against the boundaries of his own body with all his strength.

But it remained desperately still.

Piore relaxed her cruel rings and placed Shael's lifeless body back on the torture table. Her beautiful starry dress became tinged with the cobalt of her murdered sister assassin, and her feathered garment soaked up the coveted cursed liquid.

Piore's fingers slid again on her victim's skin, and with alarming delicacy, she wrapped her long nails around Shael's throat, all while under Talyvien's hateful stare. A jubilant sadism.

Piore leaned the upper part of her womanly body toward the assassin.

A silent fury seized Talyvien; a cry of rage screamed inside his mind. His jaw clenched, the knuckles of his fingers whitened as they desperately burrowed to his palms, his arms still frustratingly motionless.

The serpentine tongue of Piore licked Shael's neck with delight, visibly relishing the paladin's reaction. The Lamented offered an obscene and bestial smile.

"Mmhh. That would be too . . . easy. Too predictable," Piore purred, a perverse spark in her voice. "What do you say, paladin? *Come here . . .*"

Talyvien's body moved out of his control and stood on the other side of the torture table.

"*Stab her with your sword*," she added, handing him Tuoryn's sword.

What?! No.

Though he resisted with all his might, his arms lifted and clasped the hilt of the sword, the blade dangerously hovering above Shael.

Piore's fingers slithered over the assassin's body, and her hand stopped above her abdomen.

"*Mmhh . . . in the belly, I think*," she amused herself.

A fatal blow. Talyvien knew it.

He would resist. Always. He had to believe it. His hands began to violently tremble, the sharp metal of the sword still swinging above the assassin. He prayed to Callystrande. Just this once, not to be as sensitive to magic. He had to buy some time.

A storm raged in his mind. He felt his body seized by intense spasms. The viperal's magic fiercely clashed against his soul, against the feelings he held for Shael. Slightly opening his eyes, he saw the blade of his sword gleam with its gentle warmth. Tuoryn. He was there to help him, responding to his call.

Piore burst into a cruel laugh. "The sword of good old Tuoryn! He would have been proud of you, for resisting like that. He tried to resist me too," she said, clicking her tongue against her palate, "but you know, even he, in the end . . . didn't survive me."

A guttural cry escaped Talyvien's body. His mentor. She had killed him. He who had been like a father to him. Killed by a vulgar viperal. The only resistance against her path of domination. And they were about to meet the same fate.

The spasms in his body intensified. He would resist this magic. No matter what.

Too many lives depended on it.

His furious gaze challenged Piore's. Face to face. His quivering hands, the blade of his sword caught between his determination and the creature's perversion.

"Oh, well. Since I have to do everything myself here," she continued. The creature grew impatient. She leaned once again toward the assassin's ear. Talyvien felt panic and terror.

"*Give me one of your daggers,*" she languorously whispered to Shael.

With horror, Talyvien saw the dagger materialize above the assassin's forearm and slide gently into her palm. Her sapphire eyes met him once again. "*I'm sorry,*" was written in them.

Piore's fingers brushed the weapon in the assassin's palm and closed around the hilt.

No. Talyvien threw himself against the barrier that imprisoned his mind.

Piore's serpentine tongue passed over her lips, and an obscene smile formed on her malevolent face.

"NO!" he screamed inside. Only a muffled growl escaped his throat. Talyvien struggled mentally, his body still prisoner of this vile magic.

Piore raised the blade above Shael's abdomen.

58

The bow summoned by Teluar's magic drawn between her hands, Lucine rushed down the stairs leading to the dungeons. She hoped to arrive in time and wished that the assassin had shown patience and good sense. But despite the restraint Shael had demonstrated in the queen's chamber, Lucine knew the impulsive nature of the young woman. She had to act quickly.

The breath of the young druidess faded with each step she took. Her anxiety caused an incessant rhythm to beat in her veins. She had been forced to leave Calixte's motionless body in a corner of the corridor, trying to conceal them as best as possible. The bard, too weak and likely having lost too much blood, had passed out from exhaustion.

An unthinkable situation. An impossible choice that Lucine had to make, leaving Calixte behind. But the urgency of the events had left little room for consideration of other possibilities.

Tyrannical in length and roughness, the stone staircase seemed to extend endlessly. Lucine's terror increased her heart rate. A relentless pounding in her ears. A punishment that seemed never-ending.

Finally, the last step became visible, and the young druidess burst into the dungeons. Her bow ready to shoot, Lucine broke open the door with force, causing it to slam violently.

Her throat tightened at the gruesome scene before her.

A massive serpentine creature threatened to impale Shael with one of her own daggers. Talyvien, strangely frozen, watched helplessly, his sword in hand.

Without hesitation and without seeking to understand everything, Lucine aimed at the creature and released her prodigious arrow.

The projectile soared magnificently through the air. A sparkling fraction that exploded in Lucine's heart. She followed its trajectory eagerly, holding her breath.

The arrow missed its target by a few inches.

It shattered with an unfair crack against the brick wall behind the creature's head. Thousands of icy needles pierced Lucine from all sides, her dismay puncturing her thoughts.

She had failed. How could she have missed such a shot?

The creature, amazed by its luck, stared back at the druidess. Eyes that Lucine immediately recognized, as they transcended her memories.

Piore.

With a defiant air, the monstrous being plunged the dagger into Shael's stomach.

The assassin's body jerked violently upon impact. Her astounded eyes locked with Talyvien's in terror, their sapphire luminescence desperately searching for him.

The creature reveled in the sight of the influx of blue blood pouring under its fingers.

The paladin's body shivered violently in distress, tears streaming down his cheeks uncontrollably.

Lucine screamed at the top of her lungs, strongly enough that the walls could have trembled. Her pain turned into vengeful rage. Tears welling up in the corners of her eyes, she conjured a second arrow in her hands and drew her bow.

She would not miss this time.

"I thought you had things under control, Naja,"

A deep voice. Infallible.

Lucine's body was struck. Before she could release the arrow, ribbons of vermillion magic wrapped around her, lifting her off the ground. The light wood of her unused bow and arrow tinkled against the stone slabs.

Through one of the large openings, the nightmare of the young druidess invaded the room. The flying creature that had abducted her brother. The figure with green, biting eyes.

Valnard. In all his sepulchral splendor.

The Alaris, unperturbed, dismounted and took a few steps with hands joined. His imposing figure was clad in exquisitely woven tunic of leaves. His audacious gait, his catastrophically perfect face. An ancient beauty. Indecent for such a being.

"I did tell you to be careful with your frivolous games, Naja," Valnard said decisively. "That was a close one."

"Yes, Master," she simpered, dipping one of her fingers into the cobalt blood on Shael's still convulsing abdomen.

Then, Piore brought her hand to her mouth with delight, while giving Valnard a mischievous side glance.

"Well, it seems that all your little machinations still worked after all," he uttered, turning to Lucine.

What was he doing here? Were Piore and Valnard allies in their insane plan to destroy humanity? She recalled with horror Talyvien's and Shael's revelations. The Alaris was responsible for creating those degenerate monsters.

The situation was desperate. Talyvien's body was overcome with despondency, his features torn and focused on the assassin. Life was slipping away from Shael, her pallid skin bearing the weight of her distress.

Lucine's stomach rose in her throat.

"Where is Solehan!" the young druidess shouted, still imprisoned by the Ignescent.

"But precisely, my dear chosen one. I have come to take you to him! Together, we can restore glory to Nature and awaken Teluar!"

"You're completely mad, Valnard. I will never join you!" the young woman spat. "Where is Solehan?!"

"He's gravely injured, Lucine. And I believe you possess something that can save him. In fact, you're the only one that can truly do it. Callystrande refused to help him."

The heart of Teluar. Was that why Valnard's lychena had tried to take it from her? Or was all this just fabrication and pretext?

"What have you done to him?" Lucine growled.

"I merely showed him the truth. The ignominy of humans. Their harmful impact on the world. As I will show you too. Although I believe you've already had a good glimpse," Valnard said, glancing at Piore. "It wasn't really challenging for a viperal like her to darken the hearts of men and make them kill each other. Humans are already so . . . *vile*. Ready at the slightest excuse to satisfy their greed and perversions."

"It wasn't humans who put me on the pyre," Lucine retorted.

"And yet, I only needed to use my powers on Arthios and Cassandra," Piore chuckled. "The others followed without hesitation . . ."

"Believe it or not, the fact that you fell into Naja's clutches was not my doing," Valnard explained with irritating calmness. "Probably just an ironic twist of events, as your fate mattered little to me, to be honest. But everything changed with the emergence of your powers."

"I will never follow you, Valnard! I will save Solehan from your grasp! I will bring him back to reason!"

"Oh, do you think he has gone mad?" Valnard scoffed. "No. Solehan has simply come to understand his role. His power. His destiny. What he is capable of . . . And how *unique* he is."

Although the situation was already dramatic enough, Lucine noticed something even more sinister in Valnard's previously sly eyes. A kind of attachment, a tenderness, when he spoke her brother's name.

Horror filled the young woman's mind.

"I would have preferred all this to be voluntary, Lucine. Really," Valnard continued calmly. "But I promised your brother I would find you and bring you back. If necessary, force would have to do. Perhaps, with time, you'll understand?" He gestured toward Piore. "Naja, please."

"With pleasure, Master," the creature murmured, as she slowly circled the torture table, sliding her fingers on the wood and heading toward Lucine.

The young druidess struggled fiercely and groaned with frustration at being trapped by the Ignescent.

"*Follow Valnard, Lucine . . .*"

The words resonated in her head. The red magic filaments dissipated into luminous dust around her. The physical prison of Valnard's magic was replaced by the psychic grip of Piore.

Lucine's body moved toward the Alaris, who extended his hand. An irresistible command. Just like the first time she had heard that malevolent voice, sitting on the bench in the small caravan. She tried to resist, to scream her disapproval and hatred. But her mouth remained mute, and her feet continued to walk toward Valnard. Inexorably.

In a final desperate effort, she looked at her two friends. How could she abandon them to such a sad fate? Condemned by so much cruelty to certain agony?

No. For everything they had already gone through to get here. For all the journey she had already undertaken. For all she had endured.

She would decide when and how her story would end.

Lucine silently defied Piore. Her reptilian eyes and their pupils retracting in delight at the situation, her inhuman mouth twisting into the most sinister smile, her forked tongue passing over her lips. And a memory struck the young druidess.

Had Teluar guided her from the beginning, when she was just that naive child of the world around her? Were the hallucinations she had at the inn in Luminaur connected to the Dream of her god? Was that why she had this strange affinity with animals?

Then a new clarity revealed itself to Lucine. And she knew.

Teluar's magic took hold of her limbs, her mind, and her heart, defying the psychic bonds of her prison. Like a code she could now decipher, Lucine scrutinized the animality contained within Piore. Like a lock of which she now held the key.

With the resurgent memory of the gaping maw of the enormous serpent paralyzed in her mind, Lucine raised her arm.

And she commanded the viperal to attack Valnard.

Two conflicting control magics. The revenge of a god against the perversion of an Alaris.

The initially vicious look on Piore's horrifying face suddenly became stunned. Bewildered, her eyes dissected the druidess. Her body trembled. But despite the evident internal struggle of the creature, Teluar's magic swept everything in its path. The determination of the young woman as well.

Against her will, Piore lunged at the Alaris. Her enormous serpentine body gained momentum and rushed toward Valnard, who cried out in a mixture of surprise and rage. Not understanding what was happening and struck by events, the immortal counterattacked.

An enormous vine of Ignescent shot out of Valnard's hand. It pierced the viperal from side to side and emerged from the creature's back, causing her to stiffen before reaching her target. Impaled like this, Piore let out a raspy and aghast sigh. Her eyes still fixed on Lucine, she was seized by violent spasms, her viper tail lashing against the stone slabs. After a few horrible seconds, her body collapsed in a final gasp.

Piore was no more.

The Alaris, panting, with his back arched, witnessed the final breath of his creation before staring at the young druidess with a blank look on his face.

"Do you have control over animals?" he blurted out breathlessly.

Lucine's fists clenched with anger as she stared back with an air of provocation at Valnard with her golden and silver eyes. Knowing that the gods were on her side, she took a step toward him with renewed confidence.

A deafening uproar reverberated throughout the castle. Earsplitting. Moaning. Finally, a burst of liberated spirits, released from the torment inflicted by the High Priestess.

Freed from the creature's control, Talyvien joined in the clamor, threw his sword to the ground and rushed to Shael's body. He placed both hands on the wound, trying to stop the bleeding.

"Stay with me, Shael!" he cried, tears streaming down his cheeks.

The assassin's eyes remained fixed on him, their purple glow almost faded. Lucine was stung in the heart at that sight.

Breathless and disheveled, Valnard turned his head as the sound of multiple footsteps echoed on the stairs leading to the dungeons. The paladins were rushing down the steps and coming toward them.

"Lucine, we don't have much time left," Valnard gasped. "If you don't want to follow me, fine. But I need to save your brother. Give me the heart!"

"And what guarantees me that you won't use it for something else? That Solehan is really injured?" she growled.

"You are his twin sister, Lucine. You can feel that I'm not lying about his condition. He was gravely wounded on the flank. As for using the heart . . . I just can't lose him . . ."

And that incredible emotion resurfaced in Valnard's voice, in his features now desperate. What did the Alaris truly feel for Solehan? Repugnance swelled in Lucine's throat. She also recalled the sharp pain she had felt in her flank a few days before. Was that the reason?

"No! Lucine! I beg you . . . You can save Shael with it," Talyvien intervened with a broken voice. "No paladin will ever agree to heal an assassin of Sazaelith. And it will also amplify your brother's powers! We can't afford it!"

All of Lucine's rational thoughts crumbled. She looked at the paladin in a daze. Another impossible choice. The cruelest of all: Solehan's life against Shael's. Two men staring at her with intense attention tinged with despair.

How could she decide on this? Was this what 'using her powers wisely' as Teluar had told her meant? What a vile joke.

The footsteps of the paladins became faster, their weight more pronounced on the stone stairs. A sadistic countdown.

Lucine took the small flower out of her pocket with trembling hands, a notable consternation on her face. A cruel dilemma with no real solution. Someone would die tonight, and she couldn't prevent it.

She looked up toward the torture table. Toward Talyvien's more ravaged face than ever, swaying in the candlelight, hands still pressed against Shael's abdomen, trying to stop the bleeding. He sought to stem her fate with tragic disillusionment. How could she decide on this?

The texture of the flower petals burned her fingers. The weight of this impossible answer pounded in her heart. But she couldn't resist her truth.

"I'm sorry, Taly . . ." Lucine whispered.

And without averting her gaze from her friend, who looked back at her with devastation, she extended a shaky arm to offer the flower to Valnard. Perhaps it was an answer to a question that had no answer. An instinct she couldn't fight. For the promise she had made to him. Lucine couldn't imagine a life without her twin brother.

She had to trust the intense emotion she had glimpsed in Valnard's face. The connection they seemed to have, even if it cost her to admit it. Maybe it was the only chance she had to see her brother alive again.

"I will come back with him, Lucine," Valnard said, taking the flower. "If I can't convince you, he will."

"Don't make me regret my choice, Valnard," the young woman cut in. "You have something to do, it seems."

With a slight nod of his head, Valnard mounted his steed and disappeared through one of the openings in the wall, the powerful wings flapping. The nightmarish imprint left by Valnard dissipated like a pale figure lost in thick fog, a distant bray echoing as the only trace.

An eternity passed in the dreadful room where Lucine, Talyvien, and Shael remained. Now alone, confronting the overwhelming weight of the consequences of this heinous evening.

Navigating between the horrifying bodies of Piore and Evelyn still lying on the ground, Lucine approached her friends. Like a burning ember, guilt devoured her from within. How could she have made such a choice?

Shael's eyes, still desperately fixed on Talyvien's face, seemed to have lost their usual brightness. A last spark escaping into the shadows. A final sigh marked the end of her existence.

The soul of the assassin slid toward her goddess.

Talyvien let out a scream that tore at Lucine's chest. The young druidess fell to her knees. Sobs erupted from her chest. Her body shook.

With his face ravaged by pain, the paladin cradled Shael's upper body in his arms. He held the assassin close, placing one hand behind her head, resting it in the hollow of his shoulder. His tunic and skin got stained with that intolerable blue. Talyvien kissed Shael's cheek gently and rocked her softly in his embrace.

"I'm sorry, Taly," Lucine repeated, her lower lip trembling. "I'm so sorry . . ."

What had she done? How could the situation be so cruel to the paladin? To the assassin? Why had the gods abandoned them after all they had been through?

Led by King Arthios, about ten paladins of Callystrande entered the dungeons. An army finally freed from the viperal's control, eager to understand the outcome of this absurd confrontation. Swords in hand, they all stopped in shock at the carnage in the room.

Talyvien, still holding Shael close to him, broke into even more pronounced sobs, completely ignoring the stunned murmurs rising around him.

And finally, after so much suffering and misery, after so many trials, a goddess answered his calamity.

Golden tears streamed down Talyvien's cheeks.

 The dark and silky wings enveloped her completely. Floating in the darkness of her beloved goddess, Shael let herself be carried away by the caress of feathers on her skin. Sazaelith welcomed her with open arms and embraced her with all her strength, like the mother she had always been. A sense of fulfillment washed over her soul. She got lost among the stars of the night.

To her great surprise, dawn broke on the horizon. The long golden hair of the opposing goddess stretched across the canvas of changing colors. Callystrande approached with light steps, rivers of gold and light flowing around her graceful body. The contours of her shimmering skin intermingled with Sazaelith's darkness; their bodies wrapped in an infinite and ephemeral whirlwind. The warmth and the scent of his skin against Shael's were sublime and awakened the coldness of their embrace. An embrace she wanted to be eternal.

She gently lifted her hand to caress his shoulder, feeling the soft breath of his sobs against her cheek. A radiant light emanated from his skin. She pressed her body against his, her heart craving his warmth.

"Talyvien?"

A nearly inaudible murmur in his ear.

Hazel eyes looked at her with awe, a fine golden ring circling the pupils, bathed in long golden tears that she wiped away with her fingers.

This face. She could die for this face. She could also live for it.

"Sha—Shael?" he hesitated, his deep and intoxicating voice resonating within the assassin's chest.

Gradually regaining her senses, she observed the familiarity of Talyvien's features beside her, the contours of his silhouette flooded with the light of his goddess.

Large, radiant wings spread above them, emerging from his back.

"Your powers . . ." she marveled.

More tears of gold rolled down Talyvien's cheeks, an incredulous smile on his lips. He caressed the assassin's face, letting Callystrande's magic mark the passage of his fingers with their warmth.

Shael paid no attention to the surrounding commotion. She brought her lips closer to his, and they finally found each other.

The gold of Callystrande and the blue of Sazaelith blended on their faces, their hands, and their bodies. They kissed, lost in the miracle of the moment, their embrace a painting of divine shades. Eager to anchor the reality of this moment, Shael ran her hand through Talyvien's hair, gripping it lightly. He pressed his mouth more ardently against hers. She melted into the power of his arms and the protection they offered. The paladin's hands glided over her body, the light magic leaving its radiant mark on her skin.

Nothing else mattered but this moment. Fragile and infinite.

"Our bodies entwine in this cosmic affair,
Your skin's golden hue, my soul's bluish reign,
In this fleeting passion, a dance without compare,
As my found eyes blend with your tears, untamed."

OPPOSITE UTOPIAS

<h1 style="text-align:center">59</h1>

Days must have probably passed when the Alaris's voice once again pulled Solehan out of his torpor.

"Solehan, wake up!"

The druid opened his eyes laboriously. Leaning over him, Valnard scrutinized him with an intensity that exuded impatience. "Come with me. You'll have to make an effort," he added.

The Alaris's arms wrapped firmly around Solehan's chest, and he felt himself being lifted. Despite wincing in pain, he followed Valnard's embrace and managed to stand, the Alaris supporting him at the waist. Solehan placed his arm on Valnard's shoulder, and together, they moved toward the elaphora that was waiting patiently on the balcony of the grand bedroom.

The young druid stumbled several times, his body weaker than ever. Was Valnard taking him to some place to die? Perhaps a place where his soul could flourish alongside Teluar?

Solehan struggled to mount the elaphora, and Valnard used the Ignescent to help stabilize the young man as he climbed onto the creature behind him. Once settled, they took off swiftly. The wind slapped Solehan's face as he observed, with half-closed eyes, the balcony becoming tiny behind them.

"There's a temple of Teluar beneath the castle," the Alaris whispered in Solehan's ear. Valnard's words got accompanied by his hand gently resting on the young man's belly to keep him steady in the saddle.

After a few minutes of flight, the creature landed on a steep stone cliff, and Solehan could see the hidden entrance to the temple, with elegant inscriptions engraved around the slightly ajar door. When he looked up, he realized they were situated below the immense walls of the castle of Argentvale, where natural rock began to intersect with bricks on the other side of the city.

With the Alaris still assisting him to stand, they entered the dark stone entrance. Solehan's mind stretched slowly, the fever growing more persistent. He observed their shadows, cast by a faint greenish glow, dancing on the damp walls of the corridor as they descended the roughly hewn stone stairs.

They finally reached the heart of the temple, where a large circular pool of clear water occupied most of the space. On the other side, facing the entrance, a statue of Teluar stood proudly, with long hair and deer antlers on either side of its forehead.

So, this was where he was going to die. Exhausted and accepting his fate, Solehan collapsed against the Alaris. He was tired of struggling with his destiny. Maybe it was the right moment after all?

But the cold and austere touch of the stone floor defied the young man's expectations. When he managed to open his eyes again, he felt like he was floating. The fresh smell of the undergrowth filled the air. A curious gentleness. He found himself cradled in Valnard's arms, being lifted. Realizing that he was probably dreaming, the druid admired the Alaris one last time. Would he finally have the audacity to confess what was hidden within him before departing?

Valnard gently placed the young man on the stone steps that were submerged beneath the shimmering liquid. The cold rock of the basin's edge chilled Solehan's shoulders as he leaned his head back. Exhausted from their journey, and with his half-immersed, trembling bare chest rising and falling with his labored breaths, the young druid was ready.

Solehan gazed languidly at the magnificent engravings on the walls and ceiling. A starry dome had been sculpted in the rock above the water, and the stars seemed to dance in the celestial stone vault, celebrating the end of his existence with their vigilance.

A perfect place to depart. Reflecting the power of Teluar and his magic.

Valnard sighed, removed the top of his tunic, and straddled over the young druid, partially submerging himself in the water. With the Alaris positioned against him like this, Solehan thought that his desirous hallucinations had now clearly overtaken reality.

The warmth of the water enveloped him. His senses dulled gently. Thousands of tiny tingles invaded his vision, his skin, the tangibility of his world. With no real need left, it was the moment for Solehan's shame to take flight. He watched the water flowing over Valnard's chest with delight as the Alaris leaned closer to him.

The young man bit his lower lip, trying to silence the words that crowded his throat. The forbidden desires that consumed him to feel Valnard's body against his. But perhaps his guilt no longer mattered if he was already dreaming. If he was departing.

So, despite himself, Solehan could not suppress a final impulse.

"Valnard, before I die, I need to tell you something," he murmured with difficulty.

The Alaris looked at him with a surprised look.

"You won't—" Valnard hurried to say, placing a hand on the young man's cheek.

"Please, let me continue," he interrupted. "I don't have much time."

Valnard opened his mouth to reply, but no words came out. His eyes became evasive, almost guilty. Yet resigned. He nodded slightly. Solehan then exhaled a shaky sigh. He had no choice now.

"Don't—Don't say anything when I'm done," Solehan whispered. "I won't have the strength to hear the truth. I just want to depart, thinking it's possible, even if it's pitiful."

With a surprised and curious gleam in his eyes, Valnard nodded again and leaned closer. The young man's heart skipped a beat when their chests brushed against each other. With the immortal so close, he seemed determined to listen attentively.

His face now burning, Solehan gulped down his embarrassment. Because he didn't want to be distracted by Valnard's likely disgust, he closed his eyes to focus.

"I hesitated for a long time before telling you this . . . and I know I shouldn't, but . . . I have no choice." Solehan swallowed again, his eyes still shut. He took a deep breath. "Valnard, I—I don't know why, but . . . I can't help but feel suffocated when you're not around, as if a vital piece is missing from my life. No . . . had always been missing from my life before you came along . . . To imagine that we could have been more than this. That a future would have been possible for us. I'm sorry . . ."

Tears welled up from Solehan's closed eyelids. His sobs made his chest bounce against Valnard's. A dam had broken. His words flowed out despite himself.

"I can't help but *love* you," he blurted out between sobs.

"Solehan . . ."

"No, wait," the young druid interrupted, his eyes still shut. "I want you to know that I really tried not to feel this way . . . You have to believe me. But I ruined everything. I—I know it's not what nature desires, but—"

Valnard's lips fell upon his. They carried away the rest of Solehan's words. A fervent kiss, despite its gentleness. Terribly certain of not letting a single word of pain or guilt escape. A furious gesture, full of certainty and deliverance.

Solehan let his breath, all his emotions, the only world he knew, melt away on his lips.

The young druid opened his teary and amazed eyes when Valnard's mouth left his. His body shuddered. All of this was just a dream. Or perhaps death was finally carrying him away in the cruelest and most wonderful way. There was no other explanation.

"I never needed words to give you my answer," Valnard whispered, inches away from his face.

As if seeing the most beautiful thing of his life, Valnard wiped away the tears rolling down Solehan's cheeks with his hand. Dazed, his chest still heaving with emotion, the druid looked back at the immortal. He didn't dare speak or touch Valnard, afraid that this wondrous mirage would disappear, his body stiffened with disbelief and guilty desire, his hands clinging to the submerged stone steps.

"I don't know why you think that Solehan. Because you're perfect," Valnard murmured, running his hand through the young man's brown hair. "Just the way you are. *Exactly* as you are."

Valnard's irises shimmered with pure truth. A breathtaking truth. Was this possible?

Dumbfounded, Solehan realized how much he needed this moment. This incredible confession. Thus, amazed and with his eyes still fixed on Valnard's face, he allowed his heart to open slowly, petal by petal. And finally appreciated that someone wanted to pluck it. Finally free from the burden that had been so familiar. From the hiding place he had built.

Valnard's hand descended again to cradle the back of the young man's head. A caress on his nape. Then, with closed eyes, the Alaris pressed his forehead against Solehan's and took a long breath. As if he, too, needed to make this moment real. To feel their skin against each other as evidence of their shared feelings.

Solehan let out a choked sob of joy.

"I'd like to obliterate a second time anyone who made you believe otherwise," Valnard declared against him.

Tears rolled down Solehan's cheeks once more. His lips shivered. With his trembling hand, he managed to grasp Valnard's face in return, pressing their foreheads together even more. A final pact of love, a secret flown away.

With his dream thus fulfilled, he would now depart in peace. His heart free but his body frustrated for not having had the time to fully live their passion. He would have to be content with that.

After a few seconds spent against each other, the Alaris pulled away from their embrace.

"But I also want to believe that a future is possible for us. Your time has not come yet."

How could all this be possible? Still overwhelmed by fever and emotion, Solehan watched as Valnard took a small iridescent flower from one of his pockets.

"And it seems it's my turn to offer you one," added Valnard with a slight worried grin. "But this one is real, Solehan. A heart of Teluar."

What was he doing? Solehan strained to focus on the Alaris's face, who admired the radiant lotus in the palm of his hands. Valnard gently placed the flower on the surface of the water, above the submerged belly of the young man.

A miracle occurred.

The petals gradually detached from the heart of the flower and lazily sparkled in the liquid, tinted with a myriad of swirling magic flakes. With a disconcerting harmony, the dissolution of this wondrous flower also brought about the dissolution of Solehan's pain and weakness. The gaping wound in his chest slowly closed, leaving behind only smooth and unblemished skin. A leap through time carried away his fever and his doom.

Solehan's body and mind regained vigor and strength. His perception gradually sharpened, and he touched his flank in amazement. He felt strangely different, his magic more vibrant in his veins—a surging and unrestrained current. Finally freed from all possible feverish constraints, he fully realized the improbable situation he was in.

Valnard was indeed sitting on top of him, legs apart. The green of his eyes accentuated by the verdant reflection of the water, his tender gaze focused on the magic gleams contained in the liquid between his fingers.

With his newfound vitality, Solehan brought a trembling hand to his lips, tasting the memory of the Alaris's mouth on his own. The flavor of his improbable confession.

"Is it with a flower like this that Teluar allowed you to have Sylveah?" he hesitated. "Is that why you had it tattooed on your back?"

"Yes," Valnard admitted with a half-word. The Alaris's attention shifted to the young man's hand still on his lips.

"Why—Why didn't you use it again to resurrect her?"

"Because when you will awaken Teluar, the god will be able to give her back to me anyway," Valnard whispered. "But mostly . . . because I couldn't bear to lose you. I, too, can no longer imagine a life without you . . ."

Solehan closed the distance between them and kissed Valnard with passion. His frustration broke in an instant, the temptation he had withheld for weeks overwhelming. This mouth, this forbidden fruit he had longed to taste, touch, and feel come alive against his own.

An obsession.

Surprised, the Alaris placed a hand on his chest reflexively, while the young druid gripped the back of Valnard's head, his long silken hair slipping through his fingers.

Once the initial surprise passed, a new fervor seized the Alaris as their bodies touched. His mouth pressed more boldly against Solehan's, his lips now greedy for his kisses. Valnard's hand slid over the young man's waist as he gently pushed him back against the steps. The Alaris's weight settled on him, and his hips, full of promises, pressed with desire against Solehan under the water. A jolt ran along the young druid's spine.

Fueled by passionate curiosity, the young man arched against the Alaris in return. Their mouths still locked; his hands explored Valnard's back as he had desired so many times before. His fingers shaped the firmness of the muscles on his shoulders. He slid them down along his spine to his lower back, marveling at the wonder that unfurled beneath his touch. To feel the water droplets running down on his soft and perfect skin.

But the young man, enthralled and eager, wanted even more. With audacity, Solehan flicked his tongue against Valnard's as the lascivious undulation of his hips revealed their shared excitement. The Alaris let out a slight impatient moan.

They kissed impetuously for a long time, their long deprivation dissipating on their lips and in their caresses amid the starlit water. Their bodies intertwined with each other. Their questioning dissolved into an evident and joint flame.

Still pressed against him, the Alaris finally detached his mouth from Solehan's. His eyes were filled with a sparkling emotion. A question with an answer of crucial significance.

"Do you want . . . ," Valnard gasped between two ragged breaths as the young druid kissed the skin on his neck at the base of his hair.

"I want you," Solehan murmured in his ear. "I wanted you for so long . . ."

Their mouths found each other again. Their bodies, their hands resumed the rhythm of their frenzied exploration. Soon, the rest of their clothes were discarded outside the basin, damp and lonely on the stone floor.

With no more barriers between them, neither physical nor moral, they embraced each other, finally accepting their consuming attraction. A fantastic dream, caressed by the warmth of the liquid.

But a strange effervescence spread through Solehan. Under the exquisite touch of their bodies and mouths, an exhilarating energy seemed to fuse beneath his skin. It pulsed with the rhythm of blood in his veins and slowly reached his head.

An explosion occurred in his mind.

A multitude of sparkling particles fragmented within him. Their corporeal forms buckled against each other under the power of the blast. Their souls merged and surged all around them, creating waves in the shimmering water of the temple.

They became one with the environment, their beings consumed by electric discharges. Their minds escaped in ecstatic pulsations and seeped through the stone cracks of the temple, through the earth, roots, vegetation, animals, up to the tips of the branches of the trees rustling in the breeze around the castle of Argentvale, where the leaves eventually crackled as the magic dissipated.

Slowly, the energy returned to his head, and Solehan's thoughts realigned. The cold touch of the stone under his arms and shoulders froze him once more. Breathless, he raised his head with difficulty. Valnard was lying on top of him, panting, his face buried in the hollow of his neck. The Alaris's arms in his back held him against him as if he feared he would disappear forever.

The young druid tenderly passed his hand over the immortal's shoulder.

"What just happened?" Solehan asked, his voice faltering.

"A gift from the great city of Alar," Valnard replied breathlessly, a small laugh escaping from his throat.

An unprecedented sensation. An exultation he could never live without anymore. Still breathless and with a cloudy mind, Solehan admired Valnard in his perfection as he slightly straightened up above him. The young man delicately tucked a strand of hair behind his pointed ear. Was it possible to die from pleasure?

In some places, dark and evanescent bark could be seen on the Alaris's skin, remnants of the release their bodies had just experienced together. Solehan noticed that his own skin had been similarly affected: a few pale and fleeting scales dotted his tanned arms and shoulders. One the primordial contrast of the other. The magic contained in their bodies communed together and glorified in a fabulous prayer to nature.

Like a carnal litany that Valnard was eager to recite in honor of the young man's body, he kissed the tattoos on Solehan's chest, which rose and fell with his difficult breathing. The young druid observed the contained shame in the inked symbols dying with a majestic irony on Valnard's lips.

"Who gave you permission to be so magnificent?" the immortal murmured against his skin.

A fleeting grin appeared on Solehan's face. However, his excitement quickly overwhelmed him again as the Alaris traced kisses down his belly.

"We've taken care of the mind, now let's tend to the body a bit," Valnard teased.

Solehan only had time to catch a glimpse of the Alaris's two eyes filled with pure desire before they disappeared underwater.

They spent hours entwined and discovering each other, enchanted by a reality they never thought possible. They continued their wild escapade against the damp walls of the temple, their hands, mouths, and bodies thrilled to finally join together. Although their progress was interrupted several times, frustrated by being momentarily apart, they completed their journey under the sheets of the grand royal bed in the castle of Argentvale. A cage around his soul finally set free, the young druid couldn't stop wanting to know everything about the Alaris, from the smallest details of his body to the sounds that escaped his throat.

Exhausted, Valnard rolled to the side of the large bed. "Seems like I no longer have the stamina of your youth! You've worn me out!" he said, placing a hand on his forehead to brush aside a few locks of hair as he slumped onto the pillow.

Solehan chuckled and leaned over him, placing a light kiss on his chest.

"I must admit, I didn't anticipate this," Valnard added, tenderly stroking Solehan's cheek.

"I must admit, neither did I," the young man retorted, a teasing spark in his eyes.

Solehan ran his fingers through Valnard's hair. He positioned his body on top of his and melded the warmth of their two hearts. He had never felt anything like it. The perfection of the Alaris enveloped him completely, his green eyes reflecting something he had always desired but never thought possible. From his shame and guilt of being born different had grown the most beautiful of emotions.

"When . . . did you know?" he whispered to Valnard.

"The day you gave me the flower," he replied, understanding the yearning in Solehan's heart.

"Oh."

With the Alaris's hand gently resting on his cheek, which he delicately held, Solehan looked at Valnard's dark fingers for a moment before kissing them.

"I never asked you, but why do you seem to be marked by nature? Your magic seems to be connected to Teluar in some way. The vines of Ignescent, the bark on your skin . . ."

"Because I spent several centuries in his Dream, and it had an impact on my body and my powers. I was with Sylveah's mother, Feör'ael, the queen of the forest spirits."

Centuries? How could he compete with that? Solehan swallowed hard and scrutinized Valnard's hand interlaced with his own cautiously. A feeling of bitterness crossed the young druid that he couldn't hide in his eyes.

"What's wrong?" Valnard asked, looking worried as he straightened up. "You know I no longer feel anything for her, right?"

"No, it's just . . . you're an Alaris."

"And?"

"Even with powers, I am . . . just a human . . . One day, I will age. But you will remain . . ." *Beautiful. Grandiose. Divine. You,* he thought.

"Hey! Come here."

The Alaris wrapped his arms around Solehan, who rested his head against his chest. Valnard gently stroked his hair.

"Maybe we could ask Teluar to intervene on that too," Valnard added. "When he can admire his creation without humans, when you and your sister can finally awaken him."

"Do you think she'll agree to join our cause?"

"I think she still cares a lot about you, Solehan. She's the one who gave me the heart of Teluar."

"What! You saw her?" he said, slightly pulling away from Valnard's embrace.

"Yes, I did. But she refused to come with me. Maybe you could convince her? She's in Dawnelest."

"Do you know how to find her?"

"No . . . The way I had . . . is no longer valid."

The young druid expressed his displeasure by sighing through his nose. His fist tightened on Valnard's chest.

"Then I'll make sure she comes to me," Solehan decided. "And besides, it seems like we have some unfinished business with the kingdom of Vamentera. I think it's time to send them a clear message."

"Look at you!" Valnard teased, sitting up as well and kissing the young man's jaw. "The champion of Teluar in all his splendor!"

"But I think that can wait until tomorrow," Solehan purred, a mischievous smirk on his face. "Which means we still have a few more hours."

A small laugh escaped from Valnard's lips. "You're insatiable!"

Solehan sat on top of Valnard's body and guided the Alaris's arms above his head. Vines wrapped around the immortal's wrists, and he chuckled slightly in surprise.

"It seems I'm at your mercy, champion of Teluar. Are you trying to get revenge?" Valnard murmured, a broad smile on his face, his eyes igniting.

"It would seem so," Solehan whispered, leaning in languidly, his words a caress against Valnard's pointed ear.

The young druid felt the Alaris having a shiver when he used his god's magic to grow two enormous fangs in his mouth. With the animality expressed by Teluar's powers, Solehan licked the bite scar on Valnard's neck, his fangs grazing his skin.

60

 With a lump in his throat and a hand on the hilt of his sword, Talyvien walked along the long blue carpet that led to the throne. He had only had time to freshen up quickly after the eventful night, and now he advanced under the gaze of dozens of paladins of Callystrande. He also felt the apprehension of Lucine and Calixte directed toward him amid the golden suits of armor.

He still didn't quite understand why Callystrande had chosen to come back to him that night, but his heart overflowed with gratitude for his goddess. She had allowed him to save Shael. Absently moistening his lips, the kiss they had shared played on a loop in his mind.

When their obvious passion had to come to an end, the horrifying consequences of Piore's cruelty had struck them. In the night, a tremendous tumult had shaken the castle of Dawnelest. The truth about the High Priestess Piore had finally been revealed. The power of the abilities that was ultimately destined for Talyvien as well. On everyone's lips, he had heard the name Lamented being mentioned concerning him. Was it true? Had wings truly appeared on his back?

However, despite their incredible luck, Lucine, consumed by the guilt of her choice, had spent several minutes hugging the paladin and the assassin, apologizing profusely. Understanding the love she felt for her brother, neither of the companions had held it against her. They knew she hadn't really had a choice after all. Her whole life since that cursed eclipse had been devoted to finding Solehan. After that, the young druidess had also gone to rescue Calixte, who was still lying unconscious in one of the grand corridors of the castle.

As for Shael, with the help of several of her acolytes, she had taken Evelyn's body to honor her memory in their convent. Talyvien hadn't seen her since. He still feared her new confrontation with Cassandra and prayed that nothing would happen to her. After all, what fate awaited the chosen ones who did not fulfill their contracts?

As for himself, he had been escorted by ten paladins to a private area of the castle to wash quickly and change while waiting for an audience with the rulers, for which he had been summoned at dawn.

Talyvien didn't know what to expect when his eyes met those of King Arthios. The sovereign stood, arms behind his back, observing him with a neutral expression. Behind him, Queen Selena sat on the massive throne, still in a particularly sullen mood, a sparkling defiance in her stare.

Talyvien unsheathed his sword and knelt before the two rulers, placing it in front of him, point against the ground. "Your Majesties," he greeted solemnly, lowering his eyes.

"Talyvien Haldgard," proclaimed the king. "Former captain of the order of the paladins of Callystrande, *traitor* of the Crusade of the Dawn's Resolve, do you know why you have been summoned here today?"

Traitor. That was indeed what he was. But he had no regrets.

"I am ready to accept my sentence, Your Majesty. I am ready to accept the justice of Callystrande, and I will honor it," Talyvien replied honestly.

He knew that his king had fully regained control of his faculties. Talyvien was prepared to accept his judgment, as well as that of the goddess of light, whose magic now coursed through his body once more.

King Arthios nodded briefly. He approached Talyvien and drew his own sword from its sheath, the metal screeching against the scabbard. A chill ran down Talyvien's spine. Was this the sentence awaiting him?

He lowered his head, resigned. Talyvien felt the warmth of the light magic beneath his fingers and was grateful to reunite with his goddess in the afterlife. He thanked her once again for saving Shael, even though he wished he had more time to share with her. To have her by his side for these final moments. But asking for more than he had already received would have been greedy.

He took a deep breath.

The blade rested on the top of his head. He flinched.

"Talyvien Haldgard, I, Arthios Therybane, King of Astitan, hereby appoint you as the Supreme Commander of the order of the paladins of Callystrande, the armed force of the goddess of light."

The paladin's heart skipped a beat. His fingers clenched around the hilt of his sword.

"Where the Crusade of the Dawn's Resolve faltered, where I faltered, you have remained true to her teachings of justice, kindness, and tolerance. You are the chosen one we have all been waiting for. The goddess has made you her Lamented by your wings of light. The one who can see through enchantments and guide souls."

The cold metal of the blade on the top of his head made Talyvien shiver. A tingling sensation appeared in his eyes as the warmth of Callystrande enveloped him.

"The kingdoms of Astitan and Vamentera will forever be in your debt for the service you have rendered to them today," he continued. "May the goddess continue to guide your destiny and your heart nobly to show us the way. To protect the innocent and the weak. To vanquish the creatures that lurk in the shadows. Rise, Supreme Commander, Lamented of Callystrande."

Unsteadily, Talyvien stood back on his two feet. He stared at the sovereign for a long moment, perplexed. The absence of fanaticism now emanating from him. The firm yet radiant air on his features. Had he managed to completely free himself from Piore's control over his mind? A sense of pride for his king tinged the young man's chest. He had finally regained his comrade in arms.

In Talyvien's hand, Tuoryn's sword began to glow. King Arthios noticed the gleam of the weapon.

"You are worthy of the teachings of our mentor Tuoryn. And I am certain he would have been proud to consider you as his son."

"Thank you, Your Majesty," he murmured.

Dazed and moved, Talyvien nodded slightly. The sovereign advanced toward the assembly and assumed a solemn tone once again.

"Rise, Supreme Commander Haldgard, for today, we are in your debt. We are the ones whose knees must touch the ground in your honor. For the true Lamented of Callystrande!" proclaimed the king, raising his sword.

To his surprise, Talyvien then saw the king bow in his direction. All the paladins in the assembly unsheathed their swords and knelt in his honor. Even Queen Selena, at her brother's insistence, made a brief nod before turning her eyes away. Shame and bitterness still seemed to animate her features.

Because gratitude prevailed over what he might have expected from her anyway, Talyvien preferred to watch his brothers kneel before him. The hope of this situation. He did his best not to appear shaky and kept his head high, despite his emotions.

He was aware that he had much to do to show them the way, to cleanse their hatred. But he knew now that he was finally ready.

Two feline eyes caught his attention through one of the skylight windows of the throne room. A broad smile appeared on the face he loved so much. The young man breathed a sigh of relief. She was safe and sound.

"What will be your first command, Lamented?" exclaimed King Arthios.

"To dismantle the Crusade of the Dawn's Resolve," Talyvien replied without hesitation. His gaze remained fixed on Shael. Now confident, he continued with determination. "To impart the teachings of tolerance and kindness of the goddess. To curb the fear of differences in people's hearts and to repair the suffering caused by the crusade. So that it never happens again. And it is also time for our order to honor the relationship between Callystrande and Sazaelith. The purity of their love."

Surprised murmurs broke the solemn silence of the moment. Talyvien paid them no attention. Then, his eyes shifted to Lucine, who looked at him affectionately from the crowd, a hand on her throat.

"And to fulfill this promise of defending and protecting, of love and tolerance, the order of the paladins of Callystrande will march toward Argentvale," he added firmly. "Where the one who created perversions like the viperals resides."

New whispers circulated through the assembly. But Talyvien only had eyes for the druidess now. For the tears that gathered at the corners of her mouth as she displayed a deeply moved smile.

61

Shael watched the shining golden armor under the flames of the small candle illuminating the room that served as his office and improvised bedroom. He looked impressive behind the grand ornate desk that had been provided to him. Talyvien seemed to become aware of the enormous responsibility that had rested on his shoulders since the previous day, as a pile of various documents was spread out under his hands. Such was his destiny, his vow, and his devotion. She could not bring herself to deprive him of that. Out of love, she would sacrifice herself. Sacrifice the need of his light against her soul.

Once again, she would remain in the shadows. She was used to it.

"Here are all the documents related to what you requested, Supreme Commander," the man added, placing new documents on the already piled-up desk.

"Good. I will go through all of this. Ensure that I am not disturbed; I will pray to the goddess of light and perform my ablutions," Talyvien responded solemnly.

After bowing discreetly in agreement, the servant left the room, the door closing behind his steps.

Hidden behind the window, Shael tenderly observed the paladin removing his heavy metal armor, piece by piece. He hung it on the wooden armor rack against one of the walls and unbuttoned his shirt. Torso bare, he sprinkled himself with sacred water from a golden bowl on a small wooden altar before drying himself with a towel. The assassin admired his body riddled with scars, the marks of his battles and sacrifices, as he moved toward the desk to retrieve a small wooden box. He went to sit on a chair next to his bed and arranged the contents of the box on a table beside him—several brushes of different compositions and a magnificent golden inkwell.

The similarity of the situation and the nostalgic memory of her failed assassination resurfaced in the assassin's mind.

"Enjoying the view, Shael?" Talyvien joked, as he arranged the brushes.

A soft and melodic laughter filled the air, and Shael slipped her slender body through the window behind the desk. Her feet landed lightly on the polished and characteristic marble of the castle of Dawnelest. The paladin focused his attention on her. The corner of his mouth twisted slightly, carrying the scar with it.

That scar. Although she regretted inflicting it on him, she couldn't help but admire it. Representing everything she had been afraid of, she had passionately hated it since that night when she had been unable to fulfill the contract. No, hadn't wanted to fulfill the contract. Today, she would have given everything to be able to touch it once again. In the exhilaration of the night, she had been fortunate enough to kiss him. Now, walled within the vow he had made to his goddess as a paladin of Callystrande, she knew she would no longer have the opportunity. She would cherish this memory.

"Prayers and ablutions?" Shael teased.

"I had to find an excuse not to be disturbed. But one day, you should learn to use the door." He chuckled.

"The door . . . mmhh . . . I wouldn't be an experienced assassin if I indulged in such foolishness."

Seated, Talyvien let out another deep chuckle, and his playful eyes tenderly rested on her.

Shael approached the armor rack with quiet steps. She placed her hand on the golden metal and let her fingers follow the contours of the breastplate.

"It's strange to see you in armor," she murmured.

"You don't like it?"

She hesitated. Deep down in her heart, she cursed this piece of golden metal that now separated them, when they had been so close. She did her best not to let her selfishness take over. As he stood there, near her, so beautiful and dignified. She was genuinely happy for him.

She lowered her hood over her shoulders and moved toward him. Talyvien looked up, and their gazes met. A thin golden ring shimmered around his pupils; evidence of the connection restored with his goddess. With a knot in her heart, Shael lightly touched the paladin's cheek with her fingers.

"It suits you well. I'm glad you have found Callystrande again," she said, trying not to show her dismay.

"Is there something wrong, Shael?" Worried, Talyvien placed a hand on hers and pressed it against his cheek. The assassin's insides twisted.

"It's just that . . . nothing will be the same as before, I suppose. You've become a paladin again. You have . . . obligations. You're bound by the vows of your order."

"Oh! You scared me!" he exclaimed. A broad smile appeared on his face, as he slid Shael's fingers over his lips and kissed them.

Why did he react like that? The warmth of his kisses on her hand made the assassin shiver as she looked at Talyvien in surprise.

"I thought you didn't want to—," he whispered.

"No, no—," she replied in a soft breath. How could she not want to be by his side?

"Shael, I am now the Supreme Commander. And apparently the Lamented too," he shrugged. "I can decide the laws of the Order of Callystrande. And believe me, this matter of celibacy vow is clearly one of the first laws I will repeal."

"You can do that?"

"Like I'm going to hold back! You won't get rid of me that easily!"

Shael chuckled softly, and finally, she let her heart speak. Her desire to be close to him fueled her audacity. She straddled Talyvien's lap and put her hands around his neck. A surprised but radiant look appeared on his face, and he wrapped his hands around the assassin's waist in return.

"How was your return to the convent?"

"It wasn't easy to see Cassandra again," she sighed. "But now that she's free from Piore's magic, I was able to explain everything to her."

"How did she take it?"

"Better than I expected. It seems that, like with Arthios, the imprint left by those creatures dissipates quite quickly. But she couldn't stand being deceived and having sold the blood of the apprentices, even under the influence. So, as penance, she stepped down from her position."

"Ah. So, you'll have to find a new Mother Superior, I suppose?"

"Mmhh. The Council of Sisters convened urgently, and they've already found an apparently ideal candidate." She lowered her eyes, but a smile appeared on the corner of her lips.

"Oh?" he said, curious sparkles in his eyes.

"Someone who is devoted to upholding the teachings of Sazaelith at all costs and protecting her values and disciples."

"Mmhh," he nodded, his features becoming more joyful.

"Someone who was pardoned for not fulfilling a contract because she recognized that it had not been authorized by the goddess before acting."

"I see," he said, a teasing look on his face. "Perhaps the charms of the potential target helped in not executing the contract as well!"

"Of course!" Shael laughed again with her melodic laughter, but she could read a mixture of relief and admiration in Talyvien's eyes. "Someone who would now be honored to give her life to protect those she cherishes," she added. Moved, she caressed Talyvien's neck with her fingers.

He tilted his head to savor the touch. "Someone who made me understand the delicate balance between life and death," he marveled.

The assassin contemplated the contours of his face. Did she deserve all of this? Despite herself, a sudden twinge of shame turned in Shael's belly. "Yes, but someone who was about to take your life in that inn despite the fact that you saved hers," she said, looking down.

"No, someone who allowed me to be reborn when I thought I was dead," he whispered, pressing his hands on her waist a little tighter. "We are even, Shael."

Surprised but with a lighter heart, the assassin nodded and gently brushed Talyvien's jaw.

"I'm sorry about Evelyn," he added with a more serious tone.

"Me too. We held a beautiful ceremony for her."

"I don't doubt it," he sympathized. "In any case, I'm sure you'll be perfect for this role, Shael. And who knows, maybe we could start something new? A collaboration between our two orders?"

"Do you think you can heal their hearts from intolerance?"

"With you by my side, yes."

It was now Shael's turn to look at the young man with tenderness.

"Mmhh . . . Despite your grand speeches as the Lamented and my assassin's charm, we'll probably still have to train them not to kill each other!" she joked, making a grimace.

They burst into laughter.

"But yes, speaking of that," she continued more seriously. "I thought a few additional assassins wouldn't hurt to march on Argentvale and accompany the brave paladins of Callystrande! They are eager to avenge Evelyn's death. They know Valnard is responsible."

"Really?" he rejoiced. The assassin nodded and drew her body closer to his.

She buried her face in the crook of his neck.

He tenderly caressed the young woman's back in their embrace.

"In that case, maybe we should set an example?" she murmured teasingly against his neck.

Talyvien chuckled lightly.

Shael raised back her upper body.

"What do you suggest?" he asked playfully.

"You could . . . mark me with Callystrande's blessing," she hesitated, looking at the brushes.

It was the only excuse her courage had found in such a situation. She untied her cloak and threw it to the ground.

The paladin followed her gaze and remained speechless. But his hands descended from her waist and delicately landed on Shael's leather pants.

The assassin could read the interested curiosity and the request to continue in his eyes. "I mean . . . a blessing from every deity wouldn't hurt for the upcoming battle, and it seems that Callystrande doesn't dislike me if she allowed you to bring me back . . . ," she stammered.

Shael undid the straps of her upper armor and pulled it over her head.

Talyvien's fingers trembled on her thighs, his eyes becoming more fervent, still locked on her.

There, presented to him like this, sitting on his legs, she had nothing but the thin leather bandeau over her chest. Febrile, torn between a new, unbearable desire and the fortifications she had built to survive. Was it too much? Was it enough? Was she foolish to act this way?

Talyvien's face tinged with desire and admiration. His ardent and tender attention glided over the assassin's body. Was he afraid of hurting her? Of flaying her with his actions or his words? His eyes ended their escapade on her abdomen, devoid of any wounds, which he gently brushed with his fingertips.

Shael shivered.

"I was scared, Shael," he lamented, contemplating the skin of her abdomen without any injuries. "I was so scared . . ."

"But I'm here now," she murmured, raising his chin with her hand. "Thanks to you. Maybe we could dispel the curse and thank the goddess by marking the prayers right here?"

Where the dagger had pierced her body. Where Piore's madness had been unleashed.

With a radiant spark on his face, Talyvien nodded and took one of the brushes, dipping it into the inkwell. He placed his other hand on the assassin's waist and silently urged her to arch backward.

The cold ink made Shael flinch at first.

With small touches, like the subtle passage of an ice cube on her skin, Talyvien began to paint the symbols of his goddess on her belly. With respect and restraint. Diligently, like a studious student drawing his finest illumination, the paladin didn't take his attention off his masterpiece.

But the slowness, the imprecise rhythm of his brushstrokes on her skin became torture for Shael. An ambiguous torment of fear and delight. The intimacy of the moment overwhelmed the assassin. Had she been too forward in what she was capable of? Her agitation overflowed her thoughts. Shael had an incredibly hard time restraining her body from following the emotional movements of her anxiety and staying still.

Talyvien's hand on her waist gently compressed. He had felt her distress. As he traced the symbols, the thumb of Talyvien's other hand drew small circles on her skin to soothe her. A reminder of his presence, his protection, their shared discovery. She would never be alone again facing her nightmares.

Shael exhaled deeply. And finally, she could let her terror dissolve into a budding desire. A warmth that contrasted with the coldness of the ink on her belly. A sensation she didn't know. Could her body really react like this? Did she still have the right to?

Despite herself, the spark turned into a blazing furnace. Her body ignited. Each brushstroke amplified her torment. Shael tilted her head back, finding it difficult to bear any more. Her breath broke in frustration at the leisurely pace and reserve the paladin insisted on using. He would never betray her. She knew it.

However, the assassin listened as Talyvien's breathing also became disrupted. The muscles of his legs tensed under hers. Inflamed by a similar ardor that he tried to restrain as best he could.

Her longing for light, the unbearable deprivation her past had imposed on her, drove Shael insane. With a swift movement, she undid the leather bandeau on her chest, letting it fall to the floor.

The brush stopped.

A few suspended seconds.

Between past and future.

Between fear and courage.

Between pain and pleasure.

Revealed to him, and only to him, Shael arched even more.

Talyvien's hand on her waist tightened a little more, his agitation palpable in his silence. She didn't dare look at him.

The brush resumed its exquisite path.

The ink no longer seemed important. The perfection of the symbols on her skin no longer mattered. It meandered languorously on her epidermis in a disorderly pattern. No more prayer to the goddess. Or perhaps the most beautiful of all.

Soon running out of ink, the brush continued its course. A few hesitant, delicate strokes. Strokes that lazily made their way up between her breasts, wanting to sublimate her body with a gallant distance to the base of her neck.

Inflamed, Shael refrained from letting out a contained sigh and bit her lip. The upper part of her body arched even more. A silent request.

Still sadistic, the brush descended again on the assassin's chest. Gently, surely, on one side, then the other, it defined her shape with small concentric circles, its coldness making Shael shiver. She couldn't take it anymore. An unbearable and fascinating torture.

A small crack of raw wood on the floor. The brush.

Talyvien's lips replaced it. He let out a muffled groan. His gentleness, his gallantry now impossible. He clearly couldn't hold back any longer.

This time, Shael couldn't prevent the sigh that escaped her lips. The paladin's hands eagerly traced the contours of the assassin's body, a supernaturally warm and radiant heat under his fingers. Immensely large compared to the slender figure of the young woman, they roamed her back and chest with curious passion.

Talyvien's mouth sprinkled her skin with light kisses, moving up to her shoulders, her neck, the side of her jaw as Shael raised her head back. The lips of the young man approached hers with a timid eagerness.

Shael responded by kissing him fervently. Her blue heart exploded throughout her body. Sazaelith's blood pulsated strongly upon contact with Callystrande's magic. Shael felt the darkness of her goddess crackling under her fingers as she brushed the paladin's face. She no longer had any doubt about the love their goddesses felt for each other.

Their magics responded to each other and united perfectly—a divine hurricane that carried them away. Both sitting and bare-chested against each other, her curves against his angular lines. Shael could no longer wait. She wanted to feel him, touch him, merge with him. A leap into the unknown. The force of their kiss intensified, and their tongues discovered each other fully.

Talyvien groaned with pleasure once more. He pressed his body against hers, his sparks of light disrupting the shadows' arabesques of Shael in their embrace.

The assassin's hips collided against the paladin's as he slid his hands behind the young woman's thighs. Without breaking the contact of their mouths, he stood up with a powerful movement and lifted Shael, who wrapped her legs and arms around him. He gently placed her on the bed and positioned himself above her while still kissing her.

Talyvien's kisses were an ode to her skin. Their softness, their warmth. The weight of his body on hers.

The calloused hands firmly holding her down. The wicked smile revealing blue teeth. She was suffocating, unable to move.

"Shael? Shael!"

She caught a glimpse of Talyvien's alarmed face. Her body trembled despite herself. The paladin straightened up above Shael and gently placed one hand on her cheek.

"You don't owe me anything, Shael," Talyvien said, panting. "We don't have to do anything if you don't want to or can't. Being close to you is enough for me. Your kisses are enough for me."

Puzzled, her chest heaving, Shael looked at Talyvien. Tears rolled down her cheeks. Why couldn't she be like everyone else? Why did her nightmares have to steal this from her too?

Talyvien lay down beside her and embraced her.

The assassin buried her face in the paladin's shoulders. He tenderly kissed the top of her head.

"You are wonderful, Shael," he whispered.

Shael lifted her head. How could he believe that? A new worry surged within her as she observed the contours of his face. Having hidden behind the excuse of their differing devotions for too long, she was overcome with panic. She didn't know how to react to this new reality.

He was just a man. She was just a woman.

"You know . . . I will never be able to give you a normal life. I will never be able to marry or give you children. I don't have the heart, I don't have the body for it," she murmured. Fresh tears streamed down her cheeks. She feared losing him. Feared of not being enough for this grand adventure. Feared of having nothing to give. He, who had everything, who was everything.

As she tried to bury herself in the hollow of his neck, he gently lifted her chin, the gold in his eyes burning in the room's backlight. "It's precisely because I know what we have is special that I want to discover it with you. Create our own path. One that suits us. Far from the gaze of others, far from conventions. It's precisely because you are you. Exactly as you are. I will choose a life by your side, Shael, no matter what we go through, rather than a multitude of 'normal' lives, and I will make that choice again and again at every step we take."

The assassin's eyes welled up profusely. A mixture of relief and wonder gently shook her as Talyvien's words imprinted on her soul.

"As for children, Shael, I'd be crazy to stop loving you for someone who may never exist. I want that in the end, when we look back, we can say we lived our truth, one we intertwined together. And even after, when I'm just a ray of sunlight lost in the glow of Callystrande, and you're a shining star in the night of Sazaelith, I know I'll find you in the dawn and dusk to dance with you until the end of time." He tenderly wiped away the abundant tears from her cheeks and kept the assassin's face between his hands.

Love. That word in Talyvien's mouth resonated within her. Against all the defenses she had erected in her life. Against all the whirlwinds of vengeance and violence raging within her. This single word soothed the storms and rushed where no one had ever been before. It was the first time this word had been addressed to her. The first time she wanted to use it too.

"I don't know where we'll go, I don't know what it will look like, but I know I love you, Talyvien Haldgard."

The scar on his lips lifted slightly as his face lit up. A gentle and powerful light, just like his goddess. A light that illuminated the darkness in which she had been lost for too long.

"I love you, Shael Ymdaral," he replied in a breath.

In his mouth, her name sounded like the most beautiful thing she had ever heard. A perfection. A promise of a future that transformed her past, her name.

Shael pressed her lips against his. More convinced than ever. She would never let the specter of her haunting steal her life from her again. Her happiness. Her present. The assassin's hand slid down Talyvien's pants. "I want to experience this with you," she whispered between kisses.

"Are you sure?" he asked, surprised.

"I won't let him steal this from me either."

And so, together, they rewrote the ending of her story. A new composition synchronized, their bodies instruments of an original symphony. A pleasure she never thought possible. Because it was him. The only person in the world capable of this at that moment.

With each movement of Talyvien's hips, Shael rediscovered her body. Its unexpected wonders. Its unforeseen feats. She could finally *be* in his arms again. Her sensations were hers, his caresses desired.

Together, they crossed the bridge that led them to the stars, at the same moment. Their hearts and bodies in perfect harmony. A blissful symphony of darkness and light.

And then, still thirsting for each other, they began again. A new melody, a new chapter in the book of their life.

Still in bed, Shael was nestled between his arms, her back to him. The scent of her hair, her skin, and the aftermath of their lovemaking cocooned Talyvien in a soft cloud. He had just spent hours showing her beauty, her worth, and her bravery. Trying to give back what someone else had taken by force. But in truth, it was she who had shown him the way. How could he have ever despised her? Feared Sazaelith and her chosen ones? In awe, he gently stroked Shael's arm. He would never wish for anything else but her presence by his side. As equals.

The assassin arched against him and reached back to caress his face. Turning, she placed a light kiss on Talyvien's lips, and he tightened his arms around her.

Someone knocked on the door.

"Supreme Commander? I know you said not to disturb you, but . . . it's urgent," a muffled voice said.

Talyvien groaned in frustration, his mouth still on hers.

"I did tell you we should be wary of doors," Shael whispered, with a smile.

62

Determined—Solehan was more than ever. His moment of truth. The culmination of months of hope and learning. The impatience of the young druid gnawed at his thoughts. The intense desire and love he felt for the Alaris too.

Ever since he had seen Teluar asleep under the Tree of Ether, he had never ceased to want to annihilate the sadness and despair of the god. Ever since such profound feelings had sprouted for Valnard, he had envisioned the utopian paradise where they could fulfill their promise, rid of the pestilence of humans.

Transformed into a falcon, on the road leading to Dawnelest, he admired Valnard flying on his elaphora beside him. Solehan relished his luck. They would succeed in awakening the god of Nature and bringing back Sylveah. They would live eternity together under his blessing.

It had to be done. At any cost.

Both landed on the roof of the tallest tower of the majestic castle of Dawnelest, ribbon-wrapped in mist. Solehan resumed his human form and contemplated the vast city. Its canals crafted and dotted with bridges. Thousands of grotesque buildings piled up in chaos. A deep disgust gripped his throat. Wherever he looked, the civilization of humans spread. Parasites who reduced nature to nothing under their feet, mistreated it, and mocked it in vulgar jest.

Solehan was determined to give them a taste of their own medicine.

"Yes. Humans as far as the eye can see. Constantly reproducing. Constantly destroying everything," Valnard whispered in his ear, as he wrapped his arms around the young man.

Solehan turned around and faced him. He put his arms around the Alaris's neck and kissed him tenderly.

"It's my turn to give you a gift today, Valnard. For allowing Wuruhi to be avenged. For showing me the way. For saving my life." He brushed another kiss on his lips. "For giving me a place by your side."

"Be careful, Solehan."

With his hands on either side of the Alaris's beautiful face, Solehan nodded. He planted one final kiss on his lips and let himself fall into the void.

Sitting on the terrace of the *Opalescent Masquerade*, Lucine observed the bustling of the grand square. Her attention drifted into the crowd as she stroked Katao's head.

The large black dog seemed to enjoy it and let out a small joyful whimper.

"Thank you for everything you've done for me, Katao."

The animal seemed to understand what Lucine had just said and rested his head on her thigh, his blue eyes filled with affection.

The surprising connection she had with animals now made sense. She had always been able to understand them and feel their emotions in her flesh. Now, she possessed the power to make them obey her command. A peculiar power that she was grateful to Teluar for, considering the events they had gone through and the madness of the viperal. Perhaps that's why the swarm of birds had swooped down on the crusade when Talyvien had saved her from the pyre. Lost in thought, Lucine continued to affectionately scratch the dog's ears.

"Ah, you two! You make a great pair!" exclaimed Calixte.

With refinement and a charisma almost supernatural, the graceful steps of the bard undulated toward the table where the young druidess sat. The hardships the Alaris had faced the previous day seemed not to have affected their good humor or poise at all, as they wore a new finely embroidered tunic that complemented their colorful makeup.

"I've ordered a few treats," they said with complicit eyes.

As Calixte took a seat next to the young druidess, the waitress arrived and placed a pile of goodies on the table.

Katao barked with joy and licked his lips.

"You don't do things by halves!" Lucine said, in jubilation.

"You know, sometimes you have to enjoy the good things! Savor them before it's too late. When life is beautiful, it's a spark in the darkness. It's not meant to last," they replied with a wink, before devouring one of the delicious pastries.

"I believe you indeed have mastered that art!"

"I've been living for centuries; I've had some practice!"

Lucine then took one of the cakes and gave one to Katao, who devoured it in one gulp. The two companions laughed heartily at the animal's enthusiasm.

Calixte finished their last bite and slightly coughed. "I hope you don't mind, but I switched rooms with Shael. It seems I'm a bit . . . too much."

"Oh, really? I think you could have realized that a little earlier!" she said with a smirk.

"Well, it doesn't hurt to tease them a bit. By now, they are probably busy catching up!" they replied, gesturing with their hand and rolling their eyes. "At least now you have a chosen of Callystrande and a chosen of Sazaelith to support you."

Lucine pursed her lips and stared at the wood of the table beneath her fingers. "I'm not sure if I deserve it, to be honest."

"Why? Because you chose to save your brother?"

Feeling sheepish, she nodded.

"It was an impossible choice, Lucine. No one should have to face such a dilemma. And I also know that neither Talyvien nor Shael hold any grudge about it."

"Maybe . . ."

With a tight throat, Lucine looked at the statue of King Herald Aramanth that stood in the square before them. Several carriages were circling around it, as the guests of the Solamaris ball were finally returning home.

"Well, don't worry! By now, they probably have their minds busy about something else!" Calixte quipped, giving her an ambiguous look as they licked the sugar off their pinky finger.

Lucine emitted a light amused sniffle. The bard always had the right words to warm her heart. But something still troubled the young woman. "It's just that . . . sometimes I wonder if I made the right choice . . . and . . ." She covered her eyes with her hands. "Yet, he's my brother. I should be relieved!"

She slid her palms away from her face and placed them back on the table. In silence, Calixte observed her with compassion, seemingly urging her to continue.

The young woman sighed, her shoulders slumping. "I feel so indebted to Shael and Talyvien for finally having an army to go to Argentvale, but . . . I'm afraid of what we'll find there."

"Mmhh. What exactly scares you?"

"I think I'm afraid of realizing that I didn't know Solehan as well as I thought. I fear he may have become someone else. The images of what we saw in that village keep looping in my mind. The cruelty. The despair of those poor wretches. The fact that he attacked Shael like that and might agree with Valnard's madness. What kind of person could do that?"

Calixte's lips curved with an unusual sadness. They turned their attention away, staring at the grand square.

"Besides, how can I be sure that Valnard used the heart of Teluar to save my brother?" Lucine added. "And even if that's the case, what will Solehan be capable of once his powers are further amplified? There doesn't seem to be a best solution."

"I understand. Sometimes it's hard to realize that the relationships we choose have more value than those we don't," Calixte murmured, breaking their strange silence.

The young woman turned her head and looked at the bard with wide eyes. Were they speaking from personal experience? Lucine remembered what they had confided in her—the lack of acceptance from their own people when they had chosen a different path.

Lucine let out a long sigh. If faced with the same dilemma, would she make the same choice again?

Her appetite gone, she tried to drown herself in the frenzied dance of the carriages in the grand square. The two of them spent several minutes silently watching the curious ballet of the onlookers and vehicles.

"In any case, Lucine, no matter what the future holds, know that I will always be by your side," Calixte finally said, placing a hand on the young woman's arm. "Never doubt it."

"Thank you, Calixte," she replied, placing a hand on theirs.

They gave her a sorrowful smile. Guilt tinged their amber eyes.

Screams tore through the air. Cries of misery and sheer terror.

Katao barked and growled, his ears pinned back, his fear and anger spreading against the emotions of the young druidess.

In a bound, Lucine stood up, knocking over her chair. Her pulse thrummed against her temples.

Heads around them turned. Murmurs grew louder.

Thick clouds of smoke rose in the distance. A wave of people, begging and screaming, poured through the adjacent streets. Everyone was in a panic. A tidal wave of terrified souls, knocking everything down in their path. Some stumbled, others crawled, their fear transformed into an inhuman madness. They all abandoned carriages, terraces, and buildings, running to drown in this absurd turmoil.

"Calixte, what's happening?" Lucine asked, panicked.

The Alaris, still seated at the table, let out a deep, phlegmatic sigh. Their emotion bafflingly languid in such a situation. They raised their eyes to the sky.

A roar of immeasurable power reverberated through the city and shook the ground. Various plates and cups fell from the table and shattered one after the other.

An ancient rumble, a dreadful curse.

The toll that heralded an apocalypse.

63

 Streams of terror, torrents of crowds jostling among which Lucine, Katao, and Calixte tried to make their way to the entrance of the castle against the current. They collided with several people in their chaotic progress, overwhelmed by the panic that had possessed the population. The wafts of ashes, sweat, and terror filled the now foul air. The young druidess had only had time to grab her bow and quiver in her room before rushing out of the inn. Her magic was not an endless reserve, so she preferred to rely on something tangible. She gripped the bow's wood until her knuckles turned white. What was this new threat? She certainly wasn't in the mood for unnecessary delays; she had to get to Argentvale.

They passed through an imposing gate and arrived in the large inner courtyard of the castle. A bitter contrast formed in the young woman's mind. Just two days ago, they had taken the same path to attend the Solamaris ball. Lucine felt a surge of nausea by reflex. Instead of vibrant-colored dresses, all she saw was the bustle of a hundred golden suits of armor swirling before them.

Katao growled, baring his teeth.

"Captain Arenor of the Sixth Battalion!" a familiar voice shouted.

"At your command, Lamented!" replied one of the paladins, pressing his fist against his breastplate.

"Escort King Athios Therybane and Queen Selena Aramanth out of the city with your men, along with any essential dignitaries."

Captain Arenor made a short bow before turning to one of the groups of paladins and shouting new instructions.

"Second, Third, and Fifth Battalions, help the survivors flee the city or barricade themselves!"

"At your command, Supreme Commander!" several voices responded in unison.

Several dozen armored men rushed into the alleys adjacent to the courtyard just as Lucine and Calixte arrived. Among the sparkling crowd, they spotted Talyvien in full armor, directing and giving orders amid the turmoil, Tuoryn's sword at his belt in its scabbard. An enormous shield adorned his back, making it look like he had massive wings made of solid gold. Instead of one of the sinister golden masks, a fine circlet of gold shimmered on his forehead.

Shael, her demeanor sharper than ever, stood with arms crossed next to him in her familiar leather attire.

"Taly! Shael!" Lucine called out as she ran toward them.

"Lucine! Calixte!" the paladin called back when he saw them approaching. "Are you both alright?"

"What's going on?" asked the young druidess. "I heard a terrible roar!"

"A roar?" the assassin interjected, raising an eyebrow.

"We didn't hear anything like that," Talyvien admitted. "However, several scouts have reported outbreaks of violence and panic in various parts of the city. We must stay on guard."

"I'm going back to the convent to get reinforcements, just in case," Shael said. "You never know."

"That's a good idea, but be careful," the paladin replied, taking her hand.

"Don't worry. I don't do temporary, I've told you that before," she retorted mischievously, caressing his cheek.

With extreme agility, Shael climbed one of the walls of a nearby building and disappeared, leaving behind only a dark and fleeting swirl as a memory of her presence.

"What do we do now?" Lucine worriedly asked as she watched the assassin vanish into the shadows.

Before anyone could answer, the ground began to shake. A deep rumble of extreme gravity reverberated through their chests. Everyone exchanged bewildered looks.

The castle courtyard bathed in twilight; the sun so cherished by the goddess of light suddenly obscured. The disconcerted murmurs of the paladins of Callystrande could be heard, interspersed with the metallic clinks of their armor.

Lucine looked up. Her fear liquefied into her legs, causing them to wobble.

A new eclipse of terror. A dark star with torn edges against the blue sky.

Menacing in its flesh, invulnerable in its dominance. The epitome of a cataclysm.

A dragon. A nightmare from beyond the grave, several hundred meters long, resurrected to seek revenge for its kind's injustice.

Lucine, frozen with terror to her core, no longer felt her hands or her face.

Talyvien cursed under his breath.

The immense, sparkling creature perched above the main entrance of the castle, its diaphanous wings shrouding the atmosphere with a sinister purity as it spread them wide. Its opalescent scaled body created shimmering waves amid the layer of ash and blackish smoke. Its four legs and long tail ended in a tangle of bark, knotted branches, and imposing ebony-like thorns. An obscene splendor that belonged only in legends.

"A dragon?!" bellowed Talyvien, who seemed to regain his composure. "Calixte! I thought these creatures no longer existed!"

The paladin turned to the Alaris. Lucine followed the movement and turned her head. But Calixte had vanished.

"Where are they?" Lucine cried, in a panic.

"They must have taken cover," grumbled Talyvien. "Cowardly bard."

The paladin drew his sword, ready to face the threat, and gave a command.

The paladins of Callystrande, snapped out of their stupor, formed a perfect line and lowered their shields to create a wall of metal.

The dragon's nostrils dilated, as it sensed the anxiety spreading through the inner courtyard like wildfire. Its monstrous head bowed, its endless gaping maw revealed rows of teeth as sharp as needles.

A new roar shattered the oppressive silence that had settled under the surprise. The world trembled under the power of its cry.

Lucine planted her feet firmly on the ground and nocked an arrow in her bow. How could such a creature stand before them?

In a dizzying flap of wings, the enormous dragon braced itself against one of the massive towers of the castle. Bricks, beams, and windows groaned and crumbled under its enormous wooden claws, which easily pierced the walls that had become so fragile compared to the beast's strength. An awful, brutish crack echoed. The tower, unable to bear the weight, split in two and collapsed onto a second tower, which it brought down in its fall.

New cries arose from the surroundings, as the townspeople were devastated by the nightmarish sight. An entire section of the castle of Dawnelest had been obliterated into a heap of misty ruins in a matter of seconds.

In another resounding roar, the dragon took flight with majesty. Perhaps it wanted to prolong the pleasure? Clearly satisfied, it vanished from their field of vision to continue its path of destruction, hovering over the city like a vulture relishing the agony of its prey.

Lucine and Talyvien exchanged horrified glances. How could they ever defeat a dragon? *A dragon!*

A deathly silence descended. Unanswered questions filled their minds. Every soul in the inner courtyard apparently shared the same uncertainty.

Katao growled even louder. The dog's fear filled the young druidess's body. New cracking sounds, wailing, and footsteps grazed the cobblestones in the nearby alleys. More and more. A deadly crescendo. With the perfect harmony of their quickening heartbeats.

Lucine listened intently, trying to gather more information. The cries of the citizens had ceased.

A harbinger of death.

She should have known by now. Misfortunes never seemed to come alone. She took a deep breath to gather her courage and aimed her bow toward one of the courtyard entrances. Ready for anything.

Seconds dripped away in the fog caused by the castle's destruction. Everyone strained their ears. Lucine squinted her eyes and coughed from the settling dust. She tried to calm her apprehension and tapped her fingers on her taut bow. She must aim precisely and not tremble.

And their answer arrived.

A multitude of withered lychenas poured forth. They screamed their rage and hatred. With a surprised yet malevolent look on her face, Lucine tightened her grip on her bow.

So, Valnard was responsible for this attack. However, everything was different now. *She* was different.

"Lucine. If this is the end, know that it has been an honor," Talyvien grumbled between his teeth. He unfastened his shield from his back and assumed a defensive posture, the dust swirling around him in his movements.

"This isn't the end, Taly!" she growled. One of her projectiles impaled the head of one of the forest spirits with ruthless precision.

Slightly surprised, Talyvien nodded and offered a determined smile to the druidess. He shouted another order, and the paladins of Callystrande immediately took their positions, their shimmering shield barrier as their defense.

The wooden creatures charged at the men and their armor, creating a powerful explosion against the bulwarks. The arms of the lychenas lifted, their curse of bark a foregone conclusion. Muffled cries filled the air.

Lucine saw with horror the flesh of the men beginning to transform into wood. Even though they were seasoned fighters, what could they do against this? They would soon be lignified into wooden statues, just like her clan had been. As evidenced by the dreadful silence in the city—the unfortunate citizens of Dawnelest had also met the misfortune of encountering this ominous wave.

Concerned for her friend, Lucine turned her head to Talyvien, who charged into the fray with his sword raised. She blinked as the paladin's skin began to shine. Under the metal of his armor, a light radiated between the plates. The young druidess gasped in surprise.

She watched in awe as the power of Callystrande materialized. The goddess of light's powers healed and counteracted the lignification of the paladins' bodies, bit by bit. Temporarily affected but blessed by the deity, the paladins fought back against the forest spirits, who evidently didn't expect such resistance from their part. The goddess seemed to bless this moment with her grace. Her disciples were the only ones capable of defeating these creatures.

Lucine glanced at Talyvien, who fought ferociously. Had Callystrande sent him a sign when she was on the stake, just for this moment? Him, apparently her Lamented?

The battle, however, was turbulent and exhausting, a fierce struggle in both camps. The men slashed the wooden figures with their swords, creating large splinters, but the forest spirits overwhelmed them with their numbers.

With perfect mastery, Lucine shot several arrows, as Katao rushed at the wooden creatures. Most of her shots hit their mark, throwing the lychenas backward, where they fell lifeless with high-pitched groans.

The young woman had become unstoppable.

The confrontation lasted several long minutes: a surge of rage in each camp. The flow of forest spirits continued relentlessly. Endlessly. Lucine tried her best to stay optimistic. She had to.

Despite the goddess's magic, several paladins were wounded and forced to retreat to receive healing. Blood entangled with fragments of dead wood from the lychenas accumulated abundantly on the courtyard's cobblestones.

A tingling sensation gripped the back of Lucine's neck as she continued to fire projectiles at a bewildering speed. Thousands of prickles snaked slowly around her skull. An irritating scratching against her magic, the tip of a rope pulling at her powers in small jerks. Annoyed by this occult itch, the young woman turned around.

She lowered her bow, dismayed. A freezing current sent shivers down her spine.

Valnard had not held back. Where the dragon had previously established its tyranny above the castle's entrance, dozens of hybrid creatures were now lurking. Lucine recognized a few echarvoras among all the abominations.

"Ta—Taly! We have a problem!" she shouted.

Talyvien swiftly sliced one of the lychenas in half. Exhausted, his face covered in sweat, his skin marked with blood and the magic of his goddess, the paladin turned around. And cursed vehemently.

The young man ordered some of the paladin battalions to whirl around. They were now surrounded. Caught in a trap carefully devised by the Alaris. The forest spirits continued their wild rush from the alleys adjacent to the courtyard on one side. The hybrid creatures leaped from the heights of the building to land in the courtyard, their eyes fixated on their prey with a carnivorous gaze, on the other.

A summary execution.

At the same moment, the gigantic and malevolent shadow of the dragon passed over them and let out a roar that shook the bowels of the earth.

Lucine jolted. Was this the ultimate aim of their journey?

"Lucine! Your powers!" Talyvien yelled out. "Control the creatures like you did with Piore!"

"There are too many! I'll never be able to control them all!" she said, panicked.

"You must try! It's our only chance!"

All the hybrid creatures rushed into the fray. Already exhausted, the paladins grumbled under their masks and assumed defensive positions behind their shields. Immense abominations towering over the warriors by several meters, crashed into their bulwarks with a metallic blast. A wild and untamed wave, an anarchic combination of animal bodies and cries.

Lucine repositioned her bow on her back and raised her arms. She had to do it. She pleaded with her god, muttering between her teeth, and closed her eyes. Sweat trickled down her neck and plastered her hair. A few sparks of her magic crackled at her fingertips. Verdant and warm. Implacable and dominant.

Echoes of animality shimmered in her mind. She felt Katao's rage, as he fought and defended against any threats near her. And then, other fragments of memories crossed her mind. Images of the past lives of these hybrid beings. Of mammals and insects. Of hunting and playing. Lucine allowed her powers to take over and let go of all thoughts, of the sounds of metal and fragmented screams around her.

She struggled to get into the heads of several of the degenerations, attempting to command them to attack each other. After a few hesitant seconds, cheers arose. Bites and scratches, gurgles, and howls echoed. Although she couldn't control all of them, she had managed to take control of a few.

Lucine's arms, still outstretched, began to quiver. The young woman tried to draw on her magic and maintain control over as many creatures as possible. But she was quickly overwhelmed. Harassed by intrusive images from all sides. Memories of joy and terror intertwined, of happiness and vengeance.

A thread led her to a more vivid memory than the others. A wolf. The leader of a pack running with its peers through a forest of dark trees. The browned leaves crackling under their paws. The smell of autumn on his mate's fur when he nuzzled her. The joy of his pups playfully nipping at each other's ears.

And then, a fight to the death to defend his pack against human hands.

The scents of tanned leather mixed with the coppery taste of blood. Saddened, Lucine witnessed the animal's final moments. His desire for revenge was almost justified in the heart of the young woman, given the complete cruelty that men had shown toward him.

However, Lucine didn't have time to dwell on it, as another thought streaked her vision.

Another fellow calling the animal. A wolf with eyes of gold and silver, fixating on him. That was why this memory had been more insistent in the young woman's mind.

Solehan.

"No! Lucine!" Talyvien shouted.

Lucine opened her eyes and looked up. A massive half-wolf hybrid creature stood before her. Her stomach lurched.

The creature lunged at her. Lucine was thrown to the ground and hit it with force. The beast's claws dug into her arms, an otherworldly strength holding her back against the stone slabs. The creature's nostrils flared, sniffing the scent of blood spreading on the ground. Lucine's control over the other creatures completely loosened.

Talyvien cried out in distress.

Long fangs appeared in the hybrid's jaws just above her. Lucine heard the paladin struggling with other creatures, trying to reach her while shouting her name. But he wouldn't make it in time. Helpless against the monster's size, Katao clung to its back, biting it with desperation. Had she been naive to believe they could overcome all these creatures?

With trembling fingers, she tried to grab the dagger at her belt. The degenerate creature arched its head back. The final attack. She was about to be devoured. Her hand frantically searched for the weapon. Without success.

In a last futile reflex, Lucine turned her face away from death.

The wolf's muzzle came down upon her.

A sharp pain. Her heartbeats throbbed in each side of her head. But death didn't come.

Appalled, Lucine opened her eyes and looked at the monster still above her. Frozen, petrified. The creature's body slumped to the side; a dagger lodged in its skull. A dagger that vibrated and soared through the air in a trajectory that Lucine followed with wide eyes.

Perched on one of the higher parapets, Shael caught her blade. Several dark and incorporeal figures appeared around her. A myriad of luminescent eyes shimmering with vengeance.

The assassins of Sazaelith. The Children of Twilight.

All in unison, they let out a cry before pouring into the lychenas and hybrid creatures in a dark and ruthless tornado.

Shael slid down the wall and landed gracefully to join Lucine, who was still on the ground.

"Just in time, it seems, druidess!" Shael exclaimed, helping Lucine to her feet with one hand.

"Thank you, Shael!" Lucine blurted out, embracing her.

"Hey!" the assassin let out with surprise, returning the hug shyly. "Are you hurt!?"

"I'll be fine. It's not life-threatening."

Still concerned, Shael nodded before turning her head and exchanging a brief look with Talyvien.

A fleeting relief flashed on his face, and the paladin resumed his onslaught in the battle.

Eager to engage, the assassin threw herself back into the turmoil and joined her sisters.

Slightly dazed, Lucine leaned against a low wall and scanned the bustling surroundings to readjust her breathing. With Katao still by her side, she re-equipped her bow. Despite the pain gripping her arms and the blood seeping from her tunic, she had to keep going. She'd had a close shave. But with her reserves nearly depleted, the young druidess had almost no magic left. She would have to use it sparingly and rely only on herself from now on.

However, Shael and Talyvien were not affected in the same way.

Lucine looked on in amazement at the miracle happening before her eyes. The chosen ones of Callystrande and Sazaelith were fighting hand in hand. Guided by her two friends, back-to-back.

The goddess of shadows' magic thwarted the warriors from transforming into creatures, with the assassins having them drink their blood when necessary. The goddess of light's magic healed and prevented the lignification caused by the lychenas. Despite their obvious reluctance on both sides, all the fighters united to have a hope of defeating the threat.

The two opposites of shadow and light harmonized perfectly. Two destinies that had intersected to have a chance of survival. They were the only chosen ones capable of battling this infernal assault.

Lucine was now convinced that nothing had happened by chance. But then, if she couldn't assist them to the extent of the goddesses' magic, what was her role?

The imposing dark silhouette plunged once again through the clouds. The dragon.

Focused on the sky, and with her heart pounding, Lucine whistled for Katao. The black dog let go of a lychena's leg and ran toward the druidess. Determined, she re-nocked an arrow in her bow and started running. The horrifying shadow quickly passed over the entrance to the inner courtyard of the castle and continued to hover over the city.

With a daring that bordered on madness, Lucine decided to follow it. Perhaps this was her destiny? Her place in this battle? With Katao's help, who leaped on several forest spirits and hybrid creatures that blocked their way, they forged a path as best they could. The young woman, almost out of ammunition, pierced everything in her path toward the adjacent alleys. She had to find a clear spot to attract the dragon's attention. Maybe she could take control of it with what little magic she had left?

She heard Talyvien and Shael shouting her name in the melee, but she ignored them. If her plan was utterly absurd, she didn't want to involve them. She advanced through the influx of forest spirits, fueled by rage. Splinters flew. Her arrows ran through the lychenas, one by one. Lucine clenched her jaw with hatred.

Finally, after several minutes of this emotionally charged barrage of projectiles, she burst onto the street she had taken with Calixte a few moments earlier. Had the bard managed to escape in time? Lucine hoped that they had found refuge, but she didn't allow herself time to dwell on her concerns. She had much to do.

The flow of lychenas decreased, and Lucine spotted the beginning of one of the large bridges that traversed the city over the canals. She hurried to enter it. The wind hammered her hair and clothes as she ascended the structure and gained height. Exhausted, breathless, but finally in the middle of the bridge, at a level devoid of all creatures, she placed her hands on the stone railing and looked out over the city.

Tears flowed frenetically on her cheeks, creating furrows through the dust, ash, and dried blood. Everything in her squeezed in—her emotions, her thoughts, her body.

A field of ruins stretched as far as the eye could see. A vision of desolation.

Tides of wooden silhouettes among the debris. Almost nothing remained of the grand and magnificent city of Dawnelest and its inhabitants. Its joy and gaiety, its splendor.

Lucine couldn't hold back a sob. While they had been striving to counterattack the forest spirits and hybrid creatures, the dragon had decimated and destroyed everything.

Despite her promise to free her brother and find Valnard, she hadn't managed to save the city in time. The young woman collapsed to her knees and covered her face with her hands. A nightmare.

The sympathetic dog laid his wet nose on her arm and whimpered.

In the distance, a building collapsed. Debris of bricks, stone, and wood rolled in a new sinister crack. Lucine raised her head, her cheeks still streaked with sadness. She picked up her fallen bow, repositioned it on her back, and got back on her feet, panting.

With yet another roar of triumph and domination, the dragon flew off again, its hyaline wings vibrating in the power of the breeze.

In a gesture born of desperation, Lucine raised her arm toward the beast and focused. She allowed the last remnants of her magic to flow through her fully and followed its nebulous trail.

But it wasn't the spirit of an animal she collided with.

 Solehan perched on the dome of one of the tallest buildings in the city. He took wicked pleasure in digging his long claws into the roof, which yielded with a delicate crunch under his weight. Pitiful, laughable before his magnificence. He was invincible. Teluar's magic flowed through his limbs, through his powerful wings. Having become the image of the god himself, Solehan decided on life or death for his creation. The heart of Teluar had amplified his powers phenomenally. A titan walking among ants.

A powerful beat of his wings propelled him back into the air. The young druid savored the metallic scent of pain that tantalized his tongue. He wanted more. Even more.

What a delicious idea he'd had. Transforming into such a majestic creature to administer justice. Those same creatures that once had to perish for humans to take their place. Did Valnard admire him somewhere? Was the Alaris rejoicing with him in the success of their endeavor? Solehan hoped so, with all his heart. He wanted to give him that, knowing how much Valnard delighted in these beings. A gift that would seal their love.

As he glided toward a district that had been less severely affected by his punishment to remedy it, dozens of birds collided with his sturdy flesh made of scales and bark. From all sides, they tried to peck him with their beaks.

Was this an attack? Probably the most pitiful one he had ever seen. Solehan growled with disdain and ignored the birds. Nevertheless, he continued his patrol in search of clues.

And that's when he spotted her. After months without seeing her, lost between useless mourning and apprehension. The only link he still tolerated to his childhood. The only person he had ever loved from his past.

On one of the large bridges still standing, Lucine stared at him. Impatience drove Solehan to dive straight toward her. From a god, he turned back into a man and landed on the bridge's cobblestones. His evaporating wings were the last traces of his transformation.

"Lucine!" he exclaimed, rushing toward her.

"Don't come any closer!" she replied, raising a bloodied hand.

Disheartened, the young druid stopped running and stared at his twin sister. Lucine's long brown hair was plastered against her sweat, mud, and dried blood-covered face. An empty quiver with just one arrow left was slung over her back, and her cotton clothes were torn on both sides. With an unsteady gait, she had two injuries on each of her arms.

The black dog accompanying her bared its teeth.

"It's me . . . Solehan! Are you hurt?" he asked.

"Do you even need to ask?" she vociferated.

"It wasn't my intention, Lucine," he said, taking a step closer, his hand on his chest.

"So, not me, but the rest of humanity? Yes?" she scoffed bitterly. "Do you think you can just show up as if nothing has happened? As if you hadn't done anything?!"

"I haven't seen you in months! Months during which I thought you were dead, Lucine! And is this how we're supposed to reunite? After all this time—"

"Whose fault do you think it is?" she spat. "You decided to make it that way when you chose this path!"

"I knew you wouldn't understand," Solehan said, turning his face away, his lips tight.

"How can I still consider you my brother after this? How can you agree with Valnard's madness? Look around you, for goodness' sake!"

Breathing heavily, she waved her bloodied arms vehemently, her different colored eyes ablaze with astonishment and piercing through the veil of her hair.

"It's because where you see only ruins, I see an opportunity." He scowled coldly. "I see a fantastic future, a paradise where we can live happily! In harmony with nature, as our god wants!"

Lucine stared at him with a dismayed look for several long seconds. Her arms fell with weariness by her side. She sighed and rubbed her forehead with a hand, her eyelids closed. "Solehan," she implored, "that's not what Teluar wants." She softened her tone, looking up at him. "Humans are also part of his creation. You've lost your way—"

"They destroy everything!" he ranted. "They kill anything that crosses their path. They transform life and ridicule it! How could Teluar want that? Do you think he has been hibernating by chance?! The world is heading toward its downfall!"

"And what do you think Valnard and you are doing? The ones who destroyed everything around us are not the humans!" Lucine exclaimed, pointing to the smoking remains of the city.

"It's regrettable, but it's a necessary evil. A just revenge," he said firmly.

"Solehan, you've lost your mind . . . What did Valnard promise you? Let me bring you back—"

No! He wouldn't let her go down that path. Solehan's fists clenched and shivered. Chin to his chest, his mouth twisted. How could she doubt the authenticity of what he had experienced with Valnard? If she couldn't believe his word, then he would have to show her.

"Do you think Teluar would prefer this amalgamation of stench and disgrace over this?" he shouted, spreading his arms wide.

Solehan let Teluar's magic course through his body and explode within him. Debris, the bridge, everything vibrated. Several windows shattered under the shock. Tiles smashed into clay shards. Beams and timbers creaked horribly. The whole city was at his mercy. He would redefine the human world, reshape it in the image of his god. Transfixed by the vastness of his boundless powers, the young man arched his body, his feet rooted in the ground.

Lucine, her face terrified, almost stumbled. She clung to the bridge's railing.

Roots emerged from everywhere. Through every crack, every crevice, every opportunity. Vegetation that lifted slabs and pavement to overrun them, intruded between the bricks of every structure, and smashed every tile to establish itself. Flora that emerged from nowhere, thriving and growing—a new world, a dream of the future. Immense and ancient trees, a luxuriant canopy that replaced the sky, a marvelous forest that took root in Solehan's heart with undeniable certainty. An ideal faithful to the vision he had once had on the couch near Valnard.

On the ruins of the city of Dawnelest, a forest of incredible beauty emerged. A forest with a floor of debris and memories. Deciduous trees that had sprouted amid the devastation of the skeletal silhouette of the buildings.

Head tilted back, the young druid exhaled blissfully and lowered his arms. He turned his attention back to his sister, a smug grin on his lips.

"You've given me an incredible gift, Lucine. Thanks to the heart of Teluar, we will be able to awaken the god more quickly! Look around you! Where are the ruins now?!"

Silent, Lucine slowly straightened up and observed her surroundings. Unsteady on her legs and in her thoughts, her eyes widened like marbles. Two shining stars that grasped the extent of what was blooming around them, the capacity of her brother's powers.

The young woman's lips trembled; her eyes filled with disbelief. Unsteadily, she leaned on the remnants of the stone bridge, the canals below now turned into rivers.

Solehan approached with light steps. "I've missed you, Lucine."

A few birds chirped happily above their heads and played among the newly created trees. His sister, still in awe of the new landscape, paid him no attention. With tender caution, Solehan closed the distance between them a little more. Had this vision convinced her? Could she now envision the utopia that Valnard had allowed him to glimpse?

Full of hope, he stood beside his sister and gently brushed her arm. Upon his touch, she finally turned her head in his direction. He gently pushed aside a few strands of hair from her face.

The sadness drowning in the young woman's eyes shattered Solehan's soul. "I'm sorry, Lucine. For everything you've endured. I wish I had been there to protect you."

"Me too . . ." she sobbed, as she leaned against him.

Relieved, Solehan exhaled through his nose and wrapped his arms around her.

"Everything will be fine now," he reassured her. "I know this is hard to hear, but I'll be here. We'll both create this new world. You'll never be alone again."

Clutching her brother, Lucine timidly nodded against him.

64

Yes, she would never be alone again.

Still in Solehan's embrace, Lucine listened with bitterness to the joyful song of the birds. She appreciated the warmth of her brother's embrace that she had missed so much. But who was now so different. The mourning of a world she would have to face. Her tears dried up and gave way to a newfound resolution. She had no choice now. Hope had flown away.

So, when she let go of their hug, she held her brother's face in her hands. "I'm sorry, Solehan," she said honestly. "For everything. And for this."

"This?"

Vines quickly sprouted around Solehan's feet and wrapped around his body. He didn't have time to react as they formed a vegetal prison, keeping his arms tightly bound. Soon, they grew and immobilized him further, forcing him to kneel. Stunned by her betrayal, the young man looked at his sister as if she were a curious animal.

"Really?" he scoffed disdainfully. "And do you think this little magic trick will be enough against what I can do?"

With a haughty expression plastered on his face, the young druid tried to break free from this grip, growling, certain of the vastness of power at his disposal.

But nothing happened. Solehan seemed unable to free himself from the yoke of his sister.

"What have you done to me?!" he protested.

"Men will always underestimate you." Her heart in a thousand pieces, Lucine recalled the assassin's words.

She had not wanted to believe it was possible. And yet. She stepped back a few steps and looked helplessly at her brother, noticing the different color of his eyes, a sign of the goddesses' abandonment.

And the small wooden amulet he now had around his neck. The amulet the elders had given to Lucine. The one that had silenced her voice and magic for so long. Perhaps it would protect her from danger after all?

A sleight of hand. Nothing more. One of the many tricks she had learned from Shael's teachings. No, Lucine would never be alone again. But that she already knew.

A new opportunity had presented itself, and she had finally made the other choice. The choice to save her friends.

The choice to preserve the love between Shael and Talyvien. To honor the fragile alliance between two orders that had long despised each other. To choose tolerance.

The choice to celebrate the friendship that now united all four of them and the moments they had shared. Their common discoveries and the people they had become because of it.

The choice to honor Zaf's sacrifice, and the promise made to his daughter.

Yes. Lucine had just made the other choice.

The choice of humanity. The choice of hope.

It was an answer that completely transcended her. Greater than any other dilemma she would face in her life. She knew it.

Solehan screamed with rage and struggled even harder, the frustration of his impotence consuming him.

Hastened footsteps sounded behind the young woman. Without taking her eyes off her brother, Lucine recognized the distinctive gaits of Shael and Talyvien as they joined her on the bridge. When they reached her, she could see the savage skirmish they had just been through. Panting, weapons in hand, their bodies were covered with scratches and various wounds, dried blood speckling their armor, skin, and hair.

"Lucine! Are you okay?" the paladin worriedly asked, placing a hand on the druidess's shoulder. "We came as quickly as we could when all this vegetation started to grow!"

"Now I understand why you ran off like that!" the assassin exclaimed, glancing at Solehan with disdain. "We dealt with most of the lychenas and hybrids. The paladins and assassins are finishing the job right now, but we have to stay alert. There are probably others lurking nearby. Nice catch on your part, it seems!"

With a closed and locked look on her face directed toward her brother, Lucine's lips quirked up sadly. Was it truly a victory? Solehan, still kneeling, grumbled in frustration, his eyes replaced by daggers.

"And so, he was the dra—"

The flapping of wings interrupted Talyvien. They all looked up. Once again, Lucine was struck by the similarity between her nightmares and the terrifying vision playing out before them. A creature with formidable talons flew in their direction. Sharp, scathing green eyes.

However, this time, not a trace of fear clouded the consciousness of the young druidess. She would not back down.

Valnard landed on the bridge a few meters behind Solehan, wearing a bilious face. He dismounted with superb grace, like a raptor swooping down on its prey.

"Valnard!" the bound young druid called out, trying to twist his body to catch a glimpse of him.

"Release him, Lucine," the Alaris urged soberly, ignoring Solehan. "There is no reason it has to be this way. I'm certain we can find common ground."

None of Valnard's pale and stoic facial features betrayed any internal agitation. No tremors lurked in his deep and imperturbable voice. Yet, the emotion emanating from the Alaris was pure darkness. His presence was the very embodiment of a curse. Despite his best efforts, he couldn't conceal the scratch that marred his pupil-less irises—two bottomless wells submerged in waters of anguish.

The stakes were indeed high. Solehan's life depended on the outcome of their confrontation.

"After what you did to my brother?! What you did to all those poor victims around us?" growled Lucine. "To our clan!"

"Come now, don't be so dramatic!" Valnard retorted coldly. "What are a few lives compared to saving the world?"

"Yet we swore an oath to protect all divine creations!" a deep voice exclaimed.

It was a voice Lucine could recognize among a thousand. Behind Shael and Talyvien, who stepped aside, Calixte appeared. Intact, in all their usual splendor.

"Calixte!" Lucine cried, rushing toward them. "Are you hurt?"

The bard warmly returned her hug and made a slight negative gesture with their head, causing their long white and skies-hued hair to ripple. But as they released their embrace, Valnard burst into laughter. An insane, incongruous outburst that made the heads of Lucine, Shael, and Talyvien turn in his direction. Uncertain of his demeanor, a dubious look settled on their faces. Why was he laughing like that?

"Calixte! I should have known you were behind all this!" Valnard sneered, mockingly wiping away a few tears from his eyes.

"Do—Do you know each other?" Lucine asked, with a trembling voice. With a new weight on her chest, the young druidess turned her stunned attention back to the bard.

"Ah . . . interesting," Valnard mused. "It seems I'm not the only Alaris who has kept some little secrets!"

"Calixte, what does he mean?!" Lucine snapped through gritted teeth.

"I—I told you, Lucine," Calixte stammered, twirling a strand of their hair. "I'll always be on your side. You have to believe me!" Pathetically, Calixte silently implored the young druidess with their orange gaze.

"Answer her, bard!" Shael spat, conjuring one of her daggers and pointing it at them.

"Valnard is . . . my brother," Calixte admitted, sighing and avoiding the judgmental eyes of the young druidess with difficulty.

"Sibling!" Valnard interjected. "I suppose I still can't call you anything else. What a waste of magic!"

No. This couldn't be possible. Lucine scrutinized the bard frantically. How could they have lied to her like that and pretended not to know who was behind all of this? For so long!

Lucine felt the anger surge through her limbs, her muscles contracting, her face closing. Had she been too naive once again?

Memories collided with exchanged words. Could she have figured it all out earlier?

Feör's words.

"*My subject informs me that she found you among the ruins of a human village that had been attacked, apparently by two individuals strongly resembling you.*"

"*You know, Calixte, you remind me of someone.*"

And it all fell into place. The sorrow in the sovereign's voice when speaking of her past. Of the history she'd had with Valnard. Lucine alternated her focus between the two Alaris. The resemblance became glaringly apparent. Bitterness crept into the young woman's mouth. She also recalled her conversation with Calixte earlier in the day.

"*Sometimes it's hard to realize that the relationships we choose have more value than those we don't.*"

"How could you dare!" Lucine yelled.

"Lucine . . . I had no choice! If I had told you, everything would have changed!" Calixte pleaded.

"What would have changed!" Talyvien growled. "You lied to all of us! We spent weeks going in circles!"

"It was the only way for all three of you to be ready!" the bard begged.

"What do you mean!" Shael advanced closer, still pointing the dagger at them.

Resigned to being outnumbered three to one, Calixte raised their hands. "A few years ago, I began having visions . . . Visions of the future, of possibilities. At first, I panicked, but then I understood. After all this time, my magic was finally manifesting, merging with what I held in my heart."

"Impossible!" Valnard scoffed. "The Alaris can only use the Flow and the Ignescent!"

"And yet, a unique Alaris power was emerging within me," Calixte continued, gazing at him with their hands still raised. "So, when the goddesses came to me and revealed the foolish plans my brother had to awaken Teluar, they begged me to help find a way to stop this madness. To use this new magic to save humanity." They lowered their hands and looked at them tenderly. "They also promised that I would find what I had been seeking for so long as a reward."

"I don't understand," Lucine challenged, her features hostile.

"I spent years studying all the intricacies of the weaving of fate, Lucine. So that you would be ready to face Valnard. With the help of Callystrande and Sazaelith. Three chosen ones united."

Lucine looked intensely at the intermingled roots on the pavement.

All of this, everything they had been through—had it all been orchestrated masterfully by Calixte?

Katao pressed against the young druidess's leg and whimpered with compassion. Strangely, she felt no anger from the dog.

"Is . . . that why you prevented me from assassinating Talyvien the first time . . . ?" Shael stammered, her dagger starting to waver in her hand. "You weren't drunk! You knew I wouldn't be able to kill him later!"

"I suspected something was amiss!" Talyvien snarled. "That's also why you implanted those visions in my mind during your performance, right? Or made sure we returned to save Lucine from the echarvora in Luminaur. Or guided us to the waterfall! Under the guise of humor, you knew we would encounter Valnard and Solehan there! And the ensorcinette—"

"I did it solely for the purpose of saving all of you," the bard interrupted calmly.

"Let me guess," Valnard sneered. "Knowing your penchant for the dramatic, you even added your little finishing touch, didn't you? Making the Goddesses' chosen ones fall in love with each other . . ."

Shael and Talyvien exchanged astonished glances. Valnard clicked his tongue against his palate, satisfied.

"It was necessary for Talyvien to open his heart and be able to resurrect Shael, so he could realize his potential and become the Lamented of the Goddess of Light," explained the bard. "And it was essential for Shael to let her guard down to embody the true strength of the Goddess of Shadow and ascend as the Mother Superior. It was the only way to form an army ready to fight against your madness, Valnard!"

"You sure enjoyed manipulating us!" Lucine exclaimed. "The visions I had when I was poisoned, you arranged those with the Ignescent as well, didn't you? The serpent, the rune on the tree! It wasn't due to the poison; it was your way of guiding me to Teluar's dream and making me aware of my power over animals and hybrids! Pushing me to practice archery, getting me trained by Shael and Talyvien—"

"Is it really that terrible?" Calixte said tenderly. "I merely directed you, showed you the strength that resided in each of you. It doesn't undermine the purity of the feelings you have for each other; I have neither the power nor the desire to manipulate you like that."

Lucine didn't know what to think anymore. Would she have been truly ready to face Valnard and Solehan if Calixte hadn't acted? Would she possess all the strength and knowledge she had today without this "help"? Would she have discovered beings as important as Talyvien and Shael in her life now? Irritated by her ambivalence, she drowned her gaze in Katao's blue eyes.

And her throat tightened.

"A few months ago, during an exchange, a person claiming to be an oracle predicted that this quest for redemption would serve something grand."

"People really buy all sorts of things. For instance, the person who gave me the dog bought a broken old musical instrument from me."

The theorbo.

"You also put Zaf and Katao on my path . . ." Lucine whispered. "You played with their lives! You put me on the pyre!"

"And I sincerely regret it, Lucine," Calixte admitted. "But it was the only possibility for Zaf and Katao to discover you after the massacre of your clan. And for you to meet Talyvien and Shael. So that all four of them could save your life and make you who you are today."

Lucine took her bow from her back with a shivering hand and stepped back uncertainly. She nocked her last arrow but kept the weapon lowered and relaxed. Her magic now completely depleted; she needed this futile protection between her fingers. She needed to regain some semblance of control over this completely absurd situation. She didn't know who to believe, who to trust. Both Alaris had played their cards, used their lives as pawns on a board.

Had Calixte truly wanted to save humanity? Were they sincere about that?

"Lucine, you must believe me," they insisted, taking a few steps in her direction. "I acted only for the good of humankind. To honor the oath made to the gods."

"Why didn't you stop Valnard from kidnapping Solehan and saving my clan then?" Lucine grumbled. "Put a stop to it all from the beginning!"

"Because, unfortunately, that wasn't a viable future. You are destined for so much more than what the druids had decided for you. And because Talyvien and Shael also had a destiny to fulfill. I wish that no one would had to suffer to save your brother and that there would have been no victims, but even I don't have that kind of power."

"And what about the Augur then?" Lucine fumed. "Was that the gift from the gods you're talking about? Your *reward*? That name isn't just an homage to Feör, is it?"

Lucine caught Valnard's posture stiffening from the corner of her eye. The paladin and the assassin, still stunned in place, observed the scene with interest. Solehan, completely lost and still entangled by the brambles, looked on in disbelief at all the unfolding confusion.

"Indeed," Calixte admitted gently. "Their most beautiful gift. The only thing I couldn't foresee. The protections of Teluar's Dream are so powerful that my power of prediction seems to work only in the material plane. I imagine the goddesses were aware of that as well. But I knew you would find your answers there, Lucine."

The bard closed the distance between them and the young woman. Lucine, petrified by her doubts and the friendship she held for them, continued to stare at the Alaris as she swayed. Calixte placed their hands over Lucine's, which still held the bow lowered toward the ground.

"I may have omitted some details, that's true," they said, "but besides the nature of the Augur, I never lied to you, Lucine. I will always be there for you. I promised that to you . . ." they murmured with tender eyes.

Eyes that were now suffused with a purple glow.

Lucine pulled her hands away quickly and jumped back. "What have you done to me!" she growled.

Shael and Talyvien rushed to her aid.

Calixte collapsed onto the druidess, their body caught by the paladin before it touched the ground. The bard had lost consciousness and now lay in Talyvien's arms.

"What did they do to me?!" Lucine said, panicked again, and looking at her hands clutching the bow.

Shael, perplexed, examined Lucine's hands, while Talyvien gently laid Calixte on the ground. Katao curled up near the Alaris's body.

"A pathetic magic! Nothing more!" Valnard interjected, waving his hand dismissively. "Neither man nor woman, *they* can never reach the greatness of the true Alaris anyway. All this out of stubbornness!"

Valnard observed Calixte's unconscious form on the ground with condescension. It wasn't the first time Lucine had glimpsed that strange purple glow in the bard's eyes. Did they know what the Augur could do? Was it really the only time they had lied to her? Supported by her friends, the young druidess kept her focus on her hands, her brows furrowed.

"Well, after this lovely little sibling interlude, shall we return to the matter at hand?" Valnard resumed nonchalantly. "The fact is, thanks to my amiable sibling, it seems we now have a little problem with the deities."

"*Indeed.*"

A sharp, feminine voice rang out. Shael lifted her head from Lucine's hands and gazed at Valnard. The sapphire blue of her feline eyes had darkened like two orbs filled with black ink. Her arms became enshrouded in darkness. Large, dark, vaporous wings unfurled on the assassin's back.

Lucine pulled her hands away again and stumbled. She fell backward, a gasp of stupefaction escaping her. As she tried to make sense of what was happening, Talyvien's body arched backward. His eyes overflowed with light, streaming down his cheeks like golden rivers. The metal of his sword gleamed in his hand. In the same manner as Shael, radiant wings also spread from his back.

Lucine, still holding the nocked bow in her hand, crawled frantically backward on the ground. The earth blackened her clothes and legs. Roots, rocks, and cobblestones scratched her pants in her haste. What was happening? Had Sazaelith and Callystrande taken possession of her friends' bodies?

"*It's over, Valnard. You've done enough,*" proclaimed Callystrande, with a powerful voice through Talyvien's mouth.

"*Humans are also part of the gods' creation. Our son's creation,*" added Sazaelith.

"Impossible . . ." Valnard muttered, discountenanced. "So, you did indeed use that poor excuse of an Alaris for a sibling to harm me!"

Had Calixte told the truth about that? Lucine's mind numbed as the texture of the bow's wood and the earthy ground slipped away from her sensations. Were the goddesses really there? Her mind swirled in all directions.

"Valnard, wha—what is this?" Solehan stammered, equally astounded.

"*Your sister is right, Teluar's chosen one,*" the goddess of shadow scolded Solehan. "*You lost your way. We couldn't continue to condone your actions.*"

"*But there is still hope,*" added Callystrande, which brought a slight smile to Talyvien's face despite the tears.

"Really! And you believe that your son hibernated because he agreed with what the humans were doing?" spat the Alaris. "I merely respected our pact! To protect Nature, his creation!"

"*Solehan, you can still stop all of this,*" the goddess of light continued, ignoring Valnard.

"No! Don't listen to them," the Alaris pleaded, as he knelt before the young druid and placed his hands on Solehan's cheeks. "Stay with me. We will find a way."

In a state of utter confusion, Lucine contemplated the absurd situation they all found themselves in. A war of immortal beings in which she, her brother, and her friends had been the key players. A deliberation that would decide the fate of humanity.

Lucine's mind suffocated more and more in disarray. She observed the paladin and the assassin, stripped of their corporeal forms. The dark cleft that had become Shael's appearance in broad daylight. The blazing and resolute effigy of Talyvien's silhouette. Calixte's inert body on the ground, Katao curled up against them. Her brother still bound by the last shreds of magic she could summon.

A moment of divine grace, the resolution of everything. An original tableau of creation that she admired with confusion. Calixte had worked for this moment.

The bridge wavered. A melodic cacophony of sounds and light. Everything became blurred and yet so precise.

Lucine became lost in the pureness of the white fox's fur that shimmered before her.

 His choice was made. Long ago. Who did they think they were? "If you ask me to betray Valnard, I won't do it!" Solehan exclaimed, resolutely. "Goddesses or not, he was there for me when you decided to abandon me! You claim to be on the side of humans?! What kind of deities renounce their chosen ones!"

"*Then I have no choice . . .*"

Lucine rose with confident languor, her head buried in her hair. The black dog accompanying her whimpered and pressed even closer to the unconscious Alaris.

His twin sister passed between the deities and approached Solehan and Valnard, who were still crouched against each other.

A wave of terror struck the young druid's head and ran down his spine.

Intrigued, Valnard turned his head to see the source of his emotion. An aghast expression painted on his face, the Alaris brought his body even closer to Solehan.

Long, flowing brown hair, two resplendent golden and silver stars peering at them, two deer antlers sprouting from each side of her forehead— Lucine walked with a supernatural grace toward them.

"Teluar . . ." Solehan muttered, wide-eyed.

The arrow still nocked in the bow, the god reincarnated in his sister's body stopped a few meters from them.

"Teluar!" Valnard managed to exclaim, struggling to swallow. "You're awake?"

"*No. The blessing of the goddesses only allows me to speak through one of my chosen temporarily from my dreams,*" the god of Nature exclaimed through the young druidess. "*How dare you perpetrate these atrocities in my name?*"

"I—I had no choice! Humans ravage everything, pervert your creation!"

"*I never wanted to destroy humans, Alaris, even if their actions have caused me sorrow. They will always remain one of my most beautiful creations. I still hope they'll learn and find a solution to their situation.*"

"Please, I only sought to save this world from its demise! To preserve nature!" Valnard now pleaded, terrified.

"*No. You claim to have done all of this for a just cause, but you did it for more personal reasons. So that I could bring back your child.*"

"Understand me! I would have done anything to bring her back! Tell me what you want me to do!" begged Valnard on his knees.

"*It's too late. What's done is done, and you'll have to accept it. Nature is sometimes cruel, that's how I created it,*" Teluar continued through Lucine. "*I cannot risk leaving you with such motivation. As long as you live, humans will not be safe. But since the pact made by the ancients does not allow me to influence the fate of the Alaris, I must reclaim what was given in my name . . .*"

Valnard turned to Solehan, and panic fissured his face. Their desperate gazes met.

"No, no, no!" Valnard screamed, as he clutched Solehan's body with despair to protect him. "I beg you, not him! Anything but him! Take me instead!"

"Valnard!" the young druid panicked against him, realizing what was happening.

"I won't let them hurt you, Solehan," the Alaris sobbed, fervently kissing the young man between his tears. "I can't lose you too!"

Between kisses, Solehan glanced at his sister, who aimed her bow at them. Behind her, Callystrande and Sazaelith stood impassively, witnessing the sentence. The world around him evaporated. Only the pounding of his heart screamed against his head. His reality numbed his limbs, which he no longer felt.

So, he was going to die by the hand of his god. The deities couldn't attack the Alaris, so the arrow would pass through Valnard and hit him.

His punishment for having loved. For having dreamed of a utopian world they could have shared with Valnard. With the person who was meant for him. A perfect and lush universe. A mirage he would cherish forever.

Solehan focused his fatalistic attention back on the Alaris. On the face he loved so much, now drowned in tears. He pressed his forehead against Valnard's.

"I love you, Valnard," Solehan whispered against him. "It will be alright. I'm glad it's me who's leaving. It's better this way."

"No, no. It should be me who dies, not you. You've been perfect," the Alaris sobbed even more. "I love you . . . I will always love you, Solehan. I'm sorry. It's all my fault—"

"I'll wait for you," Solehan cut him off. "With Sylveah. Bind my soul to the tree."

He closed his eyes and gently kissed Valnard's trembling lips. He was ready. He wanted to die like this. To die forever engulfed in their kisses, in their embrace. He had always known it would end like this.

Solehan held his breath.

The bowstring vibrated. The projectile sliced through the air.

An implacable crack of bones reverberated. The Alaris's body froze against his. Solehan breathed his surprise against Valnard's mouth.

The young man opened his eyelids and parted their lips. He wanted to behold Valnard's face one last time—the masterpiece of their love.

But was death so painless when it came to claim you?

The fear that rippled in his beloved's magnificent green eyes turned to euphoria. The Alaris returned a radiant smile, a clear sense of peace on his face.

Valnard collapsed against him, the arrow still lodged in his back.

Solehan's heart ripped from his chest.

"NO!" the young druid screamed, struggling.

His pain compressed his throat, his head, his thoughts. How was it possible? He didn't want to believe it; he simply *couldn't* believe it.

The deities evaporated.

Lucine, Shael, and Talyvien all faltered and ended up on their hands and knees on the ground, breathing raggedly. The dog barked.

"What—?" Lucine began, bringing a hand to her face.

"YOU KILLED HIM!" Solehan shouted at the top of his lungs.

Lucine looked at her brother in shock, as the brambles that had ensnared him dissolved. Freed, Solehan rushed and took Valnard's body in his arms. Brutal and symbolic, the arrow had pierced the Alaris's heart from behind, between his shoulder blades. Punctured the heart of Teluar tattooed on Valnard's skin at the same time.

"No, no, no! How is this possible?!" Solehan choked, brushing a lock of hair from Valnard's face. "It should have been me . . . Valnard . . . No . . . Please, don't leave me!"

"You know what to do . . ." Valnard whispered with difficulty near his face. "Bring me to her. That's where I'll always wait for you . . ."

The tumultuous green of his eyes dimmed in a final exchanged glance. Valnard's hand slipped from his body, and he slumped in the arms of the young man.

Abundant tears erupted from Solehan's eyes. He held the body of the Alaris tightly against him and buried his face in Valnard's neck. The warmth and scent of his skin was vanishing. Everything he had been. Gone. In a terrible and impossible instant. A cruel joke of fate.

A fracture Solehan would never recover from.

65

What had just happened? The world was indolently readjusting to Lucine's consciousness. She observed the power of Teluar's magic leaving her limbs in gentle tremors as she clumsily got back on her feet. Beside her, Shael and Talyvien were also regaining their senses, crouched on the ground, all divine signs vanished in the blink of an eye.

Before them, amid the debris and lush vegetation, her brother's sadness struck the young woman. A painting of contradictions and entangled emotions. She had never seen him like this before.

"Solehan . . ." Lucine tried, taking a few steps toward her brother.

Heart-wrenching sobs escaped the young man, his face buried in the lifeless body of Valnard. He did not respond.

So, they had loved each other. As a helpless spectator, Lucine had witnessed their final moments together. Even if she did not approve of the influence Valnard had on Solehan, who was she to inflict such suffering?

Lucine looked at the projectile lodged in the back of the Alaris. The weight of her guilt burned her fingers, and she dropped her bow to the ground. Although her god had possessed her body and killed him, was she truly innocent?

"I hate you," Solehan spat with an extreme coldness that shattered Lucine's heart even more. "I have no sister anymore."

"Solehan, I didn't mean to—"

"Don't lie," he cut her off. "From the beginning, that's what you wanted. So, rejoice."

"It's not true. We had to stop Valnard's madness, but I would have wanted—"

"Enough of your whining!" he interrupted. "His madness . . . No. His *dream*, his *utopia*. But if even the gods don't seek to protect their own creation from human filth . . . Ah! Don't worry, you'll never hear from me again. Nothing matters anymore."

His face still filled with his horrible grief, Solehan tenderly caressed Valnard's cheek and closed his eyelids. The gentleness of his gesture in stark contrast to the harshness of his words. His sadness veiled in delicacy. Then, still holding Valnard's body, Solehan picked up the amulet and threw it disdainfully at Lucine's feet.

"Solehan, I beg you! Please! I don't deny your pain, but it couldn't continue like that!"

A deathly silence, an answer that would never come. Solehan gave one last look filled with pure and certain hatred at the young druidess. No more doubts, no more ambivalence. Lucine had lost her brother. They had saved humanity at this price. A cost too steep to pay. Tears streamed down the young woman's cheeks as she picked up the small wooden symbol of their childhood from the ground.

Solehan slowly stood up and lifted the Alaris's body into his arms. The browned and winged foliage creature with which Valnard had arrived approached. Solehan placed the Alaris's body on the saddle before climbing onto the mount himself.

Lucine's sobs intensified. Paralyzed by this inevitable destiny that would forever separate them. By their choices and the paths they had taken, by those they had loved.

Everything they had experienced together. Their laughter, their complicity. Gone forever.

"Are we just going to let him go like that?" Shael asked, pointing her dagger at Solehan casually.

"Believe me, he has already endured the worst punishment possible. Losing the one you love . . ." Talyvien murmured, looking at the creature as it took off with Solehan.

The assassin's face softened. The paladin had also gone through that.

But unlike him, Solehan would never have the chance to experience that love again. Though necessary, the judgment of the gods could prove to be cruel.

Lucine gazed at the silhouette of her brother shrinking against the canvas of the sky. A dark spot that evaporated and took away her last hope. He was alive. Yet still lost. A bitter victory.

Why did the arrow hit the Alaris and not her brother? Knowing the love she felt for Solehan, knowing she couldn't live with the burden of having killed him, did her god spare him? Or maybe—

"Nevertheless, he still possesses formidable powers," Shael commented, still looking up at the memory of Solehan. "Won't he pose a threat again?"

"I trust Calixte," Lucine said, turning to them.

"What do you mean?" Talyvien asked, surprised.

"The Augur . . . it's them who swapped our brothers' places. It wasn't Teluar who killed Valnard. It was them. To protect me from my guilt. To allow Solehan to live. So, we must respect that."

All three of them looked at Calixte's body still unconscious on the ground, Katao beside them. Lucine squatted down and cradled the bard's head in her lap.

"Yes, you've always been there for me," she whispered, stroking Calixte's hair. "In the castle of Dawnelest, you used the Augur so I could deliver that improbable dagger blow to the paladin. And you made me miss my shot at Piore too, didn't you?"

A faint laugh escaped Lucine, despite the tears still streaming down her face.

"So that I would be hurt?" Shael said in a shaky voice.

"No. So that I could save you. So that Lucine could discover her powers," Talyvien corrected, sheathing his sword.

"The Augur allows them to influence destiny?" the assassin asked, astonished. "They can change the fate of certain battles, of certain weapons?!"

"It seems so," Lucine added, continuing to stroke Calixte's fabulous and slumbering face. "But it costs them a tremendous amount of magic, apparently."

"They sacrificed their brother to save yours," Talyvien whispered.

"They saved us all," Lucine said.

EPILOGUE

Thunderous applause resounded. All the tavern's patrons jumped from their seats, cheering and clapping their hands. Calixte, more grandiose than ever, had obviously finished their tale in a theatrical gesture.

Seated near the stage, Lucine snorted a giggle. She could never get enough of hearing this story from the Alaris's mouth. The black dog rested his head on her thigh and barked, wagging his tail under the table, enjoying his mistress's caresses.

Lost in thought, Lucine scratched Katao's head. Despite a persistent ache in her heart, she still appreciated the joy and happiness the bard took in bringing their adventures to life. To never forget her god's oath. To never forget her brother.

Several hands shot up in the assembly, the calm returning after the excitement that had shaken the enthralled crowd.

"Is that why the city of Dawnelest was destroyed a few years ago?" asked one of the customers in the front row.

"Indeed! Despite King Therybane and Queen Aramanth's efforts to rebuild the capital, it will take several decades for it to regain its former glory, I'm afraid!" exclaimed Calixte, hand on their forehead. "However, I have heard that they decided to preserve certain parts of the vegetation in the heart of the city!"

Surprise-filled exclamations arose from the crowd. A smile crossed the druidess's face. The promise she had made to herself. In honor of Teluar, she would work for humanity and nature to coexist. A part of Valnard and her brother's delirious dream forever intertwined in the walls of the capital. An abomination transformed into hope for future generations. Their love sublimated.

"And what happened to Shael and Talyvien?" inquired a second customer.

"Ah! Apparently, our two lovebirds still lead the orders of Callystrande's paladins and Sazaelith's priestesses and assassins with an iron hand. It is even said that when the justice of the goddess of light fails, the goddess of shadow takes care of the problem! A very effective partnership, I must say!"

Laughter erupted from the crowd. Calixte discreetly winked at a couple hidden in an alcove at the back of the tavern. The hooded woman, a broad smile revealed, sat on her companion's lap and planted a fleeting kiss on his lips as he embraced her.

"Is that why the last remaining dragon defends the ruins of the city of Argentvale?" asked a third customer.

Lucine's heart clenched with sadness. She looked up at the skull of the enormous beast hanging above the tavern's bar.

"They say he doesn't let anyone approach!" someone in the tavern exclaimed. "He can be seen prowling around the castle like a scavenger. Well, who would want to go to that city now anyway? It's a tomb!"

"Yes," Calixte declared solemnly. "He vowed to protect the tree that resides at the heart of Argentvale. Where the souls of his beloved and his child have finally reunited. Where he might decide to join them someday."

The bard's tender gaze fell on Lucine. Their shared suffering. She knew that the Alaris possessed the power to glimpse the future. However, the druidess had chosen not to know her brother's fate. She would forever hold onto the hope that Solehan would return to her. Even in vain.

"So, the dragon is actually one of Teluar's chosen?" asked another person in the assembly.

"Indeed, but he renounced the deity. Today, he goes by the name of Nahelos," admitted Calixte.

Lucine swallowed her disgust. She stared at her reflection in the metal tankard she held in her hand. That familiar face. That half so terribly missing.

"And what became of Lucine?" asked a young woman in the audience.

The question startled the druidess, pulling her out of her reverie.

"One of my most beautiful encounters, without a doubt!" Calixte answered without hesitation, never taking their eyes off the druidess, whose face blushed. "She embodies the hope she never lost. For her brother. For humanity. Because she never doubted us, what we were capable of when we united and took care of each other."

Enjoyed the book ?
Support the author by leaving a review
on Amazon and Goodreads !

BESTIARY
By Calixte!

If you ever get lost with all these critters!

ANTHROPOMORPHIC AND DEGENERATE MONSTERS:

Echarvora: A creature with the upper body of a human and a spider abdomen. Its six legs resemble long, sharpened wooden stakes.

Lupinar: A creature with the torso of a man but the limbs and head of a wolf. Its fangs and claws are formidable.

Viperal: A creature with the upper body of a human and the tail of a serpent in place of legs, composed of scales and bark.

FOREST SPIRITS:

Drafelis: A chimeric creature created by Teluar in his dream. It possesses a feline body, monarch butterfly wings, and a long peacock tail composed of feathers and foliage. Its fur is deep blue, transitioning into iridescent variations of emerald and carnelian on its birdlike crests and branching plumage.

Elaphora: A chimeric creature created by Teluar in his dream. It possesses a deer-like head with antlers, large wings made of leaves, a canid body with paws ending in bird-like talons, and a tail with a plume of long leaves. The majority of its body is composed of wood and bark.

Lychena: A feminine forest spirit. While its body resembles that of a human woman, it is actually made of wood and bark. Some branches and twigs grow randomly on its limbs, shoulders, and head. It also has the ability to transform flesh into wood. (lignification)

Note and Acknowledgements

Writing this book has definitely been a great adventure that took me two years. I started in January 2022 as a New Year's resolution because it has always been a childhood dream of mine to write a fantasy novel.

Like many, I didn't feel legitimate for a long time to undertake such a project, and it took me 35 years to find the courage to finally fulfill this wish.

I've always been dedicated to doing the best I could, and I hope you'll enjoy reading this book as much as I enjoyed writing it.

I also wanted to include in this story a lot of advice I wish I had when I was younger, especially through the presence of Calixte. My goal with this character was to break the recurring patterns we often see, whether in terms of ideas, diversity, or the non-gendered writing style I aimed for, especially in the French version. That's why I chose self-publishing, as I wanted to retain full control over the work.

But this project wouldn't have turned out the same way without the help of valuable individuals I met on Insta, to whom I owe eternal gratitude. Thank you to my amazing beta readers: Atsel H, Clémentine V, Greg H, and Dahlia. Thank you for your kindness, feedback, and advice. This book wouldn't have been the same without you!

I also want to express my gratitude to Edith & Nous, who consistently did remarkable work, whether for their proofreading or developmental editing services.

I also want to thank Scribendi and the editor who greatly assisted me with the English version by revising my translation, especially the dialogues, to make it flow more smoothly in the language of Shakespeare.

Finally, thank you to my unwavering kiwi. You always have sweet and comforting words, full of wisdom. Thank you for enduring my moments of doubt and sadness and for celebrating my joys.

Thank you for always believing in us.

Milton Keynes UK
Ingram Content Group UK Ltd.
UKHW050855260324
439920UK00006B/84/J